STRONGER

MISTY PAQUETTE

MISTY
PROVENCHER

COPYRIGHT

For Chris & Sue

Your calling has been a glorious thing to witness.

CHAPTER 1

MAY 2013 - A NIGHT IN LYDIA STRONG'S LIFE, A YEAR AGO

"The thing is," I shout at Fizzy Punch, after he tells me that my hair is sticking to the counter of the bar, "I just don't care."

The music is pounding, and his mouth tastes like the booze he just sucked out of my belly button. I kiss him again, even though there is a blond chick, a natural one, angling to take my reclined position atop the bar. She tries to shove my drunk ass out of the way, but I back her off with a sharp flick from the toe of my shoe.

My bleach-blond dreads drape off the edge of the bar, but some are lightly Velcro'ed to the sticky counter, because people keep leaning on them. Like now. A creepy guy has his big ol' hammy palm right on top of one dread, as he suckles his beer and watches me kiss the guy that tastes like fizzy, tropical punch.

"I'm Shane. What's your name?" Fizzy Punch shouts over the music as he gazes down at me. The creepy guy leans in to hear, inadvertently pulling the hair that he has trapped under his bear-paw. I roll my eyes up toward Creepy Guy.

"Can you get off my hair?" I ask him. He frowns, but removes his beefy hand. Fizzy Punch helps me sit up, and the moment I do, the other blond chick scrambles onto the counter. Fizzy Punch lifts me off, and the blond throws herself down in my place, yanking her shirt up over her belly button. Creepy Guy moves in for a navel dive.

I turn back so Fizzy Punch and I are eye-to-bloodshot-eye.

"What is your name?" he asks again. I just smile at his lips. He probably won't remember my name if I tell him anyway. It makes sense, since I can't remember his name now either. All I remember is that his lips are soft and wet and candy-coated with tropical fruit liquor. I have a dozen ideas of how he'll be in bed, and all good, so what else matters?

I move in close, so that my front and his are as plastered as our minds are. I reach up and pull his face to me, trapping his kiss. Someone knocks into my back, and when I fall against Fizzy Punch, I feel the whole terrain of his muscles flex. He catches me and manages to keep us both upright. I am shocked he can do that, since I thought we were both kind of relying on one another to remain vertical as it is.

"We could go to my place--" he breathes hot, tropical fruit over my cheek. His invitation is more of a question mark that I'm happy to answer.

"Yup," I answer.

"Okay," he says, but then we just stand there, kissing, in the middle of the bar, with the music pumping and the crowd crushing in all around us. My fingers run over his ribbed, white, wife beater, my eye scouting over the scenic terrain of his chest.

Pecs. Check.

Biceps. Yes ma'am, check and check.

Hmmm...a collarbone tattoo. Checkity, check check. I squint at it. Words. Damn. I wish I could read them, but my eyes just aren't into it. All my brain wants to do is calculate the correct angle and distance I need to execute for my mouth to make a bulls eye landing on his lips.

We finally pour ourselves out onto the sidewalk, but then he can't remember which direction his place is from the bar. The way we get lost and turned around, it's almost like he doesn't really have a destination in mind, but is still fun trying to find his place, even though it's early spring and the mist in the air makes my jacket cold and soggy. The alcohol keeps us defrosted. Well, that, and every time he wrongly guesses his street, we make out under a light post for ten minutes like it's some new drinking game. It takes us hours, but we finally make it back to my apartment building.

I always remember where I live. Even at my drunkest, I can always find my way home, so we cut our loses on finding his place and stumble back to mine. In the short elevator ride up to my floor, Fizzy Punch pins me to the wall and slides his mouth down my neck. My head is in a delicious spin. The heat of his mouth is my sole focus and when the elevator does its little hop before opening the doors on my floor, I swear I almost come.

We work our way down the hall to my apartment door, groping and kissing and pinning each other to the walls at intervals. His laugh is a basket of fruit, my lips curling like their own happy peelings in response. His skin tastes slightly like the rim of a margarita glass.

Finally, we're standing in front of my door. Now, while I can always remember where I live, getting *into* the place is a whole different skill set. I drive the key toward the keyhole and miss. The bulge in his pants presses hard against me as he leans over my back, kissing my neck each time I fail.

"Are you sure you live here?" he laughs, when I can't get the key into the lock on the 60-billionth try.

"Pretty sure," I laugh too, squinting at the door. 2B. Yes, that's mine. I am positive. 2B is a great apartment number, because even when you're loaded, 2B or not 2B—it still sticks in your head. I push the key toward the lock again, miss, and groan. 2B has a ridiculously tiny key hole. Fizzy Punch grabs me then, flipping me around to face him before he shoves me up against the wall. He kisses me so deeply that I drop my keys.

"We could just do it in the elevator," he whispers.

"Nope," I tell him. "I've got a whole apartment in there. We just have to get this door open."

That's when Mrs. Lowt, from 2C, pops out of her apartment across the hall. With her midnight curlers and fat-rimmed glasses, she looks even more alien than usual. It's something with her eyes. And her face.

"Another one? Another?" My neighbor shakes her head and tsk-tsks as she staggers sleepily across the hall toward us, as if she is the one that is drunk.

"Another," I agree with a smile. She snatches my key link off the floor. She eyes Fizzy Punch up and down and he winks, long and hard, at her. I think his eyelid is stuck, until he turns to me and pops it back open with a roaring laugh.

"You're gonna get the AIDS, Lydia," Mrs. Lowt grumbles.

"So, it's Lydia!" Fizzy Punch says. I ignore him.

"You always say my name when you're mad at me." I frown at Mrs. Lowt. She should be painted green with antennas poking out of her head. I swear, her glasses are even more enormous than usual.

"I was sleeping, is all," she says with a sigh. "I know how it is, being young. I know." She pops the lock and throws open the door.

"Huzzah!" I shout, my arms in the air. Mrs. Lowt shushes me.

"It's four in the morning, Lydia! Do you want to be kicked out?" she asks. Then, she pushes the door key into my palm. "You've got to change your ways, Lydia. Too much fun is too much. You have to be in control of how you live."

I wave a dismissive thanks to her over my shoulder, as I stroll

4

into the apartment. Fizzy Punch follows me in, and I hear what I always think of as the complimentary yelp.

"That old lady grabbed my ass!" Fizzy Punch announces, as he closes the door on my horny neighbor lady.

"She always does that," I say. I toss my keys on the table near the door. They slide clean across the wood top and fall off, somewhere on the other side. "That's her payment, for opening the door. I couldn't afford her services otherwise."

"You pimp out your friends to your old lady neighbor?"

"Yeah, my *friends*." I laugh. I don't usually bang my friends. "I'm a great neighbor to have."

"I believe it," he says, pulling me to him. I kiss him and break free long enough to drag him to my bedroom, because I feel a burst of lucidity. I want my brain to absorb as much of this guy's body as it can, before my memory cells crap out. This is one man I don't want to just see naked, but I want to remember him that way. But, by the time we hit the bedroom, I know it is useless. I can't remember his name. Or mine.

But his tongue is like sucking on a slippery lollipop. He fumbles with my shirt, tries to pull it off, but my arms get all twisted up in the sleeves. I don't struggle a whole lot. It seems like it could be more fun this way, being handcuffed by my fabric appendages. It looks like I might not be the only one with restraints, either. I enjoy the show as this handsome, nameless man tries desperately to shuck off his pants.

"Hurry," I beg. He's stuck, his pants trapped over the top of his shoes. Those shoes are gumming up the whole operation. After a few yanks, it's obvious the shoes are glued on and he gives up. I am of no help with my hands still tied up in my sleeves.

Instead, he grabs me and kisses me so hard that my uvula loses its virginity. He stumbles against me, trying one last time to kick his pants free. It doesn't work. Instead, we both fall in a cackling heap on the floor at the foot of my bed.

I roll my hips against him. With his tongue down my throat, he groans, "Pants."

"Who cares?" I mumble back between kisses. "Let's just do it."

He finally gives in to his wardrobe malfunction, just like I have. Both of us, mostly naked, but shackled in different ways by our designer brands, get down to getting busy. I get my hands over his head, the torso of my shirt flopping over his face. We kiss through the material and roll across the floor together--in each other, on top of each other.

It is the best sex of my life. I'm sure of it, even when I nearly suffocate him with my shirt. He moves his hips in a way that lights me up like a flatbed full of fireworks.

But then it's over and four minutes later, the incredible nuances already begin to fade into the drunken fuzz of my memory. We climb up into bed and I fall off once, before successfully sliding under the covers. He lands beside me eventually, wrapping his arms around my waist, and I think, *okay, he's one of those.* By that, I mean, he's one of those that wants to stay the night.

All men have categories and Fizzy Punch's urge to snuggle definitely falls in one of the two after-sex-snuggler groups. He could be in the clingy group--those are the guys who usually want breakfast and another date--or he will be in the I-have-to-prove-I'm-a-sensitive-guy-that-snuggles-after-he-comes group, which means he will either sneak away the second after I drift off, or at the first trace of morning light. It isn't obvious now though. That's the way these games are played.

So, I fade off to sleep, thinking of how the clingy ones always want coffee in the morning and that I'm down to the bottom of the can. The others, though, just grab their clothes and sneak out. I'm hoping this one will be gone before I have the chance to hit the snooze on my alarm clock.

The next morning, Fizzy Punch does not disappoint.

That's what I decide that I love about him most, when I'm finally hunched over my stiff, morning cup of cream-and-sober.

Fizzy is gone early, and doesn't leave his name, phone number, or his underwear behind. The last one is probably because he couldn't manage to get his ankles out of his pants. I almost wish I could remember his face, just so I could find him and do it all again. Gotta love a man like that.

NOVEMBER 2014 - DAMN FINE NEIGHBORS

I t's only eleven in the morning, and I wake up thinking this: *gotta love apprentice moving men.*

Whoever is in my hallway obviously hasn't learned the skilled trade of silent-as-mice moving. At first, I assume, from the thunking and bumping that woke me up, that whoever is moving in next door has cheaped-out, and recruited friends to help them schlep all their crap into their new apartment. Friends always run shit into the walls and drop your boxes and laugh too loud and shout, *Where do you want this?* while the neighbors are trying to sleep.

But, by the time I drag myself out of bed, heat a cup of straight-black-and-sober, and get a look out the window, I realize I'm wrong. My new neighbor is using movers who identify them-selves with blue and white shirts, printed with HUSTLE AND BUSTLE MOVERS across the broad shoulders. The two movers are chucking boxes out of the back of their truck and arguing as they do it. I can't hear the exact words from behind my closed window, two stories up, but the mover's mouths open and close so violently, I figure they aren't the best of friends. Within ten minutes, the two of them have brought their argument up to the hall, right outside my door.

"Then don't be a lazy son of a bitch," one complains.

The other answers, "Takes a douche to know a douche."

And a third voice, thick as homemade cake, says, "Those boxes go in the kitchen. No, the kitchen! Dude, does that look like a kitchen?"

So, I decide that since these morons have gotten me up at this ungodly hour, I might as well watch the parade. I slip on my robe, swing open my door, and lean on the jamb with my coffee mug nestled in both palms. My robe sleeves fall into the crooks of my elbows.

One of the movers stands with his back to me, in the neighbor's open doorway. He turns at the sound of my first slurp. His eyes light up and run the usual track, slipping down my body, taking inventory of my robe, my boobs, my legs, and the swirl of tattoos down my arm that the loose sleeves no longer cover.

A smile spreads over his face like spilled corn syrup. That's the typical reaction I get. Tattoos = wild girl = horny girl = real live girl that might be willing to be brutalized as much as the blow-up doll he's got hidden in a closet at home. There are only two categories of new men with me: first are the ones who are terrified of my tattoos/dreads/piercings and second are those that consider my total package to be an invitation of challenge.

"Good morning," the mover says the moment he's done scanning me. He's got a scalp of spiked, blond hair, a head shaped like a bucket, and a cocky smile that just comes across making him look like a cock. No question--he's definitely Category #2.

I sip my coffee. "Are you always this loud in the morning?"

"It's almost noon, sweetheart," Buckethead says. His co-worker shoves his way out, into the hall.

"Heeeyyy," the second mover drawls, his eyes blinking rapid-fire, as if his retinas are snapping photos of me. Cocky smiles and block heads must be prerequisites for the job. But the second buckethead's eyes, when I boldly meet his gaze, dart away. Oh, he's one of *those*. The shy type that tries to be cocky, and fails. Sweet. I sip my coffee instead of answering and, a third man emerges from the apartment, into the hall.

The third man is what I call an actual *man*. And by that, I mean, man times man, plus man, squared and multiplied, into infinity...man. If I wasn't so hung over, and if he wasn't part of this problem that has gotten me out of bed so early, I would stand a little straighter and make a date with him for tonight.

"Hi," the Infinite Man says, stopping in his tracks when he spots me. He lowers the clipboard in his hand, taking in my robed attire. He spots the tattoos, but doesn't linger on them. Interesting. He is refreshingly harder to categorize. "Did we wake you?"

"I don't mind a parade," I say. It's hard to be angry at a man that looks like this, even though my hangover is clutching my brain and squeezing it like a blood pressure bulb. He's tall. He's broad. Jet black hair. A body that could stop eight lanes of traffic. Absorbing, dark eyes that deserve to see everything behind the closed door of my bedroom. Lips that belong between my thighs. I sip my coffee.

"I apologize," he says. "I'm your new neighbor, Aidan."

I lower my cup. He looks like an Aidan. He puts out his hand to shake mine.

"Aidan Badeau," he says, "and your name is?"

I don't take my hands from my coffee cup to shake. I just smile behind the rim. Oh no, I'm not going to make it easy for this miscategorized man. I don't know how to play him, so he's going to have to work for it.

"It's Lydia."

"Lydia," he repeats my name slowly, holding it in his mouth. He drops his hand with a smile. The look, along with the way he says it, sends sparks blazing straight down the ramp of my belly and crashing between my legs. "It's a beautiful name."

"Thanks," I tell him. I don't mention that I would love to

change it. Too much explaining why, why, why. The cocky bucket-head picks at the side of his uniform slacks with two fingers.

"Do you like Chinese?" the mover asks. I reluctantly turn my gaze away from my new neighbor and look back at his mover.

"Men or food?" I ask and the buckethead is momentarily confused. Aidan grins and I sip my coffee, stealing another glance. Aidan's got his own colorful ink snaking up his arms, but I don't stare. I'd be willing to show him mine, if he showed me his. I wonder how many places he has them hidden. I suck in the edge of my lip as I think of that Easter egg hunt, the tang of my lip ring on my tongue.

"Chinese *food*," Buckethead finally answers.

The shy buckethead just rolls his eyes, but whenever he looks at me, he blushes. I smile beneath the lip of my cup and watch his eyes dart away again. Shy can be fun sometimes.

"I adore it," I say and the cocky buckethead lights up like I plugged him in, until I add, "But I'm horribly allergic."

Buckethead's light goes dim then and he says, "It wouldn't have to be Chinese."

Aidan steps in.

"How about you guys finish hauling in my boxes before making dates with my neighbor?" he says. Buckethead ignores him.

"I can give you my number. Or get yours," Buckethead grumbles to me. "Do you have a pen?"

"I'm sorry, I don't." I smile dryly. "I'm not much of a writer."

Aidan slides the pen from his clipboard into his pocket. The mover shrugs.

"I've got one in the van," he grumbles.

I just smile and sip the last of my coffee, as the second, blushing buckethead follows the first one back to the elevator. Aidan slips the pen from his pocket and taps it on the clipboard.

"So, it's Lydia," he says.

"Always."

"Does your belly button still taste like a mojito?" he asks.

It's not like I am surprised by his question. This kind of thing has happened before. I've run into ex-lovers and rarely remember them. I'm a girl who has no problem enjoying my body, enjoying those of various men, and I have a diverse, sexual appetite. Sue me. It's one of the reasons why I don't tie myself down to any of them. The prissy girls would love to categorize me as a slut, but the women who love men's bodies understand me completely. They wouldn't judge me when I can't remember a name or face of a lover. They would just call me forgetful.

I squint at Aidan and kick myself for not remembering his particularly remarkable body. I can't imagine how I'd let him get away from me before I had maxed out my three-date rule. The rule is that I will date a man no more than three times, since after three it becomes a pattern and that means it's headed toward *relationship*. I don't need any more of that drama in my life.

I try again to retrieve a memory of him, but nothing comes. What a crying shame. He's obviously been acquainted with my belly button and knows one of my favorite drinks. He looks like he would've been a great time. I'd love a repeat performance, but it's a lot trickier to pull that off if he's moving in next door. I have enough sense to know that neighbors would make terrible lovers.

As I'm still contemplating, Aidan rubs his neck warily and confesses.

"Not that I've tasted it myself," he says. "But we did meet a little over a year ago. A year and a half, actually."

I wait for him to continue, because a year ago or a year and a half, it all means zero to me. It's not like I sit at home pining for a weekend. I make weekends happen every single day, so the enormous time frame he's giving me doesn't narrow it down in the slightest. He smiles. "It was at Modo's Bar?"

All I can think is *shit...I've met half the damn world down at Modo's.*

"You left with a friend of mine? Uhm...Shane?" He looks so

hopeful. As if I'll remember a name. I go out of my way to avoid names. It'd be easier if he gave me some identifying details of the guy's body instead, like tats or earrings. Maybe a severely broken nose or obvious scars. Any details that would be useful in a line-up would work for me too.

I already know that this little discussion is going to go sideways on me. I either hooked up with my new, hottie-neighbor's friend, or I turned him down. That can only mean that my hottie neighbor is about to classify me as either a slut or a bitch.

I'm disappointed already. With a body like Aidan's, I was hoping he was going to say I'd hooked up with *him* a year ago, and that he wanted to help me remember. I can think of at least five different positions that might jar my memory. And then, five more, if those didn't work.

"Sorry," I say. So sorry...and in more ways than one. "I don't remember him."

"No big deal," Aidan shrugs it off with a grin. The moment is broken by a ring from my cell, located somewhere inside my apartment...wherever I dropped it last night. I'd ignore it, except that this particular ringtone sounds like glass shattering and the sound is reflected in my spine every single time I hear it. I wince.

"Well, nice talking with you," I say and I duck back into my apartment.

Before I close the door, I catch his smile. Warm, genuine, incredibly sexy.

"You too," he says as I shut him out.

The glass shatters again. I scout the room in a frenzy, over-turning couch cushions and looking under the coffee table, before I trace the sound back to the kitchen sink. I pick up the phone as it shatters a third ring inside the basin.

"You there, Lyddle?" A deep voice asks. The name makes me quiver against my will. It radiates out of my spine and it's hard to tell, even for me, if I hate it or if it totally turns me on. He started calling me Lydie first, and then he switched to Lyddle. It's exactly how he's always made me feel.

"I'm here," I say. I step over to the coffee pot and refill my cup. "What do you want?"

"I was wondering if I could see you." His voice is as professional and detached as a physician calling with bad news.

I swing open my kitchen cupboard and take down a bottle of Jack. I slosh the last inch of the liquor left in the bottle into my cup. Swirl it. Take a burning gulp.

"I thought we agreed that wasn't a good idea," I say. He chuckles, as if I have no idea about what is good or bad.

"I never agreed and I think it is a fabulous idea. We just need to talk."

"We never *just talk*. And it hasn't even been a week, Desmond."

"But I miss you," he says, planting the soft hook on the end of his words. He knows I'll come. I hate that. "Don't forget to bring your portfolio."

I only forgot once, but he's reminded me every single time ever since, like a newspaper on the nose. I take another good slug of my begin-the-buzz breakfast, swallow it down and say, "Alright. Where?"

"My place."

"*Your* place..."

"Don't be like that," he says, but he drops his voice to a thick and sexy timbre that disguises the reprimand. He really wants me to come. That alone tingles. "We need to *talk*. Do you need me to insist, Lyddle? Is that what you want?"

"*Alright*--I said alright." Tiny grains of hope spin inside me, they always do, no matter how absurd they are. I still frown the response and hang up. If he catches a whiff of my hopes, he'll only smash them. He does it every time.

I take the last gulp of my straight-black-and-hammered and straighten my shoulders.

"Alright," I tell myself.

<<<<>>>>

*T*here is a knock on my door at the worst possible moment. I can't find my rings.

I pull on my suit coat and check my pockets, but those damn rings are still missing. I ignore the knock and keep searching, feeling along the shelves, pulling lingerie from my drawers, but there are still no rings.

There is another knock. Another.

I finally whip open the door to find my new neighbor, All-Man-Aidan-Neighbor from 2A, standing in the hall. His mouth drops open just a bit when he sees me. I take in his body as he takes in mine, but, unfortunately, I don't have time for him.

"The laundry room is in the basement and it's free, but it's dark and loaded with spiders," I say as I turn back to check the candy dishes on my shelf that have never held candy. I hope they will magically hold my rings. None of them do. He follows me into my room, silently surveying the pile of lace and heels on my bed, as I comb the top of my dresser for the rings again. "There's also the Suds Station around the corner, on Beech, down by Jack's Liquor store. If you want the grocery store, it's in the opposite direction. Take Elm to Main, turn left. It's right there. There's a Chinese place further down on Main, but there have been rumors of cat shortages, so that's up to you."

I wait for him to say thank you and leave, but he's still standing in my bedroom door, with a smirk that is so sexy, I want to put my tongue in the corner of it.

"I was wondering if you had a wrench?" he asks. "Can't seem to put my hands on mine."

"A wrench? Yeah, right. What kind of girl do you think I am?" I laugh, but I brush past him, continuing my search in the bathroom. I stopper the sink and shovel my make-up into it as I glean for the rings. A wine glass at the edge of the sink tumbles over but doesn't shatter, the little blister of dried red still secure in the bottom. "If there was ever a wrench in my apartment, it would be under the kitchen sink. I know tools have been under there before."

"This is your apartment, isn't it?" He grins as he heads into the kitchen. I expect to hear him comment on how the living room walls are all painted different colors, or how the fridge door is decoupaged with artsy magazine photos, but he doesn't. He must see it, but he breaks a record by not asking about it, and I don't have the time for a conversation to spring up. I've got things to do.

I return to my room and overturn what's left in my underwear drawer on my bed, rifling through the mound of thongs and lace panties. Still nothing. I pull out one of the rest of my drawers and do the same.

"You have a wrench in here," he calls.

"Yeah, well, people leave things here," I say. "I don't keep inventory."

His footsteps hesitate and then tromp back toward my bedroom. I peel off the lid from the coffee can in my closet, open up the cardboard pudding box huddled in with my nighties, and I feel all the way down inside the toes of my thigh-high boots beneath the bed. Still no rings. I'm under the bed, reaching for a purse strap, when I spot Aidan's shoes at the doorway of my room. From where he's standing, he's got a perfect view of my ass, stuck in the air like an offering, while the rest of me is crammed beneath the bed springs.

The thoughts that race through my head aren't polite. They involve a million things that I'd like my neighbor to do, considering his vantage point, but it's also the last thing I need right now. I've got somewhere else I have to be and being late will only make things worse for me.

I sigh and pull my head out from under the bed, along with the purse I was after. Kneeling beside the bed, I meet Aidan's gaze as I dump the contents out on the mattress. He's holding a wrench I've never seen before, and I catch him moving his eyes away from my rear. The smirk is back. I answer with one of my own, as I rifle the purse. The jackpot is at the bottom. I grab all my rings and stand up, sliding them onto my fingers one at a time. Except the last ring. I just hold that one in my palm.

"It's kind of early for a date, isn't it?" he asks. I pause, resting a hand on my hip.

"Why would you automatically think I'm going on a date?" I turn in front of him, so he can see my feminine version of a business suit: pearl-buttoned silk shirt, black suit coat tailored to my hourglass, fitted black pencil skirt, pointed-toe stilettos. "How do you know I'm not a doctor or a lawyer?"

"A lawyer with a black lace bra like that?" he asks, glancing at my chest. I glance down too and button the plunging neckline of my blouse one more button. I shoot him a *don't you-wish* look, because I don't have time for these fun and games. I step in front of the full length mirror in the corner of my room, doing my ceremonial turns and twists to make sure I have everything in place. I fasten back my dreads. The anxiety builds as I straighten, pull, adjust. I suppose it doesn't matter. Desmond will let me know what he thinks when I get there.

"And I'm guessing you're not a doctor either," Aidan says. My eyes narrow to slits in my reflection. He's got a lot of nerve to doubt me in my own apartment, holding what must be my wrench. And guessing that I'm not a doctor, in that tone of voice, is unacceptable.

"Really?" I step away from the mirror, tipping up my chin to him and lowering my tone to a challenging thrum. "And what exactly do you think I am, *neighbor*?"

His smile is so damn easy. He stares down into my eyes as if he's dropping an anchor. He doesn't look away, but I do. Damn.

"I try not to jump to conclusions about people," he says, "but doctors don't usually rush off on the weekends in suits, so you've got me curious."

I put the back of my hand up to his eye level and spread my fingers wide. He squints at the tattoo on my ring finger, but I drop my last ring over it quickly.

"What I am," I say, waggling the heavy diamond in his face, "is married. Bet you didn't jump to that conclusion, though, did you?"

A WORKING ARRANGEMENT

I'm in the back seat of the cab, bumping away from my apartment house, and I feel like a jerk. I replay the way Aidan lifted his brow after I slid on my wedding ring for the entire ride.

All he said was, "I'm not surprised, actually. Your husband's a very lucky man."

"I agree," I'd said. I gave Aidan a smile, but I didn't explain anything else. I cracked open my back-up bottle and topped off my travel mug with another healthy splash of Jack. He let himself out and I followed him, grabbing my poster-board-sized portfolio case, which I keep near the door. Aidan was standing at his own door as I locked mine.

"I apologize," he said, glancing at the huge, rectangular case, "if I offended you."

"You didn't," I said, but I felt a twinge of guilt at making him believe I was legitimate.

I don't know why I was so defensive to Aidan. He's just a guy that lives next door. Just a guy. And it's not like other men haven't made the mistake of trying to call me a whore to my face. At least he only lightly insinuated it. I've got to remember that my three-date-max rule is in place to cut down on the whore-calling, but dating my neighbor would probably end with a lot worse names being flung around. I sit back in the cab and watch the city whiz by outside, trying to figure out why Aidan's insinuation feels so much worse.

The cab jogs over a pothole and I almost spill my cup of hair-of-the-dog in my lap. We pull up in front of the security gate. It is huge and black and prestigious, rising up to a high peak that couldn't be scaled by ninjas and every time I pull up outside it, my stomach turns to lead.

Desmond is waiting just inside the bars. Even disguised by the layers of his suit, his powerful physique is obvious. The way he moves tells a story about the kind of man he is: demanding, precise, concealed. He steps through a door to the side, instead of opening the gate. He also pays the driver before he opens my door and offers me his hand.

"You look edible," he says. Once standing, I juggle my travel mug as I slide my huge portfolio out of the back seat.

"I am," I answer coolly, "but we're not eating. We're just talk-ing, remember?"

"We could do both."

"No, we can't," I say. I always start off so solidly.

He chuckles, but doesn't offer to carry the portfolio or the travel mug. Instead, he slips an arm through my free one and we stroll back through the small gate door and up the drive, toward the house.

"I want to ask you something," he says.

"I assumed that was the *talking* you wanted to do."

"Such a smart ass today." He flashes me a wicked glimpse of a grin. "You know, we could disappear in among the trees..."

"Except that I'm sure the help would never believe that your trees needed decorating," I tell him. "I'm here and I'm on the clock, so talk."

"You definitely are." He chuckles again, running his gaze over my attire, but he doesn't break our stride. "We'll talk about that, but I have another question. I'm curious."

"About?"

"Why do you come when I call, Lyddle?"

His voice drops to that low timbre that kicks up clouds of winged creatures in my stomach. What they are is hard to distinguish--dark moths or blood-thirsty bats. He rubs his knuckles and I anticipate what he will say next, like his words are actually mine and just waiting to be spoken. When I'm with him, I am nothing more than a sophisticated marionette, waiting for him to move me for his pleasure; waiting for his words to fill me, so I can say exactly what he wants to hear.

But today, I won't give in so easy.

I tell myself this every time, but I hope that today I will stick with it.

"I think you know why I come," I say.

"Oh, I know *exactly* why you come," he murmurs so softly, the words tangle in my hair, as if they are his fingers. The burn inside me begins to smolder and spread, low in my stomach. This is how it always begins and I need to fight it, but real fighting would've meant that I'd never have come here to begin with. His grin finds its way in and spreads me open. "I like to believe you don't come for the money, Lyddle, but that you come because you love me."

"Less and less each time," I say, juggling my things so I can take a healthy gulp of my spiked coffee. "I come because you pay me to do it. I need the money to survive."

"Yes, you really *can't* live without me, can you? But you're saying that you still expect to gain immunity to me one day and end all of this?"

"Of course. Don't you? You know we can't keep going like this..."

"That's where you're wrong, Lyddle. As usual. There's nothing to stop us, besides us. I still feel the same way about you that I always have. The more I see you, the more I have to have you."

"Then you should tell your wife," I say. He stops and takes my hand then, removing the coffee cup and rubbing his thumb over the enormous ring he gave me, when we began this whole affair.

"I am," he says, pulling up the ring and rubbing the skin beneath. The tattoo there is the real wedding ring he gave me, only a few days after we got married. Des had gotten me drunk to do it, then took me to a hack tattoo shop, and had his last name embedded in my skin. We fought the next morning, when I realized he didn't reciprocate with my name on his own ring finger.

"I meant, your illegal wife," I say, pulling my hand away. I wave a finger between us. "*This* doesn't mean anything anymore. I might still be your *legal* wife, but you married Claudia too and she's the one you're with. Call it what it is, Des. You're just fucking with both of us."

"Oh now. Keep your voice down, Lyddle," he growls, pulling my hand through his arm again. He brushes his thumb intimately in my palm. It's humiliating when a few more strokes make my legs quiver, but why wouldn't they? He's still my husband and his hold on me is solid. I can't blow him off like the guys at the bar. Des knows how to get under my skin, how to manipulate it and massage my ego until I open up my point of view, my heart, my legs for him. I struggle to hang onto my resolve, just this once, but he's making my palms sweat. "Tell me why you are still wearing my ring, if it doesn't mean anything to you?"

I take a drink from my mug, looking off toward the mansion beyond the trees, trying to remind myself that he's not truly a husband. Not a good one at least, and it doesn't matter how long or how well he knows me.

"I wear it because you asked me to." I jut my chin and add, "We both want what's under it to stay covered up so we can forget about it."

"So, it's going to be one of those days," he grumbles, stepping away.

"You bet."

"Maybe you were right. Seeing each other isn't such a good idea."

"The only right thing to do is get a divorce."

"You know I can't," he says, stepping closer and pulling me to him, right in the middle of the driveway. I'm an idiot to even be here.

His fingers slide to my waist. I can smell the cologne that I love on him, the stuff I know he wore just for me. His hired help will see and I try to pull away but he pulls me closer with a sexy *uh uh* under his breath. I'm like a conditioned dog. The sexy sweep of his voice, the feel of his muscles tightening against me, and the dark, enchanting scent of him all light me up inside. He knows just how to get me. The fire ignites between my legs as he ducks his head down to whisper in my ear.

"That's not really the way you want it, is it? *Poor,* Lyddle?"

"Don't call me that. You know I hate it," I say, but my argument is weak. He knows he's got me. I don't have a penny to my name and couldn't survive without the money he gives me. I've been pretending to be his and Claudia's designer for so long now, it almost feels real and thank God, the paycheck is. But, at the bottom of it all is my marriage. I loved Des from the moment I met him and as sick as it is, I still do. He continues, with a grin.

"You want me to want you...that's really why you wear it and why you come running whenever I call, isn't it? Say it is, Lydia. Please. I need you to want me too. I'm always good to you, aren't I?" This is how Des always crushes me--when he brings out the old Des, the one I fell in love with, the one who was always vulnerable and real and loyal. When he talks like this, it seems like the Desmond that I knew and loved is as trapped inside this situation as I am.

His face is so close, his breath is ruffling loose strands of hair that slipped from one of my dreads. "I want you. I know you come to get the money, but tell me it's not the only reason. Say you come because you want to *come* for me. You'll come upstairs...won't you, Lyddle?"

"Back up before the help sees us," I warn him.

It's sick how we keep doing this. It's a stupid game, but when he's standing this close, his manhood pressed against me, he is my addiction. He has been, since I was fourteen years old and he was nineteen. He taught me how to love him; he was my first. We were married on my sixteenth birthday, with my mom's consent. Des promised her he'd always take care of me.

Married for only six years, and here we are, walking up to the front of a mansion where he lives with his other wife. I blew off high school to marry him. We moved across state. Even though we had nothing, I thought we were happy until he left me two years ago to get the lifestyle he said he deserved.

He married the newly-widowed, wealthy-as-hell Claudia. She hyphenated their marriage, but never made him sign a prenup. No kids and no family to speak of, I guess Claudia was happy to have him. Mrs. Claudia Silver-Strong is now his illegal, second wife, although she has no idea that I'm still his first.

In a really twisted way, Des was good to his word to my mother, if only financially. He has kept me on his hook by refusing to get a divorce. He says filing papers would mess up things with Claudia and, as much as I hate myself for it, we both depend on her for our living. Des tells me he loves me and screws me in secret like a mistress, but he also gives me more money than I could ever hope to make on my own, even if I was stripping. He went from being my husband, to being my job, and I resent the hell out of him for it.

The worst of it all is that I still love him. My husband still turns me on, and really deep down, buried under all the deception and lies, I still feel like things could be different if I could just teach him how to love me back. Some days, when he calls me to his office and makes love to me tenderly in the sunshine that falls across his desk, I think that I've succeeded--that there is still hope for us to be what we once were.

I know. I can't help it.

I'm a head case.

The shame I feel every time I leave Claudia's estate with her husband's smell rubbed all over me, doesn't matter in this moment and he knows it. He's got me. Again.

He repeats in a soft plead, "You need me, don't you, Lyddle?"

I take a deep breath.

"I'm still your husband," he says.

"You should tell *her* that. And you should sign the divorce papers." My voice is pitiful, a whine at best. I'm drowning in him again. I've lost every friend I've had because they see me go through this rotating door with Des, thinking only that he's a married man and I'm his mistress, and over time, they get tired of my complaining. They grow disgusted when I won't end my misery and I can't say that I blame them.

But standing here with him, I can only think of my husband and how I want him to be what he promised he would on the day we were married. I try to swallow, but his scent and his fingers, pressing against my waist, shut down my most important sense-- my common sense. It's just me and Des again, standing on the rolling grounds of this palatial estate. And all I can think of is having my husband, this horrible addiction of a man, moving between my legs, loving *me* instead of his other wife.

"You know I'll tell Claudia the second that the time is right," he says. It breaks my heart to hear him lie. The right time hasn't happened in the last two years.

"If you give me a divorce, you'll never have to tell her anything," I say. He steps away. I sway toward him and have to catch myself.

"And how would you live, then, Lyddle? You think I'd let you go homeless? Become a whore?"

"I'm a whore already."

Des's eyes go to granite and then, he takes the crook of my elbow in his steely grip. He turns me toward the front of the house and raises a finger, drawing a sharp slash across the roof line, as if he's explaining something to me.

He's going to fuck me and this is part of the game. It's how he'll lead me upstairs to his home office to finalize details. We'll make a big show and he'll have shutters or gutters or shingles installed by some side contractors next week to make this 'meeting' legit, in case *the help* really is watching. It's been years and no one's ever spilled the beans yet, but even if the employees see us so close to one another, I doubt they would tell Claudia and if they did, I doubt that she'd believe them.

She believes I'm their talented designer. That's how I got tangled up in this mess in the beginning and how I'm entrenched now. Claudia loves what I don't really do with the place, because Des says he loves it. She's at ease with me because I ignore Des when she's around, and I've really sold her on how faithful I am to my own husband and our marriage. She just hasn't figured out that we're married to the same skunk.

Des's finger stops at the corner window of the roof. He turns back to me, his gaze so intense that the burn races through me like a forest fire.

"Let's go to my office," he says with a disapproving frown. He leans in close, his lips near my ear and his warm breath tingling against my skin. "I'm going to spank you for what you said to me and then I'm going to tie you to the feet of my desk and my couch in that room today, Lyddle. I'm going to stretch you wide open on the floor. And then, I'm going to screw you so hard, you're going to remember that you don't speak to me like that ever again. I'm not signing any fucking papers. You will never sell your body to any man. You're damn right that I'm your husband and you better get it straight that you will always belong to me. And if I hear one peep out of you, during anything I do to you today, I'll send you home so red, you won't be able to sit your ass down in the cab. Do you understand me?"

His eyes flash as he moves away from me. He's getting off on it even more than I am. Our sick little game Tasers the hot, aching button between my legs. Des moves his face back an inch, so his eyes are riveted on mine and it steals any sarcastic response I could give him. All I want is my husband, the disease of him, thrust into my body. His arms around me as he fills me up and makes me feel whole again. I want him more than I want my pride.

"Follow me," he growls. He turns away sharply and walks up the steps to the ornate front doors of the house.

I follow the spider, right to the center of his web.

<<<<>>>>

The cab ride home is the same as always. The scraps of my panties are at the bottom of my portfolio case. My make-up has been carefully re-applied, although there is a layer of sweat and bruising just beneath it, and there is a nice roll of cash stashed in my empty travel mug.

I try to fill myself back up again, staring out the window while I tell myself that, I can make this mug-money stretch until I find a job somewhere. I can file the papers myself. I don't ever have to go see Des again. But I already know it's a lie, because I want it to be one.

I have fantasies of never going back, of never feeling like this again, but then he calls. Sometimes I go because I could use the money. Sometimes it's because I remember who we were and what we had. Sometimes, like today, I really think I'm going to go and finish it for good. But every single time, the outcome is just an echo of all the times before it. I cave. And just like every other cab ride home, I swear I won't do it again.

I pay the cabbie before sliding on my sunglasses and stiffly exiting the cab. My rear is on fire as I drag my portfolio from the back seat. I doubt it would be any easier to walk in ballet flats, but walking in stilettos is absolute hell.

When I step through the front doors of the lobby, I stifle a groan. Less from my sore rear end and more because Aidan is standing only feet away, with his back to me, checking his mailbox. I am not prepared for a conversation right now. I need to get a few drinks in me first.

I have to slide by him without being noticed, which is impossible. He's between me and the elevator. He turns as the outside door wafts shut behind me.

"Hi," he says over one shoulder with a smile. He slips the key from his mailbox lock.

"Hi," I say. I try to glide as smoothly as I can to the elevator doors, but I feel his eyes following me, assessing my movement. Dignity and grace are nearly impossible to accomplish with an aching ass.

"Can I help you carry up your case?" he asks, and before I can pass on his offer, his warm hand encases mine. He takes the portfolio from me. I only hope to God it doesn't drop open and spill my ravaged panties. I force my gaze off of the guilty portfolio and focus instead on the doors sliding open and stepping inside. I try not to wince as Aidan presses the button for our floor. The lift jerks upward and I try to hide my wince. Aidan takes it all in. I can almost see him debating whether or not to ask what's going on with me. I keep my eyes averted, so as to discourage any questioning, and we ride up in silence.

When the doors open, I pause, hoping Aidan will step out first, but he picks a lousy day to be a gentleman. He extends an arm for me to go first and I focus on keeping my stride steady. This is the way it is sometimes, but usually it's no big deal because no one is around to notice.

We make it all the way to my door, before he asks, "Are you alright, Lydia?"

I flash him a smile. I don't wait for a response as I fish my keys out of my bag and open my apartment door.

"Perfect." I say, taking the portfolio from him. I am careful not to touch his skin. "Thanks for the help."

"No problem. I'll bring your wrench back later, if that's okay?"

"Sure," I flash him another smile, probably too stiff this time, because I can't go beating the drums right now. Not the way my body is aching.

Aidan cocks his head and returns a questioning smile as I close the door on him. I don't want to be rude, but I need a very hot bath and a very tall drink, to soothe my pride.

$\mathcal{I}$t's like there is a green light hanging over my apartment door, because the moment I'm out of the tub, still feeling tenderized but relaxed, Aidan is at my door again. I answer, wrapped in my robe and he holds up the wrench, his eyes sweeping over me.

"Yours," he says, but I don't take it.

"It's not mine, actually. Someone just left it here. You can keep it, if you like."

"I've got one of my own, someplace. In one of my moving boxes." He holds out the wrench again, but it's greasy. I swing open the door instead.

"If you can put it beneath the sink, then maybe I'll remember it's there the next time a neighbor asks for one."

Aidan steps into the room. I feel his body, even though it doesn't touch mine, as he passes by me.

"No problem," he says as he walks into the kitchen. Over his shoulder, he asks, "So, does it happen often?"

His tone is curious, almost concerned, and it throws me off.

"Does what happen?" I ask. Aidan slides the wrench into the cupboard. I notice him noticing the half-empty bottle of whiskey on the counter, and it's twin from this morning, in the trash. He turns back to me. Checking me out doesn't make me feel vulnerable, but knowing that he just eyed the evidence of my binge, does. He smirks.

"Do neighbors often come looking for tools?" he says.

"Not often. But Mrs. Lowt, from 2C across the hall? She comes looking for men, so you should know, you're not safe on this floor." I cross the room and, as nonchalantly as I can, put the whiskey bottle back up in the cupboard and smash the other down into the trash can so the lid will close on it.

"Mrs. Lowt...you mean the lady across the hall, with the glasses," Aidan says. He watches me move. "I've met her. She's already acquainted herself with my left thigh." I feel his gaze, like static, prickling over my body. "Does your, uh...work...call you out a lot on the weekend?"

"Sometimes."

"I don't think you mentioned what it is you do?"

"Design. Art and design," I say. "Home decor."

"Hmm. Interior or exterior?"

"Both." His eyebrows hike a little.

"Both," he repeats, dipping his chin as he says it. Then, "Does it always make you move like that?"

The first thing that flares up in my head is to tell him to mind his own business, but the softness of his tone--the concern is soothing and it makes putty out of my defenses.

"Sometimes," I say. And then, to stop the interrogation, I add, "Only when I stop at the gym after."

That does it. His brow is restored, and I'm pretty sure I'm off the hook, until he says, "You work out in a suit?"

Caught. No gym bag.

I smile and say, "I keep my things in a locker there."

Aidan's smile flickers.

"Well, I should get going," he says. I don't stop him as he walks to the door. The one solid pleasure of this afternoon is in taking in every step and every inch of him from behind. He's got an easy stride, so different from Desmond's swagger. Aidan's jeans are faded and soft-looking, just like his shirt. It was probably a bright, crimson color once. Now, it's faded to a soft red. While Aidan's clothing tells me that he's easy-going and hands-on, his rear end says that Mrs. Lowt is going to be after him more often than he thinks.

He pauses near the door. Since my eyes aren't where they're supposed to be, I almost flatten my face against his chest. He smiles as I take a step back.

"If you ever need anything, Lydia," he says, stepping into the hall, "I'm right next door. You're always welcome to come by."

The tacky comebacks pop into my head. *You're good with your hands...wanna check out my plumbing? I want to check out your tool belt. Maybe you could drill a hole for me. I have some holes that need filling...*but I'm not that kind of a comeback girl. And besides, he's a neighbor. And my ass is still throbbing. If I caved, there would be no explaining the welts on my rear end.

"Thanks," I say, leaning on the door. His eyes slip down the front of me, as Mrs. Lowt's door opens. She steps into the hall, glimpsing me before she refocuses on Aidan. She doesn't take her eyes off him as she says, "Lydia, your chest is showing."

I reach down and sure enough, my robe is open, exposing half of my left breast. I pull my robe shut and wiggle a *bad boy* finger at Aidan. He grins, but tears his eyes away as Mrs. Lowt advances on him.

"And how are you, Mr. Badeau?" she murmurs, with a sly grin.

She pours herself into his personal space, her pink scalp glaring through the rows of her curlers. Paired with her magnifying-glass eyewear, she looks a little terrifying as she flutters her lashes and licks her lips. "It's always nice seeing my neighbors."

I almost giggle as he squirms a step backward. It's either that, or she'll fall on him. "Thank you, Mrs. Lowt. And how are you today?"

"Better, now," she purrs. She closes the gap again. Aidan leans back as she leans in. I just stay rooted in my doorway, enjoying the show. I'm not going to save him from her today. He deserves it, since he got an eyeful of my chest without mentioning it.

"I'm glad you're doing well," Aidan says, with another desperate glance in my direction. I smile at him. Mrs. Lowt leans closer.

"I could be better," she reaches for his lower thigh.

"Oh!" Aidan yelps as she pinches him. I hide my laugh behind my hand as Aidan scoots away. Mrs. Lowt turns her attention back to me.

"You shouldn't run around half dressed, Lydia," she scolds. "Not with men like this--virile men, full of needs--running around our hallways..."

I think Aidan's going to scream. Mrs. Lowt takes another step toward him and he trips backward, until he reaches his door.

"Well, have a good day, Mrs. Lowt. And have fun, Aidan." He shoots me a horrified glance as I close my door on them.

FLINGS ARE GOOD FOR THE SKIN

This one is wild and I name him George, even though his real name is Tony or something like that. He's a tattoo artist, and the first time he drove me home and came up for a drink, he pulled out his kit to prove it. I thought he meant it as foreplay when he said he'd like to tattoo me at the bar, but when I agreed, he popped out his gun--his actual tattoo gun.

"What do you want?" he asked. He didn't bother putting on gloves.

"How about coloring in the lotus on my arm? You do color?"

"Yeah, but don't you want something original?"

"That will make it original."

I got us drinks, but even after I'd emptied my glass and started on his, George was still all business on my arm. I squinted down at his work. "Oh wait...you're making it pink?"

"Yeah. You're a girl, I thought you'd like it, baby."

"I *am* pink," I said with a smile around the glass I'd poured for him, "but I *like* red."

George smirked, but didn't stop working away on my arm. "Did you know, pink is actually a much stronger color?"

"Why would you think that?"

"Red is vicious. It's a fierce color--it's all about anger and fury and explosion. But pink, pink symbolizes change. It mixes the anger of red with the patience, balance and control of white. Anger plus balance equals change. Very powerful shit."

He leaned back to admire his work. Pink lotus, green leaves. I didn't bother to ask him what hippie bullshit green triggered for him. George had gorgeous brown eyes and lips that I couldn't help but imagine on my nipples.

"I'm a powerful bitch," I told him. "Are you ever going to kiss me?"

He dropped his gun and his pants.

The thing about George is that he made me laugh and he was not phenomenal, but decent at the talk--and by 'the talk', I mean that he was good at murmuring his appreciation about my body in a voice that made me want more.

George was a surprise, after all his singular focus on inking me that first night--he turned out to be exceptionally good in bed. He knows the game and has mastered how to play it. This kind of man is my favorite, because he's good at what he does, doesn't spend the night, and leaves me with plenty of moments to replay in my head the next day.

But, this kind of man is also a drug. He's so good, he should be classified as a narcotic, but I've only got three dates to spend with him and this is our last. He took me for dinner and we brought dessert and wine back to my place. We've been taking turns wearing whip cream underwear, but as I'm nestled between George's legs, it sinks in that this is our last date.

I even consider breaking my ultimate three-date rule and squeaking George in for a fourth, but I know I won't. I hate the thought of the buzz wearing off and the moment down the line when George will insist I call him by his real name. When that happens, he'll want me to meet his friends or, worse, his family. Knowing that we can't just remain what we are now--people who mess up each other's hair between the sheets--is a little sad.

I sink my teeth into his thigh. Nothing vicious or *red* about it, just a good love nip. George groans his appreciation. I'm going to miss him.

I think of how much I'll miss George, as he shakes the whip can and flips me over, squirting rosettes on my nipples. The cold blast makes them rise and one of the rosettes tips over. George catches it and the sudden warmth of his mouth dissolves me. He trails his tongue down my belly. Damn. Yes, this has to be the last date.

"I can't get enough of you," he murmurs between my legs. I fist my hand into his hair. George has got great hair too, thick and soft, the deep color of wet sand. His mouth is ruining me, and then--

"Move in with me, Lydia," he breathes across my thigh. "I want to wake up with you every morning."

His puff of words extinguishes the heat between my legs. I pull my hand out of his hair.

Dammit. I knew this was going to happen. The sun is coming up and I should've made him leave hours ago. I get out of bed and slip into my robe.

"Where are you going, babe?" George asks.

"To get a drink," I say.

"Now?"

"I need it."

He leans back on the pillows, smiling at me. He fills his mouth with a shot of whip cream.

"Hurry back," he says through the whip goop. I return with vodka on the rocks--God knows I'm going to need it-- and George rattles the whip bottle in midair. "Vodka cream?"

"Sorry," I tell him. "I didn't realize the time. I've got to get ready for work."

"It's Saturday. What do you do?"

"Design," I say. "I've got a client meeting. I forgot all about it."

He doesn't move. All he does is smile, fill his mouth with another shot of whip and say, "I want to watch you get dressed, babe. I like being the only one who gets to see what's underneath your clothes."

Oh no. I expected a lot better out of George. I expected, the moment I heard his incredible sex voice, that I'd be just one of his belt notches. That first night, I assumed he'd even totter off in the early morning, feeling a little guilty and hoping to God that I'd never call the wrong number he'd leave on the table. But he didn't leave a wrong number. He left in the middle of the night, but took my number with him. I certainly didn't expect a roommate-with-benefits proposal and sure as hell wasn't looking for any exclusive arrangements on who gets to view my delicates. I thought he was way more of a player than this.

"I'm in kind of a hurry," I say, but he stretches across the bed, reaching for me.

"Slow down, baby," he says, making a grab for my wrist when I don't reach back. He tries to do the playful thing and pull me back to him, but I hold my ground as if I have hooks in my heels, embedded in the carpet. "Slow down and be with me."

I let him draw me in since he's not letting go. He takes what I know is our final kiss, and then I whisper, "I really need to get out of here."

He lets go, but instead of getting out of bed, he settles back on the pillows. This is going to be a rough Band-Aid to yank off.

So, I escape.

I go to the kitchen, pour myself a tall travel mug of Jack with a splash of coffee, and skitter to the front door, still in my robe. I unlatch it as quietly as I can and let myself out on tiptoes, closing it quietly behind me. I rap softly on Aidan's door.

When Aidan doesn't answer, I take the chance and rap a little louder. George's muffled shout comes from my apartment, "Is that your door, baby?"

Aidan's footsteps approach his door and he opens it right up, no chain lock. He's wearing shorts, no shirt, no shoes, and he's glistening with sweat. His gaze rolls over my robe.

"Hi," he says.

"Hi," I whisper. "Do you have any coffee made? I'm out and I could really use some this morning."

"Sure," he steps aside and I slip past him quickly. George has started searching for me in my apartment, calling, "Babe? Baby? Where you at, babe?"

Aidan cocks his head to the side with a smirk as he closes his door. I go into his kitchen and move a box marked *dishes* out of the way, so I can get at his coffee maker. Aidan leans on the wall, arms over his chest as I add a splash to my full cup. I snap the lid back on and take a warming sip.

"I thought you'd be unpacked by now," I say.

"I'm slow when it comes to unpacking...*babe*," he smirks. Aidan's right--George has a classic case of over-babeing. I smile over the rim of my cup and take another sip.

"Babe?" George calls again.

"And some people are really slow at moving out," I whisper to Aidan with a wink.

There is a commotion next door, muted through the walls, but it's still easy to make out George's fury, "What the fuck? WHAT THE FUCK, BABE?"

"These walls aren't as thick as they should be," I whisper again as I move away, into Aidan's living room. His furniture is dark brown leather, his coffee table is square, glass. A corner of his living room is still stacked with boxes. The place screams *bachelor* and it's so sad that I can never even have a sample bite of this man. It's taking him so long to move in and unpack his junk that things could go miserable between us and it would take him years to move out. That kind of thing makes for a huge headache that I don't need. But man, do I wish I did.

"What were you doing, before I showed up?" I ask softly, taking a seat on his couch. He drops onto his chair.

"Working out." Our voices are nothing but murmurs as George's ranting continues to escalate next door. Aidan motions to

37

a thing like a crowbar that is wedged in the door frame of his bedroom. Chin ups. Looking at his arms, it's obvious that he does them a lot. "How about you...*babe*? What were you doing?"

"Very funny," I say as George stomps across the floor in my apartment. Something shatters and I wince. "I hope that wasn't my full-length mirror. It'll be almost impossible to get ready without it."

Another crash. If the last one wasn't my mirror, this one is.

"Do you want me to escort your friend out?" Aidan offers, but I shake my head. Another crash. Another. A million crashes, one after another.

"I deserve to have a few things broken," I say. I take another long sip from my mug.

"Do you?" Aidan asks.

Everything is silent for a minute before the door to my apartment squeaks open and slams shut. George's voice in the hallway is so clear that I startle on the couch as he shouts, "THANKS A LOT, BABE! THANKS A FUCKING LOT FOR SKIPPING OUT!"

Aidan and I freeze as we hear the squeak of Mrs. Lowt's door. Her muffled voice drifts in, "Who are you? You one of Lydia's? Listen, if you have a problem, you come in here. Yes, come! You can come tell me all your problems."

"Are you...what? You're ALL NUTS!" George hollers and he stomps off down the hall.

Mrs. Lowt calls after him, "Stop shouting! You want the police to come?"

I look back at Aidan.

"Sooo," he says. "He didn't sound too happy, babe."

"No, he didn't."

"That couldn't be your *boyfriend*," he reasons. "You said you were married...but I get the feeling he's not your husband either."

"He was just a friend."

"Do all your friends stay the night?"

I smile over the rim of my mug. "Some of them."

"It sounds like you don't stay friends though."

"Usually not. It gets too complicated."

"Why was he so upset?"

I shrug.

"Did he misplace his wallet or something like that?" Aidan asks. I lower my mug. Now he's going too far. I glare from my seat on his couch.

"What do you mean?"

"Nothing...I--"

"What do you think I am, Aidan?" I sit back and take him in. "Because you keep suggesting that I'm a thief...or a whore."

"I'd never suggest anything like that."

It's not surprising that he'd try to back out of it. I've never met a man that would say it in polite conversation. I think it's because they figure it could ruin their chances if it's true. The only time *whore* really gets used is when they realize they have no chance at all. Then, they splattered all over the conversation like a volcano burping lava.

However, what's unnerving is that Aidan isn't jumping to his feet to defend himself or to attack me for calling him out. I'm used to a lot more rage from men that disagree, but Aidan is keeping his tone soft, as if George is still trying to locate me.

"If you'd never suggest it, then what are you saying?" I ask.

"I was only curious about why you're hiding from your *friend* in my apartment. And why you are sitting on my couch while your abandoned *friend* is essentially being fed to Mrs. Lowt."

I take a sip from my travel mug, weighing lies against the truth. I decide to tell him the real deal, since I can never have even one date with him anyway.

"I have a three date rule," I confide with a shrug. "This was his last date and he wasn't going easy. Since you said if I ever needed anything you were right next door, well, this morning I needed to disappear. So, thank you."

I rise off the couch, clutching the terry cloth lapels of my robe

39

to my chest so we don't have another wardrobe malfunction. Aidan is my neighbor and my new friend that may be able to save me on occasion, and in his rugged, man apartment, I see the necessity in keeping him just that. He can be my personal bouncer and body guard, but it won't help to keep the lines drawn in this arrangement if my boobs keep falling out. My malfunctions have to be intentional, just like everyone else's.

"I'll come back with you," he says as he gets to his feet. "Let's make sure that your friend is gone."

"Mrs. Lowt scared him away. It's fine. I can take it from here," I say, but Aidan shadows me to the door.

"Not while you're only wearing a robe," he says.

He follows me back to my apartment. Mrs. Lowt doesn't open her door when Aidan does and I can tell that he's relieved. We sneak into my apartment and Aidan closes the door behind him, before he even takes a look at my apartment. The minute he does, he growls, "I hope you got this guy's number, because I need to have a word with him."

My apartment is exactly what we heard: smashed, crashed and shattered. Aidan puts a hand over my waist, holding me back. There are tiny shards of my bud vases and wine glasses and my full-length mirror tracked all over the floor. Shelves are torn off the walls, the coffee table kicked over.

"Well," I sigh, slipping on my boots from near the door. "That was a lot of demolition for only a few minutes, wasn't it? I never expected George would be such a bastard. He was so much fun."

"George? That's his name?" Aidan asks as I crunch across the floor to the kitchen.

"Oh, I don't know. That's just what I called him."

I round the corner and suck in a breath. The floor is flooded with booze and more bits of glass. George had opened my liquor cupboard beside the fridge and broke all of my bottles on the floor and in the sink. All my glasses are smashed too.

"Oh, *man down*," I groan, picking a shattered bottle out of the sink that is only held together by it's label. George only knew me for three dates, but he sure knew how to get me good.

I laugh half-heartedly at how I was considering breaking my three-date rule for this guy as I peek around the corner of the kitchen and see Aidan, still standing near the door, taking in the ruin of my apartment. His expression is almost sorrowful.

"You can go," I say. "I have a dustpan."

"I'll stay. He might come back."

"I doubt it. He's got to be tired. After all the smashing George did, I'm going to assume he's too worn out to come back and do any more."

"You never know. I'll stick around and help."

"Thanks, but I'll be fine. I'm confident that this is George's way of saying he's accepted my resignation from our relationship."

Aidan's angry gaze roves over the room again.

"This is pretty typical of how your relationships end?" he asks. "I'd be furious."

"Typical? No," I tell him a little coolly. His words feel like another assumption, even though there's nothing offensive in his tone, his stance, or his gaze.

Nothing, except that he looks like he's been emptied and it makes a horrible sadness well up in me where there is no reason for it. I'm not sad about George, or even what he did, at all. These things happen. But something in Aidan's expression makes me want to sit down and rest my head in my hands. I guess it's the feeling of being judged that makes me a little angry.

"I can tell you that as far as relationships go, you'll never see the assholes coming," I say, "and you usually don't see them going either. There is no *typical* when it comes to people, Aidan. Relationships are just things that happen."

"What does your husband think about that?" Aidan asks. *Oh now.* I flash a dagger of a glare at him, to let him know that he is moving into dangerous territory.

"He agrees," I say. Aidan just looks away.

"Well, if you need me, you know where I am."
"Yup, I do," I say and I throw in a lukewarm, "Thanks."

eorge does not return. I would have killed him if he did, since it takes a lot longer to clean everything up than I thought it would. Worse, he destroyed all of my happy juice that could have been a spoonful of sugar in this whole mess. The one cheerful thought I have is of going down to the Lakeview Liquor on the corner to restock. And it will be fun to get new wine glasses.

After everything is cleaned up, I take a shower and get dressed, but it is hard to see how anything looks on me when I only have a few shards left of my mirror that George didn't manage to kick out of the corner of the frame. I finally haul it out to the dumpster. The only mirror left is the medicine cabinet mirror in the bathroom and it's in the worst possible place. I have to balance on the edge of the tub and I still can't see everything I need to.

Scrutinizing my ensemble in pieces is fairly impossible. I'm not sure I can go out like this. George really knew how to sink my battleship.

This all started with Desmond. He used to insist that I stand in front of the mirror so he could assess each outfit I wore, before we could leave the house. Sometimes it would turn into a sex game, with him running his hand up under my skirt, checking to see if my panties matched the rest of my outfit. Or, if something was out of place, he would bend me over his knee and spank me for the infraction. At first I thought it was scary, then just a little kinky, but eventually, I learned to love the sting of his hand, and then his belt. When Des left me for Claudia, I continued the weird ritual of having to make sure that I was always dressed correctly, except that I never felt like I'd done it right and there was no spanking to relieve the feeling.

Now, hanging on to the shower bar and trying to fit my entire reflection into the tiny box of my medicine cabinet, I know it's ludicrous, but I can't stop. I pull up my leg to view how well my shoe matches.

It'd make sense that I have worn outfits before and could just repeat the successful ones, but that's not how it works in my head. Each ensemble has to be carefully studied each time I wear it. I've found loose threads, scuffs on my shoes, a nail pop in a stocking, a smudge of ink on the elbow of a shirt.

It's especially impossible to tell whether or not my attire is wrinkled because of the contortions I'm doing or if they will remain there when I'm finished. I put on the skirt and blouse I wore to Desmond's mansion, but I can't go out like this. The top button of my shirt doesn't look right buttoned or unbuttoned and my hands are starting to shake so much it's uncomfortable trying to mess with it. I add it to my pile of reasons for hating Desmond and one day, I'm sure the reasons will take root. At least, I hope.

I know that what I really need to switch my mood is an Alabama Slammer. Or a straight up shot of Two Fingers Tequila. That would lighten me up again. I hit the computer and order the necessary groceries from the store a street over. I'd be willing to pay a few golden eggs to have them delivered to my door, but the order is denied. They won't deliver liquor.

Shit. I need a drink.

I finally conceal myself inside a trench coat and knee-high boots and slink out into the hall. I might as well be naked--I keep my eyes on the floor as I scurry down the hall and wait for the elevator.

Riding down to the ground floor, the reflection from the steel doors is comforting. A woman from the floor above me rides down with me and watches, but I don't care. I twist and turn and try to make myself presentable in the distorted image. My sense of calm returns a bit. I'm starting to feel okay when the doors roll open and the woman steps out ahead of me. I'm about to step out when a man's face swoops in close to mine. I startle backward as I stare into the eyes of the man who's made me this neurotic.

"Des?" I say as he steps into the elevator with me. "What are you doing here?"

His eyes flick over my outfit and it's like I'm naked all over again, ready to be bent over and spanked. The worst part is that I almost crave it. I want it to relieve the tension inside me.

Damn, I am screwed in the head.

"I thought I'd come to you for a change," Des says. "A little surprise visit. Just to talk."

"I was just leaving." My eyes flit from his as he blocks my way out. A waft of his cologne drifts into my lungs like a sedative.

"I only need a few minutes. What floor are you again?" he asks as he punches the number of my floor.

The doors slide shut. I want to groan. I'm giving in again. It always starts like this--I say no, he says yes, I think of how he'll touch me and I become useless. Fuck me.

"I would've thought you'd be in the penthouse, Lyddle. Don't I give you enough money?"

I don't say a word as the elevator jogs back up to my floor. I'm surprised that he doesn't try to get closer, as elevators were always our thing. Well, everything was our thing.

"We'll have to talk about your clothing choice," he murmurs.

I can feel my resolve slipping away like a sand timer with a hole busted out of the side. I can't give in today. For once in my damned life, I've got to stand my ground. I can't let him into my apartment.

My eyes are on the floor as the elevator door slides open and I hear an apartment door open down the hall. I hope Mrs. Lowt spots Des and comes shooting out. I really hope she does. She hates him and I could use all the distractions I can get to keep him out of my apartment. I shift from foot to foot, waiting to be saved as Des steps off the elevator and into the hall.

Instead, Aidan emerges from his apartment and comes straight toward us. My stomach drops. Des turns back when he realizes I haven't followed him and catches me looking at Aidan. Aidan catches the whole eye-conversation too. The two begin eye-jousting as Aidan puts his hand on the elevator door to keep it open.

"How's it going, Lydia?" he says. "Want to share an elevator ride down?"

Desmond answers for me, "No, she doesn't. We were just coming up."

"Funny," Aidan tips his head, looking only at me. "I thought I just heard you go out."

Des puts out his hand.

"Let's go, Lyddle," he says.

"Or you could just ride down with me," Aidan returns, his voice all warm and inviting. I want to hide from them both. Des puts his fingertips on Aidan's arm.

"I didn't get your name?" Des says. It's not a friendly inquiry. Not from the look on his face. Aidan shoots him a wise-ass smile as he pulls his arm away.

"I'm her neighbor," he says. Then, back to me, "So, how about it, Lydia? You want to come with me?"

"Tell this man that you don't, Lyddle," Des says tightly. "Right now, please."

"I'm fine," I say.

"You don't look fine."

"This is none of your business," Desmond says and Aidan's glare swings at him.

"And who are *you*? What's your name, buddy? Is it George?"

"This is my husband, Aidan," I say flatly. I step out of the elevator as every trace of expression slides right off Aidan's face.

He goes silent and takes a step backward as if he's been pushed into the lift.

"Oh," he says. Des leans in and hits the ground floor button. The elevator doors slide closed on Aidan's blank face.

"Nice to meet you," Desmond replies with a little wave.

" *L* et's go have a talk," Des says.

"Not now. You can't just show up. I have things to do."

"I'll pay for your time," he says, reaching into his pocket. He extracts a wad of bills, wrapped in a thick green roll and secured with a rubber band.

He planned it this way.

He knew I'd object.

But I can use the money.

I tell myself I'll use it to get divorce papers. Yeah, right. I take the wad.

We walk down to my apartment. I slide the key in the door. Mrs. Lowt doesn't save me.

"So, Lydia." Des's voice is all smooth once we're inside, running his vocal fingers over my mental shelves, checking for dust. "Your neighbor--Aidan, wasn't it?--he's very protective over you. Why?"

"I have no idea. He just moved in," I say. I stand near the door as Des tours the apartment, observing the empty, re-installed shelves, the trash can still full of broken glass, checking the view from the window.

"Who's George?" he says.

"A friend."

46

"A friend." He takes his time crossing the room. "Lyddle, do you think that's appropriate?"

"Don't play with my head, Des," I say, raising my chin. He reaches up, curling his fingers under it and resting his thumb on my chin. "You're only my husband on paper."

"You've gotten such a smart mouth," he says, his eyes on my lips. The horrible tingle of his touch makes me feel like he's rubbing dirt all over me. Even worse, I like it. "I might need to do something about that mouth."

"I'm not doing anything with you right now."

He smirks, his eyes trailing down to my quaking fingers. "I only came to talk, Lyddle. What's got you in such a big hurry?"

"I broke my mirror. I have to go order another one."

"That explains your attire, doesn't it." He reaches for my hand, giving it a tug, so I follow him to the couch.

"Come," he says, all velvet and steel. "It won't take long, I promise."

He paid me. I tell myself that's the only reason why I sit on the couch beside him. Des reclines, his arm spread across the back, his fingertips touching my hair. He glances around the apartment again.

"This is such a small place," he says.

"That's what happens when your husband leaves you," I tell him. "You don't need so much space."

"Oh, now," Des drawls, straightening his wrist cuff. "That smart mouth again, Lyddle? Is that how this is going to go?"

"What did you come for?"

"First things first," he says. "I give you more than enough money to afford a nicer place than this, don't I?"

"This is good enough."

"Well, that's always been the problem, hasn't it, Lyddle? Haven't you learned anything from me? You should never be happy with *good enough*. Move closer to me."

I scoot over, until I'm next to him. His fingers play in my hair, massage my skin. He leans in and places a warm kiss at the base of neck. He knows what melts me. His lips on my body have had a track record of erasing all the crappy things he's done to me.

"Damn it, Des," I moan. "This is wrong. It's got to stop."

He just laughs, blowing his warm breath over my skin. "You're still my wife. And a wife is never supposed to refuse her husband."

"Tell that to your other wife." I say. His grip tightens on my arm as he drags me even closer. I fall into the dip between the cushions.

"Don't be jealous, Lyddle. You know I care for Claudia, for different reasons. I don't know why you constantly want to give me such a hard time about this. You're the one that has always had my heart. Why aren't you happy? Do you want to go back to being poor? I can finally give you whatever you want now..."

"I never wanted anything but *you*."

He softens at that. "I'm right here, Lyddle. You've got me. You've always got me." He pushes back my hair and lays his lips tenderly to my neck again, tracing the skin to my collar bone with the moist warmth of his mouth. "I miss you so much. This arrangement isn't forever. I promise."

"It's been three years," I say, but I am already losing ground, melting away beneath the heat of his tongue. Damn him. I already know I'll lie awake tonight, reviewing whatever happens in the next hour or so, hating myself for taking Claudia's money, hating him for giving it.

His hands skim over the front of me, tracing the Bermuda triangle beneath my clothes. That's what he always called it, since he said he loses his mind every time he touches it.

The stroking of his fingertips temporarily blurs the shame. His tongue moves against mine and I drink it in, nixing any further conversation.

"Now," he murmurs when I come up for air. "I want to see how you're dressed. Stand up and let me look."

I'm stupid to do it, stupid to keep on letting this happen. He's

48

cheating on both me and his fake wife in one shot and I'm helping him do it by never telling, never stopping him.

But I have a stubborn thought that I use to justify it all. He's still married to me. I still have feelings for him that I keep shored up, bulging inside my heart, as my desire roars behind them. This was the first man I ever loved, the first man I ever made love to. His presence still makes me feel like things will be okay, even though he's the one who has made everything go wrong.

"I said, I want to see how you're dressed, Lyddle. Are you wearing the right panties? Will you let me see?" he whispers.

He is my tragedy. My sick, sick addiction.

I turn away and bend over in front of him, offering him the length of my thigh, the opening of my skirt.

"Yes," I say as I close my eyes and wait for his touch.

STRANGER THINGS HAVE HAPPENED

My sunglasses make the inside of the elevator even darker on my ride down to the lobby, an hour after Des has gone.

I had to be sure he was long gone, so I could put my head back together best I could, without a drink. My hands are quaking, thanks to George's rampage. I reassure myself, as the elevator sinks past the floors, that this will be the last time I do any of that with Des, but it's a helluva lot easier to believe that lie when I chase it with a few Mojitos.

The sunglasses are all I've got, and not nearly enough, as the doors glide open and I'm standing face-to-face with Aidan. His eyes roll over me and he cocks his head.

Great. I'm not really armed for an extra shaming. I try to brush past him with a polite grin, since he's the last person I want to see right now, but, of course, he wants to talk.

"Nice shades," he says. "And a new outfit, isn't it?"

"Is it?" I say absently, as if I have no idea that the other is upstairs in my hamper, too stained to wear out in public.

"Your husband...he's an interesting character." Aidan smiles all good-natured-neighborishly.

"Yes, he is."

"Is he always like that to you?

"Like what?"

"An asshole."

I decide then and there that Aidan needs to remember what we are to each other and that I'm not the helpless princess waiting for his white-knighted ass to save me. He might be right on target-- Des is a total asshole--but the deposits he just made are still rolled in my pocket and still slick between my legs. He's still my husband.

"We're neighbors, Aidan," I say with a wry smile. "How about we just keep it that way?"

He nods with a little frown. "Alright."

"Thanks," I say, whisking past him and out the lobby doors. I'm happy to be wearing the dark shades because, for some reason, my eyes are welling up with tears.

<<<<>>>>

J order the mirror and pick it up four excruciating days later. I haven't even bothered to leave my apartment, since I can't really see what I look like in the medicine cabinet. Down to the last of the Jim Beam, I was relieved when the store finally called to say the mirror was ready for pick up. I spend three hours getting myself ready and still step out of my apartment feeling like I'd rolled in mud.

It would've taken an extra three days to have it delivered, so I decided to pick it up myself, which turns out to be a monumental mistake.

The mirror is a bitch to drag home.

It's an even bigger bitch to drag through the lobby and into the elevator.

And it's almost a totally broken bitch when I lose my grip and it tips over in front of my door. Mrs. Lowt rushes out of her apartment, nearly stampeding me in the hallway.

"Lydia, what is going on out here? Why are you making so much noise?" She circles the enormous, rectangle box as if she's a bomb-sniffing dog. She drags her finger over the word stamped on the cardboard. "Mirror? What kind of mirror is this big? A ceiling mirror?" Her smile is almost hopeful. "Is that what you got here? Are you making one of those kinky bedrooms--with mirrors and chains and the poles for dancing?"

"No." I smile at her, a little disappointed to be kicking down her expectations of me. "This is just a regular, full-length mirror. It's the kind that stands in the corner."

She's not giving up that easy. "So you can see everything in the bed?"

"No, I just use it to see how I'm dressed," I say. Why I have to add it, I have no idea, but I do-- "My professional outfits."

"A professional," she says with a knowing nod. "Oh, Lydia. Why do you want to do that? And the men...the men you bring back here--at least they're good looking. I wouldn't charge them myself, but that's not good for business to tell them that, is it? Where do you find the handsome ones that pay?"

"Oh my God, Mrs. Lowt! I'm not a prostitute! Those are my...boyfriends."

Her sly grin disappears as she plants her hands on her hips.

"Boyfriends come back, Lydia," she says. "The only one that ever comes back is the one that was here today. The one I don't like. I hoped he was gone, since I haven't seen him in a while."

"Desmond? He's an *old* friend," I say. I've been careful to never tell her that Des is my husband. She already pries too much and I'm worried that if Claudia ever decided to investigate, Mrs. Lowt would be a gold mine. "Why don't you like him?"

"He's got a mean way about him. All wrong for you. I can see it in his eyes."

I squat down to grab the end of the mirror box, so she can't see the shiver that runs through my legs. "You nailed him."

"You need a *good* man, Lydia. Just one." She skitters out of the way as I heave the mirror upright.

The elevator doors open at the end of the hall and Aidan steps out. I haven't seen him since I told him to mind his own business, four days ago. I've heard him coming and going, his door has a particular squeak, and although I thought about meeting him in the hall and apologizing for being such a hard ass to him, I didn't.

He walks toward us, a computer store bag dangling from his fingers, his gait calm and graceful. I could fall in love with his body; even if I could only fall in love with it three times--damn the rules--but those three times might be enough love to last me all my life.

"A good one like *him*, right?" I ask Mrs. Lowt with an appreciative smile, but she shakes her head.

"No, that one needs a real woman," she says, her eyes drooping seductively. They actually look more like trashcan lids being compacted behind her enormous glasses. "Aidan needs someone who knows exactly what she wants and can treat him like the man he is."

"Someone like you?" I ask with a giggle.

Mrs. Lowt licks her lips. "You got it, toots."

"Hello, neighbors," Aidan says with a two finger salute to us. His eyes dust over the box, but he gets his keys out for his door. I would swear all my muscles are about to pop out of my face from dragging this mirror as far as I have, but I'd rather just heave the fucking mirror into my apartment on my own than have to pay for his help by answering his questions.

"Neighbors help," Mrs. Lowt squawks too loud for Aidan to ignore it.

"You need help, Lydia?" he asks. But he's not just asking. He's being a wise ass.

"I think I've got it," I grunt.

"You don't have it," Mrs. Lowt says, waving our handsome neighbor over. "You come here, Aidan. Do what men do. Be a man and carry this box in for Lydia."

He plays along, sliding his keys back into his pocket. He walks over and takes the end of the box from me with a smug smile. I'm about to pass out, but Aidan hefts the mirror box like it's a chopstick. He nods to my door.

"Open up, Lydia."

I do as he says with a sour glare. He carries the box right in.

"Show off," I mumble.

"Weakling," he says, but he laughs.

Mrs. Lowt takes a step toward my door, as if she's going to follow Aidan in, but I block her way.

"Thank you, Mrs. Lowt! I'll talk to you later!" I say.

"Ohhh, Lydia!" she whines, but I close the door on her anyway. I don't want her nosing around my apartment and I really don't want to stand around while she mauls Aidan. She can do that in the hall on her own time. I just want to get my mirror set up and then have Aidan clear out.

"Where do you want me to put it?" he asks.

"In the bedroom would be great," I say. Great, indeed. I watch his lean back, tight and angular beneath his shirt, as he carries the mirror into my room. He's got a rear end that makes his Levi's look like art. He puts the box on end, in the same corner where I had the last one.

"I can take it out for you, if you like," he says. I snicker at his innuendo. I'd sure like it to be more than just words, but...no. It doesn't change the fact that he lives next door.

"It can stay where it is. I'll pull it out and put it together later."

"I could do it for you."

"You've done enough, but thanks."

He shrugs. "Just trying to be neighborly."

I cross my arms over my chest.

"Are you going to be like this forever?" I ask.

"Neighborly?"

"No, angry."

"I'm not angry at all. But how about you? Are you always going to be secretive and suspicious?"

"Damn, you're nosey."

"Seems kind of suspicious that you refuse to answer the question."

He's wearing me out, or maybe he's just wearing me down, with that lazy smile of his. I'm almost glad. I'd rather us be friends instead of enemies.

"What do you want from me, Aidan?" I almost hope he says something that will involve our tongues and/or our hips.

He shrugs as he turns away and opens the end of the box. "Friendship."

I don't insist that he stop as he slides out the mirror. Instead, I watch his muscles move as he sets up the solid wood frame. I imagine his hands on me, instead of the bags of parts.

"Can you grab me a screwdriver?"

"I don't have one."

"Under your sink," he says. Like magic, I retrieve it, slapping it into his waiting palm with a smile as he winces.

When he's finished, the mirror stands on its pedestal in the corner and it's better than the first one. The frame is carved and gorgeous. Aidan wipes the glass clean with his elbow. He stands back, suddenly grabbing my wrist and pulling me to him. We stare at our reflection and he bumps my shoulder with his.

"I think we can be friends, can't we, Lydia?" he says.

"Sure," I say, but as he moves away, I want to drag him back. I want to push him onto my bed, pull the mirror to the edge, and have him watch the hundred or so things I'd like to do to him.

Instead, he leaves, and I go to my cupboard for a drink, but my cupboard is bare. Four days of moping will do that.

Thanks again, George.

Since the liquor won't come to me, the only thing I can do is go to it. I open my closet and begin the selection. It's at least a little easier to be dressed properly now.

<<<<>>>>

*T*hree hours later, I step into the hall and lock my front door behind me just as Aidan's swings open. A woman's laughter wafts into the hall from his open door and I feel a tinge of something I refuse to acknowledge. I remind myself that I am perfectly dressed and ready to snag a dozen men as I put up my chin and walk down the hall, past Aidan's place.

"Lydia!" His voice is deep and unmistakable as he calls to me. An older man exits the apartment, brushing past me with a smile and a wave over his shoulder as people from inside shout good-byes. Two brunettes are bookends for a guy parked on the middle cushion of Aidan's couch and another guy is standing beside the kitchen bar, dipping into a bowl of chips. Aidan is perched on the arm of his recliner beside a blond, but he still motions for me to come inside.

"I'm just on my way out," I say, pointing down the hall. Comfy little gatherings like this, without any blaring music, swirling lights, or bartenders, just aren't my thing.

"Come on in and say hello first," the man on Aidan's couch shouts. He also smiles at me, while the dark-haired girl beside him eyes me with a lot less enthusiasm. The second brunette on the furthest cushion, cranes to see me.

"Is that your *neighbor*, Aidan?" She raises her fingers and visually air-quotes *neighbor.* "Make her come in!"

Make her? The small grin on my lips thickens like old Jell-O, but the younger, perkier brunette jumps off the couch and scurries toward me.

"This is *perfect!* I'm Ila, Aidan's sister. Come on in! We've heard all sorts of things about you!" She's as toothy as a sorority sister and all I can do is gape at her. What has Aidan told these people? That I hid in his apartment while George busted up my place? That I'm married to an asshole? That I'm the slut who lives next door?

"You must be thinking of someone else," I hardly get the words out before Ila is dragging me into Aidan's apartment. *Dragging.* "We're just neighb..."

"You're Lydia, aren't you?" a man says behind me.

I swing toward my name and spot the owner of the voice, the man in the chips at the counter. He's a cross between up-tight (ironed khakis) and punk rock (short, shaggy hair) and when the lemon-faced brunette jumps off the couch and goes to his side, he slides an arm around her waist. Retired Punk Rock has a tight smile, as if his girlfriend has a Jedi vice-grip on his balls.

"Do I know you?" I ask, hoping it's safe to own up to my name, since he hasn't slipped his hand off of his girlfriend's waist. All I'm thinking is, *please say you're a waiter or a bank teller or a stripper at a bachelorette party...anything really, besides 'I've seen your vagina.' Please.* My track record has shown that it is rarely a good thing for a man to admit to knowing me, especially while he's holding another woman, and it's crazy how many men just don't get that.

"You should, but I guess Aidan's admiration only goes in one direction. He's told us all about you." Punk Rock laughs and his brunette cracks a bitchy little smile. Ah yes, she hates me. I'm just a little floored that Aidan's been talking about me enough that they'd want to meet me. I'm not sure what to think of that. Flattered? Embarrassed? Stalked?

Punk Rock puts out his hand. "I'm Shane."

All I can do is blink like the village idiot.

"Shane?" I say. Oh no. *My-belly-button-tastes-like-a-Mojito* Shane? That Shane? Oh crap. He's seen my *Who*. The *Whoberry.* The tropical *Whoflower* in my pants.

I glance at the brunette girlfriend. She catches it and I watch as my shock and hesitation disintegrates her smile like dandelion fluff in a breeze. She steps away from him.

"You know each other?" The dimples in her smile tighten down like bolts in her cheeks. "How?"

"It seems like it, from all of Aidan's stories," Shane says, still sporting the dopey grin. He's looking at me, not her. He should be looking at her. *Jeezus.* And he should wipe the stupid smile off, before we both kill him. Instead, he just takes in my attire with politely raised eyebrows. "Do you bartend, Lydia?"

"No," I say, "I just tend to hang at the bar."

"Ohhh, you're on your way to the *bar*," Ila says, her tone cresting as if it was a mystery I just solved instead of a simple answer. Her eyes cut to Aidan.

I don't know why--except that Aidan's *my* neighbor--but I get this sudden burst of possessiveness, like the proximity of our apartments makes him more mine than any of theirs. Holy shit. I've got to shake that off. He's just a dude that lives next door to me.

That I kind of want to bang.

But won't.

Maybe.

"You're not hanging at the bar, are you, Aidan?" the guy next to her says. My ears perk. The mood in the room suddenly slants toward something like an intervention. What the hell? I don't care what they think of me, but I am a little offended that everyone in the room is throwing their parental controls on my neighbor.

Who belongs to me.

Who I will not bang.

Probably.

Aidan ignores the guy's question, taking me in from head to toe instead. "I like your shoes."

I slant my foot to show off the gunmetal-gray pumps, but mostly the translucent spike of the heel.

"I usually hate gray, but..."

"They look good on you."

"I used to have a pair like those. Bar shoes," Shane's girlfriend says. She air-quotes *bar shoes* separately. Whoa. Whatever they think they're looking at, it's definitely not me.

I turn back to Aidan. "You can come along if you like."

I hope he'll say yes just to piss them all off. I try to keep it casual and friendly, even though now I really, really want him to come. I want him to choose me over his pack of bossy friends.

But, it's not like I own him.

I don't.

Yet.

He looks at me and it's like everyone else has cleared out of the room. Aidan smiles.

"I probably shouldn't," he says and even though my smile lags, I hang onto it.

"That's fine," I say. "I'm going to get moving then. Nice meeting all of you."

"Why don't you stay with us instead? We're more entertaining than Mojitos," the guy on the couch says. Doubtful, but the reference to the Mojitos sends my eyes to Shane. Aidan told them about my belly button, but Shane is still acting like he doesn't have a clue of who I am. Miss Air Quotes still looks like she'd like to incinerate me. Shane steps forward.

"You're welcome to stick around," he says.

"I can't. I'm meeting friends," I say. It's not a lie. I meet friends at Modo's every night. "Have a good night."

Aidan rises off the arm of the chair.

"You sure you can't stay?" he asks. His gaze reaches for me, instead of his hands, and it's stronger than if I was trapped in his arms. I can see that he wants to make me stay, like he wants to beg me or tie to me to a chair, but I just smile.

He's got to be *just* a neighbor.

No matter how much I would love to have him begging me, or tying me to his furniture.

We're just not going there. We can't.

And I've got to get out the door.

"I'll see you around, Aidan," I say.

"Absolutely." His eyes drop, along with his smile, as I turn away.

*T*he evening at Modo's is not what it should have been. I'm annoyed and I can't put my finger right on the exact reason why. Part of it, I think, is that no one measures up on the ruler that has *Aidan* burnt into it tonight. I can't get my neighbor off my mind, no matter how many shots I down.

And then there are the drinks. They all taste flat and pissy. Every single one stirs thoughts of Aidan's next-door-soiree that seemed like a full-blown, intervention of strangers. I should've knocked Miss Air Quotes in the head and called out Shane, the one-night-wonder. I should've let her know that her boyfriend's tongue once had an intimate conversation with my belly button.

"I thought you'd be here," a man's voice says from my elbow and the voice is unmistakable. I turn to him with a frown.

"What the hell are you doing here, Des?"

"Checking up on you."

"Three times in two weeks? You're starting to act like you're my husband or something."

"You can always look at your ring finger, if you forget."

"Don't get me started," I grumble.

"You look lovely..."

"Seriously, why are you here?" I snap. "You know we shouldn't be seen together in public like this."

"Change of rules." He shrugs. Like it's that simple to just reconfigure the whole game. He steers me away from the bar, to a corner table where I can hear what he's saying. Grabbing a waitress, he orders me a Slippery Nipple and himself a Hole In One, twerking his eyebrows at me as he does it. He tips the waitress a twenty, dumping it on her tray without even looking at her, once the drinks are on the table.

He takes a slow sip, watching me over the top of his glass. I can smell the warmth of the booze clinging to his words. "I see you all the time, right beneath Claudia's nose at the house, so I thought, why *not* here?"

Yeah right. What I think really happened is that he just got a good look at Aidan and it's just like dangling a carrot in front of an ass.

"I can tell you why not here. Because Modo's is hardly a 'professional meeting' kind of a bar. You're going to blow your cushy ride if you're not careful," I say, chewing on the straw in my drink. "Maybe end up in jail. Besides, I don't want you here. This is too confusing as it is."

"There's nothing confusing about it. You are my designer. It's not like we can't meet for drinks to discuss a project. Christmas is coming. I'm meeting you to discuss plans for an upcoming party."

"That I can never attend."

"It's a conflict of interest." His eyes flash. He knows it's a veiled threat. Des doesn't do threats well. "And you are a loyal wife. Your husband's firm always schedules their party two Fridays before Christmas, just like we do. Don't forget, Lyddle, you've been part of this deal from the start. If I go down, you're coming with me." He reaches across the edge of the table and twirls the skinny tip of one of my dreads around his fingertip. "I wish I'd never gotten you involved in any of this, Lydia, but my only alternative was to divorce. You know I can't live without you. I'm not the one being selfish here. All I've ever wanted to do was give you everything. If it means a little creative license here and there, well, I guess we've proved that we can both live with that."

What can I say? He's right. I don't have any money without him. I have no skills to get a job and I can't go back home to be a burden on my mother. I gave up everything to be with Desmond and that means accepting whatever he can give me, even if it's not *him*.

My buzz mercifully kicks in, from sucking my drinks through the stirrer straws, and I don't want to kill it with this conversation. Better yet, I'd like Des to go on home to his fake wife so I can get my groove on and find a new face to focus on for the night. I set down my drink.

"Alright, I got it. You can go home now."

"I think I'll stay for a while. Claudia's visiting a retreat."

"Come on, Des. I know why you're really here," I say with a grin. He perks an interested eyebrow. "You don't have to be jealous--he's not coming. My neighbor really got you nuts, didn't he?"

"Not at all." He leans back in his chair, arm loosely extended on the table as if he's the king of this domain. I almost laugh. I like that he's a little jealous. It's a nice switch.

"The only time I see this much of you in one week is when you think there's another man around. So let me just put you at ease. Aidan's *only* my neighbor. You don't have to scout out my apartment complex anymore. I'm not fucking him."

"So crass, Lyddle" he chuckles. "You think that he's why I'm coming around?"

He reaches under the table, the tips of his fingers sliding over my leg and then under, to the tender back of my knee. It melts me more than I'd like to admit, but I manage to croak out a throaty, "Yes."

His touch is expert and soft, as if his fingers slide up into a more intimate place then just the crook of my knee. The delicate pressure he applies makes my head spin. He catches my gaze and his eyelashes flutter like the nimble legs of a seductive spider, enchanting me with their lazy dance.

His voice is deeper than the bass beat on the dance floor. "He is not the only reason, Lyddle."

WARS AND GAMES

My tongue tastes like an old shoe that has spent the night walking through a sewer. And the rest of me--my arms, my legs, the tips of my hair--is a pitiful collection of limp socks. I wake, face-down on the pillow like I was trying to smother myself. With my first breath, I suck my pillowcase into my nostrils. Jerking up my head sends atomic throbs through my skull and makes me think I should've let myself finish the job with the pillow. I lay back and try to breathe between the hyper, Richter ripples of my hangover.

On mornings like this, I have to lie very still until the throbbing ebbs and my memory can kick in again. But, today, I should've just enjoyed the pain and left it at that.

Des was here. I remember draping myself over him so he could drag me down the hall to my apartment. He felt me up for the door key. Mrs. Lowt opened her door and shut it again once she saw Des. She doesn't want anything to do with grabbing his butt.

I almost threw up in the kitchen sink. Des told me I was a mess and put me to bed. He slipped between the sheets shortly after. I scour my memories for sex and feel around, looking for clues, but I think Des only took off his shoes.

One of my nightmares woke me at dusk. I reached for him and felt the soft fabric of his pants, the tight knit of his shirt, the ribbing of his socks beneath my toes.

"I'm not going to stick around if all you're going to do is cry and make me feel like shit," he grumbled. The memories drift in and out--I remember opening my eyes and seeing Des there, looking at his phone. Then, opening my eyes again, I remember him lying on his side, looking at me.

I push my leg over the sheets now, checking to be sure he's gone. Of course he is, but he left at dawn. It's bright outside now and Des usually turns to ash any time past three in the morning. I don't know why he stayed so long. Even if Claudia's out of town, the help might report back that Desmond wasn't home, tucked in bed, after the bars closed. I'm surprised he'd chance staying the night, but then it occurs to me. I was right after all.

Des was waiting for Aidan to go out in the morning, so he could leave at the same time.

<<<<>>>>

*M*y tennis-shoe-tongue slowly ebbs away to normal-enough by midday. I'm starving, but the only things in my fridge are a jar of pickle juice, a carton of expired milk that I must've bought on some health whim, and mustard. I struggle into my clothes, check myself with only one eye open to the mirror, and I give up immediately.

Standing in my mirror, I smash a black baseball hat on my head and put on my sunglasses. The knee-high boots are a necessity and I spend thirty-five, excruciating minutes adjusting the hat and smoothing out my trench. There's no way I can make myself acceptable enough, so I need to make myself invisible instead; just any other shadow of a person moving down the sidewalk.

But, of course, it's not that easy. Aidan crashes into me as I walk out the lobby door.

"Hey, stranger." He once-overs my black *ensemb* and smirks. "Invisible is the new black, huh?"

I kind of hate that he sees right through it, but the sensual little tug of his lips, as they drift toward his right cheek, makes it forgivable.

"Shhh, you never saw me." I brush past him.

"It's hard to do that," he says, falling into step beside me. "Where are you off to?"

"Grocery store."

"That's amazing. It's exactly where I was headed."

"That *is* amazing, since you were walking into the lobby."

"I just got turned around. It happens when you're new to a place."

"Which store were you going to? There's two."

"Probably the same one you were. You know--that one with all the food."

"Oh yeah, that one," I say. I consider turning him back toward the lobby with a biting comment, but the size of him, walking beside me, does the opposite of what it usually would. Usually, the fact that I'm not dressed properly would make my skin crawl until I was alone again, but he doesn't have that effect on me. It could be the breadth of his shoulders, spreading out like a wide canopy just a little higher than my eye level, or--*damn*--his body, his face, his work boots, the scent of his cologne all over his jacket...who knows. Aidan's combinations pick my lock. I let him walk along with me.

"Thanksgiving is next week," he says. I laugh.

"There's a conversation opener," I say. "Is that what inspired you to come along with me?"

"Maybe. I've got to grab a turkey."

"Aren't you going home for the holidays?" I say it the way a gooey, holiday commercial would.

"No," he says. "Too far. What about you? Where's home?"

"You've seen it. 2B."

"Kind of tight for your whole family."

"Har har. You really are nosey," I tell him, but there's no bite to it. "They're in Oregon."

He whistles. "That's a hike from here. How did you land in Michigan?"

"My husband."

"Oh yeah, him." A blast of cold air rushes up the sidewalk after a passing car and Aidan stuffs his hands in his pockets. "He seems like a real interesting guy."

"*Interesting*. I've never heard Des called that, but it fits."

"It seems like you have a different kind of a relationship."

My instinct should be to defend what I've got with Des, but I don't even know what I have with Des anymore. The best I can do is a stiff little shrug. "You could say that."

"Does he live with you?"

I consider the question and what my answer should be for a few steps. We take the corner and head down Elm, toward Main, and I decide to opt out of answering with a subject change.

"So you're cooking for Thanksgiving. Are you inviting all your friends from the other night? They seem like a real good time."

He turns his upper lip under and chews on it a second before answering. "About that..."

"I don't think your friend Shane remembered me."

"No, I'm pretty sure he didn't."

"Well, that's good. I think his girlfriend gave him amnesia."

"Wife. Natalie." He shifts uncomfortably.

"They don't seem like they'd be your crowd. It felt more like an church meeting." I say with a little laugh. Aidan pulls a hand from his pocket and coughs into his fist.

"Actually, they are friends, and it was a gathering of recovering addicts," he says. Oh shit.

"Oh."

"I'm a recovering alcoholic. I have eighteen months."

"Well, at least that makes more sense. I was wondering why your friends got so squirrely when I invited you to the bar. I guess meetings like that don't just pop up like flash mobs." I try to laugh, but my arms are suddenly warm and a little itchy inside my coat. We turn onto Main and I can see the grocery store only a block ahead. Oh great. What's he going to think when I load my grocery cart with bottles of booze? I just want him to leave, so I can get in, get out, and get back home. Aidan touches the sleeve of my coat.

"Does it bother you?"

"Yes. I hate recovering alcoholics. They're traitors to the bottle," I say with a smirk. "No, Aidan, I don't care at all."

Except that he's probably going to be judging me now. And preaching.

"You really don't, do you?" he says and his expression is a little too sincere.

"It's not my business what you do with your liver, as long as you don't get all judgmental about what I do with mine."

"I've got no room to judge you."

"Good." We reach the doors of the Stop -N- Shop and he stands aside so I can go in first.

"I want to invite you," he says, "for Thanksgiving dinner."

"Oh, uh..." I make a big job of untangling a grocery cart from the line of them inside the door. "I don't know. I think we have plans already."

"We?"

"Yes," I say with another little frown. "My husband and I."

I call for emergency backup the second I get home from the grocery store.

Aidan has rattled me. He carried home my bag of bottles with a few groceries thrown in, to make it look like I eat, after he decided he didn't need anything from the store after all. The whole walk back to our apartment building, he didn't push for big answers, but just asked me little things- like if black was my favorite clothing color, if I like watching movies, if I ever had any animals. He spent most of Elm Street telling me stories of his childhood-he's got an autistic brother, a mom who likes to make soap, and Ila, the sister who was at his apartment party. Although he never asks me to reveal any of my secrets, when I get back inside my apartment, with the door locked behind me, I have this weird sinking feeling, as if I just told him everything.

I leave the bag on the counter, pour a shot and down it like medicine, and then I call Jan. He's the only person in my world, besides Des, that knows what's going on in my marriage. Jan is my hair stylist and confidant.

He's at my house that night with a bottle of wine, a rolling bag full of cosmetics, and a camera slung around his neck.

"New gig," he says as he rolls through my door. "I'm trying to get my faces into Voyeur magazine. So you're guinea pigging for me tonight."

"Alright," I say. "Do me up."

He starts setting up as I dump a jar of pasta sauce in a pan to heat on the stove top. I pour noodles into a colander in the sink as Jan joins me in the kitchen.

"Oh honey, you're cooking?" He takes the glass of wine I offer him and pokes at the gelatinous noodles with a cautious finger. They move in a clump and he winces. "What have I ever done to you to deserve this?"

"We can order take out," I say. Jan takes a gulp of the wine.

"No, no, you went to all that effort to open a jar. I'll eat it," he giggles. "But let's just do faces first, in case your dinner is already plotting our deaths."

"Good plan," I say. I put a lid on the sauce and turn it down on low. Jan returns to the living room and opens up his enormous make-up suitcase. I sit on the couch as he applies layers of moisturizer and primer and foundation to my face.

"So what's the emergency?" Jan asks. "I was just thinking the other day that I haven't seen you since I put in your dreads. They still look stunning, by the way. Something new with you and Des?"

"Nothing with Des. He's still with Claudia. I'm still here."

"Sad, isn't it? Everybody wants a bad boy, until they have one," Jan sighs. I know the sigh--it's the one Jan assigned to his own bad boy, Robert.

"How's it going with you and Robert?"

He groans. "He's still cheating, still coming and going whenever he feels like it. That's the real tragedy--one day you realize that he can't turn it off and it no longer turns you on."

I nod in depressing agreement.

"Des is still paying your expenses though, isn't he?"

"Yeah."

"So lucky," he clucks.

"My husband's married to another woman. That's luck alright--bad luck."

"No, it's pure skill is what it is, honey." Jan reaches for another bottle of something that he applies with his ring finger, in light dabs across my face. "I miss being a kept woman. Robert's never going to be that man. I'm the one that keeps us afloat."

"At least you can."

"I've said this before, and I'll say it again. If you hate being tied to Des's leash, you could always come and work at my salon."

"You know I appreciate the offer, but I can't afford to live on that."

"Not like you do now, no. But you could survive. Why don't

70

you try going back to night school again? Get yourself ready to get on your feet."

"It's pointless. It's still only a high school diploma. I can't get a decent job without a college degree."

"So, get a GED and go on to college."

I swallow a laugh with some of the wine. "Yeah, right."

"The academic mumbo jumbo isn't really you, is it? You're right. You should make a bee-line into modeling, like I told you from the start."

"Right." I roll my eyes, but I wonder if he really thinks I'm not smart.

Jan steps back to assess the make-up while simultaneously duck-facing me. "Yes, right...look at the shape of your eyes, Lydia. I don't have to tell you you're exquisite. You're like an edgy, punk rock Cleopatra."

"Des would never go for it," I say. Jan sighs.

"You are really sour tonight. What else is going on?"

I take a sip of wine to buy myself a moment of thought. I called Jan so I could talk to him about Aidan, but now that I'm about to, it feels wrong to do it. Like I'm going against Des. Or how it's a stupid idea to keep playing around with, since Aidan's my neighbor. I know I can't *have* Aidan, so there really isn't much use in even talking about him. Then again, just thinking about him gets me off and it's a lot better than thinking of how I'm stuck in a marriage with a criminal who's banging a widow for her cash flow.

Jan stops rooting in his make-up case. "Wait a minute. You haven't broken your three date rule, have you? Is that what this is about? A new *man?*"

"No," I say, but a grin seeps out of me. Jan isn't fooled. He squeals, scooting in close as he waves a fan brush in my face.

"It is a man, isn't it!" he says. "You have man troubles! I can see it in your eyes. Spill, Lydia. You must. Immediately."

It doesn't take much more than that for me to give in, since

Aidan's name is bubbling on my lips to be said. I smile. "I have a new neighbor."

"I thought so. Tell me everything. Start with his name."

"Aidan."

"Ohhh, that's sexy."

"Wait 'til you hear his last name," I say, sipping my wine as Jan pulls out an eye shadow palette. "It's *Badeau*."

Jan gives an appreciative groan and motions for me to close my eyes. A brush taps against my eyelid as he speaks.

"A sexy French man? Honey, you cannot ask for more than that. Tell me he looks like he sounds."

"Better," I say and Jan does a happy sigh. "He's tall, dark hair, and he's got a body that you would fight me for."

"You're killing me. Face? Don't tell me that's the problem."

I open my eyes.

"Not at all," I turn my head away to whisper against the edge of my wine glass. "He's incredible."

Jan lowers the palette and brush. "Then what's the problem? Has Des made you crazy? You should be over there right now, knocking on Mr. Incredible's door."

"If it was that easy, I probably would."

"Ohhh, I see," Jan says. "He's a more-than-three-dates risk, because he lives next door."

I nod. Jan swabs the brush in taupe eye shadow. I close my eyes again.

"Honey, have you ever thought that maybe there are exceptions to the three-date thing? Maybe you should just go down to the courthouse, file the divorce papers on Des yourself, and let it all play out."

"I could go to jail too," I say, pulling my head back from Jan's brush so I can take a sip of wine. "Just for letting it happen."

"Do you really think so? Have you asked anybody?"

"Who am I going to ask?"

"I don't know...the police?"

"What if it is and they traced the phone call back to me?"

"You really think they'd do that?" Jan asks. "I don't think you'd be in trouble. Not the way he treats you."

I look at him dully. "He gives me everything I want."

"He gives you money, honey. That's not everything."

"We both know I can't make it on my own."

"Do we?" Jan asks. "*Do* we know that?"

I just take a long drink, swirling the wine over my tongue. I don't want Jan to launch into an inspirational, pity speech. That makes everything ten times worse and no matter how drunk I get, I always remember it the next morning. Pity has a way of hanging around with the same aftertaste as vomit.

<<<<>>>>

*K*nocking at my door is never good. Especially in the morning. The only ones who come knocking are people who want something I don't want to give them, like my landlord, or one of my third-dates that won't take *it's over* for an answer, or Aidan, who lounges on the door frame with a smug grin when I open up.

"You should use the chain," he says. "You didn't even ask who's out here."

"I should have," I grumble as I step away, muddling around the mess from last night's little party with Jan. The coffee table is still crowded with our dishes of unfinished, congealed spaghetti, empty wine glasses, empty wine bottles, and cosmetics that Jan decided he didn't want anymore, scattered amongst it all like odd confetti.

"I came to get your final answer about Thanksgiving," Aidan says, stepping in and quickly closing my door as Mrs. Lowt's opens hers across the hall. "I'd love for you to come."

A smile flutters over my lips at the innuendo as I walk into the little cube of my kitchen. He had to know how he said that. I wish I could take him up on it.

Instead, I root in the cupboard for coffee filters. Of course, I'm out. I tear off a sheet of paper towel and try to shape it into the filter basket, aware that Aidan's behind me, watching. Waiting for an answer. I pour water into the machine and dump spoonfuls of coffee into the center of the paper-towel. I close it up and hope for the best.

"So?" he says.

"I appreciate the offer, but..."

"You're married," he finishes for me.

"I don't do Thanksgiving," I say instead. He smirks.

"We'll just call it dinner, then."

"I've got plans, remember?"

"Do you?" he asks and his gaze is like Superman's see-through stare, illuminating my lie as it sits on my tongue. But, I carry through with it anyway.

"I think you should have a good time with your AA friends. I can already tell, we don't mix."

He chuckles. "Very punny."

I smile, bow beside the perking coffee pot.

"How about if I promise to keep them under control?"

"No impromptu interventions?"

"Not one." He crosses his heart with one finger.

"How else would we pass the time?"

"No one would be there to judge you, Lydia. Believe it or not, even addicts in recovery have other things going on in their lives to talk about."

"I wouldn't feel right bringing wine."

"Then why bring it?" he asks casually. It still irks me.

"This is the problem, Aidan. I don't have to defend myself to you, just because I like a glass of wine with my dinner *on a holiday*." Even as I say it, my eyes travel over his shoulder to the carnage of bottles and glasses on my coffee table. Wine ended up being the main course last night. Looking at the glasses, I want some now.

"Bringing along some wine would convince you to come?" he asks. My hips hit the counter. I didn't even realize I'd been backing away from him.

"Why are you trying so hard?" I ask.

"I'm against anyone spending Thanksgiving alone."

"I won't be alone."

"No? The husband really does drop in for holidays?"

"The point *is*: I won't be alone," I say, dodging the question. I'm not big on turkey anyway. Modo's is open, so I'll be down there celebrating.

"I'd really like you to come," he says. He moves closer and his stare is so intense, it seems like there's nothing else in the world to look at. He's close enough that I can smell his cologne. I have this crazy desire to rub the sandpaper stubble of his jaw between my breasts. For a second, I nearly lose my train of thought and agree to going to his little soiree. The way he gets into my head is familiar. It's the way Des used to monopolize my thoughts. I should be running away screaming.

Instead, I do the next best thing, "I appreciate the invite. I'll try to make it."

I know damn well it's the last thing I'll be trying to do on Thanksgiving, but it gets him off my back. Aidan nods with a slow smile like he knows it too.

"I'll be looking forward to it," he says. "Dinner is at five."

THANKS A LOT

I wake up Thanksgiving day to the smell of turkey. It's that rich, dark smell and doesn't mix well with a hangover. I roll over on my pillow with a moan and knock into someone's face.

Crap. A cuddler. Now I've got to deal with that too.

The clock says it's one in the afternoon and I lie here, sorting out last night's memories and trying to glue it all together. I was at Modo's. The bathroom. That's right--this guy followed me into the bathroom. We were in the stall, it was cramped, and the girls waiting in line to pee began to bitch. But the guy's tongue was a soaked lime and with my foot on the toilet, I whispered to him, *don't stop.* He didn't, until one of the girls started kicking the stall door and the guy's teeth cracked against mine. We were laughing, but I thought I swallowed a piece of his tooth.

I don't know why I invited him back to my place. Or if this is even the same guy.

I lean across my pillow and lift his lip. Yep, chipped. It's him.

He's still out cold, but I need him to get out of here, so I can get out of here before five. I can't mosey out at 4:30 without Aidan giving me a hassle. I figure I'll go catch a movie and head to Modo's early.

I press my palm to his shoulder and give the mystery man a shake. He coughs and rolls over. I do it again.

"Hey," I whisper, "time to get up."

The guy rolls onto his back.

"Hey," he says with a smile. His junk is standing on end, as if it has static cling. His grin gets wider too. He can't be serious.

"I've got to get going," I tell him. Usually, the guys clear out fast, but this one grips himself under the covers and does a slow pump. It doesn't do a thing for me. *Dumb* doesn't turn me on in the least.

I slide out of bed and follow the horny Hansel-and-Gretel clothing path we left from the door of my room to my bed. I dump the wad of his attire on the mattress beside him.

"Time to go," I say with a smile. He grabs my wrist.

"C'mon now," he says. I twist out of his grip, but he's fast. He grabs the other and pulls me down beside him. He smells like B.O. and sticky booze. I wrinkle my nose.

"It's Thanksgiving and you've probably got someplace to be."

"Nope."

"Well, I do," I say.

"Right this second?"

"Actually, yes."

He hasn't let go of my wrist. I pull away, but he tugs me closer. God, does he stink.

"Just one more," he says. I can tell what this guy is now. I've had a couple like him. He's the kind that won't care about his chipped tooth, because he'll show it around like a hillbilly trophy. He's probably going to need more than one square kick to the nuts to get him out of here. Maybe even a solid crack from that wrench under my sink.

"Alright," I purr to him. "But let me get a little something first."

He drags me a little closer and his stink fans up my nose. "You don't need anything else than what I've got right here...baby."

At least I did one thing right and never gave him my name.

"Let me get some whip cream," I say, pulling away. It doesn't sound so sexy when I'm trying to fight back a gag.

"Oh." His eyebrows hike up and he lets go. "Breakfast. Where do you want to put it? On me or on you?"

"Both of us," I say as I sneak to the front door, instead of the kitchen, and grab my trench coat. I slip into the hall, but before I can knock twice on Aidan's door, mine swings open. Mystery Man steps out into the hall in his boxers, looking a little confused.

"Where you going, darlin'?" he asks. His excitement makes the fabric of his shorts dance. It's obscene, even for me. Mrs. Lowt's door flings open. She steps into the hall, her face wrinkled as she shoves her coke-bottles further up on the bridge of her nose.

"It's Thanksgiving, Lydia! It's not the time for your sex games all over the halls!"

"Hey," Mystery Man barks, "This ain't your business, lady. Go on and get back into your apartment."

"Both these ladies live here," Aidan says from behind me. "It's you that needs to leave."

"I don't think I asked for your input," Mystery Man says. He turns to me, his lip lifting in a sneer. "You sneaking away on me, *Lydia*?"

My name, on his stale tongue, makes my stomach turn. Aidan steps to my side.

"If a girl is sneaking away, then it's a pretty sure sign that you overstayed your welcome," he says. "How about you grab your clothes and get moving?"

"I don't need your help, Mr. America. This is between me and her."

"Last chance to grab your stuff." Aidan says, stepping in front of me.

"Fuck you, buddy," Mystery Man says and in a blink, Aidan twists the guy into a full nelson and walks Mystery Man down the hall like a body puppet. He knocks the elevator button with his elbow, struggling to hang onto the guy as he bucks and shouts threats. The doors roll open and Aidan steps inside, still hanging onto the guy.

As the doors roll closed, Aidan shouts to me, "Toss his clothes out your window. It's going to be cold out there!"

The elevator doors finally seal on Mystery Man's cursing. Mrs. Lowt turns to me, shaking her head.

"You see that the men are a problem, Lydia. You need to pick *one*. And not the one I don't like either, and not these men you bring home, but never see again. You've got a good looking man that lives right next door and you see what he just did. *That's* a man, Lydia. That's what you need."

"I think you've got a crush on our neighbor, Mrs. Lowt."

"I know a good one when I see him," she says. I laugh as I stride into my apartment and close the door. I've got some clothing to toss out my window.

I don't watch Mystery Man pick up his clothes. I shut my window and throw on the first things I can find, because I owe Aidan both an apology and thanks for getting rid of the guy. Aidan knocks on my door only a moment later and when I open it, he smiles.

"You owe me," he says. He's got a split lip.

"Holy shit, he got you," I say. Aidan wipes away some blood with the side of his hand.

"I let him. I figured if he got in a shot, he could leave with some dignity and wouldn't come back."

"You didn't have to do that."

"He looks worse."

"Good."

"Come on, then. Time to pay up." He jerks his head toward his apartment. I've never wanted to repay a debt so much. I follow him as if he's playing a flute.

Once inside his apartment, I think he's going to turn to me, flatten my spine against the door, and rake kisses down my neck. He doesn't. I follow him into the kitchen and when he turns to me, he hands me a knife. I take it, confused.

"You're going to help me get ready for dinner," he says. He pulls lettuce from the fridge and hands it to me, along with a bowl. "Everyone will be here in a couple hours, so I can use the help."

To cover the shock, I take the lettuce and shove past him to the sink. "You have to wash lettuce. You can't just chop it up and toss it in a bowl."

"That's why I wanted you here," he says. He chops vegetables and sticks them on a tray with room for dip in the center. The running water is the biggest sound in the room until he says, "You ever going to tell me who that guy was?"

"No," I say. How am I supposed to tell him when I don't know myself? I'm sure Mystery Man's wallet went out the window with the rest of his clothes and that was probably my only chance at ever knowing his name. Unless he pops up at Modo's or at my apartment door again.

"Alright," Aidan says. I shake the water off the lettuce and come around the counter, so I'm standing opposite him. He waits until I pick up the knife and start cutting, before he says, "Doesn't it bother you?"

"What?"

"Not knowing their names."

"Nope," I say. The silence hangs there, separating the chopping sound of the knife blade as it hacks through the head of lettuce.

"I've never met anyone like you, you know," Aidan says.

"No?"

"Most women want relationships. They want marriage, a

house, kids. But not you. You're running as fast as you can in the other direction." He pops a cherry tomato into his mouth. I wait for him to ask why, but instead, he says, "You sure you're not a dude?"

"Maybe I am." From my peripheral, I watch his eyes slide over me.

"You sure don't look like one, but you do act like one."

I shrug. "Yeah, well." Then, to change the subject, "This is going to be a great salad."

"You can tell everyone you made it."

"About that," I drawl, "I don't think I can make dinner tonight."

"How come?"

I hold up one finger.

"I'll show you," I say, walking backward toward the door.

"Where are you going? Don't think I won't bust down your door if you go into hiding. I need serious help here." He waves a carrot stick over the counter.

"I'll be right back, I promise." I slip out of his apartment and into mine, grab one of the two bottles of wine I bought in case I went to his party, and return with it. I plunk it down on his counter.

"This is why," I say.

His eyes are on the bottle's label as I watch him swallow. He steps backward and goes to his cupboard. He takes down a juice glass and sets it down, like he's placing a bet, on the counter beside the bottle. His eyes are caught on the label.

"You're right," he says, "it would probably be a bad idea, since they're struggling with it."

"What about you? Are you struggling with it?" I ask. I watch him swallow again. Then he looks away and wipes his nose on the back edge of his hand.

"Nope," he says.

"Then you don't mind if I have a drink?"

"Nope."

I crack it open, even though neither of those *nopes* sounded very convincing. I'm not trying to test him or be cruel; the truth is,

I need the drink. I'm all tensed up. I need to mellow out and get into the driver's seat during this conversation. Wine can usually take my edge off. Aidan's eyes flit around the room, back to the bottle, to me and then back to the bottle, to the vegetable tray in front of him. He frowns.

"I could hide it in a travel mug, if you want," I say.

"If you have to have it, do whatever it takes to make you comfortable coming," Aidan says, but the tiny muscles in his jaw flinch.

"It wasn't for me. It was to make your friends comfortable with me being there."

"*You* aren't the problem, Lydia. The alcohol is what would make them uncomfortable, not you."

I swirl the glass and take a good, long drink. Aidan watches my throat and studies my lips like a jealous lover after I lower the glass.

"Why is it so important to you that I show up?" I ask.

"I don't want anyone spending Thanksgiving alone."

"I'm not..."

"Or with guys that I have to throw out of the apartment building," he amends. He frowns when I salute him with the wine glass.

"I guess that's fair," I say.

*A*fter watching me down a second glass, Aidan puts some distance between us. He stays on the other side of the kitchen, furthest from me.

"It might be a good idea after all--to put your drink in a travel mug."

"Yeah, I don't know. Wine in a travel mug? Maybe not my best idea."

"Haven't you ever been addicted to anything?" he asks. His tone is a little desperate, his misery begging for a little company, I think.

"Sure," I tell him. "Good 'N Plenty candy. But I learned to handle myself."

He winces. "What I'm getting at is that my other guests haven't."

"And you want me to be considerate," I say. He smiles.

"I'll make it worth your while."

"Oh yeah?" My body goes on pilot, dropping my eyelids and lowering the timbre of my voice. "And how are you going to do that?"

He glances at me and grabs a towel. He dries a bowl sitting beside the sink before he slides it across the counter to me with some tomatoes and cucumbers to cut for the salad. "Get chopping and if you're good, I'll tell you stories of everyone coming tonight, so you can get an idea of who they are."

"Oh, I'm never good," I say with a leopard's gaze. It's my body's natural chain reaction to any flirtatious line that comes out of my mouth. My chin dips down while my eyes simultaneously look up at him. I know exactly what this does to a man, since I've done it a hundred times before. My predatory stare hits Aidan and he pauses with his chewable lower lip dropping open. His expression is so enchanting, the spell I was trying to cast seems to ricochet, and I'm no longer 100% sure of who is hypnotizing who.

Thank God, he clears his throat and looks away. I return to the cucumbers in front of me too quickly and nearly hack off my thumb. Whatever magic that was, it was a little too close for comfort. I really have to remember that Aidan's not my chew toy, not my scratching post, not my signature brand of catnip. He's just a neighbor. That's all he is and that's how it's got to remain.

"Leonard is my sponsor," he says, shaking me out of my spell.

"He's got twenty-five years clean and sober. I think you'll like him. Lots of wisdom in that man."

I'd bet that Leonard has a ponytail, wears sandals in the winter, and leases a permanent space at Boring Central.

"Devon and Marlisa are coming," he adds. "You met them already. And my sister, Ila, will be here."

"Cool name."

"Cool girl," he says. "She's been clean for a year. Shane and Natalie might be late, but they're coming. He's not an alcoholic, by the way."

"He's not?" I mull that one over. He must have just been out on a bender, the night he got with me.

"No." He avoids my gaze as he grabs a cloth and wipes the counter. I used to work with Shane--I introduced him to Natalie. She's been sober for eight months."

"She's a big fan of mine."

"Don't take it personally. She's hates everybody. She's still having a hard time figuring out who she is, away from the bar."

I laugh, trying to capture his eyes again, but it doesn't work. "At least we can bond on that. I'm not sure I could recognize myself in the line-up of blondes at Modo's either. The dreads help."

"She could learn a lot from your confidence," he says. *Confidence.* I almost snort. He's still not looking at me, so I figure I should go ahead and try to escort the elephant out of the room.

"So what made you quit drinking?"

He sighs, leans his hips against the counter. "I wanted to," he says and his eyes finally find mine. "Have you ever wanted to do something so badly that you knew there was no way you would fail? That's what happened to me. I got to the point of being so damn miserable and desperate that I would've been happy to die from withdrawals, rather than take another drink. Have you ever wanted anything that bad?"

I shake my head. This conversation, his eyes--it's all getting a little too intense. "No."

"Never?"

I scramble for a memory that will diffuse the pressure. "Well, there was one time...but it's stupid, compared to what we're talking about."

"Ok," he shrugs, "so let it be stupid. Tell me anyway."

"Alright," I say, dusting off my hands. "I was in ninth grade, and Maria Telecki and I had a gym class together. Maria was a bitch and so was I, but then, Maria's boyfriend, Carl--he was a senior--dumped her and asked me to go with him to the Prom.

"That afternoon, Maria bet me, in front of the whole lunchroom, that I couldn't beat her ass in a long distance race. If I won, I told her I wanted this silver, butterfly necklace she wore every day to school. I knew that if I got it from her, it would knock Maria off her high horse. But if I lost, she wanted me to swear that I wouldn't go to Prom with her guy. So, Maria and I both entered the annual 5K run in town.

"I didn't give a shit about Carl. I wanted that damn necklace and wanted it even more in the days leading up to the race, because Maria kept taunting me with it. She'd dangle it off her finger at me whenever she was around. I was ready to puke up my lungs to get that necklace."

Aidan reaches over the bar and brushes my dreads away from my naked collarbone. "And you're not still wearing your prize to this day?"

I shake my head. "I didn't get it. I was ready to puke up my lungs, but the day of the race...what can I say? Maria Telecki beat me. She was better."

"Doubtful," Aidan says. "She probably caught you on an off day."

"She could've raced me any day and won. I never bothered to train, but she did and she was fast." I lean back on the counter. "I stuck to my word though. I puked up my guts at the finish line and Maria took pictures to prove it."

"And you didn't go to Prom."

"No. Carl and I went to a motel party that night instead. That's the night I met my husband."

Aidan laughs. "Ahhh...slick. Two birds and one stone."

"Yeah, well." I shrug with one shoulder. "Shit happens."

"So you know what it's like to want something, but you don't know what it's like to do everything you can and actually succeed."

I feel this getting too preachy for my tastes. I reach for my wine glass.

"Meh," I say. "Success is overrated."

As I bring the glass to my mouth, Aidan steps forward and wraps his hand around mine. His face is distorted through the glass until I lower it.

"No more, okay?" He almost whispers it.

"It's really getting to you that I'm drinking?"

"No, it's really bothering me that you're trying to glue your pieces back together with wine." The pressure of his hand around mine is gentle. The bottom of the glass tinks as it meets the counter. "Wine doesn't work for shit as glue, Lydia."

The muscles in my cheeks suddenly go stiff, as I struggle to hold my grin in place. I see what he's doing and it's exactly what he said he wouldn't. My cheeks blaze with the humiliation as I push away from the counter.

"I've got to run," I say.

"Interesting choice of words." His expression is all deep and introspective and full of fucking pity. I pick up the wine glass and toss whatever's left in his face.

"Oh, sorry," I say. "It slipped."

He wipes it away slowly with his sleeve. I head for the door.

"Wait," he says, following after me. I spin on a heel to face him again.

"Just because I like a little wine, it doesn't make me an alcoholic, Aidan! That's *your* problem, not mine. So, if you need to be somebody's savior, then go find someone with an actual problem first!"

I make for the door again, but he grabs my arm. I jerk loose and he steps back.

"I'm sorry, Lydia. You're right. It's not my business and I shouldn't have said anything."

"Now *that's* an interesting choice of words," I snap. "You shouldn't have said anything--because it made me angry? Or because you think it's true?"

"It was just a stupid thing to say."

"But which one is it?"

"The stupid one. Can we start over?" he says and he grins. It's every bit as charming and disarming as he means it to be, but he just made me feel like a fucking, drunk loser. He can't do that.

"I'll see you later," I say as I slip out the door.

"Dinner's at five," he says, but the hopefulness in his voice wilts, just like the damned friendship we'd just started to grow.

FEASTING ON FRIENDS

I hear his guests as they show up. The trill of a women's voices, greeting each other with "Happy Thanksgiving!" and the deep gravel of the men as they greet one another. I wonder if Aidan realizes just how thin the walls are between our apartments.

Since I do, I tiptoe around and even wince when the lip of what was going to be my party-wine bottle hits the edge of my waiting glass with a sharp tink. I don't feel like going to Modo's anymore, but I don't want Aidan coming over to invite me again either. All I want to do is sit on the floor near the heat vent, where the voices from next door blow through a little clearer.

I don't know why I give a shit about listening to their conversations about the weather and construction, or pie recipes and turkey timing...but I do. I want to hear Aidan's laugh, even if it is a little muffled. I want to be sure no one's talking about me, or if they are, I want to be sure it's the right person and that he's saying the right things.

There is talk of the football game, the food Aidan's serving, complaints about work and the snow. They discuss the prices of lattes and new TVs, debate public transportation policies, quote some movie they've seen. And then comes the conversation I've been listening for.

"Where's your neighbor?" a woman asks. Curious, hopeful-- sounds like Aidan's sister.

"She was here earlier, but she had some things to do," Aidan says.

"She's not coming back?"

"She knows dinner's at five," he says and his tone comes through the wall like he's looking right at me. A guilty shiver speeds through my stomach.

"It's almost five now," someone else says.

"I better pull out the turkey then." Aidan says and the conversation is dropped. They talk about setting the table and who wants water and where everyone's going to sit.

I watch the digital clock on the shelf in my living room as it flashes through the minutes. It's meant for the bedroom, but it got moved out here at some point and I've never thought much about moving it back. I don't live by a clock. I live by calls from Des and measure my days in trips to the liquor store.

I listen as the chairs next door scrape as everyone sits down for dinner. Aidan doesn't come knocking and I can't tell if I'm relieved or just lonely. I hear the clink of silverware, the laughter, the small talk. With my temple against the wall, I consider downing the last swallow in my wine glass, sucking up my pride, and going next door. And then I hear my name.

"It looks like Lydia's not coming," a man says. Since he's not talking Buddhism, I figure it's got to be Shane.

"What *are* you doing with that girl anyway?" It's a disapproving woman's voice. Oh, that's Natalie, no doubt.

"Yes, I was wondering that too." That's Leonard. *Dull* comes through the wall loud and clear.

"We're friends," Aidan says. I think he's chewing his food. "Neighbors."

"You know, she's an alcoholic."

I don't care who said it, I only care that it was said. Those bastards! They don't even know me, but they're over there chewing up my reputation over dinner. They've never seen me at the bar. It's not like I'm out in the hallway slamming shots. They don't know one thing about me. But they're over there judging me, just like Aidan said they wouldn't. The outrage bubbles like caustic chemicals inside me--I want to put my hand through the wall and drag each of them into my world, just so I can tell them what I think of *them*. Then Aidan replies with something that absolutely floors me.

"I know," he says.

He doesn't defend my honor or anything! He should be over there telling his table full of quitters that they're all crazy, but instead, he *agrees* with them. That *son of a bitch*!

"You know you can't have a relationship with her, so what are you going to do about it?" Natalie says. I can *hear* her thin little lips flapping and picture her weaselly little eyes narrowing for an answer.

"I'm not doing anything about it," Aidan says. At least there is a little tiny bit of *back off* in his tone now. A little chivalry would go a hell of a long way right now.

"It sucks...I was that party girl once too." It's a quieter woman's voice, but not Ila, not Natalie. Must be Marlisa. "When I was using, I wanted to be saved. There was a guy in Tulsa, he offered to lock me in a room with him, do everything I needed to get me clean and sober..."

Natalie groans. "Let's not sidetrack into another Marlisa story."

"She's just sharing her experience." I think it's Shane that defends her? Or maybe her husband--what was his name? Devon. That's right, even though it really doesn't matter. Marlisa jumps right back into her story.

"All I'm saying is that I wanted to be saved. When I had the needle hanging out of my arm and the cops busted in, I wanted..."

Natalie's voice crests over the top of Marlisa's tale. "What do you think of it, Leonard? In relation to what we are supposed to be doing to keep ourselves healthy, I mean. Don't you agree that Aidan should be careful since she's an alcoholic?"

"It's not my business what she is," he says. *Huh.* I'm liking Mr. Dull a little more. "However, as your sponsor, Aidan, I will say that I don't think it's wise to date a person that could endanger your sobriety in any way."

--And now I like Leonard a little less.

"She won't," Aidan says and someone laughs. Or snorts.

"You have a very strong spirit," Leonard says, "but sometimes remaining strong requires avoiding those temptations that could weaken your will."

"I understand," Aidan says.

"In your experience, Leonard," Natalie's needling tone prickles at me, "how many guys have you known that have thrown away their sobriety because they thought they could save a girlfriend?"

A deeper voice intercedes- it has to be Marlisa's husband, Devon. "It happened to us, Natalie," he says. "Marly only had five months when we met. A lot of couples don't make it, but some do. It might be against the odds, but if it means that much, sometimes it works."

"Rarely," Natalie says.

"It is against the odds," Ila chimes in, but it sounds hesitant.

"So why risk it?" Natalie says. God, I hate her. Then, as if to set the cement on my feelings for her, she adds, "And how many thought it wouldn't happen to them, Leonard?"

"Quite a few."

"Did I tell you two to quit your relationship when Nat started?" Aidan asks.

"It's a completely different situation," Shane argues. "We were already together. Established."

"All I'm trying to say is that you kept it together and I think we can too."

"But it's a *new* relationship--" That, of course, comes from Natalie.

Marlisa jumps in with, "Anyone want to help clear the dishes?"
"Me," Ila says.

The dishes clank and throats clear and I can feel the tension that's got to be a hundred times worse over in Aidan's apartment. A simple difference of opinion and it's like everyone's dividing up and jumping into their foxholes.

I'm sure there is pie and coffee, but I don't listen anymore. I take my party-wine into my bedroom, shut the door, and strip down to my panties and bra. I slip into a long-sleeve shirt that Des left behind over six months ago. The scent of his cologne is long gone, it's just a ratty old shirt now, but it's at least good for a night shirt.

I flick on the flat screen, hanging on the wall at the foot of the bed, and bunch up the pillows behind my back. With my drink on the bedside table, any other night this would be cozy, but I can't get Aidan's dinner party out of my head.

Part of me wants to make a late entrance and fire off acidic responses to what I've heard.

Part of me wants to hide, just like I'm doing.

I drink my wine, hoping it will erase what I can't get off my mind, but after a few more sips, my mouth goes dry. I get restless, too hot under the covers, too cold once I throw them off. I retrieve my phone, and despite my better judgment, I call Des. He picks up on the second ring.

"Desmond Strong," he answers, all professional as if he doesn't have caller ID. Another dinner party murmurs in the background, silverware chiming against plates. Before I have a chance to speak, he says, "Well, thank you for letting me know about the back order on that ceiling fixture, Lydia. I appreciate you taking time out of your own holiday celebration to touch base. Yes...you too! And have a wonderful Thanksgiving with the family. Thanks again for calling, Claudia and I are delighted to have you on our team."

He hangs up and I never even said a word.

I toss the phone down on my bed and yank his shirt off my back.

<<<<>>>>

*I*t's around ten o'clock when there is a knock on my door. I ignore it, but then there's a second knock, and a third, and then Aidan starts shouting and it sounds like he's going to kick down the door. I slip Des's shirt back on, carry out my wine glass and open up. Aidan's standing there with a hefty tower of foil-covered dishes.

He gives the shirt a once-over as he brushes past me. Mrs. Lowt pops into the hallway just as I close the door.

"I see you had a million plans and couldn't make it to dinner," he says, depositing his tower on my kitchen counter. "So I brought the dinner to you."

"I already..."

"You've got to try my turkey." He says, popping off the foil on a plate loaded with meat and clumpy cranberry jelly. "It's the first one I've ever made and I want an honest opinion. Ila made the sweet potatoes. It's her first too, but sweet potatoes are nothing compared to cooking a turkey, right?"

"Aidan..."

"You're lucky I like you. I also got you a piece of the pecan pie *and* a slice of pumpkin."

He drops the foil on the counter, pushing the plate toward me, a fork clattering off the edge. I lean on the wall beside the kitchen and bring my glass to my lips. I empty the contents into my mouth. He takes the glass from my hand, set it on the counter and turns back to me.

I think he's going to speak, preach or complain, but instead, he kisses me.

He flattens my back to the wall, crushing his body against mine. My body responds, spearing my fingers into his hair and twisting a leg around his. If he's going to kiss me like this--then he's not getting away from me.

The small moan that eases out of his throat makes me wonder if it is my kiss or the wine on my tongue that he is enjoying most. He deepens the kiss and when he pulls away, he takes my lower lip between his teeth with a soft tug that ignites me. I clutch him and drag him back for more.

He complies, opening his mouth and devouring mine; his palm at the back of my head, as if I'd want to get away. All I want is more of him. I hitch my leg up around his thigh, opening to his clothed excitement. I want him so bad, I think I might choke him with my tongue, but he slows the rhythm, matching the motion of the kiss with a slow grind of his hips against me.

This is the part I live for, the sensual build up to the release. My heart is banging as hard as Big Ben approaching midnight and the beat sinks all the way down between my legs. The whole world seems like something I'm standing on, instead of muddling through. He steals my breath and gives it back to me. My body sings its siren song as my brain entertains every orgasmic daydream I've had about how good this sex is going to be with the man trapped between my thighs.

"I'm so bad for your sobriety," I murmur against his lips. I have to give him one last chance to run. "I don't want to wreck it for you."

"I wouldn't let that happen," he says with a slow smile. "But I'm going to wreck your taste for booze."

"Oh yeah? How are you going to do that?"

"I'm going to make it so all you'll want to be is sober...just so you can remember every damn thing I do to you."

*M*ornings-after are always weird, but this one is beyond even that, because I actually know the name of the guy that's got his arm wrapped around my waist and his body glued to the length of my back. And he knows mine. Maybe that's what makes it so uncomfortable.

Or it could be that I don't want Aidan to leave.

That's a really bad turn of events, considering he's still my neighbor, I'm still married, and I'm like a wrecking ball, swinging straight at his sobriety. It's not like I didn't see this coming or did a damn thing to stop it, but now that my neighbor is sleeping with his face in my hair, the whole idea of being able to handle this delicately has gone right out the window. Especially now that I know Aidan is even better between the sheets than I'd ever imagined.

Last night was incredible. A feat of stamina and control. Maybe the best surprise was that Aidan blew George out of the water when it comes to sex talk. Most guys haven't got a clue. They're full of groans and *oh baby*s, but have no idea how to say *tits* without it sounding like they just hit the whore jackpot. Or worse-- they talk about my *breasts* and *vagina* and *clitoris* like they're conducting an anatomy lecture. I mean, damn. In bed, it's a *clit;* the things on my chest are not *mammories* or *fun bags*, they're either tits or just *mmm;* and anything below my waist should be slowly admired, piece by slippery piece, in silence--but never, *ever*, referred to as a gynecological whole. And there's absolutely no reason to ever mumble even the most amorous words about my *clitoris* while trying to get some. None. Bad sex talk can get a man gone from my bed faster than anything else.

But that's not Aidan's deal. He says things in a soft-gravel whisper. Just remembering it, goose bumps rise up where his words slid over my skin. His mumble of *do you like this,* was so erotic that it French-kissed my imagination until my hips writhed up, begging for more of him.

My eyes flutter shut as I re-live the way his hands had moved my limbs, guiding me into the positions he wanted; how his body made mine tingle like a warm mitten; how his eyes were on my lips as he spoke. My legs ache from how I tied them, like a Christmas bow, right above his hip bones, and they ache with how I held tight until we both came undone.

My arms are stiff too. Probably from the way I was holding myself up at the window sill--a new and unexpected position. But not even the *most unexpected* position that came out of our four, midnight-gymnastic sessions. I had just hoped he'd be fun, but Aidan Badeau has proven himself to be an amazingly skilled surprise.

It's more than a little odd that I can follow my memory bread-crumbs right from the moment I met Aidan at the door to now. Usually my recollections of evening escapades consist of whatever I can stitch together around tattered holes of memory. Most of the time, what I can put together is as wide and irreparable as ripped cobwebs. But, here I am, knowing the man's name and able to identify the particular scent of his cologne on my pillow. I remember everything what we did and how we did it (with details that I'm going to replay every chance I get) and I even know where this guy lives.

And this is exactly why this has to stop.

Now.

It's gone way too far.

I don't know if *letting him down easy* is even an option now. Why the hell did I bang my neighbor? Damn. I knew better. But *damn*. My skin is already craving another play date with his and he hasn't even left yet. I'm seriously mulling over an amendment to the three-date rule.

No.

I know better.

This will end in absolute disaster if I keep this going for even one more date. The only apartment left where I can escape and hide is Mrs. Lowt's, and she would be of no help at all. She'd just invite Aidan right in, to help herself to a little bit of ass-candy.

I've got to end this all, before it goes nuclear.

I've got to convince Aidan that I was so drunk, I didn't know what I was doing. Or that I didn't know it was him. I'll say *I'm sorry, I'm sorry, I'm sorry* until he runs screaming from my apartment, repelled by how pitiful I am.

He shifts and I feel his morning salute rising up between my thighs. He snuggles closer, his thighs as strong and firm as a chair against the back of my legs. There's no way he could want to do it again. But I'm sure I'm wrong about that as his hips bump against me and then his erection nudges between my legs again, like a neighbor poking his head in my door.

Against every better judgment that exists in the world, I'm not kicking Aidan out. I should, but I can't. I'm nearly paralyzed with the vibration as he groans against my neck and I drop my head back, resting it on his collar bone.

"Oh, Lydia," he whispers. However, it's not the *oh Lydia* I am expecting. His voice dips into a melancholy valley; the sound is that of a worn and tortured man. I try to turn toward him, but Aidan holds me tight. His breath is in my hair and it freaks me out a little.

I should've sent him home last night. I knew better.

"What's wrong?" I ask.

"I shouldn't be..." he begins sorrowfully, but he is cut off by whoever is pounding at my front door.

*J*t's always a bit of a wild card, answering a pounding fist at my door.

It could be the landlord--he loves to complain about rent and usually asks to inspect my pipes, the pervert; it could be Desmond, although he's already made his statement to Aidan and I think that he thinks it stuck. Mrs. Lowt doesn't pound. It wouldn't be Jan--he never shows up at my door without calling. It could be any one of the third-dates I've had in the past--ultimately, they never leave here satisfied.

Since Aidan is in the apartment and, more precisely, in my bed at the moment, some of these wild cards could give me a losing hand. I cinch my robe around my waist and go to the door, since whoever it is isn't letting up.

I swing the door open to a leggy brunette. The tips of her hair hang at her waist and she's got thick, pouty lips, swabbed with the reddest, glossiest lipstick I've ever seen. Those lips are the most prominent thing on her whole face and she puts them to work right away.

"Hi, I'm looking for Devon..." she pauses, nipping her own lip with a frustrated sigh. "I mean, Aidan Badeau. Is this his apartment? The lady across the hall said he lives here."

"No, he doesn't live here," I say. I'm not telling this chick anything. She might know Aidan's name, and even his friend's name, but I don't know who she is. In fact, this is exactly why I try to avoid ever revealing mine. People show up.

"Can you tell me where he lives?" she asks.

"Not here," I say.

"But that lady knew him. She said he's here."

"I don't know what to tell you. He doesn't live here." Her hips adjust like rocks sliding into a catapult. She screws up her bright, red lipstick and puts a hand on her waist, signaling me that she's about to get down to it. Her eyes sweep over my dreads, my robe, the tattoos peeking out of my sleeve. I return the *fuck you* smile she's giving me.

"Well, do you know if he lives in any of these?"

"Why do you want to know?"

Her eyes narrow a little. "I don't think that's any of your business."

"Well, I'm not the one in the hallway," I say. I try to swing the door shut, but she slaps her palm against it.

"Wait," she says and I see the first glint of vulnerability that stops me from out and out busting off her wrist. "He called *me*."

"How come?"

"I don't know if you're his wife or girlfriend or his sister..." She pauses; I don't fill in her blanks. "I hardly know him, but he left a message on my phone saying he needed to talk to me. He has something of mine, so can you just tell me where the guy lives?"

"Oh hey," Aidan's voice startles me from behind. He's tucking in his shirt, but stops to holds out his hand to shake the girl's, as if this is a business meeting or something. Oh shit. Maybe it is. I still don't like the twinge in my stomach, twisting like rope burn, as Aidan smiles at her. "Marta?"

Her smile seems a little wiry and it throws hot, angry sparks as she takes in his face and his body--which just burns me up a little more. Still, the looks shooting between them confuse *me*. It's as if they are strangers, but not. Conspirators. Enemies? Something. I can't put my finger on it.

"How's it going?" Her tone is suddenly flat. "I got your message."

"Good," he says and finally glances back to me. Nice of him to notice. "Lydia, I need to go. I have some business to discuss with Marta, but I'll catch up with you later, alright?"

"Sure," I say. Marta? It helps only a little that he gives me a peck my cheek, but still. Business? You've got to be kidding me.

He steps into the hall with Lips and motions to his apartment. "That one's mine. Do you have a few minutes to talk in private?"

"That's why I'm here. Do you have my money?"

He leads her back to his place, fumbling his key in his door. The last thing I hear is him telling her, "Yes. I'm glad you came."

I shut my door and lean up against it. What the *fuck? Her money?*

What was all that about? Is she a drug dealer? He's remorseful in bed, about to tell me *something* and then *business* shows up at my door. Well, shit. Is it drug business? Or the kind of *business* Des and I have--a fucked up, riding-crops-and-chains kind of business. But that's not what this sounded like. This sounded more like mafia business. Hush hush, private stuff that gives no explanations and requires a closed door. The kind of business that I need to keep my nose out of.

I go into my apartment and plaster my ear to our adjoining wall, but Aidan's voice is so deep and low, it's nothing like it was at the Thanksgiving dinner party. The conversation next door isn't jovial or even held at a normal decibel. I can only hear the outline of their words, and all I hear of Miss Lips are a few murmurs of *oh* and *oh wow* and then, *I'm glad you told me.*

I want to kick in the wall. Or drill my fist through it.

Instead, I get a grip and push myself away. I've been telling myself all along that Aidan's just my neighbor and that he's got to remain *just* my neighbor, and I guess this is as good a time as any for me to put that declaration in stone. If he wants to come explain what's going on, I'll listen. Otherwise, as much as I hate it, Lips was right.

He's not my business.

X MARKS AIDAN'S APARTMENT

I take a shower and put on my make up, but I'm jittery. I expect a knock on the door that hasn't come, even after I've done my hair. I make my bed for the hell of it. I do all sorts of things I never do--organize my jewelry, clean out my purse, strip the sheets off my bed, and gather up the clothes from all over my apartment for the Laundromat.

When I'm finished, Aidan still hasn't knocked at my door. It's not that he owes me an explanation, but it was a bizarre way to leave, after the night we had. To scamper away with Mystery Lips like he did, and knowing he was the one that had called her with some kind of urgent news...wouldn't anyone else be just as confused?

It would be one thing if we'd had ourselves a little scoop of vanilla sex, but we didn't. We practiced some incredibly compatible sexual-yoga four times last night. And there's not one drunken, black hole in my memory, which is unfortunate for me. None of this would matter right now if I couldn't remember his face, or didn't know his name, or didn't feel like I could just walk next door and touch him.

Whoa. Do I really want to do that?

This man is a flu. He's gotten under my skin and made my muscles ache. When I replay last night, my limbs quiver. Goosebumps bloom all over me as I think of how softly his lips slid over my collarbone, or the way his hips rocked against mine, or the silky strings of loving words he whispered into my hair, binding me to him like soft ribbon.

Now I'm craving his fever. I'm dragging around my apartment waiting for him to knock, when I should be figuring out how to revert this relationship to one of friendly, platonic neighbors. The only remedy I know of is to get myself down to Modo's *tonight* and start sorting through the crowd for a new, three-date flavor of the week.

The burst of excitement over my recovery plan is short lived once I hear Aidan's apartment door open. All my thoughts flood back to him and I freeze in the middle of the living room floor, anticipating his knock at my door. I'll let him squirm out there with Mrs. Lowt a bit, just so he realizes he did me wrong by leaving the way he did.

I'm paralyzed for a full minute, but Aidan's knock doesn't come. Their voices are out there. I finally cross the floor and press my eye to the peep hole. Nothing in the bubble of visible range. The voices have faded. My nerves shred.

He's got to be out there, deciding how he's going to make nice with me. I grab my laundry basket and whip open my door. I step out just as the elevator doors close at the other end of the hall, but I couldn't catch who was inside. The hall is empty now and Aidan's door is shut.

Mrs. Lowt's door opens.

"Lydia," she whispers, peering toward the elevator, "what is going on? Aidan comes from your apartment this morning and goes straight into his with another girl? What was that about? Is he seeing that woman? She looked easy to me. I don't like that. *Oh, Lydia*...don't tell me there are going to be three of you going around together now?"

"No, Mrs. Lowt," I say a little sternly. "She was just a friend of his. Did he leave with her?"

Mrs. Lowt's tucks her wrists to her hips so her fingers stick out like the swag of a sucker wrapper. "How am I supposed to know that, Lydia? I'm not in charge of the hallway. I don't know what the neighbors do."

I adjust the laundry basket on my hip and slam my door so Aidan, if he's still in his apartment, will hear me leave. I fumble my keys into my coat pocket longer than necessary, waiting for his door to open up, but it doesn't. The prospect of having to do laundry is even more dismal now.

I can't believe he left. I can't believe he didn't return to let me know what was going on. I can't believe I'm going to actually go sit at the Laundromat or that I'm suddenly welcoming the idea of sitting and just watching my clothes spin.

<<<<>>>>

*F*OUR FUCKING DAYS. Aidan stays away for nearly four whole days. The 'flu' I had for him is over. I haven't seen him in the hallways, heard only a few of his bumpings-around next door, and got the report from Mrs. Lowt--he's lying low. Maybe he *is* with Lips? Maybe they had to hide a body in a river or he's waiting for his witness protection agent to find him a new place. Who the hell knows?

At least I'm back to my own comfortable position of: *it ain't my business*.

Now, in the late afternoon of the fourth, symptomless day, I step into the hall dressed for my appointment with Des and there stands Aidan, all smiles. I'm about as welcoming as a snarly ponytail.

"On your way out?" he asks. He looks like he's on his way in, from the bag of groceries he's toting.

"Yep," I say, continuing past him. His jacket is cut in a way that accents the slant of muscles across his shoulders. I remember his smooth, solid skin beneath my fingers and a wave of heat bolts into my deepest places. I've got to get out of here. This man isn't a flu, he's a disease. I get only three steps away before he stops me with just his voice.

"Lydia."

I turn on my designer heel, the lace of my thigh-high stocking itching my skin beneath my pencil skirt. "What?"

"Can I talk to you?"

"I'm kind of in a hurry."

"I can see that." He frowns. "Can I talk to you when you get back then?"

"I don't know when that will be."

"Please...I don't want to wait. It will only take a few minutes."

I roll my tongue behind my lip. Yes, waiting is a bitch, isn't it? He should try four days on for size. I don't have time for games, so I cut to the chase.

"Are you in the mafia, Aidan?"

"What? No." He laughs, his face crinkling with disbelief, relief. I can't tell. "Why would you think that?"

I glance at my wrist, as if I have ever worn a watch. "I've got to go."

"Don't you want to know why Marta was here?"

Now, that's offensive. As if I'm the kind of girl who cares about a guy's other chicks. At least, I wasn't that girl until four mornings ago. I hate him a little for that. I violated my three-date rule with daydreams and hope and look where it's gotten me. This mess, dammit. With him insinuating that I'd want to know (and I do) or even care (I've got to stop this)...

I carve him off a chip of my ice queen facade and throw it over my shoulder as I head for the elevator. "It's none of my business."

"I want to explain where I've been and..." His tone goes to soft gravel. It shreds my nerves a little more. I have to stop, just to keep my balance. "I want to tell you everything. I need to make it up to you."

The pleading in his tone pierces the one speck of softness I have left and it just about blows my whole heart open like an exploded trunk. I have to catch myself before I start gushing about how I've been thinking of him and missing him beside me in my bed each night and--

What is wrong with me?

I am not some stupid, naive girl.

I've been around the ring enough times with Des to know better than this.

I still struggle to hang on to the handle of my portfolio, instead of throwing it down, along with my travel mug of spiked coffee, and head back to Aidan. But I don't. No matter how unnatural it feels, we are neighbors and it will stay like this--with a wall between us, even if it is only an invisible one that I've built.

"Really, Aidan, I'm late. I've got to get out of here."

All of his muscles go slack. The free hand with his keys falls to his side with a flat jingle, his shoulders droop, even the muscles in his face resign from holding up any readable expression for me to see.

"Alright," he says. "I'll see you when I see you then."

"Yeah," I say. He turns to his door as I make my way to the elevator, punching the button over and over, as if it will take me down any faster.

*D*es is weird from the moment I arrived. He takes my portfolio without a word and walks off toward the mansion at such a clip that I have a hard time keeping up.

"Slow down," I growl, but he keeps going until we are standing in the grand entrance, with the heavy, crystal chandelier hanging over our heads like a hard snow.

Two women, hair in ponytails and jeans pegged up over their comfortable sneakers, busily wash the floor. They didn't even glance up at us when we entered.

"I want to surprise my wife with a remodel," Des announces. "The conservatory has some leaks that need to be addressed and I want new furniture and a new design. I want you to create a private ambience with a sitting area at the center of the greenery."

"I'm sure I can--"

"Good," Des clips me off as he heads up the stairs. "Then come with me, and we will discuss costs in my office."

"Certainly," I say. The cleaners don't bat an eye, but I don't believe they don't speculate.

Twenty minutes later, I'm tied to the palatial, leather couch in his office and all I'm doing is lying here like a dead fish as he strokes me, the lace of my stocking still itching my inner thigh. From lack of moisture alone, Desmond's anger has turned from a smolder to a burn.

"What is he to you, Lyddle?" Des asks. He doesn't have to be specific.

I can't see him through the blindfold, but his velvety tone isn't doing a damn thing for me today. The last thing that's going to kindle my fire is talking about Aidan, but Des still knows me as well as he knows the feel of his own penis. And he is very aware that something's not working right now.

"It's got nothing to do with my neighbor," I say, as if I can really sell that to him. "I'm just not into this today."

The cushion shifts as Des stands. I hear his feet move across the hardwood. He retrieves something.

"You're always into it," Des whispers. I hear the scrape of a Bic overhead. The crackle of a candle wick.

"Seriously, I'm just not."

"Shhh," he says.

"Des..."

"What did I say, Lyddle?"

A drop of wax hits my hip bone and it burns. Really *burns*.

"Ouch!" I yelp. "It's too hot!"

Another drop follows and I shriek.

"What is he to you?" Des demands, as I pull at the restraints on my wrists.

He chuckles as his fingers yank the lace of my right stocking down a few inches. This isn't our usual play. I buck at the restraints again, but they hold firm. Des designed this room for ultimate privacy, so I'm not sure that even my loudest scream would be more than a whisper outside the insulated walls and door. While it usually excites me, this time I'm unnerved. I lay there, blindfolded and bound, with the wax raising up a blister on my skin.

"I'm all done, Des. Enough."

"Tell me, Lyddle," he says. I bite my lip. A dribble of wax suddenly beads down my inner thigh. It feels like a third degree burn and I do something I've never done before. I bark our safe word. Actually, it's a phrase.

"Green eggs and ham!"

The room goes deathly silent, the smell of the candle hovers in my nose. I breathe hard, in and out, in and out, but the hot scent of the wax remains. The small patch of my thigh is on fire. The wax has dribbled a trail down too close to my most delicate and intimate folds.

"What is he to you?" Des asks again. But this time, his voice breaks. He clears his throat.

"Stop it, Des. He's my neighbor! He's just my fucking neighbor!"

"Oh no, he's more than that. I can tell," Des whispers. "I know you're lying to me."

I'm quivering in the bindings, scared to the bone for the first time that maybe Des has lost his mind. If I could see him, instead of looking into the dark center of the blindfold, I'd have a much better idea, but what's going on with my thigh is still a pretty good indication that things aren't right. We've done enough bondage before, even a little wax play, but burning me like this is so far over the line I can't even put a name on it.

Des has always known that I go to Modo's, that I pick up men, and even that I have sex with them--but he realizes, as much as I do, that this one is different. I never know any of their names and none of them stick around longer than three dates. Whether or not anything has actually happened yet, it's as if we can both feel our thin future hanging between us like an old, smoky, bar cloud.

Aidan and I have had sex--four incredible times--but we only spent one night together. Des shouldn't be complaining at all, considering I shut Aidan down only a few hours ago, in the hallway outside my apartment. Especially when I was on my way *here*, to have sex with my husband.

It doesn't matter that my heart isn't in it. That I only came to collect some money.

My God, my life is such a mess.

Des clears his sinuses with a sharp inhale. I turn my head toward the sound, the blindfold still firmly in place.

"Are you crying?" I ask. Long pause.

"Do you really think you have that kind of power over me, Lyddle?"

Yes. But I say, "No."

"Well, you're right," he snaps. "You don't."

A drizzle of wax splatters down my thigh and I curse. Des's fingers are on the restraints and as soon as he frees my hands, I rip off the blindfold and throw it to the floor. I rub away the wax. There are welts beneath it.

"Lydia..." There are a million apologies and pleadings in his tone, but I yank on my clothes and leave without looking at him even once.

<<<<>>>>

*M*y skin is still burning when I get out of the cab in front of my apartment building. It doesn't stop, even when I'm sitting on my couch with a bag of ice wedged between my legs.

I sip a tumbler of wine and stare at the ceiling, trying to separate the mess of my life by assigning different nail pops and spots in the uneven paint job to Des and Claudia, to Des and me, to me alone, to Aidan, to me and Aidan. There's too much for me to keep straight. I'm overwhelmed with how big the ceiling is and how it still isn't big enough to hold all my problems. I keep trying to straighten it out, until someone knocks on my door.

I hobble over and swing it open, expecting Des to be there, full of apologies, even though that's not his style. And it's not him. Aidan's in the hall.

"Can I come in?" he says. I lean heavily on the door knob.

"Some other time, alright? It's been a long day."

"It will only take a few minutes," he says, striding in past me. He never does seem to understand that *no* is a legitimate answer.

He takes the chair at the small end of the coffee table and watches me stagger my way back to the couch. His eyes glide up my yoga pants to where the ice pack has left a dark ring. I try not to notice him assessing my gait, my bag of ice, the open bottle on the coffee table. It leaves me with an aftertaste of guilt that is a little overwhelming, since there's nothing I can do about any of it.

"What happened to you?" he says. I shrug it off.

"Nothing. I think I pulled a muscle."

"With him?" There's an accusatory edge to his tone that I really can't handle right now. I should've never opened the door. It's my fault. I invited the vampire in--even though Aidan is the kind that sucks out my emotions, instead of my blood.

"No, it wasn't him," I lie.

"Weren't you with him?"

"I was, but..."

"Then when did it happen, Lydia? With me? Or him?" He leans forward, elbows on knees, his weary eyes searching mine.

"Neither," I say. "I just pulled a muscle, alright?"

He drops back in the chair, watching me. "I know he hurts you, Lydia."

What am I going to say? Mostly, it's a consensual pain that Des and I conjure between us? Granted, I'm the only one who limps home, but I agree to it. Do I say this is the first time I've had to use our safe word, that it's the first time Des took it up way too many notches? Do I say it was all because of *him?*

No. I'm not fool enough to spill the truth to Aidan--that these burns on my leg are directly connected to him. I don't need to light that wick.

I take a drink. Aidan studies every movement. His eyes trace my throat as I swallow and then escort the empty glass down to the table top. He inclines off the edge of the chair, and for a second, I think he's going to snatch up my glass and hurl it across the room. Or snarl in my face that he wants the truth. My muscles tighten up, ready to respond to whatever kind of assault he launches.

Aidan swoops down and I startle as he catches my bare foot. I fall back as he scoots over, taking a seat on the edge of the coffee table in front of me. He lifts my heel tenderly into his lap.

Without a word, he presses his thumbs into my sole, kneading the skin. His eyes are centered on my foot in his hands, and it takes me a few minutes to realize he's not interested in looking me in the eyes. Slowly, my body relaxes. My neck feels weak, so I drop my head on the back of the couch and look back up at the ceiling again.

The configuration up there seems different than it was earlier. A little clearer, maybe.

THE COLDER THE BETTER

Aidan keeps kneading my feet without a word. My muscles loosen to the consistency of puddles. My defenses spread thin, until I'm about as tenderized and translucent as my soul. Of course, that's when he clears his throat to speak again.

"Lydia," he begins. I spread my toes in his palm.

"*Shhh*...this feels too good to ruin with talking."

"All you have to do is listen," he says. Even his voice is a massage. I reply with a tiny moan of agreement as he presses his thumbs into the ball of my foot. He can talk all he wants. I can ignore it. We're just neighbors. He's made that clear by disappearing after the night we spent together. "There are a few things I wanted to talk to you about. The first one is the girl that showed up here the other day--Marta. I was sleeping with her about a year and a half ago, when I was still drinking. She's one of the few that I remember."

"Mmm," I say, head back and eyes closed. *Drug deal Marta?* Maybe they were doing drugs together and he shorted her. Anyway, I haven't seen her since the day she showed up at my door, so it's tomato/potato to me. *Neighbors.* Besides, it's no big deal now that she was with him a couple years ago--

"I lived with Marta for a few months. Well, actually, I crashed at her place on the nights I didn't have anywhere else to go. When I decided to get clean, I never showed up at her place again. No call, nothing." He says this, his voice tipping like an airplane on its way to the crash site.

I want to say, *don't give a shit, keep rubbing,* but, instead, I murmur, "Mmm...rough."

"She didn't know where I went or why and I uh...I stole two thousand dollars from her."

"You little thief," I say, without opening my eyes.

"I had to return the money to her. It's part of the plan that I follow now. Part of my sobriety is righting any of the wrongs I can."

"Good plan," I mumble. His fingers are expert. Every word is nearly extracted from my mouth with a low moan of satisfaction.

"I have to fix something that happened between us too," he says. *Shit, he can have all my money.* "Sleeping with you the other night..."

"I have no complaints about that." I smile without opening my eyes. "In fact, if you want to wrong me again, I'd be up for it."

That slipped out. Kind of. I bite my lip. I should be keeping my neighbor at arm's length, with my invisible wall between us, but he's already fuck-rubbing my feet, and all I *really* want is for him to climb off the end cushion of the couch and spread his body over me. His thumbs pause and I think I'm going to get what I'm hoping for, but then he starts kneading again, deeper into the middle of my sole.

"Lydia, I should've never slept with you." His thumb digs into my instep and I yelp.

Usually, an admission like that would garner a kick to the head or the demand that he leave, but I don't want Aidan to go. His tone is melancholy and remorseful and I feel like I can save him from whatever guilt is consuming him, if he just keeps his hands on me. I can forgive him, I can redeem him, by encouraging the magical circulation of his fingers to work their way up my body again.

I must've heard it wrong. He couldn't have meant what he just said, the way he said it. Maybe he meant, *I should've never slept with you, because we could've been screwing the whole time.* Or, *I should've never slept with you, because now I'll never be able to stop.*

I want him to want me. I want him to need *me*--and more than just that one piece of me that rests between my thighs. I want Aidan to need the real me, the entire one, that puts dandelions in my empty whiskey bottles, and sings old church hymns in the shower. The *me* that used to dot the 'i' in Lydia with a heart. All the ancient variations of *me* and the culmination of *me*'s that are gathered up on this couch cushion with my foot in his hands, wanting *him*.

I haven't wanted a man like this since I walked up the aisle in a Vegas chapel to marry Des.

I haven't cared enough to want any of them, until now.

"Wow. I've never had anyone complain after sleeping with me." I smirk, like it's nothing but a joke, but it's slowly tearing a hole in me.

"It's not what you think," he says.

"Maybe I wasn't really thinking anything."

"I'm an alcoholic, Lydia," he says. This is where it's going? He's going to blame sleeping with me on *not drinking?*

"Not really. You don't drink anymore."

"It doesn't change what I am."

"No, it kinda does. If you're not drinking, you're not really an alcoholic. You're just a guy that used to drink."

"That's not the way it works." He smiles. "But that's not the point I'm trying to make anyway. What I'm trying to say is that I'm nothing but a lousy drunk, still waiting for the next drink, and I knew better than to sleep with you."

I stare at him, long and hard. "You knew better..."

"You're struggling with it too and I'm just muddying the waters even more by..."

"Hold up," I say, yanking my foot from him grasp as I scoot to sit up straight. "*I'm struggling with it too?* I thought we were done having this discussion. I know I am."

He wipes his face, from forehead to chin, with one hand. "You're in denial..."

"Fuck you," I say. I jump to my feet. "Leave, Aidan."

"Lydia, I want to help you."

"I don't need your amateur psychologist bullshit!" I explode. "Don't you dare come in here and think you can transfer all your problems onto me! You keep trying to do that! I'm not a fucking drunk, Aidan!"

"I want to help, but you need to see the problem," he says, leaning forward to pick up the empty bottle on my coffee table.

"That was from last night!"

"There are four or five of these in the trash," he says. I want to hurt him. Kill him, maybe. Who the hell does he think he is?

"Get out," I say. I don't have to explain myself to him. He meets my steely glare with one of his own.

"Recognize the problem."

"You're the problem. Now get out, before I call my husband and he comes and gets you out for me."

Aidan gets to his feet, but he doesn't leave. Instead, he takes a slow step toward me.

"The husband that beats you, Lydia? I swear to God, if he showed up right now, I think I'd enjoy it. I'd beat him within an inch of his own life, just for what he does to you." I take a step back, but Aidan keeps coming. "Is he the reason you live like you do, Lydia? What's he done to you and why do you let him keep doing it? You can't love him! What is the arrangement you have with him? I don't know of many women that would put up with a husband who only comes around to beat them. Or a woman that loves her husband so much, she doesn't live with him and sleeps with her neighbor."

I slap him. My palm explodes in tingling needles as he lurches to the side.

I fully expect him to swing back.

I'm so angry, I stand there with my jaw out, offering him a clean shot.

Aidan straightens up, rubs his jaw. He takes a deep breath and another step away.

"That was over the line," he says.

"You call me a drunk..."

"I meant *I* was over the line. Again." His eyes move over the floor, shamed. Good. "I'm sorry. I guess it's the wrong way to do this, but my gut says it's the only way I can get through to you, Lydia. I don't think you have anyone else that will be honest with you. But I'm always going to be honest. Please...please see that I'm trying to help you."

"You're psycho," I tell him. I look him right in the face. "You need to get out. I'm not the one who needs help."

I feel really good about throwing him out. I'm even able to gloat a bit for the first few minutes, after the door shuts. I don't know who he thinks he is. He's a mess. I splash some rum into a glass of Coke, but my hands are shaking so much that when I try to take a gulp, it spills down my shirt.

Damn him.

I know I'm falling apart. I try to keep the shadows locked away, so no one ever sees them--especially me. But now, with Aidan chased off, I fall down on the couch, sloshing even more of my drink on me, and those shadows come crashing out.

When they come, a few drinks can't always chase them away. Lately, it's been even less effective. When the shadows absolutely outnumber me, I go down to Modo's. It's hard for the darkness to cling to me when men are vying to take its place. That's why I usually bring someone home. A warm body tends to distract the shadows, until the sun comes up.

Tonight will be one of those nights. I slam what's left of my drink and jump off the couch. I stare straight into my mirror as I walk into the bedroom, staring down the image I cast, as if it's an opponent.

Even though parts of me are still blistered from what Des did to me and other pieces are seething from what Aidan said, I've got to pull whatever's left back together.

I have to look fabulous tonight.

*D*ressed, I finally open my door and there is Aidan, standing in the hall like a mortician. I can't stand to look at him. I start down the hall, eyes straight ahead, but I feel his fingertips on my arm.

"Talk to me," he says.

"Just let the drunk get her crazy on," I say, yanking my arm away. I continue down the hall and Aidan's voice follows after me.

"You're going to Modo's," he says. "What I said got to you and now you're going to go down to Modo's and pick up some random guy, aren't you? You're going to show me that you don't need me and that I don't control you..."

I punch the button for the elevator a lot harder than necessary, but it doesn't come fast enough. Aidan won't shut up behind me. That steady voice of his rolls down the hall and crashes over me.

"I don't control you, Lydia, but I know you. Didn't it ever seem strange to you that Shane didn't recognize you? That he didn't have any recollection of sleeping with you? Do you believe that you are that forgettable, Lydia? Hasn't it bothered you?"

Hell yes, it's bothered me. I have wondered why Shane didn't remember me, but then again, I don't really recall him either. I assume he was as pickled as I was that night, although it has dented my ego a little. It still doesn't mean that Aidan can use it against me now, to make me turn around and listen to him.

I clonk the elevator button again, as if that will rush it.

"I know why he can't remember you," Aidan says. His voice and his footsteps are bringing him down the hall toward me. "Don't you want to know why?"

Damn elevator. I finally turn on my heel to face him, shooting him my most jagged glare.

"It sounds like you want me to know why, Aidan, so go ahead. Get it over with. Tell me."

He's so close, I can smell the deep, heady scent of his skin. So close, he could pin me to the wall. I keep my eyes on his lips, so I don't have to meet his gaze, and as if he knows exactly what I'm doing, he traces his tongue over his lower lip. I instantly wish we weren't fighting. I wish we were lying in my bed, raking each other over with soft murmurs of affection--instead of him spewing ex-lover riddles that I don't give a shit about solving.

"I've been in this hall with you before," he says. His lips move gently and the words are unexpectedly soft as they slip through them. "You picked me up at Modo's. Or I picked you up. I don't remember all the details of it, except that you were lying on the bar and I drank a Mojito shot from your belly button. It tasted amazing, I remember that. The best drink I've ever had. Probably because it was my last." He wipes his mouth with the side of his arm as if he's wiping away the remnant taste. He's so close now, only two steps away from me. "We came back to your place. Here. I probably would have never remembered that it was this floor or which one was your apartment door if we hadn't shared the night that we did that night."

"You're trying to tell me that you gave me your friend's name?" I say. Well, there's a curve ball. Still, I need to keep my cool. "Ok, whatever. No harm done."

The elevator doors roll open. It's empty. Aidan grabs my wrist with one hand and darts the other into the elevator and slides his palm down the panel of floor buttons. I can almost hear them all lighting up.

"I've got to tell you the rest," he says. The doors roll shut as he hangs onto me, holding me back from leaving.

"It's not important," I say, even though my head is still reeling from the realization that I've slept with Aidan before. It's infuriating that I don't have a clear recall of it.

"It is to me." He reaches out like he's going to trace my collarbone, but he pulls his finger away before he touches me. "I did that. I lied and told you my name was Shane. I used to do that when I was sleeping around."

I roll my eyes. None of this, no matter how shocking, changes that he's been trying to pin me as a drunk.

"No big deal. You didn't want anyone tracking you down, I get it. It was a long time ago, it's fine."

"That's not everything that I want to tell you though. There's more. That night, I was hoping we would have a mind-blowing, one-night stand and that was it." He pauses, his grasp loosening, his eyes dropping away from mine. "I figured I'd hit it and quit it, but I was really wasted. By the time we finished, I passed out."

I shrug again. "Happens to the best of us."

"But you woke me up."

"Lucky you," I say. I'm going to add, *lucky me too*, but I won't let myself get sucked in by the soft curve of his lips. I stay focused.

"It would've been lucky," he smiles, "except that's not why you woke me up. You weren't even awake. You woke me up, crying in your sleep."

I shut my mouth. Some of my shadows seep out of the corners and close in on me. I can feel my breath getting heavy in my chest. I don't talk about the nightmares. I try my best to never think of them.

"You were sobbing, Lydia. You kept saying that you didn't want to live anymore. It scared the shit out of me. I didn't even *know* you, but there you were beside me, breaking down and opening up to a complete stranger, without even knowing it. We'd just done one of the most intimate things two people can do together, but I was scared to death to hold you, to try and comfort you. It really did something to me. I didn't even know *your name,* and there you were, bawling in your sleep, really needing someone to just reach out and I was the only one there.

"So, I did it. I took care of you. I wrapped my arms around you and I kissed your forehead and I told you that you'd be okay. My whole chest was dripping with your tears, but you settled down. And it really, really hit me--I knew *exactly* how you felt. I knew what it was like to wake up terrified in the middle of the night and to wonder how I was going to keep going when no one was there to tell me things would be alright. My life had gotten pretty singular--all I did was spend night after night drinking and trying to drown out everything that was wrong with me.

"But then, you fell asleep and I laid there for four more hours, just laying beneath your cheek, listening to you breathe. I wanted to be sure you were okay. It made *me* feel okay to know you were peaceful, and I hadn't felt okay in so long, I didn't want to leave.

"At seven or eight in the morning, I started to realize that you would probably wake up and not remember any of it. I didn't want you to wreck the feeling you gave me, of trusting me and relying on me, even if you had no idea you were doing it. I got up and left before you woke up.

"But what happened between us that night changed me. I went

home and I couldn't stop thinking about it. I wanted more. I wanted to feel like I was needed again.

"I stopped drinking that day. I got help. I got sober and it sucked, but whenever I felt like giving in, I'd get out and come by this apartment house and I'd think of you. I never wanted to forget that. You helped me to stay sober every day for that first year. That's why I decided to move in here."

His mouth closes and I tear my eyes from it. I swallow.

"That's..." The words fade. I don't know what to say. That's a pretty heavy story and I'm not sure what he thinks I'm supposed to owe him or what he wants from me now.

My shadows dance close. It's humiliating that Aidan knows about the nightmares. I wake to a wet pillow and terror running through me a few times a week, at least. It's another reason Des won't stay the night with me, even when he could. He says my crying nightmares freak him out.

"You helped me, Lydia," Aidan says. I glance into his eyes. They swallow me up, as full of hope as every drink I've ever ordered. "That's why I want to help you now."

He reaches out, his hands moving into my hair, but I step back. I might be a little broken, but he's got to understand, I don't need *help*.

"This is the last time I'm going to tell you, Aidan. I don't have problems like you do. *Let it go.*"

The elevator returns, the doors hushing open behind me. I step in, backwards and hit the button for the ground floor before he can start arguing. I'm a little surprised that he doesn't try to stop the doors from closing between us.

I let out a deep sigh once the elevator gets moving. I need to get down to Modo's fast. I need to bring back a man that can not only beat the shadows back tonight, but one that will give Aidan the message, loud and clear, that we are *nothing* but neighbors and I don't need his *help*.

A solid message is clearly overdue.

PUT A NAME ON IT

Toward the end of the night, the guy sitting beside me has a name and can't stop saying it.

"I told you, I'm Eric," he starts with. "When are you going to tell me your name?"

"Call me *Intrigued*," I say, giving him a slow, eyelash flash. This guy is nothing compared to Aidan, but he'll do. He's got muddy brown hair and his eyes are pale and glossy--the myopic eyes of a dead fish, wrapped in plastic wrap. He ditched his rowdy friends hours ago, guiding me to the back corner where there are small, u-shaped, padded booths. The waitresses sometimes call this corner of Modo's The Kissing Corner, although that's the very least of what happens here. Eric orders us more drinks before we've finished the last ones.

A few later, he leans in and says, "So what's your real name?"

"It's a mystery," I say, chewing on the red stirrer from my drink. We're already sitting close, but he wraps his arms around my waist and hauls me onto the edge of his lap. One ass cheek on his thigh, and the other almost there, it's uncomfortable. I try to shift, but he shakes me like he wants me to laugh.

"C'mon, girl. I told you mine."

"I thought that was a game. You know--I show you mine and then you show me yours."

Of course, that does the trick. His grin goes looser and sloppier. "You wanna show me yours?"

"Maybe."

"That'd be great..." He presses a wet kiss beneath my ear. "What is your name again?"

"God, *Eric*..." I laugh and sigh at the same time. This guy might be an annoying choice for the night, but it's getting on toward closing time, and what's left in the bar looks as appetizing as week-old Chinese food. I stab my straw between the ice cubes in my empty glass. "Relax on the name thing, okay? You're you and I'm me. That's all we need, isn't it?"

He ticks back his head, squinting down his nose at me. "What's the big deal? Are you wanted or something?"

"Of course not."

He smiles then, nuzzling my ear with his wet lips. He's going to give me a rash. "Just tell me then. No big deal, right?"

If it wasn't 1:45 in the morning, I would just get up and leave, but Eric here has me in a tough spot. The shadows have been hanging around the edges of the Kissing Corner all night and when I go home, I'm going to need help keeping them away. Not to mention, I need to make enough noise for Aidan to hear what's happening; to let him know that *we're* not happening anymore.

I look back at Eric. I've been trying to pretend he's Aidan all night, but it's not working. He runs his palm up the back of my neck, gripping it the way a dog latches on to it's puppy's scruff.

"I need your name," he breathes into my ear.

"Lydia!" I say. "For Christ's sake, it's Lydia!"

He pulls back his head, his expression joyful. Or, blissfully drunk.

"Okay, baby. Good," he says.

*W*e're in the elevator, going up to my apartment, when I tear away from Eric's mediocre kiss and ask why he was so dead set on getting my name. It's been nudging my brain since we left Modo's, but the moment to ask him about it hasn't come up and wasn't going to, without my intervention, as far as I can tell.

"I had to be sure it was you," he says, diving for my lips again. I pull back, a cold drizzle of anxiety running down my spine.

"Sure? Who do you think I am?"

"Lydia Strong," he says, his smile crooked. The drizzle turns to ice and I am frozen in place. I've been waiting for this stiletto to drop from the moment Des said Claudia hadn't even mentioned a prenup. I knew that sooner or later, Claudia would get wise to Des and send her detectives snooping, to figure out what's really going on.

'Detective' doesn't really seem to fit this guy, but I've never seen him around Modo's before either. Tonight, he slid in with a bunch of frat-boy leftovers--the guys too old to be working through college, but still trying to squeeze out the last, dehydrated drops of their glory days. If they're all detectives, they're the very best kind, because they really just looked like a bunch of useless guys getting drunk.

Eric's still crammed into my personal space, flashing me his jacked-up smile. If he's not a detective, then Rule Number One in the How-to-Handle-Psychos Book (by Lydia Strong) clearly states that calm is the only way to escape psycho. It might be the only way to escape a detective too.

"How do you know me?" I ask, tossing back my head with my own sly smile. As if I'm not filled to my teeth with panic at what he might say.

"Let's just say, I was waiting my turn."

"What's that supposed to mean?"

"C'mon, *Lydia*, you know what you are," he says, ducking in to plaster another juicy kiss on me. I let him, but the sour taste of old tobacco blankets his beer-soaked tongue. It dissolves most of the buzz I've got going. I still laugh a little, to keep things calm and friendly.

"Fill me in," I say. "What am I?"

He snorts as if it's too obvious to ask about. He slides his hand around the back of my neck instead, urging me toward him with rigid fingers. It takes effort, but I manage to hold my ground. The elevator doors roll open to my floor.

"What am I?" I ask again. I'd be fine with shoving him back into the elevator and making a break for my door if I have to, but Eric softens. He lets go of my neck.

"You're Modo's Trophy Girl," he says with a wide grin. "Your name isn't just on the bathroom wall. The whole thing is dedicated to you, like a shrine. Up for anything and the best at it. You're the hottest thing in that bar and everybody knows it, so I didn't mind waiting for my turn."

What the fuck? I know a lot of guys at Modo's and no one's ever said a word about my name, or my shrine, in the bathroom. No one's ever said there was a line with tear-tickets to get with me either.

I'd continue to question him, but the whole purpose of bringing Eric home is to show Aidan that he's not the only game I've got going. Now that I'm only steps away from my apartment door and moments away from accomplishing my goal, I'm no longer sure that I want to do it with a guy who thinks it's okay to tell me I'm a slut before he's even gotten any.

"That's funny that you've heard about me," I say as Eric follows me out of the elevator, "because I've heard about you before too."

He leans in with another heady smile. "Oh yeah?"

"Yeah, I've heard a few people say you have a microscopic dick." The smile melts off his face, but just so I don't lose him, I lean in and peck him on the lips. "Why don't we go see if they're right about either of us?"

His bravado comes charging back in the form of rage. He grabs my hand and drags me down the hall, his mouth set in a grim line.

"Which of these is yours?" he growls, jabbing his mitt at the apartment doors.

"This one," I say, when we're coming up on Aidan's door. I motion to his, even though I could easily argue that I am pointing to mine. Eric does what I hope he will and grabs my keys, trying to jam them in the lock as he twists the knob.

"They're not working," he says. I hear footsteps crossing the floor inside Aidan's apartment.

"Oh, whoops." I giggle. "It's not this one, it's the next one."

We scoot over to my door and Eric pops it open like a pro. I hear Aidan's door knob twisting, but Eric grabs my wrist and drags me inside my apartment too quick. The best I can do is let out my best attempt at an excited squeal.

Still, it hardly seems worth it when Eric slams my door shut and flattens me against the wall inside so hard that it knocks the digital clock off the wall shelf beside us. He grunts like a horny gorilla and breathes stale booze against my cheek.

"My turn," he mumbles in my ear. "Now I'm going to show you just how big my dick is. You're going to choke on it, cunt. This is my turn and we're going to do this my way--"

He reaches up and clamps one hand on my throat. I lock eyes with him as he squeezes. Hard. I wasn't expecting this, but the one sick thought I have is that I need to stay focused and try to take pleasure in how loud and rough this is going to be, because Aidan is going to hear it all.

But I can't swallow and I can hardly breathe. I claw at Eric's fingers as he yanks down the zipper on his jeans. I can't scream. Finally, I just close my eyes.

<<<<>>>>

*T*here is *making love*, there is *having sex,* and then there is *fucking*. This was none of those.

Eric fucks me until I pass out. He might have even kept going. The last thing I remember is how he jabbed a finger into one of the blistered patches that Des left behind, while keeping his hand on my throat the whole time.

"I like how your face does that," he said. He dragged me into my bedroom, too far from the thin walls where I could've screamed for Aidan's help, if I could've gotten the air to do it. Eric was on a mission to prove that he had enough power under his belt to grind me to sawdust.

The whole event was full of hair pulling and hard thrusts, murmurs of *you bitch* and other forget-me-nots that weren't nearly as pleasant. And then, there was a bright dot in the middle of his face that kept spreading as he choked me, until it was larger than anything else I could see. It swallowed my apartment. I think that's when I passed out.

I'm confused when I come to, but grateful when Eric jumps into his pants and says he has to go.

He pauses at the door and turns back, glancing at me over his shoulder.

"It wasn't rape," he murmurs. "You invited me here. And you have sex with everybody, right?"

"Sure," I say, my throat aching as I force out the words. He nods. I stay on the bed as he slams the door behind him.

The shadows emerge the second he's gone, but this time, I welcome them, rather than Eric's company.

What the hell am I doing?

I stand up to go to the bathroom and whimper at how raw it feels between my legs. The burns are the least of my problems now. I catch a glimpse of myself in my full length mirror. My shirt hangs off one shoulder, my right breast dangling like a limp flag of surrender. Long threads hang down where buttons were yanked free. My nipple is blood red. I recall Eric chewing it like an angry wolverine. The closer I get to my reflection, the clearer I can see Eric's fingerprints painted on my neck in pale blue bruises. I look away. My skull aches.

The satisfaction of having made my *point* to Aidan has vanished. The only point I've proven is that I am a slut and even sluts can be raped.

I shower, scrubbing him from my tender skin, and when I'm finished, I ease myself down onto the edge of my bed so I don't have to touch the sheets that touched *him*. I drag on a dirty pair of yoga pants that were lying on the floor. I pull my knees to my chest.

As I stare out the window at the moonless night, the shadows grow in number. I have nothing left in me to defend myself. The shadows press in with the truths that I've staved off for years--

I work my way through lovers like a box of Kleenex.

I am the Kleenex, not them.

All the men who love and admire me down at Modo's--they are waiting their turn. And I am everything they say about me as they stand in line.

I stare at the wall that separates my apartment from Aidan's. He was right about me too. I can't make it through a whole day without a drink anymore, or ten. My body is a constant earthquake and a stiff shot can't always smooth out the Richter scale in my hands.

I can't stop.

I've tried.

I've tried only drinking on weekends, only drinking beer, only drinking when people are around, only drinking when people aren't around. Nothing works.

Aidan was right and I chased him away. I had to. I can't stop.

I bury my face in my pillow.

I can't stop.

The shadows gather around the edge of my bed, but for once, they don't continue to advance. They seem to know too--I can't take any more.

I can't take it and I can't stop.

SALT IN THE WOUND

The shadows don't leave, even with the morning light. I spend the night doing less sleeping and more twisting myself up in the sheets, trying to figure out how to handle what's just happened. Every trip to the bathroom, I glimpse the greenish spots on my neck and it punctuates how unmanageable my entire life has become.

I make deals with myself, to prove that I'm not as bad off as I seem.

That I'm not really a drunk.

Not a whore.

If I could just remember the first night with Aidan--

Or any of the men's names, besides Eric--

I should know names of at least a few of the men I've brought home over the past couple of years. The shadows linger and the only thing that comes to me is bottles, clinking together in my brain as if the shadows are hosting some sick celebration over my demise.

And just when it seems like it can't get worse, my phone rings. I pull myself out of my bed to find the thing and answer with a grumble.

"Lyddle, I'm outside your door," Des says on the other end. "I've been out here knocking for the last five minutes. What the hell are you doing?"

"I'm sick. Can you come back some other time?"

His tone turns to cold steel. "Is there someone in there with you?"

"No."

"Then open up. You're fine," he says. "Hurry, before that kook across the hall comes out here and rapes me."

Of all mornings to say that. I straighten up what I can of his shirt that I'm still wearing, wrap myself in a blanket that covers my neck, and pull open the door. He's standing out there with the phone still at his ear.

"You don't have to worry about Mrs. Lowt. She doesn't want you. She doesn't even like you."

Des, dressed in a dove-gray business suit, gives me a tolerant grin as he clicks off his phone and slides it into his coat pocket. He adjusts his lavender tie as he inventories the entire mess of me.

"*Everyone* wants me," he says, as he strolls in. I throw the door shut behind him.

"What do you want?"

He pulls back from craning his neck to peek into my bedroom and cocks a brow at me instead. He's got a thing about me speaking disrespectfully to him. He stares, waiting for an apology. I'm too tired and tangled up in the after-effects of last night's shadows to give a damn about apologies. He finally gives up, even though his back stays stiff as he tucks his hands in his front pockets.

"I came to see my wife. Is that okay?"

I used to melt when he called me his wife. Now, I just ease down onto the couch and wait for him to tell me what he wants. I feel him walk behind me and the hair on my neck stands on end. My throat goes too dry to swallow.

Des comes around the side of the couch and sits beside me. "What's wrong with you?"

He reaches out and moves closer, his eyelids drooping as if he's going to caress me, kiss me. His fingertips travel down my neck and I go rigid. He glances down and his eyes bulge. He pushes back the blanket I've got hooded around me.

"Who the hell did this to you?" he seethes. I'm silent. Des clutches my jaw, twisting my face to look at him. His eyes slice into my dull gaze. "Was it that son of a bitch next door?"

I yank out of his grip. "Of course not."

"Who then? Tell me who did that to you, Lydia!" He jumps up, his eyes wide and crazy. "No one lays a hand on my wife! I'm going to kill the bastard!"

Fury wells in my throat, burning away the pain that's already there. My words bubble up and burst out of my mouth.

"Stop it! Just stop it, Desmond! You do the same thing to me all the time, just in different places!"

"I have never choked you like that! That is what happened, isn't it? I can see the sick, son of a bitch's hands, for Christ's sake!"

I yank the blanket back up around my neck.

"So it's the *location* of the bruises that matter..." I sneer. His nostrils flare and I know to back off. "Just tell me why you're here and what you want, so I can get back to dealing with my own life, okay?"

The skin jumps in his jaw as he grinds his teeth. I've never called him out on what he's done to me, especially not with such pure and focused anger. It takes him a moment to regroup, finally standing tall and plucking at the front of his suit coat.

"You expect me to just stand by and take it when someone disrespects what is mine?"

"C'mon Des..." I whisper. "I stopped being yours a long time ago."

He swoops down on me so suddenly, I press my back into the couch. The tip of his nose nearly touches mine.

"Watch your mouth, Lyddle," he growls. "You are *mine,* got it? You always have been and always will be. I will let this slip *once.* Do you understand me? Once. If I see so much as a scratch on you ever again, I will hunt down the man that did it and I will kill him."

He backs off an inch, but still hovers over me, and it kills me that I do little more than cower in the shadow he casts. I'm so sick and tired of it all, but I'm too exhausted to stand my ground right now.

"I came here to give you your Christmas present and I was going to spend the afternoon with you, Lyddle, but I don't think you deserve it now." All I can do is glare up at him, but my hatred for him has finally caught spark inside me. I hope he can feel the flames of it, licking at him through my eyes.

His brow jumps, as if what he's sees on my face startles him. He takes a bigger step back.

"Don't you dare forget who you belong to, Lydia," he says, but his tone has thinned. He clears his throat. "Claudia and I are going on a cruise to Belize for the holiday. We'll be returning after the New Year. I expect you to get yourself straightened out by then. Oh, and have a very merry Christmas."

He turns to go, pausing at the wobbly little table near my front door. He removes something from his breast pocket and throws it down on the table top. He yanks open the door and he's gone with a slam.

I'm left sitting on the couch, unsure if I just won or lost that battle, but fairly certain I've just started a war to knock all other wars right out of our history books.

*I*t's not until the afternoon that I finally pick up the fat envelope that Des left on the table beside the door. Of course, it's money, but what I didn't see coming is how much that is in there. Twenty thousand dollars. It takes me a few minutes to count it out to be sure, but there it is, in cash. Big bills. There is a note tucked in the front of the envelope, but it's not in Des's writing. It's in Claudia's.

*M*erry *Christmas, Lydia. You've made our house a home. Our dreams would have been nothing without you. Happy Holidays and have a drink on us!*

I crumple the note in my hand.
Their *dreams*.

Have a drink on us. My entire body is raked with nausea. I am flooded with visions of every time I've seen Des with his arm around Claudia, playing the good husband. She has no idea what he's doing to her. My ears want to close out every lie he's whispered to me. My hands want to throw away the feeling of his skin on mine and my mouth on--

I run to the toilet, throw open the lid. I heave and the bitterness in my mouth burns. The acid Des has tried to leave in me is the kind that slowly dissolves a woman, until there is nothing left of his crime against her.

The worst part of Claudia's note is that anything I'd buy with her money wouldn't be for just my pleasure, but her husband's. Des will be expecting some lingerie, some new, leather accessories out of my little windfall.

No, the deception isn't the worst part. It is the last part. *Have a drink on us.* In lieu of everything that's happened, that line is the one that sticks in my head like an ice pick. I imagine Claudia repeating the line, with her emotionlessly-Botoxed brow and her surgically, Jolene'd lips forming a smile.

God help me, I hate her. And the very worst part of hating her is knowing that I'm hating the wrong person.

My heart is filled with empty bottles that I've been stuffing with rescue notes, but I've never sent off even one. I've always believed there was no hope in being saved.

I've known for a long time that I have no husband. I don't, maybe never did, and probably never will.

I have no high school diploma, no job, and no skills that would qualify me for anything more than flipping a burger or wiping up hair bits at a salon. I don't even know how to work a pole at a club.

The only thing I have left inside me at all is this inane need to drink, and even as I'm considering how fucked up that is, all I can think about is pouring a fifth down my throat of whatever I can get my hands on. I can't get numb enough anymore.

God, how bad does my life have to get before I can't take it anymore? I'd swear I'm at my breaking point now.

I've got to stop. Everything. And I still feel like I can't.

<<<<>>>>

I wake in the morning to nausea squirming in my stomach like maggots. My hands are shaking as if I'm being electrocuted. I poured all my liquor down the sink last night. I've really put the screws to myself and I can't take it. But I can't go out like this.

I'm enraged with how I can't get comfortable on the couch cushions, with the stupid beer commercials on TV, and with the way the rain sounds like needles rattling against my window. I'm livid that I can't hear Aidan moving around at all next door and I'm furious with how I want a drink so fucking bad, I could scream until the entire world hears my need.

But the most terrifying thing right now is thinking of what will happen if I let any alcohol past my lips. I'll have to keep on living like I have been--in hell.

I can't live like this.

Godammit!

I can't live without a drink.

The itch in me is so aggressive that I fantasize about turning myself inside out and exposing my addictions in a way that God, or maybe just the critical eyes of the world, can burn this misery away.

I pace back and forth, back and forth, back and forth, behind my couch.

Ants crawl on my skin and I swat them away even though they aren't real and I know they're not. But their skittering legs feel real.

TV doesn't interest me.

Food doesn't distract me.

Showers

and shopping

and make-up

and all the pretty shoes in the world don't interest me.

All I want is one goddamn drink. A sparkling glass of red, a rugged shot of Jack, a wide, salty rim with an umbrella. I'd take any one of them.

I just want one.

I stuff my feet into a pair of my boots, drag on my coat, and grab my keys off the counter. I've got to stop this insane itch inside me and the only place with a cure is the liquor store.

It's only one drink. One lousy sip and then--

Who am I kidding?

I could drink an ocean.

I want to.

My hand on the door knob--

I get a glimpse of someone down the hall, in my room. A flash of another entity. I freeze, squint. No, wait.

It's me. It's just my reflection in my bedroom mirror. I almost left tonight without consulting it. That's how messed up I am right now.

But the woman in the mirror down the hall catches my eye and hangs onto it. First, it's her hair that I notice. Her dreads swing with her passion to leave. Then, it's her body, thinner than it's ever been. The baggy yoga pants and the man's shirt she wears nearly swallows her whole. And then, I see the eyes of that woman in the mirror.

When did I get so sad? When did I start wearing it up on the surface like this?

My hand drops off the door knob and the keys slip from my grasp.

The woman in the mirror can't go on living like this. She's so fragile, she doesn't have the ability to handle one more drink. Not even one. One more might send her to the medicine cabinet, rutting through anything that can be taken in bulk, something that can finally stop all the pain. The misery is so sharp, it's like a cheese grater on my nerves. Pouring the idea of a drink over them makes my eyes sting.

She's at the bottom. This is what it looks like--dirty, desperate, depressed.

I leave the woman and go to the couch, laying down on it. All I want is to pour some numbness down my throat, but it terrifies me that I can't even feel who I am anymore. I can't keep living like this and I can't get relief from my life.

All I can do is cry. Dammit. It's all I can fucking do.

REAL HELP

Aidan's knock starts soft, but swells to an all-out beating on my door.

"Lydia!" he shouts. Pounds again.

"What's the matter?" I hear Mrs. Lowt join in. Aidan mumbles something about not having seen me for a couple days and Mrs. Lowt's tone escalates to a panicked chipmunk kind of pitch.

"Well, you get in there then! Lydia! Are you okay? Open up! It's Eleanor Lowt, your neighbor!"

Now there's two of them beating on the door.

The first two days, I wasn't sure I could hang on, the way my heart was beating like it was organ-donered by a caffeinated gerbil. My hands are still a little quaky, but I don't believe that I'm going to die anymore. At least, not completely, but I still don't feel up to answering the door. I've been sitting on the couch--a little afraid to leave it--in the same shirt and yoga pants from two days ago. I've been drinking water, eating crackers, and watching TV. I'm soaked through with sweat. It's safe to say that I'm not ready for company.

But Aidan and Mrs. Lowt aren't letting up. If anything, the way they're pounding, they might just break the door right off the hinges. I stand and wobble like a newborn calf, as the blood tries to climb back up into my brain.

"Lydia!" Aidan's voice is demanding, angry, panicked.

"I'm calling the landlord if she don't open up," Mrs. Lowt sounds the same. I shuffle to the door and grip the knob. It's cool in my palm, surreal, as if I've never noticed the texture and temperature of a doorknob before. The beating from the hall side stops the moment I twist it. Thank God.

I drag the door open to the two angry faces of my neighbors, but the instant they get a look at me, all of the worry and rage and panic disappear from their expressions. What's left are the faces I'd expect to see on the last two human survivors in a zombie apocalypse. The ones who are toe-to-toe with a zombie. Mrs. Lowt takes a step back.

"Oh Lydia," she gasps. "What are you doing to yourself in there?"

Aidan jumps to action. He steps between me and Mrs. Lowt, shielding me, I think, as he simultaneously shuffles me backward into the apartment. I sway and catch myself, leaning against the wall as he rushes in.

"Looks like the flu, Eleanor. I'll take care of her from here," he says. I must look like more than Mrs. Lowt can handle, since she doesn't protest. Aidan latches the door and turns back to me, muttering a curse between his teeth. "You should have called me...told me you were going to do this...it's not safe to go it alone like this."

I raise my chin, even though it makes my vision float. The wall is stable. "I'm doing fine."

"You don't smell like it."

"Go home, Aidan. I just have the flu."

"Really, Lydia? You've gotten this far and you still can't call it what it is?" he says, but when I turn my head away from him, he softens. "Come on. Let's get you in the shower."

He starts down the hall, but turns back when I don't follow. His footsteps return slowly and he takes my hand, giving me a little tug. If he does it again, I know my legs are going to give out. I'll splash down on the floor. My body is so unreliable.

"I can't," I whisper, still clinging to the wall. The shakes make my fingertips tap a faint S.O.S. against the door frame.

"That's why I'm here." He eases himself under my arm and grips my waist. We go down the hall as if I'm a life-size rag doll. Tucked in so close, I shut my eyes and breathe him in. He stops walking. "Come on now...don't pass out on me, Lydia."

"I'm not," I say. "I was smelling your cologne."

"Oh."

"It reminds me of the bar."

"I'll wash it off."

"You don't have to."

"I'm still going to."

"Aidan?"

"Yeah?"

"I think I'm going to puke."

"Now?"

I can't answer; I'm too busy letting it rip down the front of me. When I'm done, Aidan just walks me over the puddle and into the bathroom. He gives me water to wash out my mouth. We're both a stinking mess.

"Sorry," I say. "I don't know why that happened. I've been okay for the last couple days."

"It's probably from moving around." He plants me on the toilet seat and peels off my shirt before flipping on the shower. He pulls off his own soiled shirt and tosses our clothing in the sink. "They say some people get sick the first day, sometimes it's the third or fourth."

"Sorry."

"It's alright. I was sick like this the very first day." He's trying to breathe through his mouth. He smiles between breaths, holding his hand under the stream of water until he's happy with the temperature. I hang onto the counter and waver onto my feet again. He helps me undress the rest of the way, and though I'm surprised when he drops his own soiled pants to the floor too, I'm too weak to argue.

If he's expecting payment for his help, I'll do it. I don't know how, but I will.

His arms float at either side of me, safety nets, as I climb into the shower. I get hold of the towel rack and hang on with all the strength I've got left. My back faces the stream of water. Aidan steps in behind me, blocking and unblocking the flow with his movements, so the water hits me like a spastic storm. My grip tightens on the rack, but I bend over slightly, my rear end thrust out behind me in offering. I hope I don't puke again while he does it.

But instead, soap glides down my back. Aidan moves my hair over my shoulder and the tips weep down my breasts. I wait for his hands to grasp my hips. To pull himself into me. I brace for the impact.

But his knuckles, clutching the soap, sweep over my spine, into my right armpit, and down my ribs. He repeats the process on my left side. A delicate lather slides from my shoulder, down my breast, and gathers on my nipple like a tiny cluster of grapes.

Aidan slides the soap down my back, the suds spilling over my rear and down my legs. His knee caps crack as he squats to wash me, the full force of the shower finally scattering across my back. I close my eyes, enjoying the tenderness of his soft, slick hands and the pounding massage of the water. His knees crack again when he stands.

"Can you turn around?" His voice is husky. I draw close to the towel rod and turn slowly. Aidan takes my hands and threads them underneath, palms out, so my fingers grip the rod. My shoulders press back against it. Aidan blocks the stream again and I grow cold without the constant crash of the water on me. My nipples rise. I feel the heat of his body, inches from mine, and I've never felt so vulnerable. I can't even bring myself to look below his waist.

"Just try to keep yourself up, okay?" he says. I do as he tells me. There's a horrible comfort in this simple act that sits in my stomach like a soggy blanket. Des has always told me what to do and I've always done it. I've relied on it.

Aidan cleans me carefully from head to toe. The scent of vomit is quickly replaced with cranberry soap. The steam thickens to a fog and my fingertips prune in the humidity. I just hang onto the towel rack, swaying out and pressing back, focusing on the feeling of his fingers as they gently working over my skin. He touches every inch of me, gently, as if my body is something holy and valuable. No man has ever touched me like this. Not with such care and such reverence. It is...humiliating.

When I open my eyes, Aidan's looking directly into them and my gaze plummets in shame. Unfortunately, what ends up in my line of vision are his hips and the long, heavy weight of his sex, dangling loosely between them.

I expected, from all the soap and all the touching...something more. The one power I have and it has abandoned me too, along with my hope. Aidan's physical indifference to my naked body is just another brick of despair, tied around my heart. A mournful laugh dies in my throat.

"What?" he asks, seemingly amused and curious, as he turns off the water. He reaches out for a towel from the stack I keep on the back of the toilet tank. My eyes sink to his feet. Another attempt at a laugh fails.

"I don't turn you on."

I keep my head down, my eyes shut. I don't need to be staring at that monster of a failure. He takes my naked hand and deposits it on the hard crest of his right shoulder. His skin is moist and firm beneath my shriveled fingertips.

"You need my help," he says lightly, "and that wouldn't be helping, now would it?"

He places my other hand on his other shoulder before opening the towel and wrapping it around me. Help or not, he shouldn't be able to control his body's reaction to mine, unless there wasn't one to control. I don't need a savior, I need to be loved.

I feel the sting of building tears and try to hold them back beneath my closed lashes, but his touch tips up my chin and one of the tears escapes in a reckless trail down my cheek. The tears pile up, acrid and burning, until I am forced to open my eyes and release the sting. Aidan is distorted in the blur and while I'm grateful that I can't see his expression, I am humiliated that he's staring at mine.

His fingertips suddenly drift over my neck with a small groan. They move to a different position than where the tender bruises still ache, and Aidan's fingers don't grip, but lay softly on the surface of my skin. The swell of his thumb braces my jaw, holding it high, so that when the tears finally drain out of me, all that is left is Aidan's gentle gaze, locked on mine.

"Would it help?" he whispers. The question forms another tear in the corner of my eye.

Aidan brings his mouth to mine, grazing the skin so softly that my lips split apart like a waiting, baby bird. His breath is sweet and warm as his tongue sinks into my mouth. My body responds to his kiss with muscle memory, taking over and piloting my way toward this fix of bliss by pressing my breasts to Aidan's chest, tightening my grip on his shoulders, and rolling my hips toward his. My body knows the way to make a man moan, but as Aidan's interest in me surges up against my thigh, I'm the one who releases the first sound of pleasure.

Aidan breaks our kiss slowly and I sway back, my shoulders hitting the towel rack. He steadies me and I wait for another kiss, but it doesn't come. Instead, Aidan reaches out and re-adjusts my towel, dropping it like a curtain between my body and his. His awakened, throbbing beast twitches against the fabric like a scenting animal searching for my soft cave.

Aidan's eyes scan my face and flick across my neck like a checkmark. He slides back the shower drape. I stand like a carving that hasn't been finished. What he's given me was not enough, but he steps out and turns to offer me his hand. I am still frozen in place, a mixture of confusion and embarrassment. I don't know why he halted what was starting, when it's obvious that part of him so clearly wants to continue.

With his hand still extended, he closes his eyes and takes a deep, full breath. He lets it out slowly and, as if by sheer determination, opens his eyes again and smiles at me.

"I want to give you what you actually need, Lydia," he says. "Help."

<<<<>>>>

*H*e makes food that I don't want to eat. He sits at the opposite end of the couch from me and when I drift off to sleep, he's still there when I wake up. Since sitting up still makes me feel sick, he posts a bucket beside the couch and puts glasses of smoothies, with straws poking from the top, on the coffee table beside me. He rubs my feet as we watch TV.

But most of all, Aidan just talks to me. He tells me about how he grew up with a mother who blamed Ila and him for their father not wanting to come home from the bar. He tells me about what happened when his father did. But he doesn't just tell me the bad things. He tells me about a pet guinea pig he had named Norman, how he used to shovel snow for the neighbors to buy himself and Ila tickets to the movies, he fills the hours with stories of his past and questions of mine, until I'm talking as much as he is. I confess to an obsession with Good & Plenty candies, to loving the Beatles over Elvis, to wanting to travel the world. I tell him that I still don't know what I want to be when I grow up. I admit that I thought I'd be married with a big family by now. And when he asks why Des doesn't live here, I grow quiet and resistant to answer, so he gracefully reverts the conversation to the deep, gray sky outside my window. A commercial with a zip lining pig comes on.

"How about that? Have you ever tried that before?" he asks.

"Zip lining? No," I say, rubbing my temples.

"Me either. I had the chance once, but I backed out."

I don't know why, but the image of an ice cold Mojito just crashed into my head. It shouldn't be there. It can't. I rub harder as my temples are buttons that will turn off the vision.

"How come?" I ask him dryly. *Focus.* Or, *unfocus.*

"I was at a really shabby resort and the line was strung between trees that looked like they were half dead. With my luck, the thing would snap as soon as I got half way down." He laughs, but all it does is jiggle the drink in my head, slop some of the deliciousness down the edge of the glass. I actually open my mouth, as if it's a real thing that will spill onto my tongue. *Holy shit.*

"Aidan?"

"You okay?"

"I want a drink. Bad. I can't stop thinking about it. And I mean, *really* can't."

"Okay, okay," he sooths, rubbing my feet again. "Give it a minute and it'll pass. Just keep talking to me."

He presses his thumbs between my toes. I don't say a word because it would be, *Mojito.* It's never going to go away. The craving for it is as immense as Godzilla, stomping through my brain. Another commercial comes on, this one with a guy in a reindeer suit advertising Christmas savings at a department store. Aidan taps my ankle. "What are you doing for Christmas?"

He waits for my answer.

"Lydia," he says. My mind catches up, his words coming to me like I'm breaking the surface of water.

"Zip lining," I say. He laughs.

"Be sure to check the trees," he says. Then he pivots around, as if he's searching for something in my apartment. "Speaking of trees...where's yours?"

The Mojito in my head drains away. *Whoa.*

"I don't put up a tree," I say.

"No Christmas tree? How come?"

"I'm a Grinch. Totally am." I drop my forearm across my forehead, relieved that the Mojito-craving-that-could've-swallowed-Manhattan has left the building. A headache takes root in its absence. "God, my head is throbbing."

"You want some aspirin?"

"No," I say. I should say yes, but even drinking water reminds me of drinking and I'm afraid that the Mojito craving will come back. I'm afraid I'll start begging for it and that I'll get so nuts, Aidan might actually give in. Or leave. "Is this *ever* going to get easier?"

"Yes," he says and he says it so solidly, I almost believe it's not bullshit. Almost. "You want some toast?"

"No."

"Soup?"

"No."

"Eggs?"

"No food," I groan. A weather warning suddenly ticker-tapes in red across the bottom of the TV screen.

"Expect sixteen to eighteen inches of snow. Huh, they upped it," Aidan says. I twist on the couch to peer out the window. It's already coming down. When I turn back, Aidan smiles at me.

"Good thing we don't have to go anywhere," he says.

"Don't you have to work?" It occurs to me that I've never asked and have no idea what he does for a living.

"I work from home. Software design. I can take a few days off."

"A few days? Your boss is okay with that?"

"Best boss in the world," he says. "I'm self-employed. What about you?"

"What about me?" I know where this is headed--down a huge, personal slope. He knows I've said I didn't know what I wanted to be and he knows I've said I'm in home design, even though he's obviously never bought it. Feeling this sick and fidgety, with my foot in his lap, I definitely don't have the armor I need right now to deflect him the way I should. "I get by. Let's just leave at that, okay?"

Surprisingly, he shrugs and looks back at the TV.

"Okay," he says and the pressure of his fingers remains even. I lay back and stare at the TV until his steady massage puts me to sleep.

"*I*'ll be right back." Aidan wakes me with a kiss on the forehead. I push myself up on the couch and glance out the window. It's still snowing--huge fat flakes have already covered the neighborhood. The news ticker is constant at the bottom of the screen now, flashing warnings that no one should go out, the roads are a mess, the whole world is shutting down.

"How long have I been asleep?"

"A few hours," he says, pulling on his coat.

"Where are you going?" I cinch the blanket a little tighter around me as I sit up, a desperate panic building inside me at the sight of him putting on his shoes.

"Just a few supplies. Before it gets really bad."

"Look out the window! It's already really bad."

"I won't be long."

He leaves a kiss on my forehead and he's gone before I can really beg.

For the next hour, the only thing I do is focus all my concentration on staying put on the couch, instead of throwing on a coat and sneaking out to the liquor store. I drink water. Water sucks. I sip the warm smoothie Aidan made. It sucks worse. I try to envision Aidan walking through the door, as if wishes will make it reality, and then I'm furious when it doesn't work.

I get up and float around the room like a dizzy top, putting on my coat and taking it off. My mind runs a circular track of excuses and justifications, demands and resolutions, around and around again. I tell myself that Aidan will be back at any minute and he'll catch me leaving. Or worse, that he'll catch me returning with the empty bottle that I would choke down on the way back from the store. The whole thing is infuriating and humiliating. Why did he have to fucking leave?

Aidan uses my own keys an hour later to let himself back in with a grocery bag and a bag of take out from Burger Alley. I'm back on the couch, lying flat with my blanket tucked in tight around me like a straitjacket.

"You look...comfortable." He laughs. With him here, I can release myself from my fabric confinement. "Come see what I got."

I take the first deep breath that I've taken since he left. The calm he brings to me is palpable as I stand at the edge of the kitchen counter and watch him unpack the bag.

I assumed he was off getting staples, like eggs and milk and bread to surf out the storm, but he ends up pulling out a bag of flour and a canister of salt, along with two kid's paint sets. I look at the connected rainbow of paint pots, complete with cheap brushes, and then, at him. He went to the fucking store to get paint sets? While I'm fighting a fucking war here in my head? He smiles when I frown.

"You needed paint?" I say slowly. "That's why you had to go to the store?"

He nods. "I've got plenty of food in my apartment to get us through, but since we're stuck inside, we need something to *do*."

"Do," I repeat. We're going to paint-by-number? I really don't know what Aidan expects from me. It's taking all my focus to stay inside this apartment and not throw myself from the window.

"*C*hristmas is coming quick," he says, going into the kitchen. "Only a couple of weeks, so I got something to get you in the spirit. But first, we eat."

I grip the edge of the counter, still a little wobbly and still a little pissed. He unpacks the carry out next, arranging the food on two of my mismatched plates and pushes one across the counter to me.

I push it back. "I'm not hungry."

"Eating is a habit you have to get back into," he says, shoving the plate toward me again.

"No thanks."

He shrugs, biting off half of a fry. "It's not an option."

"What's that supposed to mean? You're going to stuff burgers down my throat?"

"Nope. Your recovery is up to you, Lydia. But I'm telling you, if you want to get well, you're going to have to start taking care of your body, so it can keep living."

Just what I want to do right now. Get myself healthy so I can fully enjoy this aggravated, pissed off, itching-for-a-drink bag of guts. I give the plate too hard of a push back at him. It slides straight off the edge of the counter and shatters at Aidan's feet. He doesn't even jump out of the way. He just plucks another fry from his own plate and glances down at the mess on the floor.

I feel like a dick. But an agitated, justified dick. I don't want to eat, *the end.*

Aidan steps over the mess and swings open the cupboard under the sink.

"What do you know?" he says with amused surprise. He pulls out a dustpan and mini-broom, sweeps up the mess, and dumps it in the trash. I watch his every move, waiting for a *real* reaction. I wait for him to turn and yell in my face about what I did. Or try to stuff the floor-burger down my throat.

He doesn't.

He gets down another plate. He takes out a knife and cuts his burger in half. He slides the half burger and half of his fries onto the new plate and pushes it over to me.

"Eat, Lydia," he says gently. "It will make you feel better."

Doubtful. But, staring across the counter at his serene face, I feel like an even bigger idiot. I pick up a fry and look away as I stick the end in my mouth. It tastes like greasy cardboard. From my peripheral, Aidan smiles at me and I take another.

I eat everything on the plate, even though it takes effort to get it down. The only thing worse than eating when there is zero appetite, is feeling like there never will be one again.

"Do you have cookie cutters?" Aidan asks. I snort.

"Yeah right."

"I didn't think so. How about a big bowl?"

I just stare at him. He's got to be kidding. I've got a kitchen designed by Bacardi Crocker.

"I have a blender," I say.

He opens and closes cupboards, but finally pulls out the only saucepan I have. I used it to make baked beans once.

"What are you trying to do?" I ask.

"It's a surprise," he says, but his surprise becomes annoyingly dull to me as he starts stirring his flour-water-salt concoction on a stove burner.

But then, everything seems dull. Painting my nails--snore. Going to the movies--I don't care. Even the idea of going shopping, with the fat stash Des left, doesn't ignite any sparks of interest in me. It scares me a little that I've stopped drinking and now the whole world seems a washed-out shade of nothing. I might *need* the booze just to live in color. I shiver.

Aidan catches it.

"Why don't you go cover up on the couch? This is going to take me a few minutes. Grab a nap, if you want."

A nap. I roll my eyes at him, but it makes me a little dizzy. I turn around and head to the couch. A nap. Like I'm a fucking toddler. Under the blanket, the burger and fries sink in my stomach like placing an anchor and I'm asleep in minutes

IMPERFECT SNOWFLAKES

I wake up to a full blown cookie factory happening in my
kitchen. Unsatisfied with my lack of kitchen utensils, Aidan's
dragged over most of his. There are cookie sheets and bowls and
spoons and a wire rack with weirdly shaped cookies cooling on it.

Aidan's pulling something out of the oven when I show up at
the counter. I slip a misshapen star off the cooling rack. They look
horrible, shaped without cutters. I bite the tip off the star and as he
turns around with a sheet of hot cookies clenched in a foreign oven
mitt, he catches me spitting out the bite I took. He laughs.

"No good?" he says.

"Worst *ever*! Awful! They're hard as rocks! What did you do?"

"That's because they're not cookies. They're tree ornaments,"
he chuckles. He spatulas the new cookies--majorly fucked-up
Christmas trees--onto the wire rack beside his other hideous
masterpieces. "We made these every year when I was a kid. Salt
dough. It's tradition."

They look like a little kid still made them.

I think it might be a good sign that my angst isn't rushing out of
my mouth like vomit anymore.

I inspect the bitten star in my hand a little more closely. The salt glitters a little. "You're really into this Christmas tree idea, aren't you."

"I am."

"So," I turn the beige-ish thing over in my palm before placing it back down on the cooling rack with the others, "it's going to be an ugly Christmas."

"That's what the paints are for." He nudges the kiddie paint sets. Ahhh. "We need something to do."

"We do?" I can think of far better things. Well, if I didn't feel so sick. At least, thinking of them provides a bland flicker of interest.

"To get your mind off things," he says. I wonder if he was reading my mind just now. Probably not, since he is merrily carrying on, fucking-up another batch of what I think he means to be snowflakes. I watch shape a ball of dough for a minute, before taking a glob for myself. I start shaping a fucked-up snowflake too. He glances at me from his obliteration of an ornament and a smile flicks over his lips before he goes back to what he's doing.

<<<◇>>>

e are at it all day. I use up all the white paint on three snowflake ornaments and then, to conserve on the other colors, I stick to doing only highlights on plain ornaments. Who would've ever thought that Lydia Strong, with her wild lingerie and sky-high heels, would be enjoying painting ornaments like a preschooler?

But, in between ornaments, I do try to revert back to the normal Lydia and get busy with Aidan, but he's not having any of it. He deflects it in a million clever ways.

"How are you doing those swirls?" he asks when I lean across the couch toward him for the fourth time.

153

"Great," I say, relaxing back onto my end cushion. He doesn't mention the crankiness or the attitude that I continue to throw at him. He can't, really, since he's the one causing it by refusing to kiss me.

Aidan only does a few ornaments and gives up, leaving the rest of his paint for me. Good thing, too. I'm obsessed. Painting dots and swirls and slashes on misshapen ornaments is the only thing that is keeping my mind off drinking. And keeping my mind off him...for the most part. It seems like every time I think to look at the clock, at least another hour has ticked by.

For the next two days, all it does is keep on snowing and all I do is make dough ornaments. Aidan sits on the other end of the couch, tapping away on his computer, and I huddle on the other, sculpting ornaments on top of a coffee table book that I'm using like a tiny desk.

It would be embarrassing, if it wasn't the one thing that is keeping me focused in the right direction. Aidan is like good furniture, quiet and comforting to have around. He stays over every night, sleeping on the opposite side of my bed, as immobile and chaste as an old Amish man. Even when I mold up against him, he does absolutely nothing to retaliate with the hard-on that results from the contact. When I reach out and grip it, his hand only closes over mine and then gently moves me away. It's maddening, but I don't want him to leave, so I roll over and stew quietly on my side of the mattress.

<<<◇>>>

In only days, I have reached a haughty, pro-level status in the area of preschool-ornament design. My only addiction now is getting more salt and flour when I run out. I empty Aidan's apartment before I hit up Mrs. Lowt.

"Can I borrow four cups of flour and a cup of salt?" I ask her when she answers her door.

"Lydia?" She forces her enormous glasses up the bridge of her nose and squints at me through the lenses as if I'm the alien here. "How are you doing? You look different."

"I've had the flu..."

"You look thinner, but your face has good color," Mrs. Lowt says. I smile, patiently. I need her salt. And flour.

"Do you have any craft paints I could borrow?" I ask.

"Craft paint? I don't think so."

"How about the flour and salt?"

"I have that. Come in." She walks away from the open door.

I've never once been in Mrs. Lowt's apartment and I can't remember a time that she's been in mine, other than to unlock the door when I couldn't drunkenly figure which of the three door-knobs to put my key into.

Stepping inside her place makes me feel like I'm on a weird drug trip. It's like walking into a mirror image of my place, but the furniture is all poufy and brown and the place smells like old card-board and ham. A table-top Christmas tree sits, tinseled-up, on a table big enough for two. Her apartment is also spotlessly clean. A white cat sits like a statue on a carpeted ledge affixed to the windowsill. I had no idea she had a cat.

I follow Mrs. Lowt to the edge of her wrap-around kitchen counter. As she opens gold canisters and scoops out flour and salt for me, I try to pet her cat. I reach a hand out and the moment I make contact with the hairs of its back, the animal springs up and comes down hissing at me.

"Oh, oh, oh," Mrs. Lowt clucks as she drops the measuring cup in the canister and rushes around the counter. She gets between me and her unsociable fur ball, scooping up the hissing thing in her arms. "Now Peaches...behave yourself. He's deaf, you under-stand...you just startled him is all."

The animal's ears are flat and remain so, even as Mrs. Lowt tries to soothe it with strokes down its back. Peaches shows me his exact level of comfort and acceptance with a sour, unrelenting glare and a growl that emanates from deep in his throat.

"He's precious," I say. Mrs. Lowt chuckles.

"Well, we've been together a long time. Once Patrick died, Peaches was all I had left. I've spoiled him too much for him to act like this to guests. He's just not used to visitors."

I blink at her. I've always thought of her as my obscenely nosey, horny neighbor. I had no idea she didn't have enough visi-tors to calm down her nasty cat or that she'd ever had a Patrick.

"Patrick was your husband?" I ask.

"Yes." She smiles and her mind seems to drift away from the living room, even as she continues to push down Peaches' growling head with her heavily affectionate strokes. "Forty-seven years we were together. He was a good husband. A very good man."

She snaps out of her daydream and dumps Peaches on the floor. He tears away as if his tail is on fire, his claws scratching across the carpet for traction. The last thing I see is the bent tip of his tail as he hauls ass around the corner and down the abbreviated hall to her bedroom. Mrs. Lowt hustles back into the kitchen and resumes scooping flour into a zip-top baggie for me.

"Aidan reminds me of him," Mrs. Lowt says. "Not in looks--Patrick wasn't so tall and he was a good German boy. A big man, with round cheeks and he was always ruddy, as if he'd been out in a strong wind all day."

"So they look nothing alike," I chuckle.

"No. But it's Aidan's *way* that reminds me of Patrick. My Patrick was a man that would do anything for you. Anything at all." Her eyes cut to me, over the top of her glasses. They're large and green and there isn't much sparkle to them, but for what her eyes lack in luster, they make up for in the wisdom that emanates from her stare. How did I miss it before? "I see how Aidan's been spending time at your apartment, Lydia. *Nights.*"

I'm suddenly warm, the heat concentrating in my cheeks.

"I've been sick," I say.

"Like I said, he's one of those men that would do anything for you," Mrs. Lowt says, zipping shut the bag and moving to her canister of salt. Once she begins pouring into her measuring cup, her eyes are back on me. "Don't throw that one away, Lydia. In fact, don't you let him get away. Lock him in there if you've got to."

She winks. I roll my eyes and Mrs. Lowt stops pouring to shake her measuring cup at me.

"I know what I'm talking about, Lydia. You should listen."

"I am," I insist. "It's just that Aidan and I are neighbors. That's it."

Mrs. Lowt zips the salt baggie shut and hands both to me with a sigh.

"Such a shame," she says. "Walls as thin as shoeboxes and all we are is neighbors. I live closer to you than my own son."

"You have kids?"

"Oh, just one. Howie. He's out in California. For work."

There's a whole extension of Mrs. Lowt out there? "Do you have grandkids?"

She laughs, swatting the air at my suggestion. "Oh no. Howie doesn't have time for children. He works too much. His partner, David, does too. The boys lives in Huntington Beach, just a block from the actual beach. They've been together...how many years has it been? Twelve, I think?"

I almost choke. Mrs. Lowt has a gay son? And she's talking about him as if she's completely at ease with it? I would've never guessed that any of these aspects of Mrs. Lowt's life belonged to her. By how she pinched butts and preached to me, I thought I knew enough to know her, but I realize I have no idea who she really is.

"Goodness," she says looking up at the grandmother's clock on a shelf in her living room. "It's nearly time for *Break Ins and Busts*. Come back anytime, Lydia. You know you're always welcome over here--it's just that Peaches and I have our routine. I can't break it or he'll pee in my church shoes."

She's got church shoes?

She hustles me to her front door.

"Come back anytime, Lydia. Anytime. If you ever want to watch with us, let me know."

<<<<>>>>

I'm sitting at the edge of my bed that night, looking out the window at the silvery, night sky and it's the first time I've thought of anything besides having a drink. Aidan's lying belly-down on the other side of the bed, his face turned toward my seated hip, but his eyes are closed. It's the first time I've really thought about how Aidan's been staying with me.

I'm having a hard time reconciling the last week-and-a-half in terms of my three-date rule. But this hasn't really been dates, has it? We've been sleeping together, although he's never touched me once. Having him here has been...simple.

"What are you thinking about?" His drowsy voice startles me. His eyes are open, watching. I wonder how long. I catch him doing it all the time and I'm suddenly lost on what it might mean. Long looks used to translate easily between the sheets, but it's not so simple with Aidan. I'm unsettled by how much I want him to stay. Of course, I'm not about to tell him any of this.

"Snow," I say.

"Mmm. You need a tree for your million ornaments. But I don't know if we can find a tree big enough to hold all of them."

"I told you, I don't put up a tree."

"Why not?"

"I just don't," I say. How do I tell him that a tree means home? It means this place is my home and I live here? This apartment has always been my transition place, just a place for me to wait until Des finishes his business and comes back to me. I don't know what to think of it now.

"Tomorrow, if it's not so bad out..."

"I'm not going tree shopping."

"No, I was thinking of taking you to a meeting with me."

I already know what kind of meeting he's talking about. "No thanks."

"Okay," he says with a little shrug under the covers. He closes his eyes.

That was just a little too easy. I've heard of the kind of meetings he attends. Tables full of slobbering drunks. You stand up in front of a whole room of them and admit to what a douchebag you are. As if I'm one of them. As if he is. I don't see why he even keeps going.

And it's freezing cold outside. If I have to go out, there will be a fifty-fifty chance that I have to walk in the direction of the liquor store. And if I have to walk by the liquor store--

If I even made it there, by the slim chance that I did, I bet the chairs are all the folding kind, the ones that have no padding. My ass will ache the whole time. There's nothing worse than chairs that squeak every time you move around, so everyone has to turn around and stare at you.

Then, they'll all want to preach at me with all their *stick with it*s, or their *You can kick this*, or *if I could do it, so can you*. I'm positive they'll be rattling strings of encouraging quotes heisted from t-shirts and bumper stickers like Prohibition cheerleaders. I'm annoyed with them already.

Aidan says he goes twice a week to these meetings. I've never kept tabs on his coming and going to know how long a meeting even takes. Probably an hour. Maybe two, if they sit around eating cookies and talking afterward. I chew my thumbnail thinking about that particular hell. Depending on how far away the meeting is, Aidan will be gone at least an hour and, at most, two or three hours if I don't go with him.

And that means I'll be here by myself.

I think of a couple days ago, when he went out for the salt and flour. I chomp the corner of my nail right off, remembering how hard it was to stop myself from going down to the liquor store. I don't know that I'm any stronger than I was only a couple of measly days ago. It sure doesn't feel like I am.

I don't want to go. But I'm not sure I can stay here without Aidan watching over me.

I slide down beside him. His eyes are open again. He reaches up and pulls my ravaged thumb from my mouth, tugging my fingers so I turn on my side to face him. With my forearm against his chest, he peers down at the word scrawled on my ring finger.

"That's a tattoo, isn't it?" he asks. I nod. He squints in the semi-dark to read it.

"It says *Strong.*"

"Ahhh," he says, "good choice of words."

"It's not a word, it's a name. My husband's last name. He got me drunk and had me tattooed."

"Oh," Aidan says and his frown makes me feel ashamed. I lay there with my heart stuck in my throat like a spiny peach pit, trying to put my finger on why. There are plenty of reasons to feel terrible: I'm a married woman, lying in bed with another man; I've got a husband who has not only cheated, but committed a felony doing it; I'm branded forever with my mistake's name. I'm gnawing on my thumb again and only realize it when Aidan gently pulls it from between my lips.

"I'm sorry he happened to you," he says. I force a laugh from my throat, trying to make light of it.

"Yeah, well...you don't know the half of it."

"Will you tell me about it?"

"I don't want to..."

"Never mind then," Aidan says softly. He runs the knuckles of his curled fingers like feathers over my throat. "Would you just tell me one thing? Did he give you those bruises that were on your neck a couple days ago?"

Eric's fingers jump out from the memory, gripping my neck instantly. His bruising words follow, echoing in my skull: *Girl, you know what you are. I was waiting my turn. Modo's Trophy Girl.*

I swallow turn away, looking out the window. Without any liquor running through me, the humiliation is unbearable. My eyes become bathtubs, overflowing with the sting of my shame. I'm caught beneath the surface. The room swims.

I manage to choke out, "No. Des didn't do it."

I'm glad Aidan doesn't ask about the burns on my legs. Instead, I lay there, paralyzed and praying, that Aidan doesn't make me admit that the damage came from some random guy that *waited his turn* for me at Modo's. *Slut* was such a funny word to me, a joke, until Eric showed me that it was true.

Aidan's hand moves beneath the sheets, finding its way to my forearm. He pulls me closer, turning me toward him again. I curl my head beneath his chin to avoid his eyes. My forehead pressed against his neck, I feel him swallow.

He rubs his palm against my back. The soft circle there breaks my dam. The shame spills out of me in great sobs, pouring down over his chest, but he doesn't say a word. The twitch of him in the valley between my thighs stills. He doesn't pull my hair, splaying my head back to kiss my neck. He doesn't push my head under the covers toward his hips.

He does none of the things that I have come to expect of a man. Instead, he keeps on tracing soft circles, like the links of Olympic rings or the graceful turns of a figure skater, across my back.

MEETING DOOM AT ITS OWN DOOR

"We have to get going, Lydia," Aidan groans from the bedroom door. He doesn't even try to hide the edge in his voice. I'm sure he suspects that I'm stalling and I am. But I also have to look more than just *right* for something like this. I'll probably have to stand up and confess my name along with all my sins that got me to the meeting.

I'm still scrutinizing my belt choice, my head tipped to my shoulder. I loop my thumb under it.

"Not sure if this looks right," I say. This would be so much easier if Aidan was Desmond. Des would walk right in, pointing and critiquing, and it would be done. As it is, I'm floundering in front of the mirror, making us both late to the Meeting of Drunken Doom.

"They don't care what you look like, I promise," he urges. When I don't budge, he drops a shoulder against the door frame. "If you don't want to go, you don't have to. Maybe you're not ready yet."

Not ready. Maybe he doesn't mean it to be insulting, or maybe he does, but either way, it jabs me. I can't sit in this apartment alone and be 100% sure that I won't throw on my coat and shoot down to the store for a bottle. Even though I don't want to go to this meeting, it's a *ready or not* situation.

I step away from the mirror and get stuck again. My thumbnail ends up between my teeth. With him standing there, staring at me, waiting for me to move, I finally realize it might just be easier if I ask him to do what I need. It's humiliating to ask, but I can't seem to unglue myself without it. He's stuck with me through the last few days of throwing up and looking like hell; I hope this won't be too much for him.

"Could you ask me to turn and tell me exactly what looks right or what doesn't?" I say. My voice has a soft quiver in it that I hope he interprets as sexy instead of what it is--scared. For a moment, it seems like he's not willing to feed into my sick dependency.

"Is that what your husband does for you?"

I nod. Aidan's stare is intense, as if he's putting a puzzle together in his head.

Then he says firmly, "Turn."

I do as he says, slowly. When I'm standing with my toes facing him again, I can't tear my eyes off the floor. I feel like my clothing has gaping holes over my nipples, over my crotch. It's a focused sort of vulnerability that is worse than being naked.

"You wear jeans like a rock star's wet dream, Lydia," he murmurs. His footsteps close the space between us. "And that shirt shows every reason why God, in his infinite wisdom, made you a woman and not a man. But," he pauses in front of me, his shoes pointing at my toes, "I would put your hair down."

His fingers release the knot of dreads I artistically bundled up at my crown. They rain down like Medusa's tresses. He clears his throat, cueing me to look up at him. His grin trembles.

"We're good to go," he says.

*T*he meeting is held in the basement of the Parish Street Church, a church I have never even noticed before, although I've passed it a thousand times. It's like any building, with thick, brown bricks and a cross studding the apex. It represents brimstone and confession to me. I shake and Aidan misinterprets it as a reaction to the frosty temperature. He grasps my hand to distill warmth or courage, or maybe there was no misinterpretation at all. Maybe he's hanging on so I won't bolt.

He leads me all the way around the church to the back and we descend the concrete stairs like criminals, slipping into a musty, gray, cinderblock corridor. Once the door latches behind us, with a metallic bang, Aidan lets go of my hand. I guess he figures I'm good and caught.

The hall is dim, the main light coming from an open door twenty feet away that casts a rectangular, yellow glow. The murmur of conversation spills from that doorway.

I pause as Aidan continues to walk toward the door. I think of turning back. I would, if it didn't feel like my heels just turned to cement blocks. The musty basement air seems too damn close and all I want is to get a breath of somewhere else.

"You coming, Lydia?" Aidan says, but he doesn't wait up for me to move my cement shoes. He just shoots me a grin and walks around the corner of the door.

People greet him, but I'm clinging to the shadows of the hall-way, an outsider. The people in there don't sound like alcoholics. Their voices sound like normal, everyday voices, which is worse for me.

It means that the people in there have been cured. They've got a handle on their fuck-ups and now they're swimming their way back up to the surface, to life. *I'm* the slobbering drunk I was worried about. They're going to see right through me. I step away from the door, putting my back against the cold, gray wall. I can't go in there. I'm not one of them. I'm paralyzed by my shame.

"Are we ready to begin?" a man's voice asks. It's familiar. Dull. Ah yes, Leonard. "Devon, can you grab the door?"

The door is hinged on the inside, so Devon doesn't even see me as he shuts me out with a metallic clunk. Shit. I stand there, waiting for Aidan to come out and retrieve me. Or to tell somebody in that room to throw me a lifeline. I'm drowning in shame out here.

Nobody comes. I mutter a string of curses. Now it's going to be twice as hard to walk into that room. Everyone will look up and gawk at the loser that couldn't make it on time.

I stomp my right foot and throw my shoulders back against the wall.

I'm either going to stand here for an hour and wait for Aidan or I'm going to open that goddamned door. It's one or the other, because I know that if I leave, I'm headed straight for the liquor store.

I'd trade a million karat diamond for a gulp of liquor burning down my throat, but I know I can't do it. I'm wrung out. I can't go back to the *Eric*s at Modo's; I can't sit in my apartment drowning my life in endless shots. If there's nothing else in life for me but another drink, I'm going to end up swinging from my shower rod. This is rock bottom, I suppose, and the precarious position I've been holding onto, between a rock and a hard place, has squeezed my future flat.

The door swings open with a squeak. Aidan ducks his head out, sees me plastered against the wall, and, with a grin, lifts his hand. He waggles a finger playfully at me to come inside. My chest stutters in short breaths. When I don't move, Aidan comes out, takes my hand, and leans his head down to whisper in my ear.

"You don't have to say a word. Just sit there and listen."

I nod, because if I open my mouth, I'm pretty sure that nothing good is going to come of it. I trail behind him, into the room. There are round tables with folding chairs and he drops my hand the moment we hit the one closest to the door, pulling out a chair for me to sit. I perch on the edge of the folding chair with wide eyes, waiting for all the eyes in the room to turn and critique me.

Leonard--I can tell who he is from voice alone--is standing at the front of the room, beneath a naked light bulb, droning a welcome to everyone in the room. Many of them don't tear themselves from his dull opening speech to look at me, but then, many others do. Some flash me a bored glance, a few smile, some assess me like an unwanted newcomer to the playground, before turning back around. I feel dismissed as I slide further back onto the creaking, metal seat of a folding chair. I was right about the lousy chairs.

There are no individual introductions. Thank God.

Leonard announces the evening's topic. Something about spouses, about fighting addiction while staying committed. Something like that. I can't really concentrate on the words since I'm still debating how I can bolt past Aidan and make it out the door, up the stairs, down the street, and to the counter of the liquor store.

Then my stomach sinks with the thought of downing the whole bottle in one gulp. It's a sick fantasy that nearly gives me orgasms at the part where I'm drinking, and nearly makes me throw up when I think about finishing the drink and still having to deal with my life as it is right now.

I rinse and repeat the fantasy, soiling and cleaning my mind in a frantic tumble, as random people speak from the other tables, introducing themselves and admitting their losership openly. For the first couple speakers, I'm so busy worrying that someone's going to call on me to say something, I don't really hear a thing. It's not until a familiar brunette speaks that I pay attention.

"Hi, my name is Natalie, and I'm an alcoholic. I've been sober for eight months and three days," she says. Her hair is separated in a razor-sharp, white part that runs down the center of her head.

There is a dull murmur of *hi Natalie's* that rise up from the folding chair trenches. "I've also been married for a year. I think that it's incredibly hard to work a relationship, even when your spouse is a normy and even when he's supportive of my recovery from this disease. An established relationship is hard enough, but I can't imagine beginning a new relationship and trying to juggle it while trying to get sober at the same time. The two are at odds. You have to be well and whole before you can really think about giving yourself to another person." Murmurs of agreement rise up and a few people clap. "I was thinking it might be useful to talk a little about the suggestions in regards to relationships in the first year of sobriety, Leonard? I think there are newcomers who might benefit."

She says this while glancing at Aidan and I. There's nothing else in my head but the clang of one word: *bitch.* I can't believe Aidan's own friend is doing this. Aidan is the one person who is helping me. He *got me here.*

As Natalie's eyes come to rest on me again, I can't take any more of it. It's either explode right here and now, or ditch this place and hit the nearest bar on my home.

It's not like I really have a choice.

So.

I jump to my feet. The metal chair flips, clattering across the floor behind me. Anyone who didn't know I was in attendance before, definitely knows it now. The sea of faces turns to give me center stage.

"I wouldn't be sitting here now if it wasn't for that night at Modo's! Yes, Aidan made a mistake and we had sex, but it was just his friend's name for Christ's sake! I don't even want to be here, but I am, because *Aidan's* gotten me this far. And if it's none of that--if you're giving me the death stare because your husband looked at me when I first met the two of you--then, it isn't my damn fault...quit being such a jealous bitch for Christ's sake!"

Aidan rubs his forehead with one hand, looking into his lap with an embarrassed grin. He's probably regretting everything from the moment his lips touched my Mojito-filled belly button, right up to the second ago, when I sprung off the seat beside him.

The naked light bulb in the front of the room, over Natalie's head, hums and pops off with a flash. She startles and a guy in the front wheezes a chuckle as Leonard gets to his feet. Leonard is a tall guy with a long, gray ponytail and skin that sags off his cheeks, but his expression appears gentle, and God knows, I need somebody in this room to see my side of things right now.

"Welcome to the group," Leonard says. He cracks a smile. "That was one hell of an introduction."

The crowd breaks into laughter. Aidan rights my collapsed chair. I sit. I feel like I'm about to sink through the small opening at the back. I wish I could. Leonard deflects.

"The suggestion that Natalie is referring to," he looks back over the crowd and carefully avoids any eye contact with me, "is that for our first year of sobriety, we suggest you don't change anything in our current environments. We don't move out of our houses, we don't change jobs, we don't take on a new relationship. Opposite-sex sponsoring tends to present additional challenges that just aren't necessary. We want to focus all of our energy on recovery. We don't want to be sidetracked with stressors from other situations. Our addictions are stressful enough."

"My point exactly," Natalie says from somewhere at a front table. "I'm not trying to accuse, I am just trying to help."

Hell if she sounds helpful. Aidan weaves an arm around the back of my seat and lounges against his own. He latches an ankle over his knee.

"It's a helpful suggestion," he says with a dry grin. "I think we can all appreciate that the suggestions are actually *guidelines*, not *laws*."

"They're in place for a reason," a man says without turning his head around. "Men sponsor men, women with women. That's what works."

"What if I don't want that?" I say. I can't keep my mouth shut. Fuck this whole room. Aidan's gotten me this far and I owe him my loyalty, not these strangers. Would they have wiped the barf off me in the shower?

"Well, hell. I'm not going to beg anyone to be my *sponsee*." A woman with hair like metal shavings half-laughs as she turns her back to us. "You got to want help before I'll give it. But I think Natalie makes a good point. A sponsor's job is to *help*, not create a dependency."

"Thank you all for your concern," Aidan says. "It's taken under advisement."

Leonard resumes the talk, calling on someone from a table to the left, and the meeting goes along like a wagon on loose wheels for about an hour. At the end, the crowd breaks, the chairs are stacked against the wall, and a woman announces that there will be coffee and cookies available at the banquet table on the other side of the room.

"I'm think I'm ready to leave," I say, as soon as Aidan returns from dropping off our chairs.

"Yeah, I'm ready too," he says. We exit without holding hands. Climb the stairs to ground level in silence. I gulp down the air, wishing it was a drink. I'm afraid that the feeling will never go away. That I'm going to drag this rattling chain around with me every minute for the rest of my life, always waiting for the bottle at the end to catch up and clobber me.

"So what did you think?" Aidan asks.

"I thought they were a bunch of assholes," I say.

"What they're saying is actually right," he says, keeping his hands loose as we walk around the side of the church. I tuck mine in my pockets. "I want to be the one that you lean on, Lydia, but they're right. I'm not doing you any favors as a sponsor. I'm too invested."

"You don't have to worry about that. I don't think I'm going back."

Aidan stops walking and turns to me with an expression that is both stunned and deeply pained. It sinks into me and I know right then and there, he just snuffed out any other choice I have, other than returning to that shitty church basement.

"Hey!" A breathless shout comes from behind us. We both turn back to see who's yelling. Natalie is yanking on her lambskin jacket, pulling her hair from its collar as she runs toward us. "Wait up!"

She's almost to us, and I envision her face on a punching bag. I want to beat her down. She is the reason for the sudden proposal of change in my and Aidan's relationship. I wish I could slam a drink to calm down. The urge to escape down to the bar fires up as she works her way toward us, like a vampire's ripping thirst for blood.

"Hey Nat," Aidan says as she catches up. His tone is both friendly and guarded. I am mentally preparing to grab her by the hair and take her down if she says one more lousy thing to either of us.

"I wasn't trying to be a bitch in there." A little winded, Natalie's breath puffs out of her like a steam engine. The clean part in the center of her scalp is mussed from running. "I'm trying to help."

"Help was what *he* did," I snap at her, "by getting me to come here tonight."

"Help is not calling us out in front of the whole group," Aidan adds. "Especially not on her first night."

"I didn't mean it like that," she says. She puts her hand on my sleeve, since I've dug my hands into my pockets for her safety. "I know how hard it is for me and Shane. I know what it takes to get clean. It's so hard to focus on yourself when you have to juggle the needs of a relationship too. This time should be all about you and doing this for yourself."

"I don't see where it is any of your..." I begin, but Aidan cuts me off.

"She's right," he says. "You're right, Natalie, but this is between Lydia and me. I appreciate your concern, but we'll have to discuss it ourselves."

"I'm just trying to help," she says again. She pulls a piece of paper from her pocket and pushes it into my pocket. "Here's the sponsor list. I wrote my name at the bottom. I'd be honored to sponsor you."

Aidan grimaces. "You can't do that, Nat. You know you've got to have at least a year in before you sponsor."

"Those are suggestions, not laws," she says.

"And as you pointed out, the suggestions are there for a reason," he says.

"I'm just trying this whole meeting thing out, but no thanks," I tell her. "I don't think we'd be a good fit."

Natalie's eyebrows tent with genuine concern. "If you don't get help, you know what the alternative is, don't you?"

Damn it. She looks like she's going to cry and along with what she just said, she pokes a hole in me. My anger deflates, the blow-up-clown-punching-bag fantasy I had for her, wrinkling down into pitiful despair, deep in my soul. There is no alternative.

"So, what do you say?" Natalie says. I don't know what to say. I'm a girl with dreadlocks, piercings and an arm sleeve of tattoos. Natalie's wears a razor-sharp part splitting her head in half, sensible shoes, and a grudge about the way her husband greeted me the first time we met. Before I can turn her down again, Aidan intercedes.

"If we're following suggestions, I think Lydia would be better off with a veteran," he says. He steps close, knocking me with his elbow. "Want some time to think about it?"

"Yes," I say. Natalie's smile downgrades to a grin.

"Okay," she says with a hair flip. "I'll see you tomorrow."

She turns on her heel, kind of proving the point that she's not the girl that should be in my corner.

"Tomorrow?" I say to Aidan.

"In the beginning, you should attend meetings every day."

"That's a suggestion?"

"What's the alternative?" he says and I drop my chin to my chest with a cough. I watch the dusting of snow dance out of my path as we walk back to our apartment building. I don't even notice passing the liquor store. That's how much I've run out of choices.

CHOOSE YOUR LOSER

I open the door to my apartment. I'm so used to Aidan walking into my apartment now, it strikes me how it's only been happening for about a week, but that it seems like he always has been here. He takes off his shoes, drops his coat on the pegs beside the door. I hang my trench beside his leather.

I'm antsy and it takes a few minutes to recognize the hole in my routine. I usually have a drink when I come in from wherever I've been. Especially when I come in with a guy.

We take a seat on our individual cushions at opposite ends of the couch. There is an invisible line between them. A few times, I've crossed the line, but I've been shot down each time--friendly fire, but still. I'm not letting it discourage me.

"Tonight didn't go the way I hoped it would," he says.

"Are you referring to the guerilla attack by the group, Natalie, or are you talking about the way I blurted out our business?"

He laughs and I take the cue, laughing a little too as I scoot closer. Reclined a little, his legs are stretched out beneath the coffee table, one ankle over the other, his hands laced behind his head. He's watching the ceiling as if it's going to get up and leave.

"The more I think about it, the more I think they're right," he says. "You need to have a woman as your sponsor."

"Nope. If I have to have one, then I choose you," I say softly. Closer.

"No, there are things you can tell another woman that you couldn't tell me as easily. And there wouldn't be the temptation..." His eyes swing from the ceiling to me and he seems surprised with how close I am.

"Temptation?" The look on his face sends a shiver right through me. In one flash of desperation, I drop my lips on his. His shoulders relax. I close the space between us, climbing into his lap as my tongue rolls into his mouth. It takes a few seconds to realize his arms aren't around me. He's not even kissing me back. I pull my head away.

"I'm sorry," he says. He tries to scoot me off his lap, but I clamp my thighs around his legs. I need him. After a few futile attempts to politely remove me, he gives up. I don't. He drops the back of his head against the couch and I put my lips to his neck, brushing them softly over the skin until his flesh raises up in excited bumps. I feel other parts of him raising too.

"Please," I whimper. It's a new low. I've never begged a man to touch me before. Never had to.

"Lydia," he groans.

"Please," I plead again. I hunch back on his knees a little so I can reach his belt. As I try to unfasten it, his hands grasp my wrists.

"Stop," he says. "For the first year..."

"I can't wait a year. Besides, a year is just a suggestion, isn't it?" Desperate, I lean in and purr with my teeth on his ear. "It's not like we haven't done it already before. We can say we were together already."

"It's not about having to lie to anybody else," he says, but I don't want to hear him talk. Not unless he's telling me how good I feel against his skin. He's got my wrists, but it doesn't slow me down. I lean forward, rising up and down on his thighs as I press my crotch to his. I swoop in to capture his lower lip, but he turns his head to the side.

"It's the truth...it's not a new relationship," I argue in a soft tone. He turns his head back and I suddenly wish he hadn't. His eyes are somber.

"We didn't have a relationship, Lydia," he says. "You know that. We have what you and I always had. We were players back then, weren't we? All we had was sex."

I'm not about to give in. I need something to make me feel good tonight and he's it.

"That's all I am to you?" I pout. I hope my projected lip will entice him to chew it.

"Will you tell me something? Honestly?" he asks, hoisting an eyebrow. I decide to just stare at the part I want: his mouth. Drives guys wild.

"What?"

"Did you ever want more from me than just sex?"

God, this is starting to bore me a little. "Sure."

"How many partners did you usually have in a month?" The words just lie there, flat. They jar my eyes from his mouth. My thigh muscles stiffen as I rise, to move off his lap, but he wraps his arms around my waist, holding me in place. "I'm a sex addict too, Lydia, just like you. You know it's true. We were doing the same damn thing that night we met. We were both getting some and moving on. I was usually with a couple girls each week. More if I could manage it. How about you?"

"That's nothing like me."

"It's *exactly* like you, Lydia," he says. The growl in both of our voices rises. "I always gave out friend's names instead of mine, but you wouldn't give me your name at all. It's because you didn't want me to track you down either."

I give him an earnest shove, planting my feet on the floor. I stand.

"And I didn't track you down, Aidan. You're the one that moved next door *to me*. I would've never come looking. I didn't even remember you."

"But I couldn't stop remembering you," he says, staring up at me. His gaze moves from one of my eyes to the other and back again, as if he's hoping one will show some sign of recognition. "I knew what you were before I even got you back here. I knew I'd met my match."

I stand there with a shrug weighing down my shoulders. I can't seem to throw it off in front of him.

"So let's play with each other, instead of fighting," I say. "No harm done."

It comes out sounding a little harsh.

"We can't," he says softly. "I'm not that guy anymore. You changed me. That's what I keep trying to tell you. I used to take home whatever let me..."

"Thanks."

He grasps the sides of his head in frustration. "You did the same thing, Lydia! You're going to tell me you didn't?"

"I have standards."

He groans. Then, he reaches out to me, aligning his fingertips in the same places the bruises were on my throat. They're gone now, but those harsh fingertips still haunt my skin. It doesn't take much of a touch to pull them up and have them dancing goose bumps down to my collar bone. I draw away.

"Standards," he says. His gaze is so satisfied. So fucking satisfied.

"Fuck you," I say.

"I'm not trying to hurt you, Lydia. That's not what I'm trying to do."

"No, I get it. You're trying to help me to see what a drunken slut I've been."

His eyes drop as he shakes his head. "I only want you to see how you've been hurting yourself."

The tears are right there, stinging my eyes, but to hell if I'll let him see them. I put my fingers over my mouth.

"Ok, thanks," I tell him softly. I step away from him, brushing my fingers over my neck to scatter the ghosts. "Now get out."

<<<<>>>>

J expected more of a fight out of him, but the slam of my door is just as satisfying. Picking up the nearest thing to me, one of my fucked-up snowflakes, and I whip it at the door. It shatters on impact.

I could really use a drink.

I deserve it.

But there is nothing in my apartment but water glasses and the faucet.

"Fuck you, Aidan," I snarl as I pace the floor. He pretty much said everything Eric did, the only difference being that Aidan didn't strangle me after he said it. At least, not in ways that will leave bruises.

I pace and pace until I can't stand any more of it. Then, I go to my mirror and fix myself as best I can before I grab my keys, throw on my coat, and head out the door.

Aidan's not in the hall to stop me. I board the elevator and coast all the way down, landing with a soft bump at the ground floor. I step out and stride across the lobby to the front door, hanging onto my justification like a steel rod.

It's freezing outside, as if it's dropped ten more degrees in the last hour. I slip on the sidewalk, curse, but manage to keep myself upright. Once I'm drunk, slipping on ice will look about the same as staggering home. I plan on getting fully loaded tonight.

At first, my feet take me in the direction of Modo's, but I turn myself around. I won't chance another Eric. I head straight for the liquor store.

Trudging through the snow and slipping on stealthy patches of black ice doesn't detour me. I'm busy fantasizing over flavors. I can almost feel the warmth of the liquor spreading across my tongue, the heat snaking down my esophagus and lighting up my gut. Maybe tomorrow I'll regret this--I already know I will--but maybe I can give myself this one pass and act like it never happened.

Sure I can. Aidan's not here to shake a finger at me. Nobody's looking.

I walk until the neon sign of the store flickers from a few blocks away and conjures images of the shelves within. I think of the inside of the store as the portal to an adult, Christmas wonder-land with all the colored liquor novelties, all the different brands of whiskey, the fancy vessels of wine. I miss the whole ritual of drinking, like the sound of popping corks, the ingenuity of a stop-per, the slender stem of a wine glass between my fingers. I love the sexy lip print my lipstick makes on the glass and the joy that comes from passing a bottle.

I cross the street, the neon sign reeling me in like kite string. Only about thirty more feet--

"Hey there, it's Lydia, isn't it?" a smoke-stained voice says. I blink back into reality, looking away from the liquor sign, turning my head to find the owner of the greeting.

I don't recognize the older woman in a burgundy knit cap and puffy coat with fur around the collar at first. The one thing that triggers my memory of her is the kinky, steel-wool hair poking out from beneath her hat.

"Oh hi," I say, instantly ashamed as her eyes dart across the bright advertisements papering the liquor store window. My hand on the rim of the cookie jar, I'm trying not to look.

"It's Edith, from the meeting?"

"I remember."

"Stopped off afterward for dinner. Never seems I can finish

what I'm given though," she says. She hoists a Styrofoam box to chest level like proof. "What are you up to?"

"Just taking a walk."

"Lovely night for it," she grunts, her gaze taking in the quiver of my lower lip. She nods in the direction from which I came. "I'm headed home. Want to walk with me?"

She's not begging. She's not insisting. It's just an offer.

A man walks out of the liquor store, a brown bag tucked into his elbow. He's wearing a long wool coat, sleek leather gloves, shiny black shoes. He nods to us and smiles a hello as he passes. The bag is probably a gift or a bribe for a business associate, since his eyes don't have one hint of thirst in them.

Not like me.

I want a drink so bad, I've spent the whole walk here dreaming of what and when and how much I could get down my throat in the first gulp. I was contemplating the orgasmic quality of stemware, for Christ's sake.

My eyes on the ground, I trace the man's footsteps away from the door and down the sidewalk. It looks so easy. All I've got to do is walk away. That's it.

"So, what do you say?" Edith asks. "Walk with me? It's freezing out here."

"I can keep you company," I say, turning back in the direction I came.

We walk in silence. We're a block away from the store before Edith says, "At least the wind's at our back this way."

"Yeah, that's good," I agree. I'm not up for chit-chat. For the first couple blocks, I'm still thinking of how I can ditch Edith and circle back, but by the time we reach my apartment house, I'm freezing and as infuriating as it might be, I've lost the urge to walk all the way back to the liquor store.

"This is your place, isn't it?" Edith pauses in front of my building. I said I'd walk with her and I figure she wants me to walk her the whole way home, wherever that is, but I just want to go upstairs and bury my anxiety beneath my covers. I'm just relieved she isn't much of a conversationalist. The walk back has been excruciating and relieving and awful. Nothing I need to talk about.

"Yes," I say. Of course, she must know Aidan and where he lives. I'm sure the whole meeting has already discussed how he moved into the apartment next to mine. "But I can walk you the rest of the way."

"No need," she says. She takes a few steps before turning back, her gaze first finding my hand on the apartment house door. She smiles. "You coming to the meeting tomorrow?"

Shit. I don't want to say yes. But I know the answer.

"Yeah, I'll be there," I say. I want to slam my head against the bricks of my building's exterior. Edith smiles lightly.

"Good," she says, swinging her purse to the front of her hip. She digs around in it before pulling out a card that she hands to me. "My number, if you want it. I'll see you there, then."

"Alright," I say. I slide the card into my pocket without looking at it. Edith stands there, staring at me, and I realize she's waiting for me to go into the lobby. I go in and head to the elevator, looking back out the front doors when I punch the button. Edith's shadow doesn't depart until I step into the lift.

Seeing that leaves a familiar-ish, warm tingle inside me. It's like the tingle from a date. No, that's not it. It's the feeling of getting flowers delivered to my door. No, that's not it either, but almost. I close my eyes as the elevator ascends floors, trying to locate a similar tingle from memory. It's the warmth and tingle of Jan offering me a job at the salon; of Mrs. Lowt telling me about her husband as she scoops flour and salt into plastic baggies for me.

Yes, that's it. Definitely it. Holy shit.

It's the feeling of friendship.

GOING SOLO

I stay in my apartment the whole day, until it's time for the meeting that night. I've paced the floor so much, I should've fallen through, into the apartment below mine. I know I have to go, but I'm worried that the meeting won't be at the same time or place it was last night. Hell if I'm asking Aidan.

It's bad enough that my whole apartment is a reminder of what he's done for me. The lack of bottles, the mirror in the corner of my room, the scent of him in my bed, the couch cushion where he sat, even the bathroom shower. Every inch of my place has one of his memories coating it. Especially the coffee table and kitchen counters, covered in the ornamental overflow of my recovery. The salt-dough sculptures that seemed charming before, look ridiculous and amateur to me now. I decide to chuck them all, when I return from the meeting.

We come out of our apartments at the same time. Well, isn't this awkward.

He smiles and I throw back only a dismissive flash of a grin, striding past him for the elevator. He's right behind me the whole way, I sense him filling up the hall, looming. I'm not wrong. He reaches past me, pressing the button to summon the lift. As he does it, I inhale his cologne and feel the long heat of his body stretching down the side of me like a shoreline.

We get into the elevator and ride down in silence. I watch the numbers until the doors open. Crossing the lobby and stepping out into the frosty night, he's behind me still.

I think of all the small talk I could make, as well as the bigger questions I could ask, but I keep my mouth shut. I'm petrified of going into the meeting alone, but it's not so bad if he's following me in. I figure I'll sit in the back by myself and slip out the second it's over. Or I'll sit by Edith, if there's room. It's as exciting a trip as going to the gynecologist's office, but I'm going for the same reason: I need to.

Aidan's footsteps pack down the snow behind mine. He's probably shocked that I'm not headed to Modo's instead. I hate that he's probably back there thinking he's right--the slut needed help. Or, he's just thinking *slut* and studying my ass.

I like the idea of that last part. However, any extra swish in my hips still doesn't get him talking on the way there.

I find my way around the back of the church, open the door myself, and even hold it for Aidan. He takes it, arm extended. I made it here on my own. I go down the hall without any extra enchanting shake in my stride. He doesn't deserve it.

Rounding the corner, I take the first chair I see, sliding into it like home base. There's a woman to my right, with thick curls the color of boiled hot dogs, but she's busy talking to the haggard blond beside her. I tuck my arms tightly around my waist, eyes straight ahead, as Aidan walks past.

He takes a seat in the table diagonal to this one, in the one chair that faces me. He greets the men around his table and picks up a card that a guy in a baseball cap slides across to him. Aidan nods and talks and glances, but his gaze strays back to me, again and again. He taps the card absently through his first and middle fingers, turning it end over end, as he watches me.

I don't know if I'm turned on or infuriated. Maybe it's a sick little mix of both. That seems right.

"Good evening," Edith's road-rash voice startles me. She walks past and takes the seat blocking Aidan from my view. I'm liking Edith a little bit more every time I see her. "Glad we didn't freeze last night. Looks like tonight's going to be just as bad though."

"It's supposed to get colder?" I ask. It's not like I care, but I'm trying. I don't small talk like this and especially haven't talked about anything environmental in ages--not unless I had to detangle it from a pick-up line, or it was a necessary ingredient in a drink.

Edith laughs. "You still need a sponsor, Lydia?"

"I'm not even sure I need to be here. I haven't had a drink in a week." I don't bother to mention that I think of drinking every moment of the day. What counts is that I haven't done it.

"Well, if you decide you need one, I'll sponsor you, if you like. It's up to you."

The lady with the hot dog hair leans toward me as Leonard stands up from one of the front tables and starts the meeting.

"You should really get yourself a sponsor. It helps. If you don't want Edie, you could ask any of us."

"Thanks," I whisper. She shrugs when I don't jump at the offer and melts back into her chair.

The meeting filters through me. I'm busy ignoring Aidan's stare and worrying that I just offended Frankenhair. When did I turn into somebody who gives a crap about offending anybody? I elbowed a biker in the face to get a spot center stage at a concert once; I've told more than one girl at Modo's to fuck off because her boyfriend wants me more than her. I've been downright awful on a million-and-one occasions, but in this most awful situation, I can't rise to the challenge. I'm actually worried about upsetting a pile of old ladies. I'm not sure when or how this happened to me.

<<<<>>>>

*a*idan walks three feet behind me on the way home from the meeting. The snowflakes are fat and feel like rain as they soak my hair. I'm miserable for too many reasons, the last of which is being cold and wet.

The whole meeting passed by without me really attending in any way except physical presence. Aidan caught my eye and held it a dozen times. We were a table apart with Edith between us, but when she leaned over to speak to a man at the table in front of ours, there were Aidan's deep brown eyes, watching me. His whole expression was focused and wandering at the same time. I could see him thinking of me and when our eyes met, he blinked and his focus sharpened.

I sank into his gaze. I pulled him into mine.

In the first moment, my body tried to take over. I know the feeling instantly. Lids lowering, lashes fluttering, the tip of my tongue tempting the inner edge of my lip with a lick. My body was trying to pull him all the way in, eye-fuck his irises first, if that's all it could get. It would start there, and then, my body would get to work on its magic--signaling him throughout the meeting with strategic movements of my fingers in my hair or a seemingly absent self-caress down my neck. The meeting would end and I would rise from my chair. My body would assume total control then, swaying and undulating and strutting its way back to my apartment, keeping Aidan's already-hooked irises tethered to my ass. My body would string him along with the supple waves of my walking hips--drawing him into our lobby, up the elevator, down the hall, into my apartment, onto my bed, into me.

My body knows how to lure a man as much as it knows how to breathe.

But Aidan's eyes were not trying to screw me. Against my body's feverish desire, I loosened its grip with a blink. I let myself stare back. I let him swallow my gaze, until I was the one surrounded. The connection was more intense than any iris-fucking could ever be. Aidan was all around me and inside me. His vision looked beyond Lyddle, and Modo's Trophy Girl, and Des's wife, and the unfocused addict parked in an uncomfortable folding chair. Aidan's gaze breached *me*, saw *me*.

Edith and Hot-Dog-Hair both turned when I gasped. My eyes shot away from Aidan and I didn't look back for the rest of the meeting. I couldn't. He made me feel like a virgin, deflowered in clear view.

"I'm sorry," he says from behind me. After everything that happened in the meeting, the intimacy that was as tender as our bodies sinking into one another, I can't stop walking. I can't handle it if he tells me again that *he shouldn't have*. The feeling he gave me can't be turned into a regret. It would destroy me. I only answer him from over my shoulder.

"You're always sorry," I say. He laughs.

"True."

We keep walking. We pass the liquor store. If I even thought to look at the sign, the snowflakes would blind me anyway. I keep trudging along, but then Aidan is suddenly there, catching my arm.

"I'm so sorry, Lydia," he says as he pulls me to him. My chest crushes against his as he holds me; he pulls me onto the tip of my toes as his mouth opens on mine. I take his tongue like a sacrament. My body wants to devour it, but I hold back. I don't know how long I'll be able to control myself, but the warm taste of him in my mouth, placing himself there willingly, melts me and I don't want it to stop. It is different than the consuming lust I'm used to. This is a form of trust, a form of wanting, and its taste is much sweeter.

He releases me gradually. I don't want to move away. My eyelids flutter.

"I'm sorry," he says.

"Don't be," I tell him.

"I promised myself I wouldn't do this, but..."

"Touch me," I say. I step into him again, but this time I can't control it. My body takes over; my hips roll with a sensual swell. My leg slides smoothly between his, the center of me rubbing against his thigh. I nip his jaw with pastel lips and whisper in his ear, "It's okay. Touch me."

His fingertips grip my shoulders, pull me close, and he touches me.

<<<<◇>>>>

"*Y*ou're going to keep going to meetings, aren't you?" Aidan asks. The sun came up hours ago and we're still lying here, tangled in my bed sheets together. He's playing with my naked fingers, our elbows touching on the mattress, our hands in the air. Two parts of one reckless prayer. At least, that's what it seems like to me.

"What you really mean is, *am I going to drink* if we don't work out?"

He slaps his hand lightly into mine, so we clap. "I guess I do."

"I always want to drink."

"We all want to," Aidan says. "Leonard said that sometimes he fantasizes about being told he has a terminal disease, just so he could have a shot. He said that it would be a great excuse to drink himself to death's door, but he's still not sure he would do it."

"I would."

"I'm not sure I would anymore," he says. He weaves his fingers through mine. "It would depend."

"On what?" Depending on anything is so left field to me, I can't even fathom it. I close my eyes and imagine myself being bliss-fully terminal, swallowing down bottle after bottle of everything to bring on the old numb again.

"If I have a family, for one." Aidan's voice dissipates my fantasy, like wind pushing away fog. "Kids. A wife. Grandkids. Good friends. I want all that and I'm not sure I'd want to waste one second of the time I had left with them being drunk."

I try to stand in those shoes, of having beautiful little kids and knowing I'm going to die and leave them. I gave up on the possibility of children a long time ago, but in one breath, the whole scene becomes too real. I used to have this dream of family, until Des and I had a horrible fight one night about having kids. He said he didn't want more of a mess to weigh him down. He went out that night and didn't come back home for two days. When he did return, he was happy again. He told me he'd met Claudia.

It hits me like a series of cannonballs. I wanted a family. I wanted a husband that loved me, children. I've buried away all my wants like a welfare child's Christmas list.

I think again of dying and how, if I got so lucky as to get the family and friends I wanted, an entire store full of the numb wouldn't take away the pain of leaving them behind. The terror rises up like a silver bullet, lodged in my heart. I don't want to drink away one second of time with my fake family and friends. I open my eyes to make the horrific image disappear and my focus zeroes in on my tattooed ring finger.

The epiphany keeps firing at me, crashing over the beliefs I've been carrying around in my head since Des left. I've been stuck, waiting around for Des in this broken-down bunker of a life, turning down every escape and ride out, hoping that Des would come to his senses and circle back to get me. But, it's backfired on him. I've been drinking away my feelings for him, slowly dissolving whatever love I had left for him. I hadn't realized that until now.

I want to trade in my life. Trade up. I want the kids and husband and grandkids and good friends that will give me those precious, second thoughts before ever putting my lips on the rim of a wine glass, ever again. I want that life that beats out even the most incredible numb. I don't know how I never saw that it was out there, or that I could have it, but lying here beside Aidan, I get a good long glance at it and want it more than I've ever wanted a drink. So many million times more.

"I have something I want to do today," I say. He smiles, curling our fingers up together.

"We're finally getting you a Christmas tree?"

"After," I laugh. "I want to go down to the court house first. I'm filing for a divorce."

ALL IN

Fuck the no-change-for-a-year idea.

Getting divorced, or at least filing the papers, is a lot like when I lost my virginity. I feel different, but I look the same. I come down from the courthouse steps, elated and giddy--shit, I'm never *giddy*--and when Aidan takes my hand with a smile, we tromp down the steps as if we just eloped. We walk a block or two, swinging hands.

"Can you tell me about him now?" Aidan asks. I don't give it much thought. I'm still high from signing my name to the legal documents.

"What do you want to know?"

"Everything," he says. I laugh.

"It's a long story."

"The Christmas tree lot is a million blocks away," he coaxes. "We'll stop for hot chocolate if you need more time to tell it all."

"Alright." I grin. "I met him when I was fourteen. I dropped out of high school and we moved around wherever Des thought there would be work. We got married the minute I turned sixteen."

"What about your family? Didn't your parents have a fit?"

"No," I say. "My father was long gone. My mom was a single

189

parent bringing in minimum wage. No matter how hard she tried, she could never make ends meet with my sister and me weighing her down. She wasn't crazy about Des, but she thought he'd take better care of me than she could." The radiance of a moment ago is only dulled a tiny bit by the admission. I've had years to wall out the way my mother was relieved for me to be Desmond's mouth to feed instead of hers.

Aidan doesn't give me the tragic face I expect, the one that made me stop telling people my history years ago. It's why I keep on with his questioning.

"You never finished school?"

"No."

"But I thought you're a designer?"

He's so naive. I flash him a pitying grin.

"Desmond married another woman. A rich one," I say. I take a deep breath. This is really a do-or-die moment. Telling him everything could end what we have, but I know that we can't go any further unless he knows my truths. I take his hand. "Des wouldn't divorce me, but he didn't want to struggle to live anymore. He married Claudia for her money. He knew I didn't have any skills to earn a living, so he hires me as their designer. He has contractors do the work he drums up and pays me a bullshit consultation fee." I gulp before I tell him the raw truth. "It's all a scam. It's awful and I never wanted to be part of it, but when he left, I had no other way to survive."

"So if you filed on your own, that's the end of the money," Aidan's voice trails off. I'm sure he's in shock. All I can do is nod. "And his other wife is going to find out."

"Yes."

"You could go to jail over this."

"I know."

Then he asks something I don't expect.

"Why now?" he says. "What changed?"

"*I* did." I wipe at the tiny sting in my nose that doesn't come from the rush of winter wind battering us on the sidewalk. "And I just realized that Des changed too. Probably a lot longer ago than I think."

"I don't understand why you would keep going back when he was beating you," Aidan says. "He *was* beating you, wasn't he?"

"Not like you're thinking," I say. The heat of a blush scales my neck and makes the wind burn twice as harsh on my cheeks. My eyes scramble away from his. "Desmond has always been a little kinky, but it's gotten worse in the past few years."

"Beating is beating, Lydia, and if he's doing it under the guise of sex, than he's a really sick bastard."

"Maybe."

"Not maybe," he says, tugging me to a halt. Aidan catches my gaze and his is too intense for me to break away from it. "Definitely."

The blush turns my cheeks into a stove top.

"You don't agree?" he asks. The simmer of his tone makes me uneasy.

"At first I didn't like it, but..."

"What does he do to you?" His brows steeple. "I know about the mirror, but what else does he do to you?"

I shrug. The words don't come out. Desmond and I have such a huge history together that talking like this makes me feel disloyal. It doesn't matter that Des has done me wrong in about a dozen different ways--it's not something that I want to discuss with Aidan. What can come of it but another judgment?

What I want is for Des's injustices to boil inside my skin, so I can throw them on Des like hot oil when I need to. And I'm going to need to, when Claudia finds out.

"Alright, we'll talk about this another time," Aidan says when I don't answer. He takes my hand, pointing up the street. "Right now, we need to get you a Christmas tree."

*W*e don't get a regular tree. It's not full or beautiful or even so big that I couldn't have carried it home myself, by the top, center branch. It's more like a fluffy twig, but it's the only one on the lot that I'll agree to.

"This won't hold more than a couple of your ornaments," Aidan complains.

"I don't care."

"But you can get a real tree!" He steps back, doing his best showcase hands, with his bulky man hands, in front of a Douglas Fir.

"I didn't want *any* tree."

"Well," he grins, "then this one is perfect."

"That's what I thought."

He insists on buying the tree, since I didn't want it anyway. We leave the lot and head for our apartment house, the tiny tree over one of Aidan's shoulders. The breeze of passing cars charges up the sidewalk and makes us both curl into our coats a little more.

We pass a convenience store and when I glance up at it, all that pops out are the liquor ads, adhered to the window. I look away quickly. Aidan makes a soft, understanding grunt.

"Makes you feel guilty to even look, doesn't it?" Aidan asks. A tinge of heat warms my face as the embarrassment shrinks my laugh.

"Yeah," I say.

"I know," he says. That's all he needs to say. We are both people who can't walk past a liquor store without feeling as if the neon signs are illuminating our shame. We are people that walk by, fantasizing about locking ourselves inside. I don't need to tell him that the desire burns my throat like a desert thirst. Aidan takes my hand with his free one.

"Is it ever going to get easier?" I croak. My voice is parched.

"Yes," he says, squeezing my knuckles.

"I hope you're right."

"I am," he says. I cling to the words, as I squeeze his fingers back.

<<<<>>>>

We decorate the tree so the branches droop. If they were sturdy, they'd snap, but they're flimsy, so they just sag beneath the mini lights and tinsel and three of my sober-dough ornaments.

We eat take out and we take barf-free showers together and we talk about Christmas. We attend meetings at night and I listen sometimes. But, almost every other second of my life, I'm thinking of how much more perfect this would all be with a sip of some cognac or a glass of red or even a gulp of a foamy beer. I'm still too ashamed to admit any of it when we share struggles around the meeting tables.

"What are you thinking of?" Aidan asks one night. We just got out of the shower and even though he's already wearing a t-shirt and some plaid pajama bottoms, I sit on the edge of the bed, naked, squeezing the water out of my dreads. I guess I was staring into space too long again. Or he's checking to make sure I'm not silently stroking out. I still tip my head up at him with a blush at being caught, as if my face is a movie screen, playing my guilty thoughts. He stands in front of me, tracing my collar bone with a light finger. "You can tell me anything, you know."

I pause, biting my tongue against telling him the truth, but this is Aidan. If anyone understands what I'm thinking, it's him.

"I was thinking about drinking." I frown.

193

"That's what I thought," he says with a faint smile.

"I can't stop thinking about it."

"It seemed like those thoughts would never end for me either," he says, "but they did."

"What am I supposed to do until then?" I say as he squats down before me. "I think I'm going insane."

"You're not," he says, his finger running up my neck to my lips. He smoothes his thumb over my bottom lip and wipes the errant tear that streams a single path down my cheek. He smiles up at me. "What helped me was to think of something better."

"I can't." A bubble expands in my chest, sucking up my air. It forces out more tears. Aidan slides his hand beneath my ear, his thumb fluttering over my cheekbone, disturbing the path of a second tear.

"Christmas presents," he whispers.

"I...don't...care...about...that..." The sob I'm holding in crimps each word. Aidan's touch remains constant, smoothing over my cheek.

"No, no," he admonishes softly. "Just close your eyes and listen to what I'm saying. We're going to go Christmas shopping together, Lydia. We're going to buy Christmas stockings to hang on the wall and we're going to get something for our crazy neighbor. Maybe we'll get Mrs. Lowt a naughty fireman calendar. Or a good pair of binoculars, so she can spy on the apartment house across the street."

I laugh at that, but I'm still gasping in tiny, hiccupping breaths. Aidan's voice remains mellow, soft.

"When we're tired of shopping, you'll make me carry all the bags. We'll still stop at a few shops, even though you said you were done. We'll walk around downtown and look at all the lights. I'll get us hot chocolate and if there are carolers singing for money, I'll pay them to sing *Baby, It's Cold Outside*. And I'll kiss you as they're singing. People will stop and smile at us. Afterward, I'll take you to dinner at Rinaldi's and I'll feed you ravioli across the table. It will be so sexy, all the tables around us will start whispering and they'll eventually kick us out for public indecency."

I blink, swallow. My lungs fill all the way to the bottom and I exhale one long, smooth breath.

"There," he says. He leans in, planting a soft kiss on my forehead. "Better?"

"Thank you," I say. I mean it in deeper, heavier, and more meaningful ways than I can express it.

"I told you there were better things to think about," he says with a grin.

<<<<>>>>

*W*e don't exactly go shopping first, because I decide I need to violate the no-changes-for-a-year suggestion again. Leonard couldn't have meant *hair*. But then, even if he did, I'm breaking that no-change rule all over the place anyway.

I choke down the eggs Aidan insists I eat for breakfast and leave him in my apartment so I can head down to Jan's salon.

"I want to get my dreads out," I tell Jan the second I'm sitting in his chair. His lips slant to the side of his cheek.

"You sure about this? You've got some of the best dreads around."

"I need a change," I say. Then, after darting a cautious look around the room, I whisper, "I *filed*."

"Filed, filed?" Jan says.

I nod, catching my bottom lip in my teeth as I smile.

"Well, alright then," he says, reaching for a comb. "Change it is! There's no way I'm cutting them out, though. You better have some juicy gossip about that neighbor of yours, because this is going to take a while and taking out all the snarls is going to hurt."

<<<<>>>>

*A*idan picks me up afterward. My hair feels so...*small*...but it's silky and still reaches past my shoulders.

"Wow," he whispers. There's no smile accompanying it; there's no excited incline to the word. I try not to scowl. Aidan reaches out and takes some of my hair in his hand. "I thought it was going to be short."

He lets the strands slip through his fingers, so they spill over my shoulders. He picks them up again, his focus intense and gentle, all at once, as he lets the hair slide over his palms.

Oh.

He's mesmerized.

I smile so hard, my ears pull back with it, as if they're trying to give my joy more room.

"The real me," I say. His gaze slams into mine. I blink at the impact.

"I love it," he says. Since Des left, I've made a point to never allow the praise of men to feed me, but Aidan's compliment is so genuine that it warms my stomach more than a shot of tequila. He gives me his elbow like a gentleman from the 50's. "You ready to go Christmas shopping?"

I'm ready to go anywhere he wants to take me. We take the bus down to the sprawling, outdoor mall and enter the thrall of Christmas chaos. There are carols playing from shops, the smell of sweets, the colorful splashes of scarves and the constant rustle of shopping bags as people bustle by us.

I think of how I was here last year by myself, shopping for something incredible that I hoped would blow Des's mind. I wanted to impress him, enchant him, I wanted him to leave

Claudia and come back to me. I came home with leather lingerie and a fifth of Jack Daniels. Des didn't call. And didn't call. Finally, on Christmas Day, I watched *It's a Wonderful Life* and drank until I passed out. Des called the next morning, but I was too hung over to answer. He was furious.

That alone should make booze undesirable, but here I am looking in the windows of the restaurants we pass by, wishing I was any one of the people inside, lifting a wine glass to my lips without worry. Sipping that warm, liquid heaven without wondering how much more I could hold before I threw up, or ran out of money.

Aidan adjusts his hold on my hand and I catch him following my gaze. I shoot him an embarrassed grin from behind my sober masquerade mask. I wish there was some kind of plastic surgery that could make my happiness real, make this mask permanent.

"It's gets easier," Aidan says, lifting my knuckles to kiss them softly.

"You keep saying that."

"It's the truth. Just hang in there."

"I am," I say, but it feels a little shaky and my own lack of confidence sends quivers of anxiety arrowing through me.

"You're doing great," Aidan says and with his second kiss on my knuckles, watching the smooth line of his jaw dip over my skin and the silk of his hair as it falls forward, I almost believe him. He's pumping my life full of a whole new addiction.

We walk through stores, buying Mrs. Lowt a coffee mug with the torso of a ripped guy on it. It looks a lot like Aidan. We also get her a Hot, Nude Jocks calendar with bonus months that will take her into the middle of next year. Aidan gets himself a pair of gloves and some techie thing for his computer; I get a day planner.

"Interesting," Aidan says when he peeks in my bag. There's no polite way to ask me what I'd need a planner for when I don't work and don't go anywhere, but I don't offer my reason for the purchase either. He drops it. Maybe he thinks it's for him.

We sample colognes at a perfume counter. I spray them all over Aidan and the sales girl blushes when I take too long smelling his neck, but it's the one he buys. I catch sight of the lingerie store, but as I head toward it, Aidan pulls me off the path, toward a jewelry store window instead.

"These," he says, pointing to a pair of crescent moon earrings. Glittery stones are embedded from one tip to the other and are so sparkly that they leave white specs in my vision when I look away.

"No, this," I say, moving his finger over the glass case until it rests on a black dragon ear wrap. He shakes his head, pulling his finger away.

"Too dark," he says. He studies the rows of earrings, looks at me, and then points to another pair. "Those."

I follow his fingertip to a pair of salt water pearls, misshapen and gorgeous and suspended like baby-pink pears on a silver scrolling vine. They are nothing I would have picked for myself, but maybe that's why I like them.

He reaches for the door of the shop, but I stop him.

"What?" Aidan asks. "You don't like them?"

Any other man, any other time, and I would've let buy me the earrings and probably mentioned that a matching necklace would be lovely. But this is Aidan and I am a brand new, soon-to-be divorced woman. I look down at my ring finger and frown. Des's last name, in its bold black print, glares up at me. A part of me is always going to belong to Des. He's branded me, so I can't escape him. The joy goes out of the moment.

"I have something else I want instead," I say.

"Yeah? What is it?"

"It's at the tattoo shop, at the very end. The mall's dirty little secret."

"You want another tattoo?"

I lift my ring finger so it separates our gaze. "I want to modify this one. It doesn't apply anymore."

"What do you want to do to it?"

"I'm going to change it to something accurate," I say.

"Okay then, let's go," he says.

We move down the sidewalk and I feel like I'm dragging my feet until Aidan opens the door of the shop. A tiny, metal bell rings over my head.

"An angel just got her wings! That you, Lydia?" a man hoots from the back. He steps out from the office, located behind the register and separated from the lobby by a wall with a two-way mirror in it. Of course, I know him. He's done all my tattoos, save the coloring of my lotus flower and the Des's surname on my ring finger.

I shouldn't be surprised that Angus is still here or that the guy remembers me. Des always bought the guy a few bottles of Jack to enjoy, and Angus never failed to enjoy it, even while he was tattooing. It's proof that Holy intervention exists, that Angus's work is as good as it is, even when his brains are pickled.

Angus opens his arms and I accept the hug. Considering he did my whole arm sleeve for me, it's reasonable to say that the aging tattoo artist has spent more time with me than my own father.

"Desmond, you sure have changed," Angus says, looking Aidan over. "You got a lot more muscle on you these days."

"This is Aidan," I say. "He's a friend of mine."

"Oh, I thought something was different about him," Angus says, but I notice how he glances again at the bags in Aidan's hands, searching for the usual gift of a few bottles. With the right sized bottle of Jack, Aidan could be a barking monkey and I'm sure Angus would approve. However, the old man's gaze comes up empty, so he slaps his hands together, rubbing them as if maybe something more than air will end up in them before the night is through.

"So what brings you in tonight?" he asks. I hold up my ring finger.

"I want to mod this," I say. Angus squints, takes my hand.

"I don't remember this one...that's not my work, is it?" he asks.

199

"No."

"Good, because it's damn awful."

"I agree. Do you think you can cover it up somehow?"

"What are you looking for? Butterflies or daisies or some shit like that?" He turns my hand over, inspecting the print. He winces with a small hiss. "That's some bold black lettering and there's no room to do much with it. It would be a bitch to cover it and it'd be a bigger bitch to try and remove it, considering where it is."

Aidan adds, "But you can cover it?"

Angus winces again, before shaking his head. "I don't think so. Best I can do is make the whole thing black--one solid ring."

I groan. Angus rubs his neck with his free hand, still hanging onto my tattooed hand in the other.

"You could always cover it up with a real ring," he suggests. I could kill Des for doing this to me. I need more than a cover up. I've filed to leave Des's name behind at the court and I'm not leaving this tattoo shop until I've gotten Des's name off of my skin.

"What about adding onto it?" I ask.

"Adding what?"

"An *er*," I say, "Can you make it say Strong*er*?"

"Nice," Aidan says with a nod. Angus flips my hand over again, licking his lips at the challenge.

"Here's what we could do," he says. "It goes in almost a full circle, but there's a little opening here, see it? You're lucky whoever did this was kind of a hack. I can give the whole thing the illusion of curling up and we can continue the word up your finger."

"That might look out of place, two letters climbing up your finger by themselves," Aidan says. I nod, looking back to Angus.

"Can we add a couple words?"

"Maybe," Angus shrugs. "You only got so much room though, even if we go all the way up the finger. What are you thinking?"

"*Stronger Than That.*"

"Than what?" Angus asks with an amused puff.

"Stronger than whatever *that* will ever be," I say.

*A*idan holds my other hand as Angus goes to work. I chew my lower lip and squeeze Aidan's hand a few times, just so he doesn't feel like he's not helping. And just so he doesn't let go.

"I think we got it," Angus final says, rolling away from me on his castered stool. My finger stings like it's soaking in a battery acid, but Angus has done an incredible job. *Stronger Than That* flows up my finger with the addition of some girly swirls and curls that change Des's name into a fresh, new talisman.

Inspecting it, I get the first real crashing wave of reality.

Des and I are over. I've broken ties in every way that I know how, even though Des doesn't know yet. When the papers are delivered, the storm will begin. Claudia's lawyers will pig pile in order to sort out this new snarl. Claudia will probably divorce him, we might both go to jail.

As I consider it, the depth of the horrible possibilities occur to me and I sway as I slip on my coat.

"You okay?" Aidan asks, a hand at my back. He opens the door leading out of the tattoo shop as Angus shouts a goodbye. "Don't get woozy on me, now."

I step outside, the winter chill hitting me in the forehead with a splash of ice cold clarity. What if Des manages to blame all of this on me somehow? I accepted every penny he gave me and he's always told me he wouldn't go down alone. I've kept my mouth shut because I was still stupid-in-love, but what if he actually makes good on his threat? What if Claudia is so crazy about him that she would be happy with sticking it to me as the scapegoat?

Oh my God. I'm going to jail.

"You okay?" Aidan asks. I turn back to him on autopilot. My body kicks in, takes over. I wrap my arm around his, scooting close, squeezing his bicep.

"I'm actually getting a little tired," I lie. What I want to do is ditch him, pick up a little something and head home. I want to curl up with a bottle, get numb and forget. "Maybe we should call it a night."

He squints a look at me, suspicious.

"The night hasn't even started yet and you're going to miss out on the hot chocolate."

"Next time," I say. A serpent smile slithers across my cheeks. As if I could feel any guiltier.

"Alright," he says, but his voice is weary. We trudge back to the bus stop, barely speaking. A whole choir of carolers standing on the street corner, ten feet away. Their beautiful rendition of *I Heard The Bells on Christmas Day* drifts over us, but Aidan doesn't ask them to sing anything else.

ALL OUT

We step off the bus, three blocks past the liquor store. I'll have to walk right past it to get home and then double back later. The plan is lit up bright in my head, like a kid with a flashlight, poring over a treasure map and devising routes.

The sidewalk is slick in places with invisible patches of ice that make us both slide and flail, but I am determined to honey-badger my way home. The few bags we accumulated rustle in Aidan's hands as he follows behind me. When he suddenly snags the elbow of my coat between his fingers, it gives me a sharp shot of annoyance instead of excitement. I don't want to slow down, much less stop. I want to get back to my apartment, tell him whatever lie I need to so he'll go back to his place, and then all I have to do is sneak down to the store.

The liquor store sign is just ahead, the fluorescent glow like a Christmas star among the sedate drift of the falling snowflakes. It's enchanting. The numb is hailing me with its slimy fingers and the liquor store is pinging me like a homing devise. I'm ready and willing to give up this whole ridiculous quest for sobriety in order to get some relief. I understand the grab alcohol has on me, but the fear of what Claudia might do when she gets the divorce papers suddenly has a much tighter grip. I need to escape and anything standing in the way of that it is going to be taken out at the knees. Even Aidan.

"I just want to get home. I'm freezing," I snap. He doesn't let go of my sleeve.

"It's hitting you pretty hard," he says. "I was wondering when that was going to happen."

I yank loose from him, but what he said irritates me enough to spin on him. A good battle might use up some of the fear-induced adrenaline racing through me.

"What are you talking about?"

"It just hit you that you're getting divorced, didn't it?" His voice is so damn inviting and warm on this cold street. "Do you actually love that guy?"

I snort. "Not anymore."

"Then you're afraid of him."

His statement hits me like an iron mallet, right on the head. I get that Aidan doesn't mean it as an attack, but to be so dead-on accurate, it feels like he's calling for war and it brings me out swinging.

"Sometimes you just think you know everything, Aidan, but you don't. And you don't know a damn thing about this."

"Oh my gosh--that is it, isn't it? You're afraid of him."

"I'm not afraid of anything." I turn away and resume a slippery clip toward home.

"Considering the circumstances, I think a little fear would be a justifiable response. Healthy, even."

"Well, thanks for your completely unqualified, armchair analysis."

"Lydia," he says as he reaches for my hand, but I pull away and keep walking. "I'm just saying...*damn it*, would you wait a second?"

"I'm done talking."

"You're terrified," he shouts down the sidewalk, but in a few steps, he catches up and tugs me to a halt, nearly dropping the bags in the snow at our feet. "He *abuses* you, Lydia. It's okay to be terrified. It's okay to be mad as hell. He's been playing with your life, without any regard for..."

"Let go of me!" I shout in his face as I tear my arm loose.

"What's bothering you..."

"*You*. You're what's bothering me!"

"Are you sure about that?" His calm only infuriates me more. The bags crinkle in the frigid breeze of a passing car.

"Fuck off."

Aidan puts up both hands in surrender. "Hey, I'm the good guy here."

"Really?" I shoot back. "It didn't sound like that to me."

"You're going to go drink, aren't you," he says. "That's what this is really about. You're terrified and you don't know what to do with that, so you want to drink it away. You want to get rid of me so you can go do it."

The apartment house in view, I step up my pace even more. I don't reply, because there is no defense against the truth and I'm humiliated that I'm so transparent. Aidan just trails me, in through the lobby, up the elevator, down to my door.

"I'm not inviting you in." I feel the heat of his body at my back as I twist the key in the knob.

"I know," he says flatly. "Take your bags."

I turn back and grab the bag out of his hands, avoiding his eyes. It's like killing kittens and I can't take anymore guilt than I already have. I shut the door on him.

I pace first.

Then I listen, an ear pressed to our adjoining walls. I listen for Aidan's feet next door, but I don't hear a thing. I want to be sure he doesn't open the door as I'm sneaking away. It would be humiliating to have to look him in the face and lie about where I was going. Especially if he wants to come with me. It would be a whole lot easier for him to spot my back from his apartment window, as I make my getaway down the sidewalk.

I'm antsy, but I wait, listening. Still nothing. He could be laying on his couch, trying to figure out why he ever moved in next door to a head case like me. Or he could be lying in his bed, jacking off. I instantly imagine his long legs, sprawled out and so powerful that my thirst is momentarily distracted by the ache between my legs. But then it returns--the quest for booze even more powerful than the thought of Aidan's body. If I could exchange this craving, I would. It's just too big.

I slide on my coat and inch my feet into my shoes like a thief. I check myself in my mirror and creep back to the door, grimacing at the sound of my door latch as I ease it open. I'm startled by the man on the floor outside.

"What are you doing?" I shriek. Aidan looks up from his spot in my doorway, wedged in sideways with his back on one side of the door jamb and his foot touching the other.

"I was waiting for you to come talk to me," he says, running his gaze over my outdoor attire. "It looks like we're going back out for that hot chocolate after all?"

"*I'm* going out," I say, but I don't try stepping over him. The look of determination on his face makes me think he'd grab my heel and yank me down on the floor beside him without a second thought.

"Where are you going?"

I should've had a lie ready and waiting, and the oversight costs me. The only thing flashing in my head is the liquor store sign, wine labels and shot glasses. I open and close my mouth like a guppy in his palm.

"I...well, I was...the store. I'm going to the store."

"I needed to go to the store," he says, hopping to his feet. "I'll come with you."

"No, I...I was..." It's pointless. I'm trapped and I'm so frustrated I want to sink down someplace and bawl. Instead, I take a step back and slam the door as hard as I can in Aidan's face.

<<<<>>>>

J drop the back of my head against my door and listen as Aidan resumes his post on the floor outside. He is not giving up, and while I should be overjoyed that he cares, I'm pissed off that he won't leave so I can get what I need. I stuff my hands in my coat pockets and something jabs me between the thumb and first finger. I draw out a card.

Edith Maklvoy-Jars. Across from her name is listed an address, phone number, cell number, email. The background is a surprise--a yin and yang symbol with licks of fire around the edge. I wouldn't have thought she was that type.

What the hell am I going to do? I've got hell roaring inside me and a watchdog at my door.

I pull my phone from my pocket and click the numbers on the card, one click at a grueling time. I chew my upper lip as the line rings. Edith picks up.

"Hello. This is Lydia," I say. There's a pause on the other end. "From the meetings."

"I know who you are. Aidan's Lydia, right? That Lydia?"

"Ye..yes," I stammer, "but it's just Lydia."

"Ok, fine, just Lydia. How's it going?"

Now it's my turn to pause. I chew my lip, everything inside me welling up--Des, the divorce, Claudia, Aidan. Suddenly, I can't speak. Only a sniffle comes out.

"Sounds like it's not going too good," Edith says. "Where are you at, Lydia? I'll come to you."

"No, that's--"

"Are you home?" There is very little choice in her tone. My impulse is to hang up on her, but I fight it, because I need her help. I manage to choke out an answer instead.

"Yes."

"I know the place. What's your apartment number?"

"2B."

"Okay. I'm on my way." Edith clicks off before I can argue with her. Not that I would.

"What are you?" I hear Edith's voice say in the hallway. "The cell guard?"

I can't believe Aidan's still out there. The door clunks; he must be using it steady himself as he gets off the floor. Then, Mrs. Lowt's voice joins in.

"What's going on out here, Aidan? Who's this?"

"Who're you?" Edith asks.

"This is my hallway," Mrs. Lowt retorts. "Who are you?"

"*Your* hallway?" Edith asks.

"Who is this person, Aidan? Why is she here? Is Lydia alright?"

I open the door before the trio in the hall either goes to blows or starts blasting my business up and down the corridor. The other neighbors don't seem to want to know me, and I'd prefer to keep it that way.

Everyone turns to look at me once I swing the door open.

"Hi," Edith says. She walks past Aidan and straight into my apartment, completely ignoring Mrs. Lowt's questioning.

"What's all this, Lydia?" Mrs. Lowt asks.

"Just a friend that's visiting," I say. It's like I'm back in high school, having to explain to my mother why I had a boy in my room. I turn and shut the door, leaving Aidan to take care of our neighbor.

"Sorry about that," I say to Edith.

"Nothing to be sorry for. I'm not here for them, I'm here for you." She drops her purse on my couch and turns back to me. "So what's going on?"

here's something about Edith that has me confessing like a guilty serial killer. I've been silent for so long and now I'm spewing all my secrets--everything from wanting to be with Aidan despite all the suggestions in the world to the scam I'm involved in with Des.

Edith sits on my couch, her finger resting over her mouth and her brow bent in deep concentration. When I'm done confessing, she gives it a minute to sink in before she sighs.

"You've got a small warehouse full of things you need to take care of," she says. "But it looks like the biggest box in your way, is your ex. Now, I've got a lawyer friend I can talk to. Let me ask him about this business with the double marriage. You might be in some trouble for taking the money, but I don't know. It's a lot more complex than just that."

With my legs drawn up to my chest on the other end of the couch, I just nod against my knees.

"Well, there's no sense in being worried about it until you have an answer," Edith says.

I nod again.

"So let's talk about Aidan."

"What about him?" I say.

"What's the deal with you two? Have you been together a while?"

"Sort of."

"I don't really care either way," Edith sniffs. "It's none of my business and frankly, I don't care if you two are going with the program or bucking it. What I do care about is that if I sponsor you, you are doing everything you can to get sober."

"And that means staying away from Aidan?"

Edith shakes her head. "I just said, I don't care about that."

"Then what do you want me to do?"

"Everything I tell you. If you want what I've got, which is a successful, clean and sober life, with solid and real relationships in it, then you'll do what I say. I know how to get you there, but you've got to commit to doing as I tell you."

"What's that mean? That I'm your personal assistant or something?"

"I'm doing something for you here, you're not doing it for me." She puffs like I'm an idiot. "It means that you don't drink. You come to meetings. You call me every single day and check in with me on how you're doing."

The last two sound easy at least, but what choice do I have?

"I want to drink," I whisper. "Bad."

"All you gotta do," she says, leaning toward me like she's about to impart a secret, "is stay away from the first one."

She stands up and goes to my dismal stick of a Christmas tree. She slides a soft hand beneath one of the ornaments. "You make these?"

"Yes. When I stopped drinking, Aidan had me do them."

"Ahhh, to keep your mind off things. Smart man," she says.

"Take it, if you want. I've got hundreds of them."

"Don't mind if I do," she inspects each of them on the tree carefully, before removing one from a branch. She finally holds up a yellow Christmas tree with pinched outer branches, a blue star, and green bulbs. "I'll take this one. It'll remind me of the day Lydia finally started living her life again."

Her words fill my eyes with tears. At least they don't sting.

A MILLION REASONS

I sleep, curled up like an ear.

When I open my door in the morning, I fully expect Aidan to fall into my apartment, but the hall is empty. The urge to drink lingers, it nags me like a tiny headache, but it's not so hard for me to push off this morning. All I really want right now is food--a bowl of Cheerios, to be exact.

Not that I mean to tiptoe past Aidan's door, but I do. I ride the elevator to ground level and walk out into the wintery mess of the city, breathing deep. Left is the way to the meetings, to the liquor store. I turn right and head for the market.

This morning I have on the hat I used to wear. Stretched from holding my dreads, it used to look like a sagging beehive at the back of my head, but now it looks like a huge, empty sock. My blond hair spills from the edges and over the shoulders of my coat. I wonder if Aidan is watching my back as I walk down the side-walk from his window. I kind of wish he was trailing me, or even walking beside me, cracking his jokes or giving me his unsolicited insights into the world.

I'm in line with my cereal and milk and a bag full of other stuff I found, when my phone rings. I freeze in place, listening again for the ringtone. Des couldn't have gotten the papers already. The clerk at the courthouse said Christmas might even delay them a little and with Claudia and Des away on their cruise, it can't be him--

The ringtone blasts a jersey accent, *Yo haaaairdressa is callin', pick it up!*

I let out a relieved sigh as I pull out the phone, juggling my groceries to answer.

"He's gone. Rob's gone." Jan bawls on the other end.

"It's going to be okay," I say. "What happened?"

"The bastard cheated on me..."

"He always cheats. He'll be back..."

"WITH A WOMAN!" Jan shouts in my ear. "He's cheated on me *with a woman*!"

"Oh my God, are you kidding me?"

"Nooo!" He breaks down crying again.

"Okay, listen, I'm coming. Where are you?"

"At the salon, I've put up the *closed* sign and I'm sitting here getting drunk all by myself."

"Oh. Okay," I say. *Oh shit.* He blows his nose and I can hear his heartbroken sobs. But an open bottle...it might as well be a burning stick of dynamite waiting for me.

"Can you come, honey? I could use a shoulder..."

Jan's been my shoulder through just about everything with Des. I can't fail him now, but I don't know how I'm going to do this without failing myself.

"I'm coming," I say. "Stay where you are, I'm on my way."

"*I* need your help," I say into the phone. My thumb paused over Edith's number, but it was Aidan's digits that I hit.

"What's going on?" he asks. It sounds like he just woke up from a rough night and it probably was, if he sat outside my door most of the time.

"My friend Jan needs me, but he's getting drunk..."

"Then don't go."

"I have to. He just broke up with his boyfriend and he's devastated..."

"What you're trying to do is more important than..."

"Just listen to me, Aidan. I'm going to go see him. I was just wondering if you'd come with me. I won't drink if you're there."

"When are you going?"

"Now. I'm almost to the lobby."

"Our lobby? You went out?"

"Yeah, for breakfast. You suck at guarding doors."

"I'll be right down," he says and hangs up.

He's down in less than three minutes. He takes my bag of groceries as we walk down to the bus stop.

"I'm sorry about yesterday," I begin. "It hit me all at once."

"You did the right thing. You called for help," he says, but there's an edge in his tone, as if he's beating himself up that it wasn't him that got the call.

"Next time, I'll just open my door." I say and his brow lifts.

"You could. So this friend of yours that we're going to see? He's the hair guy?"

"His boyfriend, Robert, is an asshole. He's been cheating on Jan forever, but this time, he did it with a chick."

"Ouch."

"Exactly."

"Does Jan know what you're doing...with the drinking?"

"Not yet."

"You should have a plan for how you're going to handle it before you get there," Aidan says as the bus pulls up. We climb aboard and take a seat near the front.

"I guess I do," I say, rustling the bag in his arms. "I'm planning on having breakfast."

He peeks into the bag.

"I thought maybe you *met* someone for breakfast."

"Nope, just the cashier down at the grocery store."

"Oh," he says and he grins at me.

We get off the bus and make our way to Jan's salon. I knock on the glass. It takes a minute before Jan appears and opens the door. His mascara has run down his face and he looks like hell. The smell of the booze hits me straight in the face as I step inside, but I catch Jan in a huge hug anyway.

"I didn't think you'd bring anyone," he says in my ear.

"It's okay, Aidan's great."

"I can see *that*," Jan says with a sniffly laugh. He wipes the mascara landslide from his cheeks. "It's just not the way I was hoping to meet him. But thank you for coming, honey. Drink?"

"No, I haven't even had breakfast yet," I say.

"That's never stopped you before," Jan giggles. I laugh with him, but I move toward the back break room.

"You caught me at the grocery store when you called. I brought cereal. Do you have bowls around here?"

"Mugs," Jan says, raising his mug in the air. Some of his drink sloshes over the lip. "None for me though. I have every-thing I need right here. How about you, Aidan? Would you like a drink?"

I watch Aidan swallow. "No thanks," he says.

It hasn't occurred to me that being around the stuff would still affect Aidan. He seems like such a rock, but as I watch his eyes swing to the Jan's bottle and linger a bit too long, I realize this is hard on him too. I walk back to him, giving him an understanding smile as I hand him one of the mugs in Jan's stash. I slide my hand up and down his bicep and he grins, as if I'm the one here to comfort him and help him out. Maybe I am.

We sit in the stylist chairs, Aidan and I drinking out cereal from the mugs as Jan paces, ranting about Rob and the bitch he ran off with. It takes Jan a solid hour before he begins to wind down. By that time, Aidan and I have polished off the whole box of cereal and my stomach is painfully full.

"Thank you two for coming when I called," Jan says for the hundredth time. The booze has got him monologue in circles. "Thank you for listening to my mess. Robert and I are so trapped in this cycle..."

"Not anymore," I say, but Jan sighs. He collapses in a chair and it spins until he drags his foot along the floor to stop it.

"You know me, Lydia, probably better than anybody else does. Even that fool man of mine. You know how I am. I'll be here for him. I always am."

"Maybe you shouldn't," Aidan says and Jan gives him a sad little smile.

"It's a lovely thought, but Robert is me and I am Robert. We've been together, doing this to each other for too long. He knows I won't walk away over some little twat. *Literally*." Jan's laugh is as sad as his smile.

"You've done it for me how many times before," I say and Jan perks up.

"I wish I had your courage, Lydia. What did Des say about the papers?"

"Even drunk, you've got the memory of a hairdresser," I say and Jan laughs. "I don't think he's gotten them yet. The court said they might be delayed because of Christmas."

"Well, it's about time. It's about *damn* time you did it! This calls for a drink!" Jan roar, holding his bottle high in the air.

"And, I quit drinking," I say.

"Seriously?" Jan says. He tries to focus on my face, scrutinizing. It makes me uneasy. I realize that this is what Jan and I are to each other, people who share a bottle over the constant mountain slides that we call our lives. Our relationship might not work the same without the booze.

But Jan takes my chin in his soft fingers and shakes it a little. His eyes gloss over as he speaks.

"I'm so proud of you, honey. You keep going, Lydia, you *keep going*. You're growing so far past Des, he'll never be able to catch you again. And don't you let him, my girl, you hear me?" His voice cracks. "Don't you dare let him."

<<<<◇>>>>

I draw an X over another day in my planner, close up the pleather binder and set it on my bedside table. A heap of my displaced jewelry falls onto the floor. Aidan reaches for me from beneath the sheets, his hand warm through the thin silk of my nightgown.

"It's been two weeks," I say. "Fourteen days."

"Are you feeling good?"

"I still want to drink, but I think it's getting a little better," I lay with my back against him, the heat of his body activating mine. My hips press against his, release, and press again. I've been walking so much--miles and miles a day, even in the sleet and freezing temperatures--that I think I've even gotten a little more buff. One solid hip thrust and we could be making love.

"Still worried about when Des gets back?"

"Yes," I say, freezing my excitement.

"No point in worrying until you have to." Aidan pulls me close, kissing my neck. "I think we should have a Christmas party."

"When?"

"On Christmas, duh." He ruffles my hair.

"Who's going to come to that? Everybody's got families to go to on Christmas."

"Do you?"

"No."

"Me either. And most of the people we know don't. Let's have a party."

I snort. "That would suck. Everybody sitting around the room, staring at each other."

"C'mon," his voice slithers, just like his finger, down my rib cage. "I'll show you how to party without the substance crutches."

"I know how it goes. I've been to one of your parties, remember?"

"You only walked in on one. *Being* at one is a lot better."

"I don't want to talk about drinking and drugging the whole night..."

"Lydia, they're all normal people, with other things to talk about. You'll see."

I make a sound that says he's wrong, but he just laughs, the sound as settling as muted wind chimes through my hair.

"Who do you want to invite?" he says.

"Nobody."

"Okay, sooo...Edith...and I was thinking Mrs. Lowt might want to come."

"I don't want Mrs. Lowt to know what's going on."

"You think she doesn't by now? I think she'd be happy to hear it." He nestles his jaw against mine. When he talks, his stubble brushes my skin and the hum of his voice transfers into my mouth as if it were his tongue. The warmth of his body, the melodic tone of his words--it's got to be why I finally agree to having the party.

To celebrate my flexibility, we have sex--with him on top, guiding his long, strong strokes against me like a classically-trained violinist. He strokes my hair in a way that feels much more like making love than just having sex. We've gone so far past three dates, it is impossible to convince myself that any of my old rules even apply anymore.

*I*t is Christmas Eve, and thinking of the party tomorrow, I am the exact opposite of excited. My anxiety piles up like a brick wall. It's not because I haven't thrown or attended a party, while being both straight and sober, since elementary school. It's not that I'm nervous about the judgments Aidan's friends will probably bring about our relationship, wrapped up tight when they walk in the door, but slowly unfurling as they get comfortable over dinner. It's none of that.

What is getting me is that Des will be back soon. He'll know about the divorce papers, if he doesn't already. I can't even imagine what kind of fury that is going to bring to my front door.

I was so strong when I went to the courthouse to file, but as the time keeps passing, my resolve is fading. The worry has set in. I've got to make a life without Des. I don't know how to do that.

I'm trying to make eggs when all my anxiety is put on hold by the ring of Aidan's phone.

He answers the call as he leans a shoulder on the fridge as I make eggs. "Hey Shane, you're out of bed early..."

He pushes off the fridge suddenly, staring at the floor. His back is so rigid and his stare so intense, I switch off the burner.

"I'll be right there," he says and flicks off the phone.

"What's going on?"

"Natalie," he says grimly. He's already on his way to my front door. "She tried committing suicide last night. I've got to get down to the hospital."

"Holy shit," I say. Aidan frowns, pushing on his shoes. He's out the door, circling back for his coat, and dropping a kiss on my cheek--like we're some old married couple--before he leaves. I watch him go down the hall from my door. He rubs the back of his neck as curses the elevator for taking so long and finally bolts down the stairwell instead.

Mrs. Lowt's door opens before I close mine.

"What's going on now, Lydia?" she asks. "Everything is so busy here lately."

"A friend of Aidan's...Shane...his wife tried to kill herself last night." The words are all hollow and strange coming off my tongue. They feel like lies, since I knew Natalie too. She wanted to be my sponsor. Maybe I did this to her by turning her down. It couldn't be that. But maybe that added to it.

"Poor thing," Mrs. Lowt says as my mind races to determine if I am responsible for this. Suddenly, Mrs. Lowt's hand is on my arm and I realize the *poor thing* she means is me, not Natalie. "Are you alright?"

"Yes, I hardly knew her...I only met her a couple times," I say. *And none of them were good.* I don't say that, even though I'm thinking it. The guilt accumulates, hovers.

And immediately, the haunting thought surfaces--*the liquor store is only down the street.*

"Would you like to come in and sit for a while?" Mrs. Lowt asks.

I could be there and back and drunk before Aidan returns. I could hide the bottle; he'd never know. He might not be back until late.

"That would be good," I tell her and let her lead me into her apartment, instead of retreating back into the emptiness of mine.

MERRY?

I stay at Mrs. Lowt's probably longer than what is polite, but she makes me homemade potato soup for lunch and then, when I tell her I should go, she insists on me staying for dessert with her. I'm relieved.

"I made cookies," she says, pulling a platter from the cold oven. She sets it down in front of me; a pile of red and white twists, shaped like candy canes. "Tonight is probably off, so we should enjoy them now. Have one."

I take one, close my eyes and savor the almond taste that melts on my tongue. My reaction leaves a proud smile on my neighbor's face.

"I leave the peppermint sprinkles off," Mrs. Lowt says. "They're better this way, I think."

"Me too," I say. "How many can I eat before you throw me out?"

"Oh no, I would never throw you out, Lydia," she says. The warmth in her voice attracts my eyes and I see the sparkle of lonely tears in hers. She's been my neighbor for years, watching over me and getting my door open when I was too drunk to do it myself, shouting her advise to me as she goosed the rears of the trouble I always brought home. In her funny way, Mrs. Lowt has always been there for me. I can hardly help myself as I reach across the counter and grasp her hand. Her fingers are softly pleated with age, but when she squeezes my hand back, she's got the strength of a man.

"Thank you, Mrs. Lowt."

"Eleanor, Lydia. My name is Eleanor Esmeralda Lowt, but my real friends have always called me Merry."

"That's perfect." It's hard to take another bite around my wide smile. Mrs. Lowt's reflects my own.

"Sometimes, things are," she says, saluting me with a candy cane cookie.

<<<<>>>>

We hear Aidan call my name from across the hall and Mrs. Lowt picks up the cookie tray.

"Take the cookies," she says. "I'll make something for you kids to eat later too."

I do something I never expected to do. I hug her goodbye. And she hugs back, as warm and steady as any mother. I never expected that either.

"Alright, go," she says, releasing me. "Aidan needs you."

I step into the hallway with the cookies, pulling Mrs. Lowt door closed behind me. Aidan's facing into the open door of my apartment, his back to me. Something isn't right.

"Aidan?" I say when he doesn't turn around right away. I cross the hall and put my free hand on his arm.

He turns. His eyes are swollen and red. The scent of whiskey rolls of him like storm clouds.

"I didn't mean to," he says. My gaze travels down to the paper bag he's clutching in his hand. The open mouth of the bottle, poking from the rolled edge of the bag, forms *oh* lips, as if it is as shocked as I am.

The whiskey is a sour cloud he exhumes with a small sob. He is broken, I see it all over him, but I can't help the anger that wells up inside me.

He is the strong one.

He is the rock, dammit.

If he's going to sink so easily, how am I going to make it? Who am I going to rely on?

I snatch the bottle and pound my shoulder against his as I pass into my apartment. I stomp straight into the lighted kitchen, slamming the cookie platter down on the counter. He drifts in behind me like a fading ghost. I hold my breath as I drain the rich, amber whiskey into the sink. I turn on the water full gush to wash it all away.

"I'm sorry," he says.

I rinse out the bottle and drop it in the sink. I catch sight of my ring finger then, and the tender commitment I had tattooed up my finger only a week ago. Leaning on the sink, I allow myself to droop over the empty bottle a moment longer. Then I pull up my head and take a deep breath.

"How is Natalie?" I ask.

"I'm sorry," Aidan says again. I know what he wants: absolution. When he's sober again, he'll realize that I'm not the one he needs it from.

"You need to call Leonard. If you don't, I will," I say. "But before you do, how's Natalie?"

He sniffles behind me, pulling in a breath. "She's going to be okay. They pumped her stomach." His footsteps turn, retreat, and I whip around from the sink.

"Where are you going?" I ask.

"Home."

"No you're not," I tell him. "You're staying here and sobering up."

"It's over," he says softly. "I blew it."

A fast-moving panic pierces my heart. I imagine losing Aidan-- losing him lying beside me in bed, sitting at the end of my couch as he works on his computer, making dough ornaments, and walking me to meetings. When I try to erase his presence from my life, I can hardly breathe. If it's over, we're both lost.

A second wave of panic crashes into me. I really thought I could quit seeing Aidan at any time and just go about my business. I figured it might be a little sad, a little uncomfortable in the halls, but I had no idea that it might make me feel like this. Paralyzed. Destitute. Impossible.

Addicted.

In love.

I go to him, laying a hand on his shoulder, and he turns to me. His face is wet with tears. Mine quickly reflects it.

"You're staying here," I tell him as I draw him into my arms. "You need to be here, with me."

*M*rs. Lowt delivers more potato soup, with biscuits, through the sliver of my open door, without questions.

"Merry Christmas, Lydia," she says. "Don't forget, I'm right across the hall if you need me."

She is like a fairy godmother without the wand or sparkles or musical number. As I juggle the food to close the door, I realize that Mrs. Lowt is more magical than any of that. She is more like a mother.

Aidan reeks, but I don't shove him under a shower. I don't prolong his drunkenness with coffee. Instead, I watch him laugh as struggles to feed himself, dumping a load of biscuit crumbs down the front of himself and drooling soup from the corner of his mouth.

I've never really seen this side of drunkenness before--the part where stupid, nothing things are hysterical and where every moronic, useless thought seems insightful. Only one of us thinks he's brilliant right now and it's not me.

I think he's repulsive this way. The Aidan I know and his appeal is completely gone. He's gone from remorseful to happy, horny drunk and I can't stand him. I shove and push him off, I can't even bring myself to laugh at this version of him.

He appears at the door of my bedroom, his belt undone.

"Fuck me," he slurs. "Come on, Lydia. You're beautiful and pretty and you smell like...cake. Fuck me."

"Shut up and go lie down," I tell him.

"You're going to come and fuck me then?"

"Yep," I say flatly. "Go lie down on the couch and wait for me. I'll be there in a few minutes."

He moans my name a few times and I ignore it. I'm relieved when he finally passes out.

NOT JUST SNOW FALLS

I didn't expect any of my Christmases to start like this. I wake up to Aidan, still fully clothed and sitting on the opposite edge of the bed, rubbing his skull as if he can buff out his hangover. He pushes off the bed and I hear the call to Leonard minutes later, going on in my bathroom. I hear the whole story, of how he saw Natalie and it blasted him because he'd contemplated the same thing. I had no idea. His humiliation leaks through the locked door.

He emerges almost an hour and a half later, following a long shower, but his eyes are still swollen. I'm on the couch, a bowl of cereal waiting for him on the coffee table.

"Merry Christmas. I made you breakfast," I say, nudging the bowl toward him with my toe. He falls onto his usual cushion at the opposite end from mine.

"I'm not that hungry."

"You've got to eat. You have to re-learn the right habits," I say. I give him a tiny grin as he takes the bowl. He stares into the cereal.

"Aren't you going to ask me about yesterday?"

"No."

"I fucked up."

"I know."

"I think you should know why it happened though," he says, putting down the cereal bowl.

"I'll listen if you want to tell me."

He nods. "I was okay being there for Shane. It was awful seeing Natalie, but I was still alright until I was riding the bus back home. There's something I haven't told you, Lydia. That first night I spent with you over a year ago, I was where Natalie is right now. That night I met you, I expected that you were going to be the last fling of my life. Everything about that night was going to be the last night of my life. That girl, Marta? Her whole family is a bunch of gun enthusiasts. I had a loaded gun waiting in a drawer at her house, waiting for me to come home that night."

"Holy shit, Aidan..."

"I know. I didn't tell you this part at first because I thought that it would be all you'd ever see in me--the lowest part. I thought it would scare you away. I didn't want to tell you because it isn't me."

"Of course it's not."

"My addictions had sucked me dry." His voice quivers. "I didn't think I could ever stop drinking. I was sure I couldn't. I was more messed up then I'd ever been. I was with different women every night, my business was starting to fail because I wasn't doing the work to keep it going--I was too busy partying and I didn't even care. All I wanted to do was feel *good*, but I got to that place where no amount of anything could even make me feel just *okay* anymore. That night I met you, it was like a death-row inmate's last meal. I was going to do everything and do it up big, come home, and swallow a bullet."

The tears stream down both our faces, but we stay on our opposite sides of the couch, connected only by his memories and my empathy.

"But then, I met you. We came back here and had sex. It was phenomenal. I *felt* it, but then you passed out and I didn't want to leave. I wanted to wake you up and feel what you made me feel all over again. Then, in your sleep, you started to cry. But when I held you, you stopped crying. I realized that it wasn't just about what someone else could make *me* feel. I could get a bigger rush by making someone else feel good. It changed how I was thinking about everything. I never went back to Marta's. I went to Shane and Natalie's house and met Leonard. I've never thought about doing anything like that ever again."

"Until last night." I can hardly say the words, but Aidan moves across the couch, taking my face in his hands.

"No, not even last night," he says. "But I got overwhelmed. I was scared that I'd ever gotten to that point before, that either of us might ever be where Natalie is. I started to panic, thinking about what I would do if it ever happened and the thoughts kept going. I let them pile up. I should've called Leonard, but instead, I caved. I got a fifth and I fucked up."

"You should've called me," I say, wiping away his tears as he wipes away mine. "You can't do that again. You call me if you're in trouble. I need you to be stronger than that."

"I will."

"But what's going to stop you from doing that again?"

"Me," he says. "I feel like shit. I choked down every swallow last night and it didn't help anything. I'm still sick about it all this morning and I have this hangover on top of it--I fucked up and it wasn't worth it. It didn't change anything."

"Not a thing," I say. "I'm glad you see that."

He sits back on the couch. I pick up his bowl of cereal and hand it to him.

"Thank you," he says.

"Friends make friends eat breakfast, right?"

My words make him miss a beat and I immediately start searching for what I said wrong. He frowns, softly stabbing his spoon into the bowl.

"Yes," he says a little tightly, "that is what *friends* do."

I realize the mistake instantly, but the vibe in the room is suddenly too steep for me to go back on what I said. He's probably thinking that I'm friend-zoning him because he screwed up, but to say it out loud might be shaming. After all he's done for me, I didn't think anything could be this awkward between us, but it is.

And then another thought chimes in: it doesn't have to be awkward. *I've* got the ability to turn this all around, just like Aidan has done for me, time and time again.

"So do friends who are a lot more than *just* friends," I say. His eyebrows lift a tiny bit.

"What are you trying to say?"

"I'm just saying, people like to--should--help each other out. You know."

"That's not what you said before, you didn't say *people,*" he teases, leaning toward me, over the middle cushion.

"You know what I meant."

"I'm not sure I do." He smiles. "Tell me."

He catches my wrist and pulls me toward him. We clunk foreheads but stay there, cross-eyed as we stare at each other. I giggle. When have I *ever* giggled?

"I was saying...we're a little more than friends."

"A little?" he asks. I feel the crinkle of his eyebrows as they rise.

"Maybe a little more than that."

"I am hoping for a lot more than that," His irises widen, drinking me in. They search for my answer, jumping between my eyes.

I can't answer. What do I say to him?

I'm still somebody else's wife.

I haven't figured myself out yet.

And *yes, God, I want you, I want you more than I want to be whole.*

"We're a couple of drunks." My laugh whispers away as I close my eyes. His thumb grazes my jaw bone.

"More or less," he says. "But don't let that be all we are to each other, Lydia."

There he is, my sober Aidan. The man who sees beyond the moment and rises to it. I open my eyes, allowing myself to swallow down every detail of him. The endless depth in his dark eyes, his caramel skin, even the equator of his facial hair--the angular lines drawn between the areas where it is smooth and where there is stubble. I reach up and run my fingers over the rough patches. My tattoo glances at me. Aidan takes my hand and moves my fingers higher, so they glide across the soft skin of his cheek bones instead.

I smile and he smiles back, as though neither of us needs my answer anymore.

*S*hane shows up at my door that night. He looks like hell partially digested him and spat him back out.

"She's going to be okay, whatever that means," he says, dumping his phone on the coffee table. He's never been in my apartment before, but his level of fatigue and distress has him dropping onto my couch like he lives here. He leans forward, his head in his hands.

"When did you eat last?" Aidan asks.

"I don't know," Shane says. It's pretty obvious that all he's been chewing on is his misery.

"You've got to eat. I'll get you something." Aidan gets up and goes into the kitchen. I move a little closer to Shane, quietly stalking around him. I don't know what to say to him and I know it's not reasonable, but getting in too close, the guilt of Natalie's attempted suicide is too contagious. I think of her, after the meeting, running after Aidan and I in the snow, asking me to let her help. Letting her sponsor me might've been the help *she* needed and I turned her down.

"How are you doing?" I finally ask. Shane pulls up his head, as if he didn't realize anyone else was in the room. He clears his throat, but it does no good. His voice still cracks.

"I'm okay. I'm going to be okay."

"She's conscious?"

"Yeah. She has been all along, for the most part. She was out of it when they brought her in, but she didn't like having her stomach pumped."

"She was awake for that?"

"Yeah," he says. I sit on the edge of the chair, furthest from him. He scrubs his head with harsh fingers.

"Do you know why yet? Why she did it?" I ask and he lets out a long sigh. Maybe asking is going too far, but Aidan sets a hot bowl of Mrs. Lowt's soup on the coffee table and answers for his friend.

"It's pretty common for addicts. Part of the disease."

Shane eyes the bowl, but doesn't lift the spoon. "She was in a bad place for a while, I knew that. I just couldn't figure out why. I could see her sinking, but I didn't know what to do for her. I should've tried harder to figure it out."

"Figured out how to fix it?" Aidan asks. "Come on. We've all been at the low spots before. You know you're the only one that can get you out of it."

"I was sixteen," Shane says. "It was completely different. And you were the one that straightened me out."

Aidan shakes his head. The two of them have entered into a private world, a past that I can only observe from the side lines. This is part of Aidan's history that he hasn't told me yet and it intrigues me.

"Overwhelmed is overwhelmed," Aidan goes on, "and you

straightened yourself out. The only thing I did for you was need my best friend."

"I need her."

"I know you do."

"But I've always needed her," Shane says, his tone collapsing, the breaks in his thought process mirrored by the way his voice fails him. "It hasn't been enough, or we wouldn't be here."

"I turned her down," I blurt. "Natalie asked me to be my sponsor. She wanted to guide me and I turned her down. I think I contributed to this..."

Her husband's eyes find mine. "I guess we all did."

"Knock it off, both of you," Aidan admonishes us softly. "No one knew Nat was in this bad of shape. She made her own decisions." He wipes his mouth with his hand, as if he's wiping away the memory of last night's fifth. "We can't blame ourselves for what someone else chooses to do."

Shane's gaze sinks to the floor. "But I should've..."

"You *couldn't have*."

In the break of our voices, Christmas carols and laughter permeate the wall from some other neighbor's apartment, and Shane begins to cry. Aidan and I move in, surrounding him, leaning and being leaned on, like a tepee of souls, trying to kindle enough faith to send up a genuine signal of hope.

WHO I AM DEPENDS ON WHO YOU ARE

The day after Christmas, I give Aidan his Christmas gift. My most elaborate, heart-shaped, salt-dough ornament. And I'm wearing lace lingerie with thigh-highs when I do it.

Three days after Christmas, Aidan gives me a gift. A pedometer, to keep track of how much I walk. That's what I do now. I bundle up and walk the streets like a sober, post-visit Scrooge.

Five days after Christmas, Shane texted to say that the hospital released Natalie. He asked if we would take her to the meeting with us in a couple of days.

Six days after Christmas, Aidan decides to run some food over to them.

"You don't want to come?" he asks, but I still feel partially responsible for what Natalie did and I don't know what I'd say to her.

"We're not friends and with everything that's happened..."

"I get it," he says, kissing my forehead. "I'm not going to stick around too long."

It occurs to me that I don't *have* to have him in the apartment. I don't need a constant babysitter to keep me from the booze anymore. I'm doing that for myself now. "I'm going to go walking anyway."

He chuckles. "I don't know if you want to do that. Have you looked out there? It's not just freezing--it's windy today too."

Once he leaves, it takes about ten minutes before I'm pacing. I need to keep busy. I suck at baking and making ornaments has lost all its appeal now that Christmas is over. My eye catches on a film of dust on one of the shelves. Aha! Spring cleaning. I've got all the supplies, but the last time I did it was...when I moved in? I've got all this energy and without being able to walk it off, I know by now that I've got to do something to keep my mind off of what it always floats back to: fucking up.

I tie back my hair with a bandana and it takes me only a half hour in the mirror to be sure that I am dressed correctly enough to clean. I laugh at that as I drag out my bucket and mop, turn on my music, and get to work. Within five minutes, the first unhappy neighbor is pounding on my door.

I swing it open, ready to apologize, but it's not a neighbor.

Des shoves his way inside, slamming the door behind him. He whips my music port off the shelf, shattering the thing in pieces on my newly cleaned floor.

"What the fuck, Lydia!" he shouts. He's got the divorce papers wadded in his hand. "Do you know what you just did? DO YOU?"

His anger is contagious. "It had to happen sometime..."

"It NEVER had to happen! We were fine, until you did this!"

"*You* were fine--I never wanted to live like this!"

"Well, you sure as shit don't have to worry about living like *this* anymore!" He waves a hand around my apartment. "Claudia's legal team is crawling up my ass with pliers!"

"Did she throw you out?"

"Listen to me, dumbass," he snarls, "people as rich as Claudia don't *throw you out.* They throw your ass in a dungeon and cover the whole thing over with cement!"

"Give me a break. She's not mafia--"

Suddenly, he shuts his mouth and clasps his hands in front of him. Ducking his chin, his words growl from between his bared teeth, as dangerous as a feral dog guarding his food.

"What the fuck are you not getting here, *Lyddle*?" he asks. He takes a step toward me and I quickly wish he was yelling again. His anger rolls from him. "They want to charge me with extortion and bigamy. They're going to charge me with so much shit, I'll never see the sun again. And I told you, I would never go down alone. So, I'm going to make sure they get you too. How do you like that? How do you like knowing you fucked us both, you little *cunt*!"

His eyes dig into me like drill bits, trying to drive into my core and ignite. He stalks me and I stagger backward, falling over the pail, sloshing small, dirty rivers across the floor. When he's standing over me, he is as ominous and solid as any impending prison.

He spots the Christmas tree Aidan insisted on, still sagging with my handmade ornaments. Des's smirk is savage as he reaches down and snatches the bandana off my head.

"Are you playing house, you little bitch? Is that why you did this to me?" he shouts, and then the blows rain down on me, his feet, his fists, one after another without hesitation.

*Cunt, bitch, whore, slut...*he snarls the words as he beats me.

I get a glimpse of the door and imagine Aidan bursting through it, but as the hard toe of Des's designer shoe catches me in the face, the hope of rescue dims. His attack pauses at my moan and I pray to pass out as I hear Des's belt slither from his waist.

He doubles the leather in his fist and strikes me across the stomach. I curl up, flipping over to protect myself. He whips my back, the buckle digging into the flesh at the base of my neck. I feel the welts rising up beneath my shirt as I try to scurry away.

Someone has to come.

Someone has to save me.

He's going to kill me.

Des lands a kick to my thigh with so much force that I tumble across the floor.

Someone has to come.

Someone has to save me.

But the door is locked. Mrs. Lowt would be pounding on it, if she heard, or calling the cops. I don't hear any sirens.

No one is coming.

Des slips as he tries to cross the wet floor and crashes down a few feet from me.

I see the fury of his veins popping up on his face.

My God, no one is coming.

If I'm getting out of this, I'm going to have to do it on my own.

Des crawls across the floor toward me, the belt still trapped in his fist, spitting words at me that my brain won't translate. It doesn't matter what he's saying--I know what he means.

He means to kill me, if he can.

And I'm not going to last until a hero gets here.

I plant my hands on the floor. Something hot and stinging runs into one of my eyes, but I still make out the words on my bloody ring finger. *Stronger Than That.*

As I watch Des inching toward me, his broad shoulders tight against his tailored shirt, I realize I might not be stronger than *that.*

But as I get to my feet, I know I'm stronger than *this.*

My body takes over. My foot fires out, landing a kick to Des's jaw. The sound out of him fuels me as I kick him again. He lands on his back and I tower over him, my hip raising my whole leg, ready to send it down like a dull guillotine on his neck.

He grabs my sole.

He shoves me backward. I land with a grunt, but my body plunges adrenaline through my veins.

"You little bitch!"

I skitter out of the way as he grabs for me. I make it to my feet before he does. I make it to the door.

"You ruined my *life*!"

I twist the knob.

His footsteps are behind mine as I whip open the door and burst into the hall.

He grabs a handful of my hair, ripping locks from my scalp.

But my body doesn't run away. It doesn't cry. It turns and fires me straight at him like a cannonball.

His eyes are wide as I bear my teeth. The blows rain down on him, one after another, until I've pressed him against the wall.

"Do you know what you've done to me?" I feel the words shriek out of my chest. "You ruined *my* life!"

I drive my knee up between his legs, sinking it hard and giving an extra jerk at the peak.

His groan rushes into my ears and the blood rushes out.

My hearing returns.

Des collapses onto the hallway floor. I stand above him, waiting for him to attack again. My breathing fills my ears. I glance up. Mrs. Lowt's door gapes open, Mrs. Lowt is behind me, a frying pan clutched in her hand.

"Lydia!" she shrieks. It is the last thing I hear before I hit the floor.

BRING IN THE NEW

The addiction is a hollow spot that sits like a dust valley, waiting for the deposits of all my rotten luck. Everything that I used to dump there rusts and decays, sending up a choking dust. The only thing that used to help keep down the suffocating proof of my imperfection and weaknesses and mistakes was to pour booze all over it. Bottles full of hot, wet, numbing liquor was all I needed to keep the rot from wafting into my consciousness and whatever brain cells resisted my attempts, I smothered by the pint.

I was sure that after what happened with Des, the valley would be calling out to me. Clawing at me, even. I thought that what just happened would need taming and suffocation, but it doesn't.

Maybe it's because Des broke my nose. Maybe it's because my face is so bruised. But I think it's because I've filled in the valley myself, topped it off the minute I kicked Desmond's nuts into his throat.

"How are you feeling?" Aidan asks. He hasn't left my side since the moment he tore into the emergency room, shouting at the nurses until he insisted that he was my husband and they let him in to see me. He broke down, sobbing at the side of the gurney I was laying on, until I rested my hand, with its chipped fingernails and bloody tattoo, on his head.

"Don't drink," I whispered. He pulled up his head and took my hand. He turned it over in his and kissed my palm, the last of his tears dropping into the center.

"We are stronger than that," he said.

He brought me home from the hospital and didn't tease me for looking like a walrus with all the gauze packing. After he put me to bed, Mrs. Lowt filled him in on how the cops came, but had to take Desmond away by ambulance before they could arrest him. I still don't know when the cops will come for me.

Aidan called Edith and Leonard too, so the last couple of days, people from the meeting have stopped by to drop off lasagnas and casseroles, plates of cookies and cake. Aidan gave a heap of it to Mrs. Lowt, since he said there is more than we will be able to eat in a month. Mrs. Lowt comes by three times a day at least, with soup and other soft things that are easiest for me to eat with my bruised jaw and broken nose.

But even with Mrs. Lowt's visits and the people from the meeting oscillating in and out, Aidan is the most attentive by far. He waits patiently to hear my answer to the same question he asks each time he passes by me.

"I'm good," I say. He still re-fluffs the pillow beneath my twisted ankle. I don't want him to move anything else because it kills my bruised ribs and I can't stand to ask him to stop, so I'm relieved when his fussing is interrupted by a knock at the door. He goes to it, but answers now with the door chain in place, the opening only as wide as a fist. We only know Desmond is being detained, but don't know if or when he might be released.

I hear the soft lilt of a woman's voice, but Aidan doesn't open the door right away. I'd push myself up to see who it is, if doing that didn't make me feel like I was suffocating.

"Alright," Aidan says. "You can come in, so long as it's just talking."

He closes the door, unfastens the chain and opens up. I hear the click of heels across the floor and a woman comes into view.

I know her instantly.

Claudia.

She stares down at me, gaping a moment before her rich manners kick in. She looks behind her, sees the chair and settles herself on the edge of it, her beaded handbag placed genteelly on her knees.

"I'm sorry," I say, as needles of pain shoot through my cheeks. Embarrassment floods my face, the rush of blood stinging the bruises. Aidan stands at the foot of the couch, between Claudia and I, his arms crossed over his chest like a watchful body guard.

"*He* did this to her," Aidan says, the accusation and pleading both twisting in his tone. Claudia puts up a soft hand, halting any further speech from either of us.

"If you don't mind," she says, her lips twitching uncomfortably. She focuses solely on me. "I'm not sure what to believe anymore, so I wanted to see you for myself. Now that I have, I would like to ask you some questions."

"You're not going to grill her," Aidan begins, but I shush him through my swollen lips.

"It's okay. Ask me whatever you want, Claudia. I'll tell you the truth. We both deserve for things to finally be out in the open."

She shifts on the edge of the chair. "Do you love him?"

"No," I say. "I thought I did, but somebody who loves you," I have to pause to pull in a painful breath, "wouldn't do this."

She nods once. "Did you take my money?"

"Yes." I figure there is no point in lying, no point in trying to explain, but she fidgets with the beading on her handbag.

"Do you want to tell me why?"

"I married Des before I finished high school. When he left me, to marry you, I didn't have any way to survive. He came up with the designer job for me and I didn't see any other way around it."

"That's an excuse. I'm sure you could have done something else besides steal from me."

"You're right. Stripping. I could have done that." My tone is not feisty or argumentative or seeking pity. It's as flat and unadorned as the bare truth of my words. She tips her head to one side slightly, considering it. I add more humiliating truth. "You're right that it's an excuse too. I could have done something, but I really thought I was stuck. I didn't see that I wasn't. I still loved him, back then."

"Desmond is very convincing," she concedes, scratching something from the corner of her eye.

"He's convincing and I was weak."

"Was?"

"I am. But I'm working on it. That's why I filed for divorce. I don't want to be weak anymore."

"I can see that." She chuckles, pushing her rear end back a little on the seat cushion. "Why didn't you ever say anything? How could you see me and never tell me what was going on?"

"Des told me that if I said anything, he would be sure we would both go to jail."

Claudia's lips flatten out, an empty line beneath her nose. She clears her throat with a tiny, delicate grumble before flipping up her chin. "As you still may. Just because I'm here doesn't mean that I won't be pressing charges."

"I know," I say.

"But I do give you credit for stepping forward first and filing for the divorce. That, at least, alerted me to the problem."

"Filing for divorce wasn't for you, it was for me. I couldn't live like that anymore."

Claudia's eyes shift around my apartment. "Well, it's not a penthouse, but it doesn't look like you've done so badly with my money."

"I drank it all away."

Her bottom lip drags open. "You're an alcoholic?"

"Yes."

"She's getting help," Aidan interjects. "She started attending meetings almost three weeks ago and hasn't had a drop in that time. There is a whole room of people who will tell you the same."

Claudia eyes him skeptically and then returns her attention to me. "You've been sober for three weeks? Is that true?"

"Not quite three weeks," I say. "And I don't know if it counts anymore, since I got pain killers at the hospital after this happened."

Claudia leans back in the chair, studying me.

"Did you two ever..." she begins, but the question fades off. I already know what she wants to ask. I don't want to tell her, it's humiliating, but she needs to know.

"Yes. In his office upstairs."

"You did that, in my house." Her words are slow, as if they're still processing.

"Yes."

"When?"

"Whenever he called."

"You were his...his call girl?" Her lips squeeze out the sour words. She ends with a puckered, hard swallow.

"That's when he gave me money. It's how I lived."

"It doesn't sound much like living."

"No, it wasn't anything like living."

Claudia clears her throat, clasps the opening of her purse. "I'm sorry that you made the choices you did, Lydia, but I appreciate you speaking with me about them. I think you could have done much better by both of us, but I can understand how difficult it must have been."

"I appreciate that."

"It doesn't mean I can let you off the hook."

"I don't expect you to."

"No?"

"No."

That seems to surprise her. Maybe it's my busted-up face or the pride in my words, maybe she can see and hear that I mean what I say. Claudia lifts her chin.

"I think you owe a huge debt to me, considering you syphoned money from me for the last couple of years. I would expect to be paid back, but I don't know how you would go about doing that."

"I could go to jail."

"That's punishment. Not repayment." Claudia stands, tucking her purse under her arm. Aidan opens his mouth, but she speaks before he can. "My accountant is drawing up an estimate of how much you received from me. I would think that if you would agree to repay me, I might consider dropping charges."

"That is a great offer," I say, "but I don't think I'll ever be able to repay it. My friend offered me a job at his hair salon, but I won't make enough to live as it is."

Claudia rolls her tongue in thought. I figure she's going to bolt for the door, but instead, she stays put.

"I believe Desmond delivered a twenty thousand dollar bonus to you for Christmas?"

"Yes."

"Then I have a proposition. I would be willing to gift you that money, if, in return, you take the job at the salon and attend night classes to achieve your high school diploma."

"Are you serious?"

"Quite."

"Why would you do that?"

"Look at you," she says, motioning from my damaged face, down to my ribs, all the way to my messed-up ankle. "This isn't only the aftermath of a woman who loved a thief. This is the body of a woman who wanted to break away. You made the first steps. I don't know how my professional team didn't find this first, but I may never have known about any of this deceit, if it wasn't for you. Therefore, despite what I believe my team would advise me to do, I'm going to follow my intuition here.

"If you complete high school, earning a diploma, I will not

require you to return the bonus. I'm assuming you still have most of it?" she asks.

"Almost all of it." I rub my tattooed ring finger.

"Good. You can live on that until you graduate. When you graduate, if you are willing to go on to college and complete a four year degree, then I would be willing to release you from your debt; the money Desmond gave you throughout our shared marriage."

"Why would you do that?" I whisper.

"I would like to see you succeed, Lydia. I truly would. None of us are without addictions and I know firsthand how they can lead a person in the wrong directions. But I think you are worth my investment, Lydia, and seeing what Desmond's done to you, on some levels, I even feel as if I owe it to you. I had no idea that he was capable of such violence or deceit. And I may never have known that the man I fell in love with was married to another woman."

"Thank you," I say and Aidan echoes it softly.

"You are welcome." She smoothes down her jacket as she stands, but I stop her with a question.

"Do you still?" I ask. She turns back to me slowly.

"Love him?" She shakes her head slightly, sending a soft, elegant wave through her carefully-styled hair. "I did, even a few weeks ago, I did. It's going to take me some time to digest all of this still, but love? No. I can't. Not after all this."

"You're a strong woman," I tell her. Claudia smirks.

"We both are, aren't we?" she says.

EPILOGUE

The pile of slippery coupons Jan gave me slides out of my hands and down the steps.

"Shit, shit, *shit!*"

I'm never going to get into the meeting room on time. Not when both work and classes each end at 5:30 and the meetings on those same days begin at 5:45. But I won't miss even one. I'm religiously five minutes late to all three of the meetings each week, but I haven't missed a meeting yet and Edith tries to stall Leonard until I arrive.

I scoop up the coupons, some of them wet and muddy from whatever got tracked down the church's steps. Holding them close to my chest, the coupons still flutter out of my grasp as I stomp down the hall toward the meeting door.

Edith leans out of the door miscategorizeat's going on?" she asks as I approach. "I could hear you *shitting* all the way down the stairs."

"Could've used some help," I grumble, but I also laugh. Of course, Edith doesn't offer to take the muddy coupons. All she does is laugh at me.

"Looks like you can handle it. What is all this anyway?"

"Jan could use some advertising. I'm giving him a hand."

"Haven't you given him about fifty hands, by now? Isn't managing his entire business enough? Now you're advertising for him too?" Edith snorts.

"I'm a marketing major." I shrug. "Business management is only my minor. Jan's my guinea pig."

"And he doesn't mind a bit, since she's tripled his business," Aidan adds as he comes to the door. He steps past Edith and helps gather up some of the coupons. He swoops down, leaving a kiss on my mouth.

He makes sure to kiss me every single time that we've been apart. That started back when I had to testify against Desmond, five years ago. I told the judge and jury everything and during the break for lunch, Desmond managed to follow me to the bathroom. He told me that he would get me for testifying, for turning Claudia against him, for betraying his trust. His fucking *trust*. When I started screaming at him, about what he'd done to *my* trust and how he could go fuck himself, that if he ever tries to come and get me, I would bury his nuts in his nostrils again, he bashed me in the face. The court bailiffs saw him do it, but didn't get to him fast enough to prevent me from doing just what I told Des I would. I brought my knee up into his groin so hard that the bailiffs had to scrape Desmond off the floor. Aidan got to court late that day, after everything had happened, and kissing my quickly-bruising face, he told me over and over and over again how grateful he was that Des hadn't done something even worse. Now, years later, our kiss is like a prayer. It is not an asking prayer, but one that has been answered, and it is the way we show how grateful we still are to have one another.

"How's my almost-college grad?" he asks. "Only a week until graduation--"

"That just makes me more tired," I say, but I do it with a smile. He wraps his free hand around my shoulders and gives me a squeeze and another kiss on the top of my head.

"But you made it here."

"I always make it," I murmur playfully. He straightens the coupons and hands them back to me. I give him one more kiss. "Now go sit with your *men.* I'll see you after the meeting."

"You can count on it," he says. Then, dropping his voice to a whisper in my ear, "Don't forget, Mrs. Lowt is making us dinner and then...it's *baby night.*"

"You think I would forget? Thursday is my favorite day of the week," I say. We've been trying for the last couple of weeks. Since Fridays are our only day off each week (we're trying to save up enough to move out of Aidan's apartment and into a real house) Thursday nights are dedicated to staying up all night and having our fill of each other's bodies.

Aidan crosses the room to his table full of guys and I follow Edith to our regular table, in the back. Natalie tips back in her chair, smiling when she catches sight of me. She waves for me to take the seat beside her.

"Hey, Aidan said that Desmond called you?" she says. I nod.

"I don't know how he got phone privileges, but yeah. He called to tell me again that he was going to get parole and hunt me down."

"That *bastard*!" Nat's voice climbs. It still sounds funny when she swears, but she's picked up my bad habits. I guess that's what happens when you have a best friend that talks like a sailor. "You notified the authorities, haven't you?"

"I did one better," I say. "I told Claudia. She's got enough connections and money to keep him right where he is. He's not going anywhere for a long, long time."

"Well, I'm glad for that, but I don't like that he can even get on a phone."

"Nobody does," I say. I flick my chin at the new face on the other side of Nat. "Who's this?"

"This is Cora," Natalie says. The woman beside her, sweatered and sniffly, looks annoyed, or maybe it's bored. She dabs her nose with a tissue, eyeing the room before her gaze settles on me with a mild hatred. "Cora, this is Lydia Badeau, the one I was telling you about. You might want to ask her to be your sponsor. She's married to that guy you were eyeing earlier."

"I wasn't *eyeing* him, I only *noticed* him," the woman says as she turns her eyes on me. "Just so you know, I'm not here for me. I'm only here to support my husband."

She doesn't have to point him out. I know everyone in the room, but the hulking biker dude in the corner is particularly unmistakable. Especially his scowl. But, they wouldn't have let this Cora girl in here too, unless she was an invisible-card-carrying member of our little alcoholic club. I don't call her out on it. I just pull a card from my purse and slide it across the table.

"If you want some help, you can call me," I say. Cora flashes me a dry smile as Leonard stands up, calling attention. He clears his throat so loudly that it rings in my ears, even at our back table, but the room doesn't really quiet down until Edith sticks her two index fingers in her mouth and blasts us with an ear-splitting whistle.

"Tonight, we have asked a few members to speak. Our group has grown and I think we would all benefit from hearing where some of the people in this room have come from, how they manage their addictions and what they've learned in their journey thus far. So, tonight, instead of breaking into our small groups, we're going to do an open talk. It is a night of lessons, and I've asked a few members in particular to share. Each will begin by telling us what they believe is an important lesson they have learned up to this point in their sober journey, as we might all benefit from their knowledge."

One of the newer guys harumphs. Leonard twists, searching the room and I feel the back of my neck prickle as he says my name. I knew he was going to do it, but I'm not sure I'll ever love standing up and speaking in front of a whole room. At least it's not as bad as it used to be.

I look around the room at these people who have become my friends and support. My gaze finally rests on Aidan and he smiles his encouragement from his table full of men.

"Hi. I'm Lydia, and I'm an alcoholic," I say. The room greets me, the voices of my friends are recognizable. I wink at Aidan. "Leonard asked me last week to talk on this subject and I've spent all this week thinking about it. I've learned so many things since the first time I set foot in this room, it was hard for me to narrow it down to the most important ones. I guess the first thing I learned was that I was an alcoholic. That was a shocker."

There is a low rumble of laughter around the room.

"But once I learned what I was, what my weakness was, the other pieces of my life started to fall into place. When I first showed up here, I was still trying to convince myself that I didn't care about anything, but I think part of why I am an alcoholic is because I cared *too much* about all the wrong things. The truth is, I was terrified of the choices I had made up to that point, but I didn't think I had any control over it. I let everyone else take my wheel and steer me however they wanted through my life. So, I've learned that I do care and need to care and that I had to grab the wheel and make the choice to steer myself."

There is a low murmur of agreement and even an *amen* from Karyn, aka, Hot-Dog-Hairzilla. I still call her that in my head, but she was the one who arranged the surprise wedding shower for Aidan and I. She was also the one who caught the bouquet at our wedding. Watching Leonard put the garter he caught on Karyn's leg, while she was simulating an orgasm, was something to remember.

"Tell them the best one, Lydia," Aidan pipes up from his seat. "The one we talked about last night."

Edith shushes him for speaking, but I nod. It is the best lesson, the one that I told him when we were out walking, hand in hand. It came to me as he rubbed my ring finger.

"I was telling my husband last night," I say, with a smile to him, "I've learned that I...*we*...are all stronger than we ever give ourselves credit for. Too often we believe that we are alone and fighting our own battles by ourselves, when the truth is that we're all in this together. Just about everyone in this room has fought and is still fighting alcoholism. Or narcotics. Or both. Or something else, even. We may not have fought our battles together, but the we're all in the same war and we need each other to win. We're here to draw on the strength of others in this room and give it back to whoever needs it too, because that's what makes us *all* stronger than the obstacles that come our way. The world is filled with addictions and it really doesn't matter which particular one grabs your steering wheel. It matters more that when you lose your grip, you know who can help you get it back. Addictions might *feel* overwhelming, but we are *all* stronger than that."

THE END

Like STRONGER?

Continue below for a free preview of Misty Paquette's WEEDS of DETROIT— a story based on true events from the author's past. A teen runaway moves into a Detroit hotel and tries to survive the streets of the city.

Want something less gritty?
Check out the preview for Misty Paquette's steamy HALE MAREE, the first book in the Crossed & Bared series, about a shocking arranged marriage between a billionaire's suspected playboy son and a girl whose father was in the wrong place at the right time.

SPECIAL THANKS

Thank you, God, for putting all these people in my life. It is always about you.

Thank you Pook, Little Rocker Chick, and Poley, for dealing with this crazy job I do. I love you guys more than anything.

Thanks to the back table at 5:45! This book would be nothing without your wisdom. Thank you for so much for openly sharing your insights and stories. I am humbled by your journeys and honored that you would trust me with your personal histories. Your candid truths helped me to create what I hope are authentic characters and an authentic story that captures the same type of bravery each of you exhibit in your daily lives. Thanks again for your help.

Love and kisses to my incredible Beta Babes: Candace Selph, Delphina Miyares, Jackie McPherson, Lisa 'Pisa' Ammari, Heather Love King, and Kathryn Grimes. Your enthusiasm and willingness to help is above and beyond, your suggestions always make my books stronger. Thank you for getting on my roller coaster ride, yet again!

Huge thanks to Tom, Kenny, Bill, and Paul for taking the time to hang out.

Thanks to Violet Duke for being so incredibly generous with her endless, awe-inspiring talents. I am grateful beyond measure.

Thanks to my mom, for always listening to the ideas, and to my dad, for always handing over the phone. It's no small job.

FREE PREVIEW OF WEEDS OF DETROIT

FROM AUTHOR MISTY PAQUETTE

A sheltered, suburban teen runaway moves in a Detroit hotel and tries to survive the streets of the city. Based on true events.

THIS IS HOW IT STARTED...

When I was a kid, I swore I was an angel stuck in a human's body. My mom adored that. She made me tell all her friends when they came to visit, and she hustled me out in front of the relatives to recite my belief at Christmas.

She didn't do that when I told her I'd also be dead before I hit sixteen.

My mother—a staunch believer in ghosts and psychic powers and rocks that make you feel better—flipped. She told me there's no way I could know that for sure, so I should stop saying it. She tried to tell me that I didn't know what I was talking about for years.

The idea of death never scared me as a kid, because sixteen was as far off as a thousand. Even as I got closer to what was supposed to be my last birthday, I didn't worry about it. I accepted it, like that's how things were going to be, and I figured it'd be a quick death because I'd been nice in school and did what my mother asked me to. I was sure that God would go the distance and make my death a * poof * kind of event. A gun shot, a car crash, I'd die in my sleep...something easy.

My sixteenth birthday was tense from the minute I woke up until the minute I woke up again on the morning of my seventeenth birthday. My seventeenth came and went with cake, a new sketchbook, and a metal box of specialty drawing pencils. I like art. My mom gave a tremendous sigh of relief, but she waited to congratulate me until the day after my birthday, when I was officially and solidly seventeen years old.

"You made it. You're not dead," she told me over breakfast. She was triumphant, like she'd won some battle with me. I shrugged with my mouthful of Fruit Loops. I knew what she was getting at.

"Maybe I got it wrong," I told her. "Maybe I'm not supposed to live past my teens or something like that."

"Nope," she said, with one shake of her head and her nose held high. "You always said sixteen, and now you're seventeen. You had your chance. No more dying."

I swallowed my cereal.

Here we go, I thought. *Here* is where we always went.

"I didn't make it up, mom. I told you, it was just a feeling. Maybe I'm still here because I screwed up, I don't know. Maybe I didn't finish what I'm supposed to do yet, so here I am."

My mother turned a little pale. At that point, we were fighting most of the time, so even on a morning when there seemed to be a semi-truce, it was still a bonus if I could make her miserable.

"What could you possibly have finished at sixteen?" she snapped.

Truce...over.

Every word became a brick I wanted to drop on her.

"I. Don't. Know," I said flatly. "Maybe that's why I'm still stuck here with you."

My mother sniffed with a second, high-nosed shake of her head. "You forget that I've already been sixteen, Lael. I know exactly how it feels, and I can tell you, you don't know enough to have finished anything yet."

"Maybe I'm a little smarter than you." *Oh, that was a good one.* My comment sent a scowl trolling across her face. She deserved it, as far as I was concerned. The score board was finally even, and I knew she hated that more than anything.

We glared at each other across the table until she finally looked away. We finished eating in silence. She made a huge show of ignoring me, so I chewed with my mouth wide open, letting bits of cereal fall out on the table. Screw her. But I knew she wouldn't let it go that easily.

"I was just trying to say," she started in again, "that sixteen is very young to have finished much of anything. You have a lot of growing up to do. That's all." No eye contact.

Yeah. That wasn't some heartfelt Hallmark moment between us. It was said to put her ahead on the argument leader board, and her 'that's all' was meant to cap the conversation, so I wouldn't start another one.

When I was little, I would get intimidated by the edge in her voice, but I'm seventeen now. Who got the last word was more like gripping up a baseball bat, our sentences like layering fists to see who would make it to the top first, claim the bat, and swing it at the other.

I picture my victory—winding back with my last word bat and swinging at my mother's head like a ripe melon. It comes off clean, sailing through the air, her mouth still moving as I point into the distance. I would be free to round the bases once her mouth was far enough away that I couldn't hear any more of her criticisms.

But there was never a top of that last-word bat, and never, ever, a winner.

"Oh yeah," I sneered at her, "I forgot—you know it all, mom.

Seventeen is too young to do anything worth doing. Too young to know anything, according to the wise old cow."

She ignored the insult and raised her chin. "That's not what I'm saying, Lael."

"That's what it sounded like." My hands curled into fists and she glimpsed them.

"You know what?" she said, standing up from the table. "You're seventeen and you're alive. Happy Birthday."

She took her coffee cup and went out on the front porch, letting the screen door slam behind her.

I officially hated her. Walking out was winning in her book, and we both knew it. She always had to win.

"Happy freaking birthday," I grumbled. "Too bad I'm not dead yet."

ONE
August, 1986

This one ramps up before dinner this time. It is a stupid fight, like all of them are. I can't stand the sound of my mother's voice after she's taken a big, fat dose of her nerve meds.

I tell her I wish she was dead.

She runs off crying into her room, howling over one shoulder that she just can't handle it anymore.

I'm the *it*.

This is how most of our fights go.

This time, when my mother runs away, she leaves the water gushing over a heap of baby spinach in the sink. My step dad, Bob, and I sit opposite each other.

Through the layers of his suit, I can smell Bob's pickled liver all the way across the table. He's a little crooked in his chair, but my mother has tucked a napkin around his neck, and he manages to stay upright. Bob's what my high school health teacher would call a career alcoholic. At the moment, he's a pissed one too.

His bloodshot glare rolls over the table top and lands on me. It's awkward, because neither of us wants the hassle tonight, but we don't know what to do next, in order to stop what is coming. We never know, and it never stops.

Bob gets up, stumbles over to the sink, and turns off the water. He whips back around, his finger aimed at the dead center of my face.

This argument, like every single one, is going to end without being finished. We have not finished an argument since I turned thirteen, four years ago. Instead, Bob will hit me, or ground me, or tell me he's taking away the car that I bought with my own money. That's how it always ends—with a resolution that trails sparks, instead of extinguishing them.

"You had to do it again, didn't you," he says. My mother is not a quiet crier, but I swear she's howling for extra effect now. Every sob cranks Bob's eyebrows down a little lower between his eyes.

"She did it to herself," I grumble.

"She's trying to help you become a responsible adult."

"Help me?" I fire back. "How is being her puppet going to help me? She's a control freak!"

"I think you could use some control." His tone separates us. I am not his little girl anymore. He liked to claim me as his when someone complimented me. But now, glaring at me through his bloodshot eyes, I am not even a step-daughter to him; I am nothing more than an intruder that makes his wife cry.

"I'm not a little kid that you can boss around any..." I start, but Bob's shoulders drop, and I know to stop even before his hands clench into fists.

"In my house, you will follow my rules!" he booms.

"*You* moved in with *us*!" I scream back.

My mother's wailing gets louder down the hall. Bob's jaw tightens. He draws himself up. He has no idea what to do with me, or about me, anymore. I've gotten taller, but he's still bigger than me.

"Go to your room!" he shouts.

But I can't let him win. I cross my arms over my chest. "No."

My plan is to flee like my mother did, except I'll jump in my car and get the hell out of here—but even with Bob juiced, he's big and he's between me and the front door. And he ain't moving.

The good news: I have a car key in my wheel well, if I can just get to it. I gotta try. I step toward the door and Bob gives me a hard shove backward, down the hall, toward my room. I trip on my own feet and throw out a hand to steady myself against the wall.

"Go!" he barks, jabbing his finger at me.

I get my balance and root myself in the mouth of the hallway, shooting him my best *screw you* face.

It's a stupid move, and something that I know better than to do to Bob. It sends him into bar-fight mode.

He gives me another hard shove. I stumble backward again, but this time, I go down. I land hard on my tailbone with a yelp.

With one push, he's won this fight the same way he always does: he is stronger than me.

I get to my feet and retreat the four steps back to my room as he advances. Once inside, I slam the door with everything I've got. The walls shake.

I yank a chair from my closet—the green one with the hand painted flowers on the back that my mother used to make me take time-outs on when I was five. I wedge it up under the doorknob. Screw them both.

My mother is still sobbing. I hear her through the wall. Bob's voice joins hers in their bedroom next door. His voice is soft and gentle now, agreeing with her that I am out of control. Agreeing that they need to do something about me. Agreeing that I am the one who is wrong for not agreeing with them.

I let the tears slide out then, but I don't make any noise. I will not sob the way my mother does.

The corner windows in my room that overlook the roof of our garage light up as the sun breaks from behind clouds. The rectangular glow expands and falls on my dingy, baby-pink bedroom walls. Years of smudgy fingerprints and secret crayon drawings show.

I hear my mother sniffle between questions about the cost of tutoring and boarding schools. She thinks the only problem we have is my last report card and that I don't listen to her.

Oh, I listen—I just refuse to be her robot.

It occurs to me that my window isn't just a window. It's a dusty, screen door to freedom. My mom and Bob might hear the floor boards creak if I tried to sneak out down the hall, but they would never expect I'd go out my window.

Window, window, window—door. My mind won't think anything else.

I drag my school backpack from beneath a pile of trash in my closet and empty it on the floor. I travel circles around my room, collecting things that I might need or can't leave behind. My brain won't think in straight lines. I have never packed to leave forever.

I stuff all the money I have in my pocket. I pile in clothes and a couple bottles of nail polish that drop to the bottom.

Bob soothes my mother, but of course, she won't stop sobbing. She lives for this.

I wedge my sketchbook inside the pack and stuff my drawing pencil box into the side pocket. Some underwear. An extra bra. A bottle of Bath & Body vanilla bean lotion. Two pairs of ankle socks. My night light, a blanket I've had since I was born. I squeeze in my little jewelry box on top, guarded by a broken ballerina who still tries to spin when I open the lid. It's all that will fit. The zipper teeth strain to close over my mouthful of belongings. I stuff my car keys in my pocket.

Balancing on the top of my dresser, I push out the window screen and fling it away. It lands in the grass without a sound.

Now I've got to leave if I don't want to get caught.

If I stay, I'll have to apologize to my mother. Agree that there's something wrong with me every time I don't agree with her.

Maybe go to boarding school. I'll have to promise to do everything she commands. But I've tried that and failed.

The only smart thing to do is escape.

I push my backpack out the window.

It tumbles off the edge of the roof and hits the ground with a thud. I freeze, listening to be sure my mom and Bob didn't hear it, but my mother is still sobbing and Bob is still reassuring her that he is going to straighten me out once and for all.

I climb over the window sill, onto the garage roof. The pitch is steep, but the gritty shingles stop me from sliding. I'm sure my skin has just turned fifty shades lighter than I've ever been. I'm scared to death of heights and even though I keep telling myself to jump down— it's not that far, it will only hurt a little—I can't.

Our next door neighbor's screen door swings open and I scuttle back, flattening myself against the siding of the house, my ankles slanted on the roof to keep me in place.

The Masnen's door hangs open for a hundred moments, while I hold my breath. Then I hear Mrs. Masnen's sharp voice, "Go all ready!"

I'm positive she is talking to me until Annie, the Masnen's raggedy old Lhasa apso, wiggles out the door, aided by the toe of Mrs. Masnen's house slipper. The door slams shut and Annie pauses on the walk. Through the tangles over her eyes, she spots my backpack, sniffs the air, and barks twice.

Mrs. Masnen shouts at her dog again, "Go!"

Annie waddles off with her tail wagging.

I can't stay up here any longer.

It's not so high up, I tell myself.

Be a spring.

Be a coil.

Be Tigger's tail.

I jump.

The ground comes up fast, but I'm too full of adrenaline to even feel the landing. I splat and hop up, grabbing my backpack and scurrying to my rusty Granada in the driveway. I throw my bag in the back seat.

No one comes running from the house as I start the car. I shoot out of the driveway and then gun it up the street, watching our mailbox get smaller in my rearview mirror. No one rushes out screaming for me to come back.

I'm not sure I feel anything until I'm passing under the expressway signs that guide me into Detroit, but it's then that I start to feel two things.

I feel seventeen.

And I feel scared to death about having no place in the world to go.

TWO

I flex my foot against the gas pedal.

At the ramp for the express way, I go west. The cars glide around me like we are caught in the same current. I am swept under sign after sign, all of them leading me into Detroit.

Having been raised on the petticoat fringe of the suburbs, getting closer to the city is terrifying. All my life, I've heard news stories of downtown Detroit. Drugs. Murder. Armed robberies. Whores. The city is filled with lowlifes that don't have the sense to choose anything better.

I grip the steering wheel and follow the gush of cars anyway. I just want to get lost, even though every rapist, junkie, and car jacker within city limits will know I don't belong there, just by the way I push down on the gas pedal at yellow lights, or peer across my dashboard at red ones. At least, that's what my mother would say when we visited downtown and she'd smoosh down in her seat, afraid to look out the window.

My reckless desire to be lost only holds up until I am ... lost. As fast as I go, I am barely keeping with the tide of traffic. They fly all around me.

When I see the city water tower, I take the Woodward exit and spill out into Royal Oak. Royal Oak at 11 Mile, has a fairy-dust ambience of safety blown over its artsy streets. Punk rockers and freaks on every corner, the little town is still on the verge—only separated by a flimsy strip of Ferndale from the Arab-saturated edges, and solid black blocks, of the ghetto.

But I get out on the boulevard, traveling through the main artery into the inner city. I inch in, mile by mile. I cross over 8 Mile and pass the State Fairgrounds where the news reported people shot during carnivals. Graffiti tags and metal bars spring up on store fronts. Grocery marts are replaced with corner liquor stores, and crumbling motels that blink hourly vacancies like shell-shocked casualties in the broad daylight.

Past 7 Mile, I take my foot off the gas. The cars have to slow down, jerking their brakes and honking at me as I coast toward a red light. The driver behind me lays on the horn and swings her car into the lane beside me. I glance over with a nervous smile and am met with a black woman's furious glare. With a flick of her wrist, she backhands the air over her dashboard. Her nostrils flare as she angrily mouths, "Bitch, GO!" to me before the light turns green and she speeds away.

Traffic is moving too fast and nothing here looks like home. Cars keep honking, drivers gunning it to get around me, flipping me off as they pass. I inch past light after light. I spot a motel on the opposite side of the street. I double back toward the burnt-brick building with the white shutters. A white, wrought iron balcony makes the place look like Scarlet O'Hara's plantation house. The building seems ancient, but the motel sign is one of the only ones I've seen without gaping holes in it. It says *Starlight Hotel* and beneath it is another sign, attached with chain links, advertising free triple X movies with every room. A sign taped in the front window promises reasonable weekly rates and it's not as dirty as the others, so I pull onto the side street and follow it around to the parking lot at the back.

I'm going to rent a room. I'm going to do it. I might be sick first.

I park in the tiny lot and turn off my engine. My mom and Bob will never think to look for me here. They'd be as afraid to come here as I am right now.

I throw open the door.

My backpack slung on my back, I throw open the door to the motel lobby. A shrieking alarm triggers, the sound erupting over my head, as loud and startling as the fire drills in elementary school. But, the moment the door slams shut, the thousand steel pots, beaten with a thousand metal spoons, goes silent.

The lobby is deserted and eerily quiet in the wake of the alarm. The adrenaline pumping through me screams, *get out of here*. My eyes gulp down everything in the lobby, without really seeing it, as I search and sift for imminent danger.

The place is empty, and instead of being seedy and creepy, it's clean and smells like fabric softener. The walls are the color of black cherry ice cream and a spotless, plum runner extends through the lobby like a celebrity carpet, leading to an ascending staircase. A fake fern drapes off the counter, and another leaks from the top of a snack machine. After the string of burnt out buildings on the way here, everything in this lobby is weirdly charming.

On my left is a line of useful machines: a pay phone set in a wood cubbyhole that suggests, but would not provide, privacy; a squat little box of an ice machine with a lopsided crown of plastic buckets. A fake fichus tree punctuates the line up, its branches smashed against the tall pop machine beside it. The fern-topped, snack machine is at the end, right before the stairs, with rows of metal, curlicue fingers clutching snacks behind glass.

To my right, one look at the counter, it's obvious that this is a counter that means business. As impenetrable as a highway guardrail, the monster takes up the entire right half of the lobby. Baked-bean brown and marbled with black veins and flecks of gold, it stands as high as my chest near the lobby door and only slightly lower at the payment window. The very center of the beast's back is embedded with a deep track, from which bullet-proof glass, at least a half-foot thick, extends all the way up to the vaulted ceiling. The office is wedged like a foxhole between the bulletproof barrier and a wall of tall windows that looks out at the oil change shop next door. Room keys, hung on a peg board inside the office, shiver on their hooks as heavy footsteps clomp down the stairs behind me.

"You just usin' the phone, or you lookin' to git a room?" A woman asks from above me. I step away from the counter and peer up the staircase to the first floor landing.

A black woman, more bottom than top and dressed in violet hospital scrubs, stares down at me. I'm frozen by her stare, although my blood is pulsing.

Her eyebrows rise. "Well?" she asks. "Whuch'ya gonna do?"

"A room...I think."

The woman sidesteps down the stairs. One foot goes down, the other joins it, and that's how she gets to the lobby floor. Once she's there, her nostrils flare like an exhausted horse. She drags a ring of keys from her purple cotton pocket and unlocks the office door. Once inside, she locks the door behind her, like I'm a criminal.

"So, okay," she wheezes. "Whu'chu wanna do?"

I stoop to speak into the trough.

"How much are the rooms, ma'am?" My eyes slide up to meet hers and the returned stare is stony, one eyebrow cocked over it. I can't tell if she is annoyed with, or confused by, me. Maybe I was too loud or not loud enough. Still hunched over near the trough, I raise my eyebrows, wondering which it is.

"You ain't gotta do dat." Her eyes flick to the trough. I scoot back and stand up straight again. She taps a round vent over the trough.

"This one here's fo' talkin'," she says. "Rooms is twenty-eight a night; eighteen fo' a short stay." Her eyes sweep over me and I

264

assume she sees my confusion again because she adds, "Short stay's three hours. You don't want no waterbed, do ya?"

"No," I shake my head. "I thought your sign said you rent by the week? How much is that?"

"It's one fitty a week."

"What does that include?"

"Include?" Her head swivels back, her whole face puckered. I've said something wrong again. "It *includes* housekeepin' once a week...towels, a bed, soap...whuch ya wan' it ta include?"

"I just didn't..." I let the words fade as I shift from foot to foot. "I'll take it, okay?"

She rolls her eyes, blowing out a sigh. "Ahright."

I stand there, not knowing what I need to do next, figuring renting a room is probably like going to the doctor's office. She'll probably give me papers to fill out and I wonder how she'll get them through the metal trough hole if she does. When I look up, she's staring at me.

"You gotta pay fo' it," she says flatly.

"Oh. Okay." I swing the backpack up from off the floor and unzip a front pocket. I wish I had more common sense to know what I was supposed to do, instead of always having to be told. I pull out my money, folded over so it looks like a thick, green wallet. Everything I've got equals about two weeks rent, maybe two and a half.

The woman's eyes dart to the door, then the stairs, and when her gaze returns to me, she looks angry.

"Ain't you got no sense, girl?" she hisses. She's leaning in toward the round slot now, so her voice is louder. "Put dat money back in yo' pocket. *Right now.*"

I do what she says and this time, my face feels as dark plum as the runner beneath my feet. I look up at her, wondering why she's mad and how she expects me to pay for the room with the money in my pocket.

Her expression is a little softer with the money hidden away, but she's shaking her head again. "You don't go flashin' no big stacks a' money roun' a place like dis! Ya only take out whachya need and *da's it*."

I nod my understanding. This time, I reach into my pocket and use my thumb and index finger to peel back bills, trying to count them as I do it. My eyes travel up the bulletproof glass to where it meets the ceiling. When I think I have the right amount, I pull out the money, keeping it in my palm like a magic trick. I nod to her, to let her know I have it, and she lets out another long sigh with another eye roll.

"Well, go on." She taps the shiny metal trough. I pass the green wad of bills through, clenched between my finger and thumb, but hit a glass partition in the center. It stops me from being able to just pass it straight across to her and it seems impolite to just push the stack over the top and let the bills spill out all over the desk on the other side. I don't want to make any more mistakes with her, so I wedge my wrist into the opening and crook my arm so that I can thread my fingers up over the center lip and pass her the bills pinched between my fingertips.

Once the money is bulging out on her side of the partition, the woman just stares at it, and then at my arm, wedged awkwardly through the slot. I smile at her and wiggle the bills so she can see that I'm making an effort to be helpful. My arm is starting to ache.

Her lips pull into a silent, sour whistle before she reaches out and takes the wad. She counts the bills I've given her in plain view.

"I need aotha' twenty," she says and shuffles through the bills again, so I can see that I'm short. I pull out another twenty and pass it to her, but this time I let the bill drop once I get my fingers over the partition. "An' a license."

I can't give her that. It won't read the right age. I blush as I lie to her, "I don't have it on me."

"Mmm," she eyes me knowingly as she flattens the bills into a drawer beneath the desk. "How old are ya?"

"I'm...uh...I'm eighteen," I tell her. She only glances back up, but I'm sure she can see the lie engraved on my head in bold, black just-turned-seventeen block print.

"Huh," she says as she takes out a pen and a wide, spiral-bound book. "Fine. It don't make no difference ta me. Jus' gimme yo' name." She sighs, spreading the book open on the desk.

"Lael," I say.

"Lael?" she repeats under a quirked, not-buying-it lip.

"Like...snail. Or fail," I tell her. "My mom's a hippie."

"Da's yo' firs' name? I jus' need yo' las'."

My hands are sweating. "Wallace. My name is Lael Wallace."

"Ahright," the woman says with a long look before she puts it on the paper. "Weeklies stay on da third floor. *Complimentary room cleanin' is included.* See dat lounge ova' there?" She points the pen straight out the side door of the office. I look in the direction she's pointing, but have to walk around the corner to see what she's actually pointing at.

There is a walkway I hadn't noticed at the end of the counter. In the middle of it is another staircase leading down to a bottom floor, and just past it is an opening into the room she's calling the lounge. I follow the walkway and look in.

The lounge has a saggy couch on the outer wall and a fridge and microwave across from it. At the far end of the room is a door to the boulevard with a red bar across it that says EMERGENCIES ONLY. Paper signs are taped all over the windows, blocking the daylight with advertisements for triple X movies, cheap rates, clean rooms, new management.

I'm pretty sure I've seen everything I was supposed to when I hear the woman clear her throat from behind the office door. I return to the counter and she is glowering at me from behind the thick glass. I've screwed up again.

"I saw the lounge," I tell her. She stares at me like she's trying to wrap her head around what I'm saying. I let my shoulders rise and fall in a loose shrug, unsure of what I've done to disappoint her again.

"Yeah, ya did," is all she says. "Weeklies can use the fridge and microwave ova' there. Mark yo' food, but we ain't respons'ble fo' anythin' dat go missin'. Clean up afta' yo'self too."

"Okay," I say. "Thank you."

That seems to throw her. She rolls her tongue in her cheek.

"Where you from?" she asks and then, just as quick, she shakes her head. "Neva'mine. You welcome." She takes a key off the pegboard behind her. "I'll show ya yo' room."

"Okay." I say and again, "Thank you."

"Uh huh." It doesn't impress her this time. She takes the key in her palm and unlocks the office door, steps out, and locks it up again from the outside. She tries it once and when it doesn't open, she stuffs her ring of keys into a pocket where I am surprised they fit.

As we climb the stairs together, the woman is quiet except for her labored breathing.

"What's your name?" I ask when she pauses on the second landing to catch her breath. The landing extends further out, creating a little alcove that is blocked by the stairway rail. A fake fern droops over the edge of the jutting ledge and if I lean a little over the rail, I can see the entire length of the lounge below.

"Name's Lavina," the woman pants. "I clean da rooms. And don't go leanin' on dat rail too much. Ain't nothin' too sturdy roun' here."

It starts sinking in that I'm really staying here as we reach the top floor. A tingle of anxiety shivers my spine. I rented a room for a whole week. I'm not going home. Part of me wants to race down the stairs and back to my car, but the other part just wants Lavina to hurry up, so I can see my first 'place'. However, Lavina goes up the stairs the same way she came down, so it takes a while to get to the next level, which opens to the third floor.

Electric romance-lighting flickers from wall sconces, turning the deep plum carpet the color of a seasoned bruise. Lavina waddles down the hall in her purple hospital scrubs, her thick hips swaying like a violet hippo, to the very last door on the right.

"If there eva' a fire, dat door dere is da emergency stairs." She waves a hand to a recessed door across the hall. "It goes down ta tha groun' floor. I'd jus' use the reg'lar stairs if I was you though. Them emergency stairs ain't lit good and God knows what's walkin' round in dat stairwell at any minute."

Deep in the recessed hall, I imagine the dark ear of a shadow pressed to the other side of the emergency door, listening to us right now. The shadow waits for Lavina to turn away, so it can reach through the door and pull me into the stairwell, quick as a spider. Another shiver rolls through me, and this time Lavina sees it. She flattens out her brow. Her glare wipes all the shadows from my imagination, and for a second I'm more afraid of Lavina than what could ever be hiding in a stairwell.

"Jus' stick wit' the reg'lar stairs," she says. She rattles the room key into the door knob and swings the metal door open. She shuffles into the pitch-black room while I stand frozen in the hallway like a moron. She pops on the bathroom light and calls over her shoulder, "You comin'?"

Years later, I'm sure I will think of this room as a very standard room, but at the moment, in my mind, it's my first apartment. I have paid the rent and, from wall to wall, this place is all mine for now. Well, at least for a whole week. Being mine stretches the four walls so much, this room is a mansion to me.

Lavina flicks on the bedroom light and I step inside.

The bathroom to my left is pristine. It is white, with white walls and a white tiled floor, a white bathtub, and a white shower curtain, a white counter, and a white toilet and sink. White towels and washcloths are stacked on a slatted, silver shelf. Besides the silver faucets, mirror, and shelf, everything else is blindingly white.

"You done in there? I got thin's dat need doin'." Lavina's voice is impatient.

"Sorry. It's just so..." As I come into the bedroom, I can't control the grin spreading across my face.

"What?" Lavina asks.

I throw out my arms. "It's beautiful!"

"Pshh..." She rolls her eyes.

The bed is huge, compared to the twin size I have at home. The thin bedspread is tucked around two pillows at the head; it reminds me of my boobs in a tube top. There is a dresser on the wall opposite the foot of the bed, with six wide drawers and a huge mirror on top. It's screwed to the wall. I run my hand over a drawer handle, wanting Lavina to leave so I can inspect my new 'home' by myself. A television set is attached to a high wall platform and slanted so the best view is from the bed.

Lavina goes past me to the window, pulling a silver chain that opens the blinds. As the slats scoot open, the motel sign looms right outside. I could probably reach out and swing the Triple X sign that dangles from the bottom on a chain.

"If dat sign botha's ya any—" Lavina starts.

I cut her off. "It doesn't."

She doesn't need to know I'm afraid of the dark. She really doesn't need to know how carefully I packed my night light and that it is slung over my shoulder right now, along with my ratty receiving blanket and a box full of jewelry that turns my skin green if it gets wet. All she needs to know is that I'm a grown-up who just rented her very own room.

I look down on the boulevard from my new castle view. All sorts of garbage is blown up against the curb. Cars race by, sending discarded burger wrappers and sheets of shredded newspaper flying like tattered fairy wings. A woman dressed in a ratty, winter coat pushes a rickety grocery cart filled with garbage bags and returnable bottles down the cracked sidewalk.

I suck in a breath. This is my home for the next week.

I am Rapunzel now, with short hair.

"Dis one's tha *on* button fo' da TV," Lavina begins, but I'm barely hearing her instructions as she explains the TV remote and how to use the phone.

I shake off the vision of the dirty street outside and the excited tingle returns. This place is mine. I want Lavina to leave so that I can open all the drawers and put my stuff in them. I have to fight the urge to dump out my backpack on the bed while she's still talking.

She says something about the coffee pot downstairs and when I have to pay rent for the next week. Rent. I'm a girl who pays rent.

She opens a metal flap on top of the metal box beneath the window and says something about the dials and I nod, but don't hear a word. It is like listening to Bob talk about tire pressure after I'd just got my first set of car keys in my hand. I just want Lavina to leave so I can jump on the bed.

"There's three locks on da door," she goes on, bustling over to the door. She demonstrates as she instructs. "Da knob locks up on it own, but ya gotta turn tha dead bolt yo'self, and there's a chain ya slide inta dis track here at the top..."

"I'll figure it out," I say with a grin and she smirks.

"You fo' sho' *now*, ain't ya? Ah right, then. I'm roun' if ya need anythin'."

The metal door clangs behind her. I am almost dizzy with the joy of it, my own place, my very own. I put my forehead on the closed door, my eyes shut. No one can come into this room and tell me what to do, when to do it, what to say, or what not to say. I can eat in bed, I can watch TV whenever I want, I can make a person *leave*. And I want to remember the very first moment that I turn around, open my eyes, and see my very first place.

I take a deep breath and slide my forehead across the door, ready to turn for that first look. But I brush up against something that moves.

Images of fingers and spiders shoot through my head as I gasp and push myself away from whatever touched me. I open my eyes to the chain, dangling off the door frame. It swings like a hangman's rope, or like it is trying to throw itself into the empty artery of the lock.

I take the cold end of it in my hand. The chain makes a gritty sound as I push the worn nub into the track. I turn the deadbolt with a heavy clunk. I wonder if I will ever get used to locking all these locks when, at home, we never bothered to lock our front door.

This is my home now. Behind three locks and a metal door.

I clear my throat. The sound doesn't echo, it falls. The dark carpet eats it whole and then there is only the hum of the florescent light from the bathroom. I flatten my back against the icy door of a place that already seems much smaller than it did moments ago. It smells like vacuumed carpet.

Instead of running and jumping on the bed, I sit down on it with my backpack nestled between my ankles as where I am sinks in. I think I'm going to be sick.

I try telling myself that it will not be too dark at night.

I remind myself that there are three locks on the door.

I tell myself that I am an adult now.

I can do this, I say.

I repeat it out loud. Twice.

Then I hunch forward over my knees and cry.

I put my clothes in the dresser drawers while a thousand disconnected thoughts spill around my head.

Why didn't I bring my pink shirt?

If someone knocks on the door, do I answer?

Where am I going to get a job?

What about my Senior year of high school?

Are the police going to come looking for me?

How many people are going to be raped or murdered in the city tonight?

Will I hear it happen?

Am I absolutely positive the locks are all locked?

Do my parents even know I'm gone yet?

The concerns flow in a stream, but gather in a flood that water-logs me. Each fear bounces to the surface, then pushes aside to make room for the next. My optimism sinks, dragging my heart down with it.

Why didn't I grab that pink shirt?

I pick up the remote and flip away from the news. I click past a dopey sitcom and land on channel three. A woman screams from the speaker and I nearly drop the remote. On screen, a naked man spreads the woman's legs wide open. She's not exactly screaming in pain. She throws her head back and grunts as the man mounts her. She talks about the size of his penis as it slides into her, center screen. Porn. On the TV. The remote bounces off my foot and onto the carpet.

I've never seen porn before. At seventeen, my mother always explained me to friends as a 'late bloomer'. I even overheard my mother's friend refer to me as 'shielded'. I thought all their labels made me sound clueless, but I've read books, and had health class, and I've even had boyfriends. I've been kissed. I've been fingered. But all the movies I've seen always spotlight how important it is to the guy that the girl is a virgin on their wedding night. It's romantic. I'm saving myself for the right one.

Yes, it's all that. And I'm scared to death of actually doing it.

Even though I'm blushing, I can't look away from what's happening on the TV screen. How it's happening. None of the books I've read could detail what it's like the way this does on the screen.

The man drives his penis into the woman. She stops screaming and starts cooing like he's singing her a lullaby instead of pounding against her so hard that her hair bounces. She seems to like it. The shot switches from their full bodies to a close up of his penis, stiff as a baseball bat, ramming through her pink folds.

273

I get hot between my own legs.

They change positions. She's on top of him now, pointed out toward the camera, her heels balanced on his thighs, her legs spread open like butterfly wings. I can see everything.

It's embarrassing.

And hot.

I have no idea what to do about the pulsing ache between my legs. It's as if my heart has slipped down between my thighs and is running for its life. I've felt that before—that pounding beat—but I've never been able to relieve it.

I switch off the TV.

And turn it right back on.

I stare at the screen. My buttons just aren't pushable, it seems, but this pulse is going to kill me.

I switch off the TV and drop down on the carpet beside the bed. I do 300 sit-ups without stopping, until my tail bone aches and my burning abs calm the drumming between my legs. Wet with sweat, I change into my pajamas—a tank top and shorts.

I lay there until my heartbeat finally returns to normal. My stomach rumbles. I didn't eat dinner before I left home.

It's dark outside and the hotel sign kicks on, illuminating my room with a glow through the open blinds. I close them and it blocks out the sign pretty well, but it leaves the room spooky dark. I turn on the lights and my stomach growls again, like it's chewing on itself.

I'm afraid to unlock the three locks, but I'm starving and there were vending machines in the lobby. I take the room key Lavina left me, dig three bucks out of the backpack I've hidden under the bed, slide the chain out of the track on the door, and unlatch the deadbolt with a clunk.

Before I can get the door open, a man in the hall shouts, "I ain't fightin' with you no more!"

I twist the lock back to where it was, thunking it into place. My stomach growls again and it makes me angry. I go to the bed, sit on the edge, and pick up the phone. I can't remember what Lavina told me, so I press "0".

"Front desk," a man's voice says. I kind of expected Lavina, so I stammer a minute, scrambling to find words.

"I...uh...I wanted to make a call."

"Press 5, and then 1, if it's long distance, and then the phone number." The guy sounds bored.

I nod, like he can see it. "Okay, thanks."

"Uh huh." He hangs up.

I dial 5 and 1 and punch in the number which has always meant home. My mother answers on the first ring.

"Hello?" Her voice is high and stringy, not like she's been crying, but like she's annoyed.

"It's me," I say.

"You better get home right now, young lady. You think it's okay to jump out a window? The things you said to me were unacceptable!"

"Bob pushing me around isn't acceptable either."

"You have ten minutes to get back here!"

"Or what?" I say. She puffs and chuffs on the other end. Ha. I really got her. She has no idea what to say and she doesn't know where I am. Ten minutes? Yeah, right. It would take me 45 minutes and that would only be if the streetlights were green all the way.

"You're already grounded," she bristles. "Don't make this worse than it already is."

"We're sending her to fucking boot camp!" Bob shouts in the background.

"Tell Bob he can go fuck himself!" I shout into the mouthpiece. "I'm never coming home."

I slam the receiver down on the cradle, hoping it will ring in her ears all night long. I grab my room key and without bothering to put my shoes on, I go to the door, flinging open the locks.

THREE

I stomp down the empty hallway in my bare feet, the carpet coarse beneath my toes. Thieves, rapists, murderers, and every other criminal I've ever seen on the news...they could all be waiting for me outside my room. And I don't care.

I shoot down the stairs and the landings fearlessly. In the back of my head, I'm almost hoping that I run into trouble, because nothing can hurt me with all this adrenaline pumping through my blood. I'm sure of it.

On top of my roaring heartbeat, what's pounding in my brain is how my mom said I'm already grounded. Like I'm still the little kid she used to shove into the time-out chair. I'm vibrating with how I told her that Bob could go fuck himself.

I should've told her they both could.

I step onto the lobby floor like I own the place.

"What the hell do you think you're doing down here like that?" a man barks from the office. It's muffled by the bullet proof glass, but the startling sound of him drains every drop of adrenaline from me as I spin around to see who's talking.

A guy in a grungy plaid shirt glares at me from behind the high edge of the counter. His face is a round, rotted squash, with angry, red acne scars pitted in his cheeks. From the looks of the harsh furrow in his brow, he probably spends a lot of time scowling.

I stop dead. "Are you talking to me?"

"Who else would I be talking to?" he growls, standing up from his chair. His eyes straggle down my body, stalling on my boobs. "Lavina told me a little redneck from the sticks moved in here today. Guess she wasn't kidding, huh? You must be Lael Wallace, room 46. Paid in full. I'm Ned." He leans toward his side of the glass partition, eyes plunging into my cleavage best they can. He grins.

I cross my arms over my chest. My pajamas suddenly seem

scandalous. The spaghetti straps too flimsy, the shorts too short. I notice my nipples rubbing against the fabric and my face heats.

He glances at my face. "You want change for the vending machine?"

I stand there, staring back at him, clutching my dollars in my palm the way Lavina told me to—my second magic trick of the day. Were all those insults his way of joking? I can't tell, now that he's softened his tone. Maybe I misunderstood him. Maybe making me feel like a roach is his way of being funny.

When I don't move, he jabs a finger toward the metal trough. But his brow has smoothed out. Either he's really bad at joking, or he thinks I'm stupid. Maybe it's both.

"Well, come on then!" he says. "I don't got all night. Put it in already." He half-laughs, flicking his fingernails against the glass like he's bored.

My stomach snarls as I step closer to the counter. I don't twist my arm into the slot this time, but shove the bills in, up and over the lip in the center, letting them spill out on his side.

He picks up the crunched roll of singles, pulling them apart and smoothing them out.

"Sweaty," he notes with a creepy grin. He deposits the bills in the drawer under the desk, and counts out three bucks worth of quarters. He drops the coins, one by one over the lip, but as they hit the trough, they roll out in all directions and roll across the counter. I try to catch them before they go off the edge. A couple hit the floor anyway and I scramble to trap them beneath my bare feet so they don't roll under the machines. When I stand up with eight coins in my hand, I catch Ned with his forehead pressed against the glass, staring down the sagging front of my tank top.

I slap my hand holding my room key over the center of my shirt, trying to block the pervert's gaze.

He waggles his wiry eyebrows at me, dropping the last of my change through the slot. "No bra. Niiice."

I block the coins from rolling away this time, slapping my free arm down on top of them, but I have to fit them all in one fist because the other is still shielding my boobs. Once I've got them, I glare at the guy behind the glass.

He chuckles, like I'm a lame joke and he's being generous.

I turn my back to him and shove the quarters into the machines. My butt and legs are on fire as if his stare is a magnifying glass aiming a laser of sun on them.

A can of Coke drops into the chute with a thunk and a cellophane-wrapped package of Suzi Q cakes drop into the bottom of the vending machine. I squat to open the door flap, scooping out the cakes as the office door knob jiggles behind me. Ned is coming out.

I grab my Coke and shoot up the stairs, taking the steps two at a time. I am already on the second landing when he shouts up, "You dress like that around here and the least you're gonna get is stared at!"

I sprint down the third floor hall to my room, my heart racing like the white rabbit racing down his hole.

I fight the key into the knob and drop my Coke as I fumble to get the door shut. I lock all three locks.

Breathing hard, I back away from the door as a sob struggles up through my pinched throat. The cellophane cake package is stuck to my fingers, the cakes smashed in my fist.

FOUR

I wake every hour throughout the night—when a door slams, when a woman howls, when a car honks on the boulevard, and when nothing happens at all. I wake up and stare at the red-numbered alarm clock, bolted to the side table. The hotel sign outside my window illuminates the room with a murky glow.

The room is sweltering hot, but I'm still too freaked out to get out of bed and turn on the air. I figure if I don't make a sound, no one will know I'm even here.

As the sun finally rises, I am triumphant. I'm still here. I'm tougher than I thought and my courage builds, the brighter it gets outside. The sun takes over and snuffs out the hotel sign. I re-check the door locks once more and change into my other pair of shorts and a fresh t-shirt. I wish I'd brought more clothes.

It's after eight now. Thursday. That means my mom and Bob should be at work, which also means I might be able to sneak home and get some of my stuff. They might be standing guard or have already changed the locks, but it still might be worth a try.

I'm starving again. That feeds my bravery too.

I could take Ned on now in the bright shine of the day. Lavina's probably here too, and I don't think she's going to be very happy knowing how he treated me. She seems protective like that—like this is her hotel and I am her customer, even if she is just the maid. I'll bet she gives Ned what and for when I tell her what happened.

But the thing I'm most proud of, what is singing in my veins, is that I made it through the whole night. The monsters that shouted and slammed doors, groaned and banged headboards all night— they must all be sleeping now.

I pull open my room door like nothing can cut me down. And just like I thought, the place is a morgue. I make my way down to the snack machines in dead silence.

Breakfast is two packages of neon orange crackers with a smear of fake cheese between them, and a can of root beer to wash it down. Lavina startles me before I have a chance to grab the pop out of the machine chute.

"Well, good mornin'," she says. She's wearing slate blue scrubs today and continues on her way, bustling past me and side-stepping down the stairs toward the lobby. Over her shoulder, between pants, she asks, "Was yo room good?"

"No," I say.

She pauses, but I'm not sure if it's to talk to me or to catch her breath. "No? How's that? What's wrong wich'ya room?"

"I guess it's not the room, it was the guy at the front desk last night."

She gives one nod and continues down the stairs. Still clutching my can of root beer, I follow her down to the lobby and then down the steps leading to the basement level. I want her to know about Ned. She turns down a dark, narrow hall on the left and waddles off into the shadows. I don't follow. It's as black as a cave.

A naked light bulb clicks on and I glimpse Lavina taking a left into another dark room. Another light pops on.

The smell of fabric softener billows up as I follow down the hall and turn the corner, into a laundry room. Three washers and four dryers—non-industrial, just like ours at home—line the walls, and at the far end, towers of folded towels and sheets are stacked on top of a wood board suspended on cinderblocks. Lavina goes to a unit of raw, metal shelving filled with bottles and cans of cleaners. "Now who was it give you trouble las' night?" Lavina gives me a long, knowing look. "Or is it jus' that you homesick? This is yo firs' time out, ain't it? You missin' yo' mama?."

It strikes a nerve. Deep. I expected her to be on my side, to be fired up and ready to kill Ned, but she's acting like whatever happened was just because I'm a child.

"No," I snap, "I'm not a baby. My problem was with the guy behind the desk. Ned."

"Oh yeah? What he do now?" Lavina asks, but she's not all that interested. She's busy sorting through the cleaners on the shelf. When I don't answer, she doesn't ask. She doesn't say anything until she's got her bottle of blue liquid in her hand and is making her way toward the laundry room door where I'm standing, blocking the exit. "Well?" Her eyebrows peak. "You gonna say what he done to ya, or you just gonna stand there an' keep me from doin' mah job?"

I move and she walks past. I scramble to follow her once she turns off the light and the whole laundry room goes black. All I want to do is explain what happened with Ned, how he was looking down my shirt and kept tossing the coins through the window slot so they'd roll away. I want her to be on my side. But it all sounds like tattling now that she's accused me of missing my mother.

"Ned's rude." I tell her.

Lavina goes up the steps to the ground floor, across the lobby, and up the second flight without a word. I follow behind her, listening to her breathe. Her nostrils flare like a bull.

"He's really rude," I repeat.

"He rude," she puffs. "I heard ya."

Why am I still following her? She doesn't seem to care what I'm saying at all. But there is nothing for me to do but go back to my room and sit alone. Maybe watch porn again. I could do that.

"So...what'd he say to ya?" Lavina stops in front of her cleaning cart parked in the middle of the hall. She grabs a roll of paper towel and goes into the room beside it. "I swear, girl...talkin' to you's like pullin' teef!"

"He's a pervert," I say, leaning in on the doorway frame. She squirts window cleaner all over the dresser mirror. The bed is messy, but otherwise, the room looks clean. The mirror was already spotless. "He dumped my money in the slot so it rolled out all over the floor and he could look down my shirt."

After a moment of thought, she nods. "Yeah, that sounds like Ned. I'll talk to 'im. Pro'lly won't do nothin' though. He got a nasty way 'bout 'im sometimes, but if he don't listen, I'll be sure to talk wit' Clive too. Dat make you happy?"

Kind of insulting, but yeah. "Who's Clive?"

Lavina pauses at the mirror. Stares at me like I'm an idiot. "Jus' the owner of dis' hotel." She *huhs* and goes back to wiping the glass.

Was I supposed to know that?

Lavina shifts gears and changes the subject. "So how come a white girl like you's lef' da country to live down here and live in the ghetto?" Lavina asks just as the lobby door alarm goes off. I flinch at the screech, but Lavina just pulls away from the mirror and throws down the soggy paper towel on the dresser top.

"Ain't nobody kin come in while I'm still downstairs, now ken they?" she grumbles. I jump out of her way, so she doesn't mow me over walking out of the room. She goes down the hall, her enormous hips cycling like mammoth bike pedals.

With nothing else to do, and her interest in me finally showing, I decide to follow along behind her again. She harumphs her way down the steps, but Lavina groans the minute she hits the lobby floor.

"C'mon now...not you ag'in!" she says.

A giant woman is standing in the lobby, wearing a cornflower-print dress with a frilly bodice that reminds me of my grandmother. So do the woman's beige, thick-soled heels. The difference is that this woman is at least six foot three, with skin as dark as a Friar plum and red-blond hair that seems to shift when she turns her face toward Lavina and me.

I gape the minute I get a good look at her.

She is not a *she* at all. *She* is definitely and unmistakably, a *he*.

A thick, five o'clock shadow conceals his cheeks, although it's only about nine in the morning. The wig slapped on his head drips synthetic curls down his temples and over the top of his wiry, black sideburns. I've never seen anything like this. Back home, a man dressing up in old lady clothes would be carted off to the hospital for treatment.

"Lavina! Baby!" the man squeals beneath his trembling wig. His voice is as deep as a well, but he delivers his words with the same flair a woman would. I can't stop staring.

Lavina isn't caught up on the details of him the way I am. She just scowls at him.

"Donch'ya *baby* me, Yolanda," she scolds as she rises up on tiptoes to look out the front door at the parking lot. When she goes flat again, she turns and glances over her shoulder, up the stairs. The scowl is still firm when she looks back at Yolanda. "You know you ain't s'pose to be in here when Clive could catch ya!"

"I didn't see his car," Yolanda explains, raking his long fingers through his wig. I'm shocked it stays in place. "So he in't here, is 'e?"

"He could pull up any second," Lavina growls, yanking the office keys out of her pocket. Once she's in the office with the door locked behind her, she leans close to the speaking vent in the glass. "So whuch'ya want, Yoyo? A night? A week?"

Yolanda's snaggle-toothed smile is grisly, but his reply is sweetly feminine. "A week, please, darlin'."

"An' you know you gotta stay outta sight," Lavina adds the reminder, still holding tight to her scowl. Her eyes dart to the front door and back.

"I know, baby," Yolanda says.

"Donch'ya fo'git now, this could cos' me mah job, if he catch you."

"He ain't gonna catch me again, sweetie, I promise you that. He bust off my tooth that las' time, remember?" Yolanda opens wide, pointing to the jagged, half tooth in the front of his mouth. "And I still din't tell him it was you who got me that room, now did I?"

Lavina sighs, motioning for Yolanda to send the money through the slot.

He glances out the front door again before pulling a wad of cash from the frills guarding his cleavage. He licks his finger, smearing it with purple lipstick, and fingers through the bills gingerly. It ends with a frown.

"Hang on now," Yolanda murmurs and then hikes his dress up to his hip, fishing around in the elastic waist band of his panty hose for more cash. I can see his shiny, purple panties and the thick club of his penis wedged in them. It's compressed against his body. He catches me looking and flashes me his gap-tooth, busted up smile as he drops the hem of his dress back around his knees.

He passes the cash to Lavina through the slot and flicks his stubbly chin in my direction. "This one a friend of yours?"

Lavina barely glances up. "She a new weekly."

"Oh, a neighbor!" Yolanda squeals again and sticks out his hand for me to shake. "Nice to meech'ya, honey. I'm Yolanda."

I'm not sure what to do with Yolanda's extended hand. I've seen news stories about junkies, car jackers, hookers, and murderers, but no one like Yolanda. All I know about Detroit is that the news, and my mom, and Bob, and our neighbors, and everyone I know says the same thing: Detroit is full of dangerous criminals and freaks. Yolanda must be what they meant by *freak*. Bob always says the people here would kill you as soon as scratch their head, so I'm not sure what Yolanda's going to do once he gets ahold of my hand. I don't really want to touch him; I don't even know what he is.

But he towers over me, and as his hand hangs there and his smile fades, what my mother taught me overrides everything else in my head. She taught me to always be polite, no matter what.

I put my quivering hand in Yolanda's, sure he's going to feel the tremor of my nerves. I hope he doesn't kill me for it. Instead, Yolanda's smile breaks wide open as he nearly crushes my bones. He shakes hands like a big man too.

"What's yo' name, sweetie?" he asks.

"Uh...Lael."

"Lael? I don't think I ever heard that name before." His eyes wander out the front door and scan the parking lot one more time.

"I know," I say. "It's a weird name."

"Naw, not weird. It's pretty." Yolanda shoots me a gap-toothed grin as Lavina drops a room key in the slot. It's only then that he lets go of my hand.

"Rememba now," Lavina shakes her finger at him, "stay outta

Clive's way, or botha us is gonna be in trouble, an' I ain't 'bout ta lose my job 'cause a you."

"You ain't gotta tell me twice, girl." Yolanda plucks the key from the slot. He brushes past me, heading up the stairs. He doesn't have any luggage. Over his shoulder he says, "I don't need no more busted teef."

I'm standing, mesmerized by Yolanda, when the door siren wails again and another customer throws open the front door.

A white woman, stick thin and tiny, comes in first. A black kid, only a thread shorter than her and with messed up glasses, trails behind. She holds the door for him, the alarm screeching as she curses and barks, "Jesus Christ, get the fuck in here, Will...now."

When the kid finally fumbles over the threshold, she mumbles good boy and lets go of the door. I think she's the mom and he's her son, but they're different colors.

I can't help but stare at the two of them. Side by side, they are strange, sharing almost the exact same height and weight, but one is black and one is white. I've never seen that before. She has a delicate nose, he has a broad one, but their eyes and lips are the same, even if his look ten times larger behind the thick, glass lenses. She's weathered and pale, with blond hair that is so dry it looks fuzzy. He is a sallow brown, with kinks of black hair shaved close to his skull and glasses bandaged all over with tape. He chomps a hunk of gum with his mouth open.

The woman pauses at the edge of the counter while the kid sticks to the opposite side of the lobby, sliding his shoulder against the front of the machines until he reaches the wide window of the snack vendor. He flips over, pressing his back against the machine. He stands there, working over his juicy mouthful of gum, only pausing when he has to gulp down the sticky overflow of saliva. He's got way too much gum to do anything but chew like a beast. When he sees me watching him, all the joy in chomping escalates. He chomps and swallows and smacks his lips even harder.

Lavina's eyes settle on the woman after a quick glance at the kid, and she tips her chin only just enough that I think she's telling me to pay attention to the two newcomers. I step back toward the stairs, making room for them at the transaction window.

The woman steps up to the window and dumps her loose, liver-shaped purse on the counter. I could probably stare at them all day, since the boy seems delighted in me noticing him and the woman seems oblivious to it.

"How much is a room?" she asks, leaning toward the window vent on her tiptoes. I see now that her mascara has had time to drain off her lashes and onto the puffy pillows beneath her eyes. She pushes back her hair, but her bangs stick to her forehead.

The kid inches closer to me, squeezing into the space between his mother and I. He pivots toward me on a dirty sneaker and when I meet his gaze, he freezes like a mannequin—one arm up and bent at the elbow, the other at his waist. He stays that way, his dead stare fixed on my forehead.

He holds steady until I look away. From my peripheral, I see him quickly change positions, widening his stance and slumping his torso to one side. His body is rigid, but he lets his arms swing at the elbows like a busted robot.

"Fo' how many?" Lavina asks.

"Me an' my kid," the woman says. "He's ten."

"Twenty eight a night fo' tha single. Thirty fo' tha double. Thirty-six fo' a waterbed," Lavina tells the woman.

The woman feels through her pockets, all of them, one at a time and then back through the cycle again, as if she can't find her money. "How much for a week?"

"One fitty," Lavina says.

"We want a week." The woman drops her hands from her pockets and reaches for her purse, unzipping it and poking around under the surface.

I glance at the kid again. He's still swinging his arms.

"Quit the robot shit," his mother snaps when she sees me looking. He falls out of it into a stoop, but keeps pumping his gum as his mother pushes the money through the slot to Lavina. "I'll pay the single rate now and bring you the rest tonight. I can do that, right?"

Lavina shrugs. "Sho'. Long as you git it ta me 'fo you s'pose ta check out tommor'ah." She puts her hands on her thighs and pushes herself to her feet. "Check out's eleven tomorr'ah mornin' if you ain't paid the rest. An' I'm gonna need a license."

The woman doesn't even look in her purse.

"I don't have no license. Can you use a Food Mart card?"

"It got yo' name an' face on it?" Lavina asks. When I told her I didn't have a license, she just wrote down my name, but Lavina seems determined to have more from this woman.

"No. Just a name."

"Whuch you got wit' yo' name and face on it?"

The woman groans as she digs through her bag. She comes up with a blue, plastic coated card. "I got a MovieBuster card. That's it. There ain't a picture on it, but it's me."

"I need somethin' wit' a pi'ture."

"I don't have nothin'." The woman waves the card in the air. "I swear it's me, alright? Can't you just take that?"

"I ain't s'posed to fo' weeklies." Lavina lets out a long, annoyed sigh before tapping the tips of her fingers into her palm, signaling the woman to pass the card through the slot. "C'mon. Give it here."

"Thanks." The woman shoves the card through the slot. Lavina takes it and turns it over twice in her palm as though she's still not sure.

"It's me," the woman insists. "Penny Grayson. I swear it's me."

"I believe ya. It's one fitty fo' da week," Lavina says, but her expression says she doesn't believe any of it. She takes a pen from the desk and writes down the woman's information in the big spiral book as the woman passes the bills she's counted twice through the payment slot. The kid scoots over toward the snack machine, punching all the numbers and checking the coin return.

"He a retard?" Lavina whispers to the mother. Lavina keeps her chin dipped toward her chest, just like the tone of her voice, but the boy turns from the machine as soon as she says it.

"You a fat nigger?" the kid asks her, shoving his glasses up on the bridge of his nose.

Lavina stares at him so hotly, I expect the kid to burst into flames. He doesn't. He stands there, staring back at her, his eyes magnified as big as tennis balls behind his taped-up, paper-clip-rigged glasses.

Lavina's gaze switches to the kid's mother. "You let yo' chil'ren talk like dat?" she says.

Penny Grayson replies flatly, "He can talk however he wants to anybody that come at him like that. He didn't call you retard."

Lavina doesn't touch the bills in the payment slot. "That might be, but you wanna rent a room from me. Not tha otha' way 'round."

The woman's chin juts, her teeth combing her upper lip. She turns to her son. "Will, don't you call this woman a nigger. If she calls you a retard again, you just call her a big, dumb bitch, but don't you call her a nigger. That ain't nice."

Lavina reaches forward and takes the money, straightening the wrinkles out of the cash before she slips it in the drawer. She drops a room key into the trough.

The woman grabs it and swings around, heading for the stairs, hoisting her purse over her shoulder. She doesn't call for her kid to follow, but stomps as she goes up.

I meet Lavina's gaze just as I hear the pop can I'd left sitting in the chute behind me being lifted out of the machine. I turn to see the kid holding my can of root beer.

"That's mine!" I say. The kid's mother is already up on the third floor. The kid slinks toward the stairs holding my can with both hands.

"Hey!" I step toward him. "I paid for that!"

The kid turns around and stares at me with his empty, robot face. He feels for the step behind him with the toe of his filthy, flapping sneaker. When he locates the bottom step, he puts his foot on it and backs his way up the stairs.

"Are you deaf? I said that's mine." I say again, pointing to the drink in his hand.

The kid just shakes his head at me, expressionless, as he retreats up to the third step.

"I found it," he says.

"This ain't no treasure hunt," Lavina shouts to him from the office. "You *foun' it* 'cause she jus' *bought it*. That don't make it yours."

The kid freezes on the step, staring at me. He's got a weak chin that dangles so I can see the enormous wad of gum stuffed in his cheek. His hands stay tight on my pop can. I know he's not giving it back to me. Not if I can't catch him and I know I can't. From the looks of him, I assume he's got a history of being fast.

I sigh and sweep him away with one hand.

"Just take it."

The kid doesn't wait for me to say it again. He turns and shoots up the steps with my root beer clutched to his chest.

"You could've said thank you!" I shout after him, but all I hear are his sneakers making a fast get away. They sound every bit as fast as I expected too.

I look back at Lavina. Her lips are pursed.

"Now what'd ya go an' do dat fo'?" she says.

"I wasn't going to get it back."

"He a punk kid! You jus' gonna let 'im steal yo stuff like dat?"

"I was trying to do something nice."

"Dat wasn't doin' somethin' nice! Dat was plain ol' givin' in. Watch now, 'cause dat kid's gonna cause you all kinds'a trouble 'cause he knows you jus' gonna let him. Jus' you watch."

"He probably never gets anything like that."

"Naw, dat ain't all there is to 'im. He a thief."

I hate how she's talking to me like I should know better. I turn away to roll my eyes and head upstairs.

Rounding the corner to the third floor, the kid is squatted on his heels outside Room 36's closed door. Arms hanging between his knees, he's drinking my root beer with both hands around the can. The second he sees me, he pauses as if I'm going to try to wrestle it away from him. When I don't, he goes back to it, gulping it down as he stares at me over the rim of the can.

"I hope it's good," I tell him. I'm even angrier with him since Lavina barked at me.

He keeps on drinking.

I'm a few feet down the hall when I hear him hum his response behind me. "*Mmm mmm!*"

I just ignore it and keep walking. At my room door, I do the careful, ritual look over my shoulder to make sure no one's standing in the recessed hallway behind me. There's never been anyone there, but it always feels like there is. I glance at the kid down the hall.

He's standing now, with my empty pop can lying at his feet. He's dangling at the waist like a busted robot again. His forearms swing like dead men hung from trees.

I go into my room and lock the door behind me.

I've made it through another night, but I'm exhausted in the morning because I still couldn't sleep with all the strange noises outside my room. It's like groundhog day—I get crackers and pop from the vending machines and find Lavina on the second floor again. I watch her clean a couple rooms. I sit with my back against the wall out in the hallway, staying out of her way.

She's good at what she does. She doesn't short-sheet the beds, skip any toilets, or forget to check all the drawers in the dressers. Her system is to start off in a bathroom, working from the sink to the toilet to the shower, then she checks under the bed, in all the drawers, empties the garbage can, makes the bed, dusts, and finishes it all off with the vacuum. She could be a crime scene specialist, she's so thorough, and every room smells like lemon cleaner when she's done.

"How long have you worked here?" I ask when she drags out her vacuum and shuts the door.

"I bin here jus' 'bout every day since Clive bought de place, two years ago."

"You work every day?"

"All 'em but Sunday." She pushes the cart down to the next room. I get up, pull the vacuum along with me and leave it beside her cart before I slide back down the wall to my sitting position.

Lavina doesn't thank me for the help.

Instead, she shoves down the pile of soiled sheets that are barfing over the edge of the cart bucket. She's ruthless, cramming them down with a determined grunt. When she comes up for air she asks, "How come you wanna watch me clean all day, anyway? Ain't you got no place to go?"

"I'm going home today," I offer.

"Fo' good?"

I tap the back of my head against the wall. "No, just to pick up some more of my stuff."

"Where 'bout's home?"

"The country." I don't want to give her the exact location. I still don't know if she would try calling my mom. Or the cops.

It seems unlikely she'd do either when she shrugs and grabs a stack of fresh towels from the middle cart shelf. "You live in a nice house?" she asks as she goes back into the room.

"I guess," I say.

"Well, you here 'cause yo' daddy beat you?" she asks.

"I have a stepfather. He doesn't beat me—just pushes me around a lot."

"Huh," she says, carrying out and dumping a wad of soggy

towels in the front bucket of the cart. She pauses for a breath. "He leave bruises on ya?"

"No," I say.

"He touch ya where he shouldn't?"

Ew, yuck. "No."

"Yo mama beat ya or touch ya?"

"No."

Lavina leans over the edge of the cart, staring down at me. "Then why da hell you here, girl?"

I shrug and look away. Her smirk is a slap in the face, minimizing all the reasons I left home. Bob's drinking. His shoving. My mom's need to control my every move.

But Lavina doesn't stop. "How come you not sleepin' on yo friend's couches? Why you wanna be here?"

What I want to say is: because I don't have friends and my mom and Bob won't come looking for me here. *They're too scared of people like you.* But I keep my mouth shut. I don't need Lavina getting insulted and mad enough to report me.

I shrug her question off again, but decide it'd be better to end the conversation altogether. I slide up the wall, my back flat against it and my thighs burning as I push myself to my feet. The lobby alarm sounds and my escape is delayed by a man's husky shout from the lobby.

"Lavina! Where you at, girl?"

"Glory days! You see what I mean?" Lavina says to me as she throws down her cleaning rag. "Do everyone gotta wait 'til I'm busy to need somethin'?" She turns her face toward the stairs and bellows, "Jonah! Secon' flo'!"

Heavy footsteps clomp up the stairs and a man in navy blue pants and shirt appears around the corner, walking down the hall toward Lavina and me. He's holding a zippered, blue vinyl bag that looks like a pencil pouch.

"I got your change from the bank," he says, waving the bag at her.

I look to Lavina, expecting her to yell at him for announcing it and waving around his money like that. It should be in his sock or something.

But she doesn't say a word. She only smiles at him. "Thank you! I appreciate that."

I look back at him and catch his gaze traveling up my thigh. It takes a second for him to reach my face, but when he does, faint lines of amusement break out around his eyes and his broad smile nearly glows against his skin.

I'm sure plenty of women would find him attractive. He's got the high, fine bones of an African warrior and skin the rich color of a wet, wooden spoon. Meticulously groomed, his hair is trimmed close, with three, fine lines shaved from one temple and reaching just past his ear. The lines remind me of the ones drawn in cartoons to show that a character is running fast. Thick enough shoulders, solid boots.

If I was into black men, who knows.

Lavina takes the bag from him and starts for the stairs. He doesn't move. He's too busy staring at me, smiling. And kind of blocking my way from following Lavina. My toes carve dips in the soles of my shoes as I wait for him to move. I don't know what he wants from me.

"Lavina," he calls over his shoulder, "you gonna introduce us?"

He's got to be ten years older than me at least.

Bob would call this man a porch monkey or a jungle bunny. He always says it is *them people* that ruined the city because none of them knew how to keep a job. Bob says black people are all savages. I think Bob should look in the mirror.

But Jonah, in his grease-smudged uniform and heavy, well-worn work boots looks like most of our factory-working neighbors back home. His uniform actually looks a lot like Bob's. And the way Jonah talks doesn't sound like the way Lavina does, but more like the people back home.

Lavina glimpses back with a wave of her hand. "Dat's Lael.

She a new weekly. Country girl. And dat dere's Jonah. He da manager next door at da oil place nex' do'."

"Lael," Jonah says my name like it's hard candy. "That's unique."

The way he stares right into my eyes makes me think maybe he's a savage after all. I am paralyzed until he looks away. I scoot past him—he's at least a head taller than me—and catch up to Lavina. I can feel the heat of his eyes on my back. Well, maybe a little lower than my back.

We follow Lavina down to the lobby. She locks herself in the office, so I'm left out in the lobby with Jonah. I back up against the ice machine, jarring it and sending the plastic buckets tumbling all over. Jonah laughs and grabs the buckets that roll off onto the floor.

I blush.

God, I'm just useless.

Jonah restacks the buckets, moving closer to me. I back away until I'm flat up against the pay phone cabinet. He lets me retreat with a soft chuckle, and turns back to Lavina when she says his name.

"Thanks ag'in," she adds.

"Sure thing," he says. "Anything else you need outta me, Miss Lavina?"

"Dat oughta do it. I kin git to da bank mah'self tomorr'ah, thanks."

"Glad to be of help," Jonah's voice drops to such a deep octave, I feel it in the pit of my stomach. He raises a hand in a parting wave. "Lemme know if there's anything else ya need."

"Yep, thanks." Lavina steps out of the office, locking the door behind her. She doesn't give him a second look as he leaves, but Jonah's eyes pause on me, and he grins, the high cheekbones underlining his almond eyes.

"It was nice meeting ya, Lael," he says.

I dredge up a smile and shoot past him to climb the stairs

behind Lavina. The door alarm goes off and the door shuts after he leaves.

"Look ta me like Jonah's got eyes fo' ya." Lavina gives me a smirk once we reach her cart again.

"Oh, I'm not into black guys," I tell her.

"You not? Well, da's good, 'cause ya oughta leave 'em ta us African Queens who kin handle 'em." She pulls a couple towels from her cart and carries them into the room, talking over her shoulder to me. "But lotsa black men wanna chase you white girls 'stead'a keepin' wit' their own. And I think Jonah the chasin' type."

Lavina's words might as well be stirring the neon orange crackers in my stomach with a dirty spoon. Jonah's a lot older than me, practically an old man. He's black. He's a guy, and I'm not looking for one of them right now.

"Well, I'm not the catchin' type," I tell her.

"How old is you ag'in?" she asks, dragging out a pile of soggy, dirty towels. She doesn't wait for my answer. "Don't matter none. Every girl's da catchin' type. Dat is, 'til she bin caught once or twice."

Thank you for reading the Weeds of Detroit free preview. If you'd like to continue reading, click here to buy Weeds of Detroit.

FREE PREVIEW OF HALE MAREE

CONTEMPORARY ROMANCE FROM MISTY
PAQUETTE

"WE GOT ENOUGH FOR TWO, don't we?"

This is how my father comes in the door at three in the morning, yelling and drunk, but laughing. I don't mind him so much when he's like this. I call it beer-drunk. Beer-drunk is when he drops the dishes, but doesn't mind that they're broken, spills things, and grins like his face is made of modeling clay. If I have to pick, I'll take this version over the whiskey-drunk one, when he can get angry at the color of the carpet.

"Yeah, Dad," I call back from the kitchen, "there's enough for me and you."

Then I hear the second set of footsteps following my father into the kitchen, and realize what he meant. He meant company.

A man, who would probably be considered handsome when his eyes weren't so blood shot, comes in behind my father. I like it better when my dad brings home women. While none of the men he's brought home have ever succeeded in laying a hand on me, lots of them have tried, and I've learned to spend the night in my room with a chair wedged up under my door knob. At least, when I get a good look at this guy, he doesn't look like he'd be a creeper. It's not like I ever know for sure, but this guy's smile is friendly, as my dad horseshoes him around the neck with a crooked arm.

"Hale," my dad says, nearly poking out his friend's eye with the indicating jab of his finger, "this here's Otto. From the old neighborhood! We were..."

"At the bar. We were just at the bar." Otto dips his chin like he's correcting a toddler, instead of my full-grown, totally-blasted father.

"Yeah, yeah, I know, I know. The bar on Fifth, not Main."

I take a good look at my dad as he staggers toward me. He's got a dark spot around his eye that doesn't disappear when he moves out of the shadows.

"Did you get into a fight?"

Otto shushes my father under his breath. My dad swishes away the admonishment with a flutter of his fingers.

"We got enough, right?" my father asks again, instead of answering my question.

"Yeah, sure." My smile fades. Otto waves his nose over the small saucepan of chunky beef stew that I've got bubbling on the stove.

"Smells absolutely delicious," he says to me. His way of talking sounds kind of fancy, even though he's plastered. His head swings back toward my father like his neck is a wobbly piece of rope. "Your daughter...she's an incredible cook."

"It's from a can," I say.

"She just turned eighteen. She knows her way around a kitchen," my dad tells his friend, and then he breaks into a guffaw, like he's the funniest thing in the world. Otto thinks so too, and the two of them collapse against the fridge, rattling the cookie jar on top. They both look up like it will drop on their heads and then they laugh even harder. I scoop the stew into two plastic bowls.

"Watch out," I say, maneuvering around them. They manage not to barrel into me, but they're doubled over on each other, still laughing. I dump the bowls on the table and grab a bag of chips off the counter. At least I'll have something to eat when I barricade myself in my room for the night. But, as I walk down the hall, away from the kitchen, Otto says something to my father that turns my face red and freezes me in my tracks.

"So, let's get this settled," Otto says. "She's a good girl, isn't she? You know what I mean."

"Of course she is! What the fuck do you think?" My dad laughs his reply, but there is still enough growl in it that I think I know what kind of 'goodness' they're referring to. What the hell? But then my dad says, "What about Oscar? Good kid? Clean?"

"Hell yes," Otto says. I scoot into the shadows around the corner, as I listen to the two men stagger to the dining room table and drop onto the chairs. "He's a man! The girls adore him. He knows what he's doing. That's why I want him to settle down. It's time he starts a family and takes over the business. Especially now."

"Well, if we do this...damn it! Watch the soup! That shit is hot!"

Otto's voice streams from the kitchen, deadly sober all of a sudden. "Jerry, this isn't an 'if' anymore. We left 'if' at the bar a few hours ago."

"I know, I know. Loyalty. I got it."

"With our children married, we both have insurance—that you trust me to keep your daughter safe..." he says, and his frigid, sinister tone drops about another ten chilly degrees as Otto adds, "and that I can trust you to keep my business quiet."

The sinister tint in his tone almost erases the words. Their children *together*? Why are they talking like mobsters? My dad's only got me, so Otto's got to be talking about his own kids, but none of this makes any sense.

"We grew up together, for Christ's sake. You know you can trust me, Otto. After everything that happened tonight, you gotta know you can trust me by now, right? Right?"

There is no answer. I hold my breath in the shadows until my father resumes, feeling only a little better when his voice raises this time, as if he's sliding a bargaining chip across our dining room table.

"But if we do this, Otto, your boy—I don't care what he does with other women, but he better never hit my girl. You hear me, Otto? She comes back to me with scratches even, and I'll cut his balls off!"

"His balls?" Otto laughs. "You're a tough bastard, you know that, Jerry? You don't have to worry. Oscar's not a maniac. He's a soft touch with the girls."

"Not too much of a castlenova!" My father laughs. Chokes. "I want grandkids, you know!"

"Castlenova?" Otto sputters.

"Yeah, you know! A ladies man, dumbass!"

"Casanova? Is that what you mean?"

The two of them break into peals of laughter, while I stay pressed to the wall, sweating. I have no idea why they're having this conversation, but it totally concerns me, and it sounds like they're planning things they have no right to plan. I just don't get how it all fits together, and why they're talking about my goodness, and Oscar's fists, and his Casanova-ness. My father must be even more drunk than he seems. Grandkids! I don't like them talking like any of this is going to happen, and I especially don't like them talking about my baby-making features. It freaks me out in about ten different directions.

"What are you going to do if she doesn't like him?" Otto says.

"She'll like him. I know my kid." My dad's laugh starts to sound like a braying donkey. I'm sick from my stomach up to my jaw, and he keeps hee-hawing. "So, we're business partners now, right?"

"Right," Otto says. They clunk something. I think it's their soup bowls. They've got to be off-the-scales-drunk if either of them thinks that my dad has a business, or is in business, or can run a business. He's been laid off and collecting state aid for the last three years.

"We buy the tractor tomorrow," my father says.

"With my money," Otto adds with a slurp.

"And I cut the lawns."

"Until you build up the business," Otto says. "Then you retire."

"Can't thank you enough," my father slurs.

"We're family now, Jerry. Loyal and trusting family, right?"

"Of course, right!"

There's a pause, and then, a wet clap of their hands, in what I assume is a handshake on the deal.

"Ok, so let's drink on it," Otto mumbles. "We need to make a toast!"

"There's no toast here," my father says. "There's nothing here, but my daughter."

I suck in a breath at the implication, but the two just laugh.

"You have a beautiful daughter, Jerry!" Otto says. "My son will be very happy to have her as his wife!"

"Of course he will!" my father shouts and I escape down the hall in absolute panic.

*S*her picks up my call on the first ring.

"Hey," she says. "What up, my sista?"

"My dad's drunk…"

She yawns. "So, what's new? He didn't bring home another weirdo, did he? You want to come over here? I can come get you."

Sher would, too. She wouldn't come over and knock on the door though. Sher and I devised an emergency plan years ago. She comes over, stands under my bedroom window, catches my gym bag, and holds the end of the knotted sheet that I use to escape. We finally figured out, the second time we did it, that we had to weight the end of the sheet with rocks and toss it back through my window so that Mrs. Coley, from downstairs, wouldn't call the cops about it. One time she did and the cops got my dad for drunk and disorderly, because, when the cops show up, my dad always gets even more disorderly.

"No, listen!" I hiss into the phone. Instead of being mad or hanging up, Sher goes quiet on her end. No one in the whole world knows me like Sher does, and she knows that this is serious if I'm hissing. "He brought home some guy named Otto and, dude...they started talking about my *virginity*. I'm totally skeeved out."

"Holy crap," Sher says. "Ok, I'm coming to get you. You got the chair under your door knob already, right?"

"Yeah, but wait. It's not like that. My dad and this guy were talking about going into business together, I think they're...I don't know for sure, but it sounded like they're going to be cutting lawns. They're buying a tractor tomorrow. And then they started talking about me marrying the guy's kid. His name is *Oscar*."

"What the fuck?" Sher says. "An arranged marriage? What are they, from the old country now?" She puts on a foreign accent and continues, "I swap you two turkey for my daughter's pussy. Yeah? Yeah? You like? You want?"

I'd answer her, but I am finally getting brain-whomped by what just happened in my kitchen. Sher keeps going, in my absence.

"And what kind of name is Oscar anyway?" she squawks. "That's the ugliest name I've ever heard. Oscar the Grouch, Oscar from the Old Couple..."

"Odd Couple..."

"Oscar Meyer Weiner!" I hear Sher slap her own head on the other end of the phone line. "You're not marrying any old *wiener* your dad drags home, Hale. I won't let you. You know this kid's got to be a hot mess with a name like..."

"My dad can't do this."

"No! Hell no! You're going to be eighteen in a few months!" Sher's tone is sure, but then there's a long pause. "It's gotta be against the constitution or something. He can't make you do anything you don't want to!"

"Even if he's my dad and I'm living in his house?" I rub my damp palms against my knees.

"You don't have to do anything you don't want to." Her voice is so tiny and scared that a new coat of sweat breaks out on my palms. "You wanna run away and live at my house? I'll come hold the sheet for you."

"Nah." I try to laugh. I can't go live at Sher's. Her family is even more broke than we are. Her mom's trying to raise five kids on her own. When I go there to spend the night, we have to squeeze into bed with Sher's younger sister, who wets the bed when she sleeps too deeply. Sher's mom is nice, but always worn out from work, and too exhausted to sit there and listen to problems that belong to other kids, let alone her own. Even when my dad was thrown in the slammer for his last disorderly and I went to stay with them, she listened warily for a few minutes, and then patted my knee mid-sentence. She told me I could stay, but, I'd eventually have to bring my own food.

"Maybe they're just talking smack, because they're super drunk." The frightened pity in her voice makes me cringe. "Dude, they're just drunk. Who has arranged marriages in the United States? I mean, we are in the new millennium and shit, right?"

<<<<>>>>

I un-prop my chair from the doorknob in the morning, but I feel kind of sick. It's that icky feeling of waking up and thinking everything is okay, only to remember the night before and realize things might still be messed up. I scope out the hall, listening for foreign snoring, or signs of wreckage, but the apartment seems in order and I hear the coffee pot burbling. Someone is awake.

I creep down the hall and catch sight of my dad at the table, his head cradled in one hand as he looks over a newspaper. I let out a relived sigh. He scours the ads every morning, over his cup of sobering coffee, but gives up by the afternoon and heads off to the bar. It's a familiar rinse-and-repeat cycle, but it's reassuring this morning. If he's searching the want ads, then it's got to mean that all of last night's crazy business talk, and backroom-vagina-deals, were just drunken musings.

"Hey, Dad." I scope out the kitchen for visitors, but we're alone. "How are you feeling?"

He looks up from his paper with his hung-over, hound dog eyes, and the father that I love, the one who I stick around for, is the one at the table this morning. His coffee mug is at his elbow, while the percolator still clicks and dribbles on the counter. He never waits for the pot to finish before stealing a cup. I sit in the chair opposite my dad, instead of the drunk moron that tried to barter his daughter to a buddy.

"Hey, honey," he says. Dad folds the paper and pushes it to the side of the table, takes a deep breath, and lets it out. I hold my own breath, so whatever's left of last night's keg, still on his tongue, doesn't pummel me.

"I got good news," he begins. I lift my eyebrows encouragingly. Sometimes good news means he's found under-the-table work and, sometimes, it means the lights won't be turned off, but the heat will. I wait to hear if there is a bad news chaser, before I commit to any variety of excitement.

"Me and Otto Maree were out talking last night," he says.

"I know. You were here. Eating soup. Remember?"

"Oh yeah." My father smiles and, for a second, his eyes meet mine, before diving back down the length of the table. "Well, we got to talking and we came up with a plan."

"A lawn cutting business, right?"

"Right. Lawn cutting. I guess you heard most of it, eh?"

"Not everything."

"No?" He licks his lips and leans back a little in his chair, but he's still not looking at me. "Okay, well, I had to make a decision. Otto's got a good bit of money and..."

"How do you even know him?" My dad always thinks *everyone* else has a ton of money. I assume it's because, in comparison to us, they do, but even a guy with twenty bucks in a savings account is rich in my dad's eyes.

"We grew up together. Our parents were neighbors. Good friends. We were buddies from way back, but when I left high school, to bust my ass in the factories, Maree went off and got a fancy-pants degree. He's done real good for himself with it too. He's made a helluva lot of money, and he said he wants to help me out, since we're old friends. He wants to make an investment. In a business. With me."

"Dad," I sigh. These investments, no matter who they're with, have a historically bad track record when they include my father. My dad tried flipping houses and we were trapped beneath that epic financial failure for years. He's sold 'green planet' soaps, magazines, and used computers from the back of his car. He's telemarketed, and he's collected scrap metal. Nothing's worked, and pretty much every time he's tried, we've ended up a little worse off than we were before.

"I know what you're going to say," he says. "But don't say it. Not this time, honey. This isn't a pie-in- the-sky kind of work. This is real, honest-to-God, blue-collar stuff. Lawn service. We might not end up rich, but we're definitely going to get ourselves out of the red for good this time."

"Cutting lawns," I repeat, hiking up a doubtful lip. He frowns.

"You got to have a little faith in this one, Hale. This is an old friend. Our families go way back. I know it's going to work. It has to. Otto's got money to invest and I've got nothing to do but work, so it's going to work. He's gonna set me up with a van, and a trailer, and all the stuff I need to do lawns."

"That doesn't sound right. What's he getting out of it?"

"Money." My dad shrugs, but he looks away as he sips his coffee. "He just wants to give a good ol' friend a hand up, and I'm taking it, Hale. Damn it, we're taking it. We need a hand up. That's the other thing I have to talk to you about."

My stomach does a back flip, the kind that fails mid-leap, and my guts fall straight into my feet. I think of the whole Hale's-a-virgin-Oscar's-not-a-beater-let's-have-grandkids discussion from last night. My dad rubs his nose a couple times with his palm. He does that when he's trying to think of how to explain something to me that I'm not going to like. I take a deep breath and start for him.

"I heard you talking to that guy," I say.

"Honey, it ain't what it seems like." He rubs his nose again. "Well, it is, but I made a deal and we're going to follow through with it. Even if this came our way under different circumstances, you know we're running out of chances, Hale. Both of us. I don't even got my high school diploma. But Otto Maree's got a lot of money and I was lucky enough to be in the wrong spot at the right time. This is gonna work out. Neither of us is going to have to be on the state aid anymore. You're going to have a future. But Otto's got to know he can trust me, so we decided to go a little further than a partnership here, baby. We're forming a family alliance. An arranged...relationship."

That's what they're calling this. A pretty face on a big, ugly deal.

"Why is it so important that he trusts you? What happened last night?" I ask.

My father seems to fade with the question. He gets a really distant look in his eyes, like he's looking straight through my head, at the wall. The moment stretches on longer than it should.

"Dad," I say, "are you seriously thinking I'm going to marry some guy I've never even met, just because you say so?"

My dad straightens up in his chair. The open collar of his worn, plaid shirt droops to one side. He flexes a fist on the table, and I see his muscles respond, all the way up to his neck. My dad's a powerful man, and even though he's never once laid a hand on me, he's put a fist through the wall before. Even though it only happened once, it stuck with me and makes me worry that he'll do it again, or that at some point, he'll lose his control and slam his fist through me.

"You're gonna meet Oscar as soon as I get the business stuff in order," he tells, with a strained, but gentle, tone. He flattens his palm on the table when he catches me staring at his hand. "And that's that. We're beyond broke. We got nothing. We're going to end up homeless in another couple months, unless we figure something out. What's happened with Otto...I can't talk about it, Hale, but I can say this: it couldn't have happened at a better time for us."

"Whatever it is, we can figure something *else* out," I say, but he only shakes his head. He's glued this ridiculous idea to his brain, and there is no pulling it off.

"We've already figured it out. Otto's got his mind set on what needs to happen and it's going to happen. It benefits us all, if you just think about it the right way. You gotta see it for what it is. You play these cards right, and you won't be eating out of soup cans all your life. You won't have to worry about *ever* being homeless. You'll have a house and a family and..."

"And a life I didn't want!" I shout. My father rubs his chin.

"Hale," he says softly. He's my dad again, the guy he used to be before my mom couldn't take it anymore and left us both. He reaches over the table and puts his big, bear-paw on mine. "I'm pretty sure the life we're living right now ain't the one you want either, honey. But this is the best I can do for you, so you're going to have to make it work."

<<<◇>>>

I'm in the truck with a double box of lawn-cutting fliers on my lap. My dad got a zillion copies made, and he's bent on plastering them all over town. He wants every tree to have a flier stapled to it.

The name of the new company was Simmons and Maree Lawn Services, but due to lack of space, it's now S & M Lawn Services, and I can see loads of problems with that. My father, however, doesn't. He's sitting behind the wheel of a brand new Silverado that we could never afford, even if we stopped eating for a year, and there is a shiny, new trailer attached to the back, with sparkling new lawn equipment that squeaks as we careen over the bumps in the road. We're on our way to drop off the lawn crap at Mr. Maree's house, so he can inventory the stuff my dad bought, and have his loser son, Oscar, meet me. I plan on making it the worst meeting ever.

Oscar. The name only conjures up garbage-green monsters and sloppy, old men. What kind of name is Oscar anyway? Not a name I want anything to do with, I know that.

This whole ride started out badly. My father got me out of bed at eight this morning and announced that we were handing out fliers for his brand new business today. I said *no*. Just that. *No*.

My dad grabbed hold of my sheets and yanked them off me. He carried them out of my bedroom, and told me I wouldn't get them back until I started cooperating. It's the most we've said to each other since 'the talk' two days ago.

When I finally threw on some wrinkled up, ripped up clothes and appeared in the kitchen, my father gave me a look up and down, and frowned.

"You ain't going like that," he said.

"Good, because I don't want to go at all."

He sighed. It wasn't one of those *'we'll see'* sighs or even a *'you'll see this is for your own good'* sighs. It was a *'you better get your ass moving'* sigh, and, out of my father, a sigh like that isn't something to be ignored or argued.

So, I'm sitting beside him, in too cute of a tank top and jean shorts for the occasion, and I'm not talking to him. I keep my eyes trained out the window, my legs trapped under the massive box of kinky business fliers on my lap.

"This kid, Oscar," my father starts, and I cut him off.

"It's a loser name."

My dad's got to be high on new-car-smell, because he just ignores what I said and continues. "Otto says the kid's a looker."

"Of course he did! It's his kid! What does it matter to me, anyway? I'm just a cow in this."

"What are you talking about?"

"You're treating me like an animal! Like I don't have any say in this!"

My father looks away. "I haven't met Oscar, but he's got to be a good man."

"But you don't really know and you're still telling me to marry a guy you've never even met! You're supposed to be my father, *not a pimp!*"

"Don't you dare talk to me like that!" he explodes. "I am doing what's best for both of us, *dammit*! So you'll have a life!"

"That I don't want!" I explode back, but I see the dangerous vein rise in his forehead. Instead of going any further, I shove the box off my lap so it makes a barrier between us. My father roars commands at me and I keep my mouth shut for miles, fuming as I stare out the window, but I'm starting to feel hopeless. He's not relenting and I don't have choices.

By the time my father turns onto a winding black-topped road that snakes through clusters of trees, he's calm again. I'm not. The weight in my stomach just gets heavier as the truck coasts up the drive and a mansion of a house comes into view.

The truck tires jump over the cobbled drive leading up to the main entrance. We pass a recessed building with four garage doors, nestled in the carpet of sprawling green lawn, and other rooftops peek from behind the front structures. This isn't Mr. Maree's *house*. It's the *Maree estate*.

My dad pulls up by the garages and a greasy-jeaned guy comes out to unhook the trailer. After a couple of minutes, my dad is back in the truck, heading for the front door of the mansion.

"Nice, huh?" My father lets out a low whistle, guiding the truck along at a crawl. "Get a look at the kind of life you can have, Hale. Didn't I tell you? Didn't I?"

"That you're trading your only daughter for a truck and tractor? Yeah, I think you mentioned it."

He doesn't bother to respond. Instead, he steers us to the epicenter of the half-circle driveway, pulling up right between the enormous fountain and the front door. My father puts it in park.

He honks the horn and it takes only a few minutes before a chiseled, young man steps out of the front door. While the hard sculpture of his body catches my eye, it's his dark gaze, sifting me from this rolling scenery, which sends a sharp tingle straight through the center of my stomach.

The gorgeous stranger moves down the front steps, to my father's open window, and my breath disappears. He moves like smoke, easy and graceful—like smoke that could get in my head and make the world go fuzzy.

He leans his palms on my dad's open window. The stranger's dark eyes flick immediately to mine, and his lips twitch a tiny grin of acknowledgement, before his gaze returns to my father.

"You Oscar?" my dad asks.

The man nods and puts a hand through the open window to shake my father's. His eyes flick back to mine, and pause, as he answers in a dark chocolate kind of voice, "That's me."

Sludge drops into my stomach, crushing the butterflies. The idea of what my father wants me to do ultimately destroys any interest I have in the handsome stranger. I turn my face away, looking out the passenger window at the ridiculous plumes of water rushing out of the hands of the three angels at the center of the fountain. They're surrounded on the far edge by pristinely manicured bushes. What it takes to operate the fountain, or to maintain the grounds, could probably send me to college.

A bright red speck catches my eye. I hone in on the last angel. Someone's adhered a pair of striped, red panties to it. I snort a tiny laugh. It's so out of place that I can almost believe that the Marees are human and not the demigods my dad makes them out to be.

"I'll just grab my phone," Oscar says. I turn back as Oscar jogs up the front steps and through the opulent front doors of his house. Smoke in the wind, that's what he's like. I knock my forehead against my window twice. I've got to clear him out my head. When his smoke clears, what he said doesn't make sense to me.

"What's he doing?" I ask.

"Getting his phone."

"I heard that, but why's he getting it?"

"He's coming with us."

"Oh, no he's not." I say, but my father smirks.

"Sure he is. And from the looks of him, you got nothing to complain about, Hale. He's a nice looking guy and he sounds responsible."

"Because he was getting his phone? Are you serious?"

"Pipe down," my dad growls, as Oscar reappears, pulling his front door shut behind him. I sulk and admire him all at once, as he crosses in front of the truck. I don't know how he walks like that. Smooth as drifting smoke. I tear my eyes away as Oscar opens the door and there's nothing else I can do at that point, but scoot over, heaving the box of fliers back onto my lap, and give him room to sit. He climbs in next to me, his thigh brushing against mine as he closes the door and settles back on the seat.

I glance at him with a ready scowl, but he shoots me a quick grin that says *hi* and *sorry for the leg bump* and I drop the scowl without meaning to. But, then, his eyes scan me and I turn away and level my scowl straight ahead, out the window.

What an asshole.

He's checking me out.

He thinks I'm a cow, after all.

And that's fine with me, because now, he's going to have to deal with one mega-pissed-off bovine.

Continue reading by clicking HERE to purchase your copy of
HALE MAREE

ALSO BY MISTY PAQUETTE

ADULT BOOKS

Literary Fiction

WEEDS of DETROIT

STRONGER

Science-Fantasy

THE FLY HOUSE

Contemporary Romance

THE CROSSED & BARED SERIES

HALE MAREE (Book One)

FULL OF GRACE (Book Two)

Erotica

THE BROWN BAG SERIES

THE RELEASE CLUB

YOUNG ADULT BOOKS BY MISTY PROVENCHER

Young Adult Paranormal Fantasy

THE CORNERSTONE SERIES

#1 Cornerstone

#2 Keystone

#3 Jamb

#4 Capstone

A SHIFT IN LOYALTY

Young Adult Sci-Fantasy

THE DIMENSION THIEVES SERIES

Book One (Episodes 1-3)

Book Two (Episodes 4-6)

Book Three (Episodes (7-9)

Book Four (Episodes 10-12)

Young Adult Urban Fantasy

MERCY

ABOUT THE AUTHOR

Misty Paquette is a long-term wife, mama, and author. The first two are a bit more recent, but Paquette's writing roots date back to hieroglyphics she left in her mother's womb.

While Paquette can ride a motorcycle, knows how to Karate chop, and has learned enough French, Spanish, and Sign Language to get herself slapped, Misty's life is actually just the ruse she uses to connect with people. She is totally enchanted with them and spends her days trying to translate the soul bouquets of her muses into words.

Misty Paquette lives in the Mitten. Knock on her internet door and join her news letter at:
http://mistyprovencherauthor.com/ and find her wherever great coffee is sold.

For more information:
mistyprovencherauthor.com
misty@mistyprovencherauthor.com

Made in the USA
Lexington, KY
21 December 2018